PRAISE FOR CHARLIE GRACIE

"When we were starting out with The Beatles, the music coming over from America was magical to us—and one of the artists who epitomized this magic was Charlie Gracie. The spirit of the times was captured beautifully by one of his big hit songs 'Fabulous,' and I loved it so much that I used to perform it live with the boys. For me, those were times which were indeed truly 'fabulous!'"
  —SIR PAUL MCCARTNEY

"Charlie Gracie is one of the first in rock & roll—and the first rock & roll singer to come out of Philadelphia! He started it and made it possible for all the rest of us!"
  —CHUBBY CHECKER

"It was his big electric slap-echo sound that was brilliant."
  —GEORGE HARRISON

"When one wants to know about the history of rockabilly and rock & roll, one has to get back to the beginning of the music that changed our lives. Charlie Gracie was there at the start. His concerts in the late '50s in Manchester, England helped me to become who I am today. My sister Elaine and I watched him perform with wide-open eyes. She still has the cigarette butt that he discarded when we got his autograph after the show. Musical magic indeed."
  —GRAHAM NASH

"There is one man I know that is dedicated to his craft...sweet, kind, and undoubtedly one of the finest guitarists and singers I've ever known! Thank you, sugar, for blessing me and the world with your talent."
  —DEE DEE SHARP

"Charlie['s] talent is unbelievable! [He] can play anything: rock blues, swing...I'll name it, [he] can do it! Anyone who meets [him] becomes an instant friend. I'm glad I was one of those people."
  —FREDDY "BOOM BOOM" CANNON

"Charlie Gracie is a rarity in the music business. An accomplished musician, skillful guitar player, true entertainer, and above all, a man of integrity. Through all the ups and downs of the music business, and his personal trials and tribulations, Charlie's passion and love for the music and his audience never wavered. I am proud to say it's been an honour working with him over the years."
  —JODY H. KLEIN (CEO, ABKCO)

ROCK & ROLL'S HIDDEN GIANT

The Story of Rock Pioneer Charlie Gracie

Alfred Music
LEARN · TEACH · PLAY

LOS ANGELES

To my wife, Joan, the love of my life and constant companion.

To my son, Charlie, Jr., daughter, Angela, and daughter-in-law, Kim, for their love and devotion.

To my parents, Sam and Mary Gracie, who had the vision to see a future for me as a musician and showman—and the belief and determination to make it happen.

To my loving brothers Frank and Robert.

Alfred Cares. Contents printed on environmentally responsible paper.

CONTENTS

ACKNOWLEDGMENTS

My sincere thanks to John A. Jackson, my talented cowriter and now a dear friend, for his expertise, hard work, and dedication to this project; to my son Charlie Gracie, Jr., who worked tirelessly on this project, devoting much of his time to this as well as numerous endeavors of mine; to Laurie Hawkins, my diligent literary agent, who believed in the importance of my story and encouraged me to tell it; and to Ronald Sklar, whose extensive Pop Entertainment article was the springboard for this book.

Thank you to Paul Barrett, my U.K. agent and dear friend of 35 years, and to the late Bernie Rothbard, my agent for 36 years and a father figure to me.

My deepest appreciation to the folks at ABKCO Music and Records: Jody Klein, president of the company, for his continued support and affirmation; Teri Landi, gifted sound engineer and archivist; and Joe Parker, vice president of sales and distribution. Also to Link Harnsberger, vice president and editor-in-chief at Alfred Music, for the great honor of this publication.

Special recognition to Nancy Bragin, for providing vital contact information for this undertaking; to actor and author James Rosin for his support and counsel; and Paul Russo and J. Paul Simeone for their creative energy and assistance with preparing the photographs for this book.

Also to Joe Harnett, broadcaster and producer of my weekly radio program, *A Fabulous Hour with Charlie Gracie* (Cruisin' 92.1 FM WVLT); Quentin Jones, president of Lanark Records, talented musician, and skilled music director; Fred Kahn and Terry Bortman, loyal and talented musicians, and dear friends with whom I've shared many local and regional stages; Gary Lefkowith, talented musician and musical director; George Manney, filmmaker and Philadelphia pop music historian; Father Matthew Phelan, O. de M. and his religious community for their prayerful support and friendship; and Shawn Swords, skilled film producer and director who created my life story in a documentary for public television.

And finally, thank you to my legions of fans around the world, without whom none of this would have been possible.

–Charlie Gracie, 2014

I—along with millions of other people around the world—first discovered Charlie Gracie in 1957. That was the year I reverently added his orange-labeled Cameo recording of "Butterfly" to my nascent record collection.

I first communicated with Charlie in 1992, while writing my book *American Bandstand*. I telephoned him to ask for an interview. Charlie was unassuming and knowledgeable during the couple of hours we spent on the phone. I thought I came away with a slam-dunk interview. That is, until I played the tape back and heard nothing but my voice asking questions, followed by long gaps of silence. A sickening feeling overcame me as I realized I'd incorrectly hooked up my new-fangled telephone recorder device. "My God!" I thought. "How can I call this man and ask him to repeat a two-hour interview after squandering his valuable time because of my ineptness?" Of course, I knew I had to do just that. After mustering up enough moxie, I called Charlie again, anxiously confessed my bungled interview attempt, apologized profusely—and then held my breath. "Geez, that's a shame," Charlie responded in a most empathetic manner. "When do you want to do it again? Just call me back and let me know." I exhaled in relief. When I did get back to Charlie, he handled our second interview as if it was the first.

That's Charlie Gracie in a nutshell—tremendously talented, amiable, and genuine. Following that interview, I spent the next two decades feeling as if I owed him—big time! Charlie's life story is an affirmation of the maxim "do what you love and you can't go wrong." It has been an inspirational and rewarding experience assisting him in documenting it.

Charlie, I hope I've repaid my 20-year debt to you.

–John A. Jackson, 2014

OTHER BOOKS BY JOHN A. JACKSON

Big Beat Heat: Alan Freed and the Early Years of Rock and Roll

*American Bandstand: Dick Clark and the
Making of a Rock 'n' Roll Empire*

A House on Fire: The Rise and Fall of Philadelphia Soul

FOREWORD

Everyone has a story to tell. No one who succeeds in the recording world has done it easily. We just seem to appear overnight, doing our thing, and fame looks easy to come by.

I heard "Butterfly" and "Fabulous" on the radio, and the DJ said it was Charlie Gracie. I went out, after saving up my pocket money, and I bought them! So there he was, famous, and in my record collection.

This book will allow you to see that nothing comes easy. Success comes with hard work, disappointments, and some artists suffer betrayal by those they trust.

Knowing now what Charlie had to go through to achieve his "overnight" success only makes me admire him all the more! So glad you happened, Charlie!

Good luck always,
Sir Cliff Richard

"Charlie Gracie put [Cameo Records] on the map."
–DAVE APPELL[1]

"Charlie was a damn good singer. He should have been a bigger star."
–KAL MANN[2]

1

DESTINY

Destiny smiled sweetly on Charlie Gracie in 1957. The 20-year-old singer-guitarist who had been making records for five years suddenly hit the big time with his recording of "Butterfly." "You talk about destiny, you talk about luck," Gracie recalled. "By March, I not only had a hit record, I had a number 1 hit. My God. A number 1 hit. It was a dream come true for the Gracie family. You know, just like James Cagney in the movie White Heat: "Made it, Ma! Top of the world."

"Everything came so fast. Before I knew it, they wanted me to play here, play there. I was running around the country, performing at all kinds of places. I headlined the Brooklyn Paramount Theater with Alan Freed and then The Ed Sullivan Show, *which was the pinnacle of show business in those days. If you performed there you were a star."*

"Butterfly" was a huge hit record for Gracie, not only in America, but also across the pond in England and in several European countries as well. He continued to perform in the choicest of showplaces, both in the States and Great Britain. A follow-up Top 20, "Fabulous," threw off any fears of having the stigmatized "one-hit wonder" appellation added to Gracie's legacy.

A film appearance followed, as did a second triumphant tour of England. It was "a whirlwind," he recalled. "Just like in a movie when they show a series of events on the screen and someone's life flashes by in 20 seconds, that's how fast it came to me."

Barely two years later, in a twist of fate, destiny revealed its crushing side with might and main. Gracie was unmercifully blackballed by the spiteful owner of his recording company and then banished by his beloved parents from the family compound he had recently purchased for them in the suburbs of Philadelphia, Pennsylvania.

Accompanied by his bride of 18 months and their infant son, Charlie Gracie sported little besides the clothes on his back and with tears streaming down his cheeks he pulled away from his family and his home in his sleek white '58 Coupe de Ville. Suddenly and stunningly, Charlie's prized Caddy became the last vestige of the spoils of fame and fortune. "My guitar and my amplifier were in the trunk," he recalled. " I figured I could always go to work somewhere."

Talk about destiny, man. I believe in destiny. Or as the Arabs call it, "kismet." Que será, será, whatever will be, will be. I believe in that—to a certain extent. I also believe that while God has His hand in everything, you still have to try to shape your own destiny. I couldn't just sit home and expect the phone to ring, and for somebody on the other end of the line to offer me a shot on *The Ed Sullivan Show*. No way. You have to go about your business, do what you have to do to hone your craft, and get on with your life. That way, if a break comes your way, you're ready for it.

I never had what I'd call a "day" job. Shakespeare wrote: "All the world's a stage, And all the men and women merely players; They have their exits and their entrances, And one man in his time plays many parts, His acts being seven ages." All my life I never did anything except sing and play my guitar. It's all I ever wanted to do. Performing really separates you from the crowd. A lot of people believe they could make a living doing what I do, singing and playing the guitar. It's like calling a plumber to your house to fix a leaky pipe. You watch him as he works and you think, "I could do that." But when you do it, the pipe leaks all over the place, because you're not a pro. Professionals make something look easy, even though it's anything but.

I thank my father and mother for giving me the opportunity to become a musician. It all worked out for me. At least it did for a while, until everything came apart. So much time has passed that it's hard to recall my mental state when that happened, but it was pretty dreadful. I never contemplated anything as dire as killing myself—I was too strong for that. But try to imagine how it was for me to headline London's Hippodrome and Palladium, and then, within two years, settle for work at a bar called Hoagie Joe's in Havertown, Pennsylvania. I did five sets a night, six nights a week there for $300 a week. I endured that indignity for 52 weeks—and then they extended my contract! People who remembered me from when I was on top saw me perform there and asked, "What are you doin' here?"

"I'm making a decent, honest living," I told them. "I have a wife and children to support."

It wasn't easy for me to swallow hard and walk into joints such as Hoagie Joe's with my guitar in hand. That would have been cause enough for many guys to get drunk or jab needles in their arms night after night. All I ever did was smoke too many cigarettes!

As I look back on my life now, I'm proud to say I'm a pretty fortunate guy. But I lived through various difficult stretches where things got really rough, and it still pains me to think about some of them. However, the way I see it, if I'm going to recount my life story, I have to tell it all.

2

BEGINNINGS

Lying at the tip of Italy's "boot," Sicily is a 10,000-square-mile land mass created by Mount Etna, Europe's tallest active volcano, which spewed molten lava and volcanic ash into the Mediterranean Sea for hundreds of thousands of years. To this day, the island's prehistoric past remains a matter of conjecture. Although Sicily lies less than 100 miles from Africa, when a small band of what is known today as the "ancestral population" emigrated from that continent some 50,000 years ago, evolution's convoluted path led them in other directions. It was not until 10,000 years ago that human feet first trod on Sicilian soil, marking the beginning of that population's transfiguring journey into the future.

Sicily, the largest island in the Mediterranean, is considered to have three indigenous societies: the Sicani, the Sicels, and the Elymians. First to arrive, probably from the Iberian Peninsula and possibly via Africa some 8,000 years ago, were the Sicani, who settled in the southwestern part of Sicily, where the province of Agrigento is located today. The Sicels, for whom Sicily is named, crossed the Straits of Messina from Italy and arrived on the island around 3,400 years ago to occupy the eastern, most fertile, part of the island. The Elymians came from Anatolia (what is now

Turkey), probably by way of North Africa, around 3,200 years ago.

The Sicani, Sicels, and Elymians had Sicily to themselves for more than two millenniums, until about 800 BC, when the Greeks and Carthaginians established outposts on the island. This marked the beginning of Sicily's written history. Over the ensuing years, the Elymians assimilated with the Greeks and eventually all traces of that indigenous group disappeared from the island.

Around 580 BC the Greeks established the city of Akragas, where they constructed seven monumental Greek temples. When the Romans captured Sicily in 210 BC, Akragas became known as Agrigentum. After the Roman Empire fell in 410 AD, for the next 1,500 years Sicily was ruled by a succession of nationalities, including German Vandals and Goths, Greeks, Arabs, Normans, Spanish, Italians, French, and Austrians. With the unification of Italy in 1861, led by Guiseppe Garibaldi, Italian rule was permanently established. After such prolonged domination by foreigners, it is entirely possible that descendents of the original inhabitants of Sicily may no longer exist.

Meanwhile, the ancient Greek temples of Agrigento were excavated, and were partially restored. Those disinterred edifices are a fitting testament to the twisted ancestral lineage of Calogero Graci, who was born in the town of Sant'Anna, municipality of Caltabellotta, in Agrigento Province on November 14, 1878.[3]

I come from a working-class family. All of my grandparents were from the island of Sicily—from Agrigento, the southernmost province. You could almost row to Africa from there. So we're full-blooded Sicilian, otherwise known as "Islanders." A lot of Greek and Sicilian blood has been mixed over the centuries, to the extent that the Greeks and the Sicilians are hard to tell apart. There's an Italian expression, *una facia, una razza*—one face, one race—which I think fairly characterizes the situation. *Everybody* conquered us Sicilians. We don't know what the hell we are!

My grandfather's name was Calogero (pronounced: Ka-LOH-ge-ro, "Charles") Graci. His surname is pronounced "GRAH-chi" in Italian; in English it's "GRAY-cie." My grandfather never talked much about life in the old country. But I do remember him saying that the entire family worked for a local landowner and they were treated like serfs. The landowner provided a little shack for them to live in and every so often he'd give them a loaf of bread and a few onions so they could make soup. My entire family worked the land, often 14 or 15 hours a day. The time eventually came when my grandfather told his father, "I'm going to save my pennies and go to America, because there's no future here!" Just before the growing season began in 1903, my grandfather and a younger sister named Josephine (known to us as Aunt Pepina) said goodbye to their family and caught a steamer from Palermo to Naples. At the beginning of April they, along with a thousand other emigrants, boarded the steamship *Marco Minghetti* and sailed to America.

Prior to 1909, when direct steamship service from the Mediterranean to Philadelphia began, the majority of Italian immigrants headed to Philadelphia disembarked at Ellis Island in New York. My grandfather was 24 years old when he, like so many other immigrants, traveled that route. When he left his family in Sant'Anna he kissed them goodbye, and that's the last time he ever saw them—or even *spoke* with them. That might sound strange, but you have to realize that my grandfather, like most people who arrived here from foreign countries in those days, had never gone to school; he didn't know how to read or write. Communication by telephone was not an option because none of my family in Sicily had a telephone. So once my grandfather and his sister left the old country they never again saw or talked with their parents. Can you imagine that? It was sort of like dying!

My paternal grandmother's name was Angela Olivieri. I don't know much about her background other than that she was an Italian woman with some Greek blood in her on her grandfather's side. She was born September 28, 1880 in Santo Stefano Quisquina, in the Sicilian province of Caltanissetta, and had several sisters and half sisters. My grandmother actually arrived in America before my grandfather did. She, along with her sister Rosalia, also sailed from Naples, on the *Burgundia*. They arrived at Ellis Island on November 26, 1900. I'm not sure how long my grandfather was here in America before he met my grandmother, but that happened in New York City, where my grandfather was staying with one of his cousins. In those days matchmaking was the tradition, and it was likely that my grandmother's sisters paired her with my grandfather. However they met, Calogero Graci and Angela Olivieri were married in New York City in 1906.

Economically speaking, things were pretty rough for my grandparents. Like most other immigrants in those days, they were uneducated, unskilled, and unable to speak English. But they were good, decent, hard-working people, and to this day I miss them very much. When my grandfather left Ellis Island he was penniless. Shortly after my Aunt Josephine was born on March 27, 1907, my grandparents left New York for Tampa, Florida. Chances are they knew someone in Tampa or at least knew *of* someone in that port city; at the time, 90% of Tampa's Italian community had roots in Agrigento Province. In Tampa, Calogero and Angela became migrant farm workers. The money they earned picking crops during the summer tided them over during the winter, until the planting season began the following spring.

While living in Tampa, my grandparents had two additional children: another daughter, Carmella, born on June 14, 1911, and a son, Santo, born on February 24, 1913. Santo Graci was my father. Although his birth name was Santo—"saint" in Italian— my grandparents decided to call him Sam because it sounded more Americanized. My father always signed his name "Samuel" Graci and everybody called him that; everybody except for his nephews and nieces, who called him Uncle Santo because someone else in the family was named Uncle Sam. (His gravestone has "Santo" engraved on it.) Around 1918, my grandmother contracted malaria, and the doctors advised my grandfather to move her to a cooler climate. I'm not sure why he chose South Philadelphia, but evidently there was some kind of family contact there, and that's where they headed.

The City of Philadelphia is made up of wards, each of which takes in maybe 8 or 10 blocks. My grandparents originally moved to 515 Carpenter Street, which is in the Second Ward, District 46 in South Philadelphia, near the Delaware River (thus known as one of the city's "river" wards). They shared that Carpenter Street row home with three other Italian families. Back then there wasn't a lot of movement within the city. Once people settled into a particular ward they usually spent their entire lives there. My grandparents were still living on Carpenter Street when the federal census of 1920 was taken.

That particular section of South Philadelphia was known as Southwark, one of the city's oldest communities. The Swedes, who settled the area in 1643, had called it Weccacoe, or "peaceful place." The Dutch were the next to control the area, before ceding it to the English. In 1682 William Penn renamed the settlement Southwark, after an English town on the south banks of the Thames. Because of its location on the Delaware, by the early 1700s Southwark was a growing maritime and industrial center. But no one wanted to live in such a grimy place, so only the poor did. Violent gangs were common in all of South Philadelphia, but particularly so in Southwark, where flocks of newcomers caused overcrowding and unsanitary conditions. With different ethnic groups thrown together in close quarters, their lifestyles clashed and disorder and mob violence was rampant. As late as the mid-1800s, South Street, which ran east to west and was the unofficial boundary between Southwark and the rest of the city to the north, was like the Rio Grande in those old cowboy westerns. If a suspect fleeing the police reached that liberating boundary, he was home free. The cops wouldn't dare follow him into Southwark.

From the 1840s to the 1870s, the Irish fled the ravishing famine of their homeland and settled heavily in Southwark. And then the tide of humanity began to turn against them. After the 1861 unification of Italy, the migration of Italians from the south of that country—including Sicily—to Philadelphia began in earnest. As late as 1870 no distinct Italian neighborhood yet existed in Philadelphia, but by the time my grandparents and their three young children came north from Tampa in 1918, Southwark contained the oldest and largest settlement of Italians in the city. They had replaced the Irish as Philadelphia's largest group of foreign-born residents.

When my grandparents and their children arrived in South Philadelphia they didn't speak English very well; only a few words here and there. Like most Sicilians, they were dark-complexioned

Roman Catholics who, as did their Sicilian neighbors, experienced a lot of prejudice. Much of it came from the Irish, who arrived in South Philadelphia before them but now felt crowded out by the new Italian majority. The Catholic Church in Philadelphia still consisted mostly of Irish parishes, and the Irish didn't accept the practice of Italians worshiping alongside them in the same buildings. Eventually the Italian majority in South Philadelphia formed its own parishes and built its own churches.

By the time my grandfather Calogero arrived in Philadelphia there were a lot of cigar factories in the city, and he became a cigar maker for a company called Royalist Cigars. Not only did my grandfather hand roll cigars, as was the practice in those days, he also smoked them. I can still see him sticking the tip of his cigar into his pipe and lighting it up the way he used to when I was a young boy.

By the 1920s, most of South Philadelphia was lined with block after block of row homes. Many of them had taken the place of the dilapidated and cramped three-story structures derogatively referred to as "trinities." As soon as my grandparents had saved enough money for a down payment, they said goodbye to their cramped quarters at 515 Carpenter Street and bought a tiny two-bedroom row home located at 731 Pierce Street in South Philadelphia. Their new home was situated between 7th and 8th Streets, with the Delaware River about four blocks to the east, just past Water Street. I think they paid $600 or $700 for that house. I remember it well—I was born there.

Those row homes were not very wide, maybe 12 or 15 feet at the most. At 731 Pierce Street you walked up white marble steps to the front door and then into a foyer. To the left was the parlor, and directly through the parlor was a very small dining area. The final room was the kitchen, the only room with a concrete floor. The only source of water was a cold tap in that room. Hot water had to be boiled on the coal stove, also located in the kitchen. The stovetop had four grates for cooking. We made toast by holding the bread over one of the grates. As the flames from below shot up through the grate, the bread became toast. Not only did we heat our water and cook our food on that stove, for a time it also served as our only source of heat. My grandparents eventually replaced that old cast iron stove with a more modern gas range, but I still have strong memories of opening the belly of the iron monster and tossing coal into it—and of eating a lot of burnt toast!

We never had a coffee pot. My mother just threw some coffee beans into a regular pot of water and boiled them. She then poured the coffee into a sockette, which was shaped like a cone and looked like the windsock you'd often see at an airport or on top of a building. The sockette served as a strainer to separate the coffee from the beans. Like everybody else in those days, we also had an icebox to keep our food cold, and a breadbox—a little metal compartment outside the kitchen window—to keep our bread fresh.

Those row homes were two-story structures. Ours had two bedrooms, one to the left and the other to the right at the top of the stairs. My mother and father occupied one room, while my grandmother and grandfather had the other. I slept in my parents' bedroom until I was about five or six. I was then moved to my grandparents' bedroom, where I spent my nights until I was about 10 years old.

My father started school in South Philadelphia, but just a couple of years before the Great Depression began in 1929, he left the eighth grade and went to work so he could earn some money to help our family survive. Despite his minimal formal schooling, my father eventually became quite a self-educated man. (After completing the seventh or eighth grade, my mother Mary also joined the work force.)

My mother was born in 1916, to Michael and Josephine (nee Pirro) Pilato. Michael was a coal miner, and the Pilatos lived in Pittston, Pennsylvania, in coal-country near Scranton. Tragically, in 1917, when my mother was only nine months old, both Michael and Josephine developed influenza and died almost simultaneously. They had been close friends with Frank and Maria Cappizzi. Like my grandfather Michael, Frank was a coal miner. What's more, Maria and Josephine came from the same village in Sicily, San Cataldo. When Michael and Josephine died, Frank and Maria (who came to be known by our family as "Mary") adopted my mother, her two sisters, and her brother. They went on to raise those four children as their own. Frank and Maria Cappizzi lost their home in Pittston when the Great Depression got the better of them. They then moved to South Philadelphia, most likely because of a job opportunity. Had they relocated anywhere else, you wouldn't be reading my story today. It was in South Philly that Mary Pilato Cappizzi and Sam Graci met. Sam and Mary married in 1935. As was the Italian custom, they then moved in with my dad's parents. That was a step backwards of sorts for my mother, who had to adjust to living in a house with no bathroom, or even a toilet!

In 1936 my mom was pregnant with me. That year my grandfather Frank, who had struggled with a serious case of black lung disease, passed away at age 62. Although I never got to meet my grandfather, over the years I did get to know my grandmother very well. (Some time after Frank died, Mary met a widower who owned a home in Atlantic City who was looking for a companion. She eventually married him.)

My father was a hard-working man who found employment at the world-renowned John B. Stetson Hat Company soon after he and my mother were married. Founded in the late 1860s, Stetson was once one of the largest hat manufacturers in the world. During the company's peak years in the 1940s and 1950s it employed more than 5,000 men, who worked around the clock in three shifts. (Stetson enjoyed boom times until John F. Kennedy, after becoming president in 1960, refused to wear any type of hat. JFK's fashion statement caused men's hats to quickly fall out of style, and the entire industry suffered badly.)

The Stetson factory was located at 5th Street and West Montgomery Avenue in North Philadelphia, which was quite a walk from where we lived in South Philly. Even at a brisk pace, it still took about half an hour to walk there, so for most of my father's life he rode the trolley car to work and back. The working conditions at Stetson were terrible. The air was always fogged with steam and the floor was constantly covered with hot water. To absorb the sweat produced from actively toiling in temperatures that routinely reached 120 or 130°F, most of the workers wore those old low-cut undershirts with the shoulder straps. As if that wasn't bad enough, roaches flew about as the hats were manufactured.

My father was what they called a "sizer" at Stetson. Using both his hands in a karate chop motion inside the unfinished hat, he banged the felt out to a specific size—seven and a quarter, seven and five eighths. For eight hours a day his hands would move side to side in front of him: chop, chop, chop, chop, chop, chop. The skin on his hands and forearms became permanently stained shades of purple, green, and black from the dyes used to color the felt for the hats. Eventually my father became so good at his particular task that Stetson put him in charge of making their signature hats, the ones worn by Hollywood cowboy stars such as Buck Jones and William Boyd (Hopalong Cassidy).

Stetson was just a horrible place to work. It must have been a bitch for my dad. He toiled in that factory five days a week for six years, until the war started in 1941. Then, just as he was about to get drafted into the army, Uncle Sam exempted him. Instead of going into the service, my father got a war-related job in a meat-cutting plant where, for the next three or four years, he cut meat for the army. When the war ended, he returned to Stetson's hellhole.

I was born at 7:30 in the morning on May 14, 1936. (Bobby Darin was born the same day, that same year.) That morning my father was ready to head for Stetson when he heard a frantic knock on the front door. A boy who'd run there from the drug store across the street gasped, "Mr. Graci, you're wanted on the phone." (My family didn't have a telephone in their home then; none of our neighbors did.) My father hurried to the phone and was told my mother had just given birth to a baby boy. In his excitement he was almost hit by a car as he carelessly dashed back to his house.

"Hey, what's a matter with you?" the driver angrily shouted.

"I'm sorry, pal. My wife just had a baby boy. I'm a father!"

They named me Calogero, after my grandfather. When I became old enough to understand the significance, I considered it quite an honor. I also learned that on the day I was born my grandfather took a long and hard look at me lying there and exclaimed to my father: "I see a star over that kid!"

That's how my life began. It quickly got worse before it became better. When I was nine months old I developed what was then called double pneumonia *and* whooping cough. Both were deadly diseases, as there were no antibiotics to fight them in those days. The family doctor came to our house, his little black bag in tow. After examining me, he informed my parents that I faced a nine-day "opening." If I made it through those nine days I'd be fine. If not, my life would be over. Evidently it was God's will that I pull through. My grandmother Mary, who had been a midwife in the old country, used whatever little bit she still knew about medicine to nurse me back to health.

I was fortunate to have had a great childhood. My mother and father were wonderful to me. Even if I wanted to concoct a negative story about them I couldn't. My earliest memories go back to when I was five or six years old. Naturally, many of them were of my mother. She was a very good cook, and although we didn't have a lot of money, there was always healthy food on the table. None of us ever went to bed hungry. My mother was also a cleanliness nut, so we never slid between anything but freshly washed sheets. Besides running the household, my mother worked in a garment factory, where she made dresses and other women's clothing to supplement the meager salary that my father brought home from Stetson. My grandmothers took turns babysitting me while my mom worked. She kept that job right into the 1950s, up until the time I got a little lucky and she was finally able to quit.

My father was also a very loving person, as well as a reliable provider. There were many times when he sacrificed things intended for him so that he could offer me whatever he thought I should have. If my father and I both needed a new pair of shoes, he'd buy them for me first. He was that way about many things. My father was also a lot of fun to be around. He was also my pal, and usually the life of the party.

Before I was old enough for school I spent a lot of time around the house with my grandfather. He was extremely proud of me. I was his fifth grandchild—my Aunt Josephine Manzi and Aunt Carmella Spizziri had three daughters and two sons, respectively—but I was the first to bear the surname Graci. Of course, I'm sure he was just as proud of his other grandchildren.

Up until I was four or five, we had no heat in our house except for that kitchen stove. As a family, we'd all gather around that black cast iron box for hours upon hours, talking, eating, and socializing. Since we had no upstairs heat you can imagine how cold those bedrooms got during the icy depths of winter. We always had heavy blankets to keep us warm through those frigid nights. My worst memories of winter involve having no inside bathroom or toilet. On the most raw, windy days (and especially nights) of winter, we had to stumble outside into the back yard and make our way to the outhouse to do our business. (I can't say we were alone in our suffering; a lot of families had outhouses back then, even those located in the city itself.)

Aided by the money my mother earned at the garment factory, we were eventually able to install a coal furnace in the basement of our row home. Of course, somebody had to go down there every four or five hours to shake the furnace grate, remove the ashes, place them in a bucket, and add additional coal to whatever was left of the fire. There were times when the fire burned itself out, temporarily returning us to our pre-furnace days, shivering as we waited for the heat to build. When it finally did return, wafting up through the big metal grate in the floor of our parlor, it reminded me of those manhole covers in the street as the heat from the steam below rose from them. There was no way to control the heat output from our furnace, so we lived from one extreme to the other. At times the house grew so damned hot it wasn't funny. I can recall many a night listening to the radio in January or February, sitting there in a t-shirt, with the windows open wide.

I was six years old in the fall of 1942 when I started first grade at Southwark Elementary. The school was located at 8th and Mifflin Streets, about a three or four-block walk south of my house. Partly because of the menacing neighborhood in which we lived, my mother was very protective of me, to the extent that she was reluctant to send me off to school.

"When it's time, Charlie," she used to tell me. "You'll go when it's time."

When I eventually did start school I was bilingual. We spoke Sicilian full-time in our house. The entire family kibitzed and told stories in the "mother tongue." Not only could I speak fluent Sicilian, from that dialect I learned to speak French, Spanish, a little Greek, and a little Arabic. I attended Southwark Elementary through the sixth grade. At that time most people flocked together because they felt there was safety in numbers. As a result, neighborhoods tended to become ghettoized. If you had a *paesano*, he was most likely from your neighborhood. Except for two Irish families, only Italians lived on my street. During the few times we ventured out of our neighborhood we usually visited fellow Italians (of which about 95% were Sicilian). Through the sweltering heat of summer and the bone-chilling cold of winter, the old Italian men spent hours rolling solid balls on the street, playing bocce. In the winter they'd build bonfires at a nearby park and play long into the night. People ate, slept, worked, paid their bills, and raised their children in those local surroundings. For the most part, that was it. There were no Disneyland family vacations. Although we were surrounded by many different nationalities, including Irish, Poles, Jews, and blacks, there was something we all had in common: poverty. But it was no big thing, because everybody else around us was poor. It was also a pretty rough neighborhood, but we never did anything really damaging. If anybody had a fistfight or some other violent disagreement, they'd shake hands when it was over.

Even though I came from one of the toughest areas in Philadelphia, I never went near the river because it wasn't in my ward. I knew that if I went into somebody else's ward, I was a stranger there to everyone except for the few guys who might have known me from school. Chances were that some stranger would see me and shout, "Hey, what are you doin' in our ward?" Not that I faced a beating or anything of that sort. It wasn't as if we were enemies. I just felt uncomfortable whenever I ventured into another ward, realizing that I really didn't belong there. For the most part I stuck within my own jurisdiction.

There were some pretty rough characters in my neighborhood. Most of them never seemed to have what people considered "real" jobs. Instead they were involved with number writing (bookies), loan sharking, and other things of that nature. They weren't hard to find. Benny Abruzzo, one of my father's cousins, used to make a buck under the table by writing numbers. Benny was what we called "connected." He didn't have enough money to cover all the bets he took, so he handed his wagers to the local mob and they let him keep a small commission. That way, if somebody hit a number for a large jackpot—say $1,000—the mob, not Benny, would pay the winner. Although I wasn't one of those local characters, I always felt safe in Southwark. I knew enough to keep away from whatever their business was. As long as I didn't bother them, they wouldn't bother me. Because we lived in the same ward we'd inevitably pass each other on the street. But when we did, the exchange was usually a simple, "Hey, what's up. How ya doin'?"

There were some, such as the Mirena family, who became well known outside our neighborhood. Angelo and Philamena Mirena had nine children, and I knew them all. The Mirenas lived at 829 Morris Street, just two streets up from Pierce, near the church I used to attend. One time I needed some money in a hurry and borrowed $10 from one of the Mirena brothers, who was a loan shark; borrow 10 and pay back 11, one of those arrangements. Somehow my father found out, and I quickly forgot about any potential problems with the Mirenas. *He* wanted to kill me!

"If you need money you come to me!" screamed my dad. "If I don't have it, then you don't need it."

You may have heard of another Mirena brother. He was named for his father, but this Angelo wasn't known as Angelo Mirena. As Angelo "Dundee" he became one of the most famous boxing trainers of all time, working with Muhammad Ali and other boxing greats. (Angelo and older brother Chris both used the Dundee name professionally.) Very few people know that my father, tough son-of-a-gun that he was, was an amateur boxer who taught all of the Mirenas—or Dundees—how to box.

Today I'm able to chuckle when I think how I incurred my father's wrath over that loan sharking episode. I now understand it wasn't the money my father was upset about, it was the fact that I'd put myself in a dangerous situation. I don't think I would have been hurt over 10 bucks, but who knew? It was common knowledge that if you owed money to the wrong people it could be bad for your health. They'd warn you once. They *might* even warn you twice. After that, they'd smack you around a bit until you paid them. Only if you owed them a *lot* of money were you in serious trouble. They'd break your legs! And if *that* didn't work they'd take you to League Island Park, which was located on the Delaware River, not far from the old Philadelphia Naval Base. As kids, we all knew that if you were tossed into the river nobody would ever see you again. My friends and I called that "goin' down the lakes."

I also remember the time somebody was shot and killed on a corner where I used to hang as a young fellow. He'd gotten into an argument with some other guy at a local bar, and pounded him into a pulp. But the loser of the fight returned home and grabbed his gun. Then he came back to the bar and shot and killed the unlucky soul who'd administered the beating. The shooter eventually went to jail for murder, but he didn't stay there very long. His family and some friends went through the neighborhood collecting money, and soon after that the shooter was released. During those tough times a couple hundred bucks was sometimes enough to buy someone's freedom.

Probably the most respected individual from our South Philadelphia neighborhood was Angelo "the Docile Don" Bruno. Up until the 1940s, organized crime in Philadelphia had been run by the Jewish mob. The Italian gangsters stuck to their own territory in South Philly, but eventually they took control throughout the city. Angelo Bruno, the son of a local grocer, ran the Philly mob in the '60s and '70s. Despite the power and wealth Bruno amassed over the years, he remained very unassuming, not at all the John Gotti high-profile type. Bruno resided in a modest row home on Snyder Avenue, not far from me, and was loved by everybody in the neighborhood. When I think about it now, I realize that we probably lived in the safest neighborhood in the city!

The "Docile Don," who ruled the local underworld despite his controversial refusal to deal in drugs, acquired his nickname because he lived by a philosophy of reconciliation, not violence, to settle differences. But he only lasted so long. In 1980 someone from a rival faction put a shotgun in Angelo Bruno's mouth and blew his head off. No way could I have imagined it when I was a youngster, but my path and that of the "Docile Don" were destined to intersect.

Midway through the 1940s, World War II ended just as I was getting started. Like any other youngster, I couldn't fully appreciate my situation at the time. My years at Southwark Elementary were the secure footing of what was to be a sound education, something fate had denied my mom and dad. As a rule, parents want their children to have a better life than they had, and my mom and dad were no exception. But at that tender age in my life I wasn't fully mindful of their sacrifices. Nor could I have imagined I was about to experience what would be one of the greatest personal losses of my lifetime.

3

ROCK THE JOINT

Philadelphia's renowned South Street, with the heart of its storied commercial district stretching west from Front Street near the Delaware River to 7th Street, is almost as old as the city itself. But it wasn't always known as South Street.

By 1800, Philadelphia was the largest city in the United States. Cedar Street marked the traditional southern boundary in William Penn's original design, while just below it was the area's initial settlement of Southwark.

During the colonial era the area around Cedar and Lombard Streets (from 5th to 7th Streets) became a magnet for free black settlement, and by 1820 the so-called "Cedar Street corridor" contained nearly two-thirds of all of Philadelphia's black families. During the antebellum period the "corridor" was the center of a prominent free black community that, at one time, was the largest in the United States.

In 1854, when Southwark was incorporated into the City of Philadelphia itself, Cedar Street was renamed South Street. Over the decades, South Street developed into a bustling marketplace lined with commercial shops that sold every kind of fish, fowl, and produce available, as well as a wide array of manufactured *merchandise. Families lived above the storefront shops and children played in the alleyways. Between 1880 and 1920, an influx of Eastern European immigrants, mostly Russian Jewish, began to replace the long-settled African-American population along South Street.*

With its large number of men's suit stores and other clothing shops, South Street and the busy commercial corridors just below it became Philadelphia's commercial hub for wholesale and retail men's apparel. Generations of Philadelphians, including Sam Graci and his family, purchased their new suits and wedding gowns there. In 1946, South Street played a part in what was perhaps the most influential event in the life of young Charlie Graci.[4]

W hen I was almost 10 years old my parents moved to a larger row home. At that point they had two children—my younger brother Frank and me—and with my youngest brother Bob about to be born we needed more space than the two bedrooms my grandparents' house provided. It was a mighty stroke of luck for us when the neighbors, just two doors away at 735 Pierce Street, put their row home up for sale. That dwelling had three bedrooms, plus a bathroom that not only contained a toilet, but also a tub where my growing family could now take baths. The house cost my parents $3,000 or $4,000, which, in those days, was a lot of money. I thought it was really great that they were able to buy the place. Once they did, I was given a small role in helping our family to keep it: After my father put a down payment on the place he let me go to the real estate agent and make the monthly mortgage payment, which amounted to $11.

When we moved to 735 Pierce Street, my grandfather and grandmother remained in their house, which, by that time, they owned. Like my grandparents' house, this one had a little yard that extended out about 10 or 12 feet behind it, surrounded by a wooden fence. It wasn't much of a yard, and because it was covered with concrete my parents did what most of our neighbors did: they grew things such as tomatoes and basil in little flower boxes and pots. As with my grandparents' place, there were steps of white marble in the front of our new house. (Most of the steps in our neighborhood were constructed of marble, and to earn a nickel or a dime I used to scrub them.) Situated underneath and behind the front steps were two little basement windows. When the coal truck stopped in front of the house to make a delivery, the driver placed a coal chute through those windows and six or seven tons of coal tumbled down the chute into the coal bin. One load of coal usually got us through the winter, but if the weather was particularly severe during that season we'd sometimes run a little short.

As the oldest of the three Graci sons, I had a wonderful childhood. Considering the age gaps between us, we were as close as any brothers could be. There was a six-year difference between Frank and I, and a four-year difference between Frank and my youngest brother, Bob. When Frank and I were young we often played together around the house. Bob, as the youngest, always had his little group of playmates. Later on, as I reached my teenage years, Frank and Bob remained closer, and I began to hang with a different crowd.

My friends and I did all the things that young children did back then, including flipping baseball cards and playing marbles. I always loved sports and games of any sort, particularly the ritual urban pastimes of handball, stickball, slap ball, and football. Since we didn't have any grass available, we played everything on concrete playgrounds or in the streets. We couldn't afford to buy any kind of equipment so we improvised, wrapping tape around some wadded-up paper to make a football and cutting the wooden handle off a broom to fashion a bat. There were bona fide neighborhood baseball leagues that played on Southwark Elementary's large grassy schoolyard field during summer evenings. When they did, we'd go buy a cup of water ice for 3¢ (a nickel if you wanted the big cup) and sit and watch the games. We also formed teams of our own. Of course, we had no uniforms, so additional improvisation was in order. Some of the guys wrote their names on their shirts with a piece of crayon. Then, uniforms or no, we'd wait for our chance. When that elusive schoolyard diamond finally became available we'd pounce on it for our own use. We had some memorable contests, too.

With the love and care projected by all our kin, my brothers and I grew up with strong family values. Being Roman Catholic, we attended St. Nicholas' parish in South Philly, which was run by the Augustinians. Baptized and confirmed at St. Nicholas', I was one of those youngsters who *always* went to church. If I missed mass just once I'd catch hell. One of the things I loved most as a youngster was that my grandmother and grandfather were nearby all the time. I recall one typically steamy South Philly summer afternoon, the kind with absolutely no breeze, when you could see the heat radiate up from the sidewalks. My grandfather was out in the street playing bocce and I was dying for an ice-cream cone. My mother had given me a nickel earlier in the day, so I wasn't about to ask her for another one. Instead, I went to my grandfather and said in Italian, "Grand-pop, could I have a nickel?"

He smiled as he opened his little pocketbook—the kind that Italian men carried around like a purse in those days—took out a nickel and handed it to me.

"Oh, *grazie* grand-pop!" I said with heartfelt thanks as I gave him a big hug. Then I ran to the corner store and bought that ice-cream cone.

I'll also always remember those times I sat with my grandfather at the kitchen table, going through my geography lessons. The poor guy had never gone to school and he wanted to learn in the worst way. We'd have a map in front of us and I'd fascinate him by pointing out various countries. My grandfather was enthralled with maps, where various countries were located, and things of that sort. He told me many times, "I wish I could go back in time and become educated like you. You keep your nose in those books!"

My grand-pop died on September 26, 1946. I still consider it one of the darkest days of my life. I was 10 years old, and we had been in our new house for only a few months. That particular morning had begun just like so many others, with my grandfather leaving for the cigar factory where he worked. But the day ended very differently. My grand-pop never came home. He'd suffered a couple of minor heart attacks in the past, but none ever disabled him. At first he took some sort of medication for his condition. But being the tough, stubborn, old guy he was, my grandfather complained that the medication made his legs feel heavy. Against everyone's advice, he stopped taking it. We later found out that he'd suffered a coronary thrombosis on the trolley car that morning. Evidently he felt ill, because he suddenly got off the trolley and flagged a cab. But when he tried to tell the cabbie his address, all he managed to get out was "731..." Before he could add "Pierce Street," he fell dead right there. To complicate matters, my grandfather had inadvertently left his wallet at home that morning, so nobody knew his identity or who to notify. His body was taken to the city morgue.

That evening everybody in our family was waiting for grand-pop to come home. He always came straight home from work, usually arriving around 4:30 or 5 o'clock. When it got to be 5:30 and he still hadn't arrived, we knew something was wrong. My father hurried across the street to the drug store and telephoned the cigar factory. "This is Sam Graci, Calogero's son. My father hasn't returned from work this evening. I'm wondering if something's happened to him."

"Well, Mr. Graci never came in this morning."

That very instant my dad felt a lump of anguish well up in his throat. My entire family was struck dumb when they heard my dad relay the heartbreaking news. It wasn't until about 7 o'clock that my Uncle Jimmy Manzi finally gained enough presence of mind to say, "Let's call the police."

"Well, we did pick up a male body in that area today," said the sergeant on duty. "It's here at the morgue. If you want to take a look at it, you may."

My father hastened to the morgue. As the drawer holding the body in question was opened, the first thing he saw was a Stetson hat, the same type of hat he'd given my grandfather as a gift. He didn't need to see any more. His worst fear had been confirmed.

Early the next morning my cousin Angie roused me out of my bed. "Charlie, wake up! I have some bad news. Grand-pop died yesterday."

Holy God almighty! My whole world fell apart the very second I heard those dreadful words. Angie and I then broke into tears. We loved him so much. My father took his dad's death very hard, too. He was the only son, and he loved his father dearly. For days, my dad couldn't eat or sleep. He refused to go back to work for six weeks. My grandmother took her husband's passing equally as hard. Grand-pop was so beloved by our entire family; we all were completely devastated.

In those days the deceased was typically laid out in the bereaved family's home. For some reason my grandfather was laid out in a funeral parlor. When I saw him there he was covered in a quilt-like shroud right to his head, and his face appeared shockingly white. I became so hysterical at the unfamiliar sight that I actually ran from the funeral parlor. And I never went to my beloved grand-pop's funeral; it would have been too traumatic for this 10-year-old to bear. Some time after the funeral, when members of our family began to gather my grandfather's possessions, they found $20 tucked away in one of his shoes. He'd been saving what money he could, most likely to buy something for us kids. My grandfather was a great man. I still go to the cemetery and cry for him. I'm sorry he never got to see me when I began to play the guitar, and never got the opportunity to see my professional success. He would have been so proud.

My grandmother lived alone for a few months. Then she sold the home at 731 Pierce Street and moved in with my Aunt Josephine, who, by that time, had married Jimmy. My grandmother received $3,000 for the sale of her house. Can you imagine? Three thousand dollars was all she had to show for a lifetime of work. Of that money, my grandmother gave $1,000 to each of her three children. That was her legacy.

My grand-pop's death taught me that whatever the depth of grief over the loss of a loved one, life goes on. It was a rough lesson for a 10-year-old to learn, but one made somewhat more bearable by my growing interest in music. In that respect, I give thanks to both my parents. They were always 100% behind me. Each of them had a true love for music and they surely encouraged me to follow suit.

With no television in those days, the family radio was constantly on, and I remember hearing plenty of music around our home. My dad was into the big bands and swing: Tommy Dorsey, Benny Goodman, Harry James, and Sinatra-type vocals. My mother went for that, too, but she absolutely *loved* country. I'd call her a real country music "freak." She loved Eddy Arnold, Tennessee Ernie Ford, Hank Snow, Ernest Tubb, Hank Williams, and many others. So I grew up in an environment influenced by the sound of big band swing, country singers, and pop crooners. Thanks to my own curiosity and access to a revealing radio dial I also discovered rhythm & blues and jive, and added *those* to the mix. It was a musical mélange that, in the years to come, would be a vital asset to my own career.

I can't say there's any one singer I admire most; I never idolized any of them. But I've thoroughly enjoyed the talents of the likes of Louis Prima and Louis Jordan. Another of my favorites is legendary blues shouter Big Joe Turner. As a kid I loved everything about Big Joe's music—the way he sang, his arrangements, and his style. If the phrase "rock and roll" had been in vogue as a musical genre when Turner began his career back in the 1930s, he would have been called a rocker.

My dad was quite musically talented himself. He sang a bit, played the harmonica, and also knew two or three chords on the guitar. While he always had an interest in show business (he was also a great tap dancer), it was never in the cards for him to become an entertainer. But he wanted to make sure that at least one, if not all, of his children had that opportunity, and he wasted no time implementing his plan.[5]

As a 10-year-old fifth grader, I had no inkling that my dad harbored plans to prepare me for a show-business career. I found out about those plans in December 1946, as Christmas Day approached. My dad was in need of a new suit. He'd managed to save about 15 bucks (you can imagine how long it took him to amass that amount, given his weekly salary of $35), knowing that up on South Street he could score a suit with two pair of pants for that price. "C'mon, Charlie, let's take a walk," my dad urged on that fateful December day.

In those days South Street wasn't the hip, swinging area that it is today. You may be familiar with the pop song "South Street," describing that particular street in Philadelphia. It was a big hit for my friends Stephen Caldwell and the Orlons back in early 1963. But in the late 1940s, people went to South Street to shop, not to party. They may have purchased some clothing and perhaps a pair or two of shoes. And if they needed some additional cash to close a sale, quite a few pawnshops beckoned on South Street.

It was about a 15-block walk from our house to South Street. (Thankfully they were short ones!) As we approached the rows of clothing stores that lined both sides of the street, we passed the first of the area's many pawnshops. My dad hesitated for a moment as he scanned the inconsistent collection of articles visible in the storefront window. He seemed to be searching for something in particular. We walked on a bit farther, passing a haberdashery and arriving at another pawnshop. Once again, my dad lingered, peering through the shop's window before we began walking again. Eventually we arrived at a third pawnshop, a popular depository for all sorts of "hot" merchandise, operated by some oddball known to the locals as "the fence." The two of us silently stood there as my dad again perused the items in the shop's window. This time he spied what he'd been searching for. "You know what Charlie?" he blurted out of the blue. "I don't want you to work like a donkey the way I have all my life. I want you to *make* somethin' of yourself. The heck with my suit!" With that, he pointed to the pawnshop window and told me to "pick out an instrument."

My dad had caught me by surprise. But I must have wanted a musical instrument more than I realized, because I didn't hesitate for a moment. "All right, dad," I replied. The trumpet-playing Harry James was quite famous at the time, and I knew my father was a big fan of his. I gestured toward a well-worn horn. "How about a trumpet? You know, like Harry James."

"Nah, you don't want a trumpet," my dad replied. "You'll just blow your brains out with a horn. Get a guitar. Then you could be a one-man band."

A guitar? I hadn't even noticed a guitar at first glance. But sure enough, a closer look through the plate glass revealed one resting vaguely against the rear wall of the window display. I never questioned my father. In that foreknowing moment we simply walked into the store to get a better look at the guitar. On closer examination we discovered it was a Harmony flat top acoustic, one whose better days were certainly behind it. I'll never forget that sorry sight. That guitar brought to mind a bow and arrow, kind of bent in the middle, so you could play only in the first position. As I reflect on it now, that instrument was in *horrible* condition! Of course, I was just a kid who didn't know the difference between a good "axe" and a bad one. My dad handed "the fence" the 15 bucks he'd saved, and I came away from the pawnshop with my first guitar.

As I mentioned earlier, the idea for me to get into show business was my dad's, not mine. I was 10 years old. What the hell did I know about show business? Up until that point we'd never even had a guitar in our home. But that was no great matter. No sooner had we returned home, my dad sat me down and my lessons began: "Charlie, here's a D-chord, here's a C..." My dad may have known only three guitar chords, but he somehow made those three do for every song he sang.

Still blissfully ignorant to my father's intent to develop my musical talent, I soon received his message. At the time, I was prepared to go out in the neighborhood and shine some shoes to make a bit of money. I'd even taken the time to painstakingly build my own shoeshine case. I was quite proud of my crude handiwork, but when my father set eyes on that case he grabbed a hammer and smashed it to bits. "You're not shinin' no shoes!" he screamed. "Get that through your head. I sacrificed my suit and bought you that guitar so you could make somethin' of yourself. That was the whole idea. Now you get in your room and practice on that guitar! I have a friend who plays better than I do. He's already agreed to give you a few lessons."

My father's guitar-playing friend turned out to be one of those half-assed musicians who played here and there on weekends. He was a guy who played the guitar, yet couldn't *really play* the guitar. What I mean is, I could teach you four or five chords and you could take your guitar to a party and have a lot of fun. But that doesn't mean you're a guitar player. I liken it to a guy who can play "Chopsticks" on the piano (we all know at least one, don't we?). While playing *on* the piano, he's not necessarily a piano *player*. As it turned out, my dad's friend wasn't a bad guitar player. But after about two weeks he'd taught me everything he knew. I was surprised to find how easy it came to me.

When my dad saw how quickly I'd picked up his friend's limited musical knowledge he decided to move things along at a faster pace. "You know what, Charlie? That's enough horsing around. Let's get you a teacher who's an expert. That way, you'll learn how to play the guitar the right way; you'll be a really good musician."

I have to admit it, when it came to developing my talent my father had a keen vision. He went out and quickly found the appropriate teacher for me. The instructor's name was Anthony Panto, a cousin of the great pioneer jazz violinist Giuseppe (Joe) Venuti. He was a wonderful, inspirational man, a great musician, and an excellent teacher. For three bucks a lesson, Mr. Panto came to my house one day each week and taught me how to play the guitar.

Mr. Panto's lessons involved reading music. I started at the very beginning, with "do-re-mi-fa-so-la-ti-do." Although I was still a youngster, I learned quickly and soon had the entire process down. Soon, Mr. Panto and I began to play songs together, he on his mandolin and I on my guitar. He obviously was pleased with my progress. I was thrilled to death just to be able to *play* something.

I still had no idea my then-rudimentary talent would one day lead me to become a professional performer, but I did learn one thing. I *wasn't* going to be a worker at the Stetson hat factory. I'd been inside the plant just once in my life, and that was enough. Soon after I began taking guitar lessons with Mr. Panto my dad said, "C'mon, Charlie, I want you to take a walk with me. I want you to see where I work." We walked up to Stetson, where my father went to great lengths to point out the worst aspects of toiling in such a vile workplace. Confident that I'd witnessed up close the foul working conditions he was subjected to each day, my dad delivered his message: "Charlie, if you don't learn how to play that damned guitar, here's where you're gonna work for the rest of your life."

"No way, man!" I exclaimed. As soon as we returned home later that day I grabbed my guitar and began to practice like crazy. Putting my budding talent to practical use, I took on a new role among the guys I hung with. I became "the entertainer." It was easy for me to take my guitar out at a party and have some fun. All I needed to know were four chords. Play four chords? I could do that *before*

Mr. Panto started giving me lessons. I have to admit, I enjoyed being the life of the party. Sometimes it didn't even take a party to get me to play. One of the guys would say, "Charlie, get your guitar and meet us on the corner," and I'd be off. We'd hit the streets and sit in front of places like the South Philadelphia Tap Room over on 8th Street and Morris. We'd stake out some territory and I proceeded to sing and play. As people walked by, some tossed money my way—a quarter here, 50¢ there—and I'd go home with a buck, a buck and a half in my pocket. I began to see my dad's point: Some of my friends *did* have to shine shoes to make that kind of money.

In the fall of 1948, after attending Southwark Elementary for six years, I entered the seventh grade at Furness Junior High. Furness was located at 3rd and Mifflin Streets, about 10 blocks from my house, heading east toward the Delaware River. Although Furness wasn't that far from where I lived, it was located in a different ethnic ghetto, more Irish and Jewish than Italian. That was uncharted territory for a 12-year-old such as I. I attended Furness for three years. While I was there, for the first time in my life, I began to sense I was finally on my way. Such premonition was largely brought about by my passage from elementary school to junior high. I still had no idea what the future held for me; I just felt that I was on the move. I can't even say my expanding interest in the guitar was a factor. But that was about to change in ways beyond my imagination.

Sometime while at Furness, probably in 1950, my mother and father took me to see a performance by Bill Haley. It was so long ago that it's impossible to remember the exact date. I was already studying and playing the guitar, so I must have been about 14 or 15. I also can't recall who was more excited to see Bill Haley that day, this young but advancing guitar picker or his country-music-loving mom.

In those days, once you got outside of Philadelphia there were quite a few country and western type attractions in the city's rural surroundings. The most popular one was called Sleepy Hollow Ranch, then regarded as the country and western capital of the East Coast. The place had been built back in 1940 and was operated by the Newman Brothers and the Murray Sisters, two popular country acts who'd merged under the name Sleepy Hollow Gang and became the attraction's resident performers.

Sleepy Hollow was located in a corner of Bucks County, near Quakertown, Pennsylvania, maybe 30 miles northwest of Philadelphia. It was a beautiful attraction, built on about 20 acres of rolling greenery. Each Sunday and holiday they offered a mix of square dancing, family games, and pony rides for the kids. They even had a rodeo, complete with bull riding. There were food stands on the premises, too, although most guests preferred to bring their own picnic lunch.

In spite of all that hoopla, the main attraction at Sleepy Hollow Ranch was its country music. You name the greats, they performed at Sleepy Hollow: Roy Acuff, Eddie Arnold, Gene Autry, the Carter Family, Roy Rogers, and on and on. Such national stars regularly attracted audiences of up to 8,000 to Sleepy Hollow, while less-famous regional performers commonly drew respectable crowds of up to 1,000 people. (In 1963, a fire destroyed the popular but under-insured attraction.)

The day I attended Sleepy Hollow the musical draw was a regional outfit, Bill Haley and the Saddlemen. Hailing from Chester, Pennsylvania, just down the highway from Philly, Haley and his band hadn't traveled all that far to make the scene. Not yet reincarnated as the Comets, Haley's Saddlemen wore cowboy garb wherever they performed. That day Bill sported his outsized cowboy Stetson, perhaps made by my own father. It wasn't so much the Saddlemen's cowboy outfits that grabbed my attention, nor was it the type of music the band played—mostly standard country fare done with the conventional country lineup of guitar, steel guitar, and bass. What interested me most was the Saddlemen playing some numbers I'd never heard before. It wasn't very long into the program when Bill announced the band was about to play a version of a song they'd only recently begun to experiment with. As Haley spoke, a drummer joined the group onstage.[6] "A drum?" I wondered. "Who used a drum to play country music?" Before I had a chance to muse any further, two jarring chords from the combo startled me back to the moment at hand. Then, just as abruptly, the group behind Haley fell silent as Bill began an a cappella rant about how he and the Saddlemen were going to "tear down the mailbox and rip up the floor," and then "smash out the windows and knock down the door." Suddenly I experienced some very *unconventional* music coming from the stage at Sleepy Hollow as Haley began to sing about *"rocking* the joint." I'd never heard anything like "Rock the Joint." It was a number so raucous that whenever the Saddlemen broke it out at local bar gigs the crowds—particularly the younger patrons—went wild; so wild that Haley's manager began to hound him to record the song.

"Rock the Joint" wasn't country by any stretch of the imagination. It was country-*ish*, but with a different tilt. On it, the Saddlemen projected a sort of "thucka, thucka, thucka, thucka" sound, bolstered by a "DIT-did, DIT-did, DIT-did" backbeat. They called it "cowboy jive," but it was really a forerunner to rock and roll.

"Holy smoke." I thought. "That's really great!"

We spent the entire day at Sleepy Hollow Ranch. While I never got to meet Bill Haley, I did get to speak with a couple of the young musicians in his band who were very gracious in taking the time to do so. The day's experience left a vivid impression on me. Captivated by Bill Haley's "new" sound, I became more enthusiastic toward becoming a musician and an entertainer.

During the 1930s and 1940s, big band guitarists very seldom took the lead on a number; they mostly played rhythm. But as the 1950s began, quite a few notable guitarists appeared, some of whom began to influence me. I thought a fellow named Danny Cedrone was the most outstanding of all. (He was with Haley and the Saddlemen the day I saw them perform at Sleepy Hollow.) The authors of *Legends of Rock Guitar* called Danny "perhaps the most technically accomplished rock player of the '50s,"[7] and I couldn't agree more. Playing a Gibson ES-300 (now on display at the Rock 'n' Roll Hall of Fame in Cleveland), Cedrone developed a technique of his own. I always knew when Danny was playing. When you hear that famous guitar break—arguably one of the most recognizable in rock and roll—in Bill Haley's classic recording of "Rock Around the Clock," you're listening to the artistry of Danny Cedrone.

Danny was a South Philly guy, too, although I never met the man. He was more of a studio musician than a performer, but in

1951 Danny and rhythm guitarist Bob Scales (nee: Bob Scaltrito) formed a group called the Esquire Boys and enjoyed regional hits with "Caravan" and "Guitar Boogie Shuffle." They never caught on nationally, however. Bob Scales' father was in the olive oil business, and my parents bought their olive oil from him. I'd sometimes be practicing with my guitar when Bob came to our house to make a delivery. He'd poke his head in my room and tell me, "Hey Charlie, that sounds great. Keep it up, kid!"

Bill Haley finally got around to recording "Rock the Joint," his first true rock song, and it eventually became one of his signature numbers. It was beyond my imagination that observing Bill Haley and the Saddlemen that day at Sleepy Hollow was to play a pivotal role in jump-starting my own career in show business.

4

BOOGIE WOOGIE BLUES

Tiny independent record labels had been in existence since the Golden Age of Radio, which began in the 1920s. Most of those labels did not survive the Great Depression, and as America entered World War II its recording industry consisted largely of just three companies: Columbia (formed in 1889), Victor (1901), and Decca (1934). Upstart Capitol made it a foursome in 1942. When the United States entered the war, government regulations and restrictions forced these "major" labels to cut back on their wide range of musical genres, particularly "race," or black music. Thus, "race" and other musics outside the American mainstream became the domain of a new generation of small independent companies that began to spring up during the war.

When the war ended, the floodgates opened. Mercury Records was formed in October 1945, a mere month after the Japanese officially surrendered. During the second half of the '40s, independent labels continued to spring up at an accelerated pace, and that trend continued into the new decade.

Charlie Graci first recorded for Cadillac Records, a label formed in Detroit, Michigan in January 1950 by Park Avenue Music Publishing. Cadillac's proprietors were songwriter, vocalist, and former bandleader Jerry Harris and veteran bandleader and arranger Graham Prince. During the summer of 1951, Cadillac, with seasoned bandleader Charles Boulanger now its president and Graham Prince its musical director, moved from Detroit to New York City.

Cadillac's best shot at a hit record came with its very first release. Shortly after setting up shop in Manhattan, the label made its debut with the philosophical, emotion-laden ballad "Cry."[8] But Cadillac's version of the song never stood a chance. One of the dozen or so copies (known as "covers" in the trade) that quickly followed the original recording was sung by newcomer Johnnie Ray, an Oregon-born singer who gained immediate attention because of his histrionic style of nearly breaking out in tears as he performed. Ray's visceral interpretation of "Cry" turned the song into a mega-hit in the fall of 1951. It sold more than 2 million copies and assured that Cadillac's original version of "Cry" remained stillborn. The little record company never again came close to having a hit record.

My guitar lessons with Mr. Panto continued for about five-and-a-half years. During that time he never referred to me as his student; he called me his *pupil.* "There's a difference, Charlie," he explained. "It's mandatory that a student go to school, but a *pupil* enlists himself." Pupil or student, everything came easy to me. I had a good ear, which I inherited from my parents. I'm convinced that my ability was a gift from God. You either have it or you don't. And if you do have it, it becomes enhanced over time and you become a better musician. While studying with Mr. Panto I discovered that I had the "gift." It was in my ears, it was in my head, and it was in my heart. After a while I could really play the guitar. You should have seen Mr. Panto then. He was thrilled to death. One day he told me, "Charlie, I taught you everything I know. I can't teach you any more. You play better than I do. You're on your own."

To celebrate, I visited a local music store called Wurlitzer's and purchased a new Gibson guitar. It cost $375, which I had to pay on a contingency plan: a small amount down, followed by payments of $12 a month. I still have that old Gibson, which didn't legally become mine until I made the final payment more than two years later. But I very seldom pick it up today. It lacks the cutaway in the body that enables you to get your hand down around the neck. They hadn't thought of such an innovation in those days. Also, that vintage Gibson has just one pickup and it tends to feed back when you move too close to the amp. Despite the new Gibson's drawbacks I was able to further develop my talent and open a few doors. But even as I continued to hone my skills, I didn't realize I was destined for a career in show business.

My former instructor Mr. Panto was responsible for one of my first radio gigs. By the early 1950s, many Philadelphia-area immigrants continued to listen to Italian-language radio programs. The announcer for one such program (whose name escapes me) was Ralph Borrelli, by then a household fixture in many Italian-American homes. Mr. Panto, who was employed as a musician on the program, was instrumental in my joining the cast. I still remember one particular show when female singer Dillya Galante sung in Italian as I played "OOMP-blink-blink, OOMP-blink-blink" on my guitar, accompanied by Mr. Panto on mandolin.

During the early phase of my career I also appeared on various television programs. My very first such appearance occurred in 1948 or 1949, on *The Children's Hour*. That show was sponsored by the Horn and Hardart automated restaurant chain. You talk about long-running shows. *The Children's Hour* was first heard on Philadelphia radio in 1927. Its televised life began in 1948, broadcast Sunday mornings from Philadelphia by CBS-TV's WCAU. *The Children's Hour* was a variety show featuring a cast of youngsters and hosted by long-time Philly broadcaster Stan Lee Broza. (I'll never forget Stan and his little pencil moustache.) The show didn't involve any competition; it was simply an opportunity to gain exposure. You just went on and performed. And man, was it tough to get on *The Children's Hour*. *Everybody* had to audition, and it wasn't unusual for scores of acts to vie for each available spot. I appeared on the show a couple of times. Some of the other "kids" who got their start there included the trumpet-playing Frankie Avalon, the Four Aces' Al

Alberts, Rosemary Clooney, Eddie Fisher, Connie Francis, and Kitty Kallen. The thing that sticks in my mind most about *The Children's Hour* is that, despite being sponsored by a restaurant chain, they never provided any food on the bloody show. But the audience at home loved it. (*The Children's Hour* proved to be so popular that a New York version hosted by Ed Herlihy was developed by NBC-TV.)

After appearing on *The Children's Hour* I didn't have to wait long for my big chance, that one opportunity every aspiring entertainer needs to kickstart his or her career. Mine came on the Philadelphia-based television show *Paul Whiteman's TV Teen Club*, emceed by the legendary bandleader. Originating in 1949, *TV Teen Club* was broadcast nationally on Saturday evenings over the ABC network (emanating from WFIL-TV in Philadelphia). Whiteman's show featured dancing teenagers long before Dick Clark became famous by utilizing the very same concept on his landmark *American Bandstand*. But it was something other than dancing that drew me to *TV Teen Club*. As part of Whiteman's show he conducted a weekly teenage talent competition, for which auditions were held to select seven or eight acts for the televised competition. During the actual show a jury of teenagers determined how loud the audience clapped for each act. The top three acts received prizes and the overall winner was invited to compete on the following week's show. Winners were limited to five appearances, after which they were "retired." Whiteman's prizes to the top acts were pretty valuable and included items such as home appliances.

By the time I'd reached 15 I was no Segovia on the guitar, but I was an accomplished musician. Even at that tender age I could play with anybody. During the summer of 1951 I breezed through *TV Teen Club's* preliminary audition and qualified for the televised competition. I figured I might catch a break with the publicity I'd receive from a televised gig and I just might win a nice prize for my family.

Bill Haley and the Saddlemen's booming interpretation of "Rock the Joint" had opened my eyes (and ears) to the excitement that rock and roll (although as yet unnamed) was capable of generating. With that pounding drumbeat from the Saddlemen's Sleepy Hollow Ranch appearance still bouncing around my head, I decided to pin my *TV Teen Club* performance on replicating Haley's dynamic performance. But I sensed a potential problem. Paul Whiteman's big band drummer would offer no help in generating excitement for my number. What did *he* know about *rockin'* the joint? I knew that when my turn came, I'd be out there on my own—in front of a television camera.

Since witnessing the Saddlemen at Sleepy Hollow I'd made it a point to develop a certain guitar technique. As I played, I twanged the strings and then momentarily silenced them with a slap from my hand. This produced a kind of backbeat—boom-chicka, boom-chicka, boom-chicka—giving the overall effect of multi-instrumental sound, with my guitar also sounding like a drum. I'd discovered this method to create a fuller sound and developed it until I thought, "Hey, I'm pretty good at this!" Facing the biggest performance of my young life, I figured it was the perfect situation in which to put my backbeat prowess to the test.

Whatever you do, you have to go out there and do it with confidence: "Hey, you know what pal? I'm *good*. Watch me!" For instance, when I play the iconic tune "Guitar Boogie" nowadays, I play it extremely fast. I invariably draw a standing ovation, which results in a great feeling, like somebody's patting me on the head. (As a performer, you *have* to have some sort of ego. But if your ego ever takes over, I think it becomes your worst enemy.)

My *TV Teen Club* competition was a black lad who sang and a girl who sang while she played the piano. Both were impressive, but when my time came I went out there and won that contest. My prize that night was a Kelvinator refrigerator. I was pleased with my performance, but I was *elated* for my mother. That gleaming Kelvinator was our family's first refrigerator. No longer would my mom have to empty the water from the icebox every three or four hours. After five weeks of collecting prizes, the powers that be "retired" me from the *TV Teen Club*. But not before I'd won some additional prizes, including a $100 bond and a 45 RPM record changer with $100 worth of records of my choice. (Remember those tiny 45s with the big hole in the center? In those days they were a new-fangled invention; now they're history!) At that point in my young life I thought I'd hit the jackpot.

Besides television appearances, I played my guitar at weddings, serenades, and various social gatherings as I strove to earn a couple of bucks for my family. For a typical wedding gig I'd arrive at the bride's house the night before the ceremony. Beneath her bedroom window I'd play my guitar—plink, plink, plink, plink, plink—and serenade her with "I Love You Truly." For that I'd receive 10 bucks, which I took home to my mom. I'd hand her the dough and say, "Mom, let me keep a dollar for spending money."

During the fall of 1951 I entered the famous high school located at South Broad Street and East Snyder Avenue, about 10 long blocks west of where we lived. Its official name was South Philadelphia High School for Boys, but we all knew it as "Southern." High schools in Philadelphia weren't coed in those days. At Southern the boys and the girls went to class in separate buildings. My friends and I used to hang out of the third story windows of our building and scream and wave at the girls outside on the athletic fields, dressed in their bloomers. Some years after I graduated—I think in the early '60s—those old granite buildings were demolished and replaced by contemporary modern structures. To me, the new architecture seemed kind of ugly. As you might expect, Southern's students represented a conglomeration of South Philadelphia's various ethnic groups. Many famous entertainers graduated from that high school, including guitar virtuoso Eddie Lang, who at one time played for Bing Crosby, and Mr. Panto's cousin, the violinist Joe Venuti. Both Lang and Venuti were great jazz musicians.

Southern graduates of my generation included Al Alberts of the Four Aces, Eddie Fisher, Armando "Buddy" Greco, Mario Lanza (Alfredo Cocozza), and Al Martino (Alfred Cini). All but Lanza (who was born in 1921) were about 10 years ahead of me. The next tier included James Darren—we knew him as Jimmy Ercolani—who's my age and Frankie Avalon (Francis Avallone), who is three years younger. Chubby Checker (Ernest Evans), who I know very well, is five years my junior. Fabian (Fabiano Forte) is almost seven years younger. If you haven't figured it out yet, Eddie Fisher and Chubby are the only non-Italians in the group! I could also give you a list of non-singing alumni celebrities—including Joey Bishop and Jack Klugman—that would knock your socks off. Some great talent went through that building. When Southern celebrated its 75th Anniversary, each of us at that reunion was given a T-shirt with the names of its famous alumni printed on it.

I was quite the athlete at Southern. Too small for the football team, I found a sport I could successfully compete in. I played soccer, a game that wasn't particularly popular at the time. Truthfully, it was a pretty dull sport back then. I earned three varsity letters and even received a college soccer scholarship. Unfortunately, I had to decline that honor. By the time I graduated from Southern I was already bringing home more money with my guitar than my father was from Stetson. My earnings were needed to help support the family.

I can't recall the exact moment I realized I wanted to pursue a career as an entertainer, but I'm certain it happened while I was in high school. Besides the monetary rewards, I loved to perform for the sheer joy of it. I'm not embarrassed to say the acclamation that I received really turned me on. The girls loved me and so did the guys. I was a local celebrity, and even if I never made it out of South Philly I felt I was *somebody*.

I might have remained a local celebrity had it not been for a gentleman named Graham Prince. Graham deserves all the credit in the world for getting my career off the ground. He gave me my start in the entertainment business. When I first met Graham, he and his family were living in Flint, Michigan. He was originally from Charlotte, North Carolina and still had (as he always would) a slight southern accent. Graham was a very talented guy, a fine musician who played the xylophone. He also had a record company called Cadillac Records, located at 1619 Broadway, inside the Brill Building in New York.[9]

One Saturday evening while driving from New York to Philadelphia, Graham Prince happened to be listening to *Paul Whiteman's TV Teen Club*. (Besides being televised, the show was simulcast on Philadelphia radio.) As luck—or destiny—would have it, I happened to be in the midst of my five-week run on Whiteman's show the night Prince was listening in. The next morning I received a telegram from Graham, indicating he'd like to talk to me about cutting a record. A *record*? The thought had never entered my mind.

Graham and I met a few days later. I was only 15 and not of legal age, yet neither my father nor anybody else ever became involved in my dealings with Prince or Cadillac Records. As interested as my father was in seeing that I got into show business, he was a working man, a laborer. He didn't know anything about the recording business or its contracts. If somebody wanted to record his kid, that was good enough for him. So there never were negotiations or anything of the sort. My dad and I never thought about contracts. We were just tickled about the opportunity that suddenly lay before me. "Come to New York and we'll record," Graham urged. We shook hands and that was it.

The people at Cadillac were thrilled to death with their latest acquisition: a promising new face, who they thought had a fresh sound. Me? I didn't know what the hell was going on. I was just happy to be recording. We cut the first record in New York City. All those tunes I made for Cadillac were done there. Each time I went to New York to record I'd stay at my Aunt Lena and Uncle Dominic DiPrisco's home in Brooklyn's Williamsburg section. I spent a lot of time with my cousins Joey, Dominic, and Mike. It was fun because we were close to the action. We'd simply hop on the subway to Manhattan, so I got to know the Big Apple pretty well.

I can't remember the exact recording dates for any of those records I made for Cadillac. It was so long ago that I'd be lying if I gave an exact date. But those records were definitely made when I was in high school. I recall hearing my records played on neighborhood jukeboxes back then. I also remember that Johnnie Ray's "Cry" was released before my first recording session took place. That stands out in my mind because Johnnie left a lasting impression on me. When I first heard him doing "Cry" I thought it was a girl singing. That was during the fall of 1951, so I'd say I cut my first record in the latter part of 1951 or perhaps early 1952.

When we went in to record for the first time, I remember being knocked out by the size of the studio Graham had booked for the session. It was much larger than I'd expected. Then again, that was the first time I'd ever been in an actual recording studio, so what the hell would I know? Before we got started, Graham asked me if I had any songs of my own that I wanted to record. I was just 15 and didn't know much about writing songs. But I had written a little number called "Boogie Woogie Blues."

"Let me hear it," drawled Graham in that southern accent.

I reached for my guitar and played the song for him.

"Ooh, Chahlie, that's goood!" he exclaimed. "We gonna *do* that." Graham paused for an instant. "And how about something for the other side?" he added.

Among that batch of records I'd won on *Paul Whiteman's TV Teen Club* was Fats Waller doing "I'm Gonna Sit Right Down and Write Myself a Letter." Written in 1935 by Joe Young and Fred Ahlert, that song was an absolute classic. I loved it and I loved Fats Waller. "How about 'I'm Gonna Sit Right Down and Write Myself a Letter'?" I asked. "That's some great songwriting. You can't go wrong with that tune." Graham agreed, and that became the second song on the day's agenda.

Graham Prince had been a bandleader in the 1940s—all of Cadillac's recordings retained the dying influence of the big bands—so the musicians he employed on that first session were top-notch. We cut both songs with me playing guitar, accompanied by a string bass, piano, and soprano sax. The bass player was Bobby Haggart, who had enjoyed a huge hit with "Big Noise from Winnetka" in 1938. Luther Henderson, a great black jazz pianist who had done a lot of work with Duke Ellington, played piano. And we used a fantastic soprano saxophone player who played on radio's *The Lucky Strike Hit Parade* band (he was a stubby Italian fellow whose first name was Andy; I can't remember his last name to save my life). Because there were no drums on those first two songs we laid down that day, my technique of playing the backbeat on my guitar came in handy.[10]

Talented musicians or not, we needed about two hours of rehearsing before the arrangements for the two songs we planned to record were completed. First I made several trial recordings, which were caught on tape and played back in the studio. Then we proceeded to lay down the final tracks.

As I said, when I made those first recordings Johnnie Ray and "Cry" were hot items. Some people who hear my early recordings today claim that I tried to *sound* like Johnnie. I was always a great fan of his; I loved his style of singing. And while I did try to *phrase* like Johnnie did, I never intentionally imitated him. Because of Johnnie's intense body movements, how he ripped his shirt when he sang, and because of his other histrionics, some call him the first rock and roller. Johnnie was certainly a forerunner of rock and roll, even before Elvis. And if you look back on some of the numbers I cut with Cadillac around that time, you can detect an early hint of rock and roll in my music, too.

Because Cadillac was a small label, Graham Prince worked out a deal for his records to be manufactured and distributed by Gotham Records, a company based in South Philadelphia. Ivin Ballen, who owned Gotham, was a pleasant fellow who reminded me of the heavy-set English actor Sydney Greenstreet. How Mr. Ballen and Graham Prince met, I don't know, but Gotham had a record-pressing plant right alongside its recording studio, and Cadillac's recordings were pressed there.

It's possible that Cadillac didn't release my first record (Cadillac 141) immediately after it was recorded. By the time it did come out, in the spring of 1952, I was nearing the end of my second year in high school.[11] There were two luncheonettes directly across the street from Southern High. The guys I hung with at school survived on meatball or cutlet sandwiches because most of us were Italian and the only place we could get such things outside of our mom's kitchens was at those luncheonettes. As you might expect, besides serving teen-oriented lunches, those high-school hangouts had well-stocked jukeboxes. When "Boogie Woogie Blues" came out, the shop owners played it constantly on those jukes. They pushed those boxes right out onto the pavement and cranked the volume to attention-drawing decibels, hoping to lure more students into their establishments. Sometimes my record would be spinning on the jukes while I was in class, dreaming about my forthcoming lunch period. "Hey Graci, tell your hoodlum buddies to lower that damned thing," a teacher would inevitably implore. "I can't teach with that music going on!"

"I can't control what they're playing on the jukebox," I'd reply. We never meant to cause any trouble. Most of my classmates were simply proud of me. Back then, kids our age didn't make records. That was quite an accomplishment, whether you had a hit record or not. So I was very popular. I even played at some high-school assemblies and similar events.

Though I recorded for Graham Prince in New York, the two of us worked together in Philadelphia, albeit in a very different capacity. When Graham wasn't devoting his time to Cadillac Records he was a musician on a televised circus show called *Big Top*. Sponsored by Sealtest, a company well known for its ice cream and other dairy products, *Big Top* was first broadcast in July 1950 out of Camden, New Jersey's cavernous Convention Hall. The show was seen nationally on Saturday afternoons from noon 'til 1 p.m. on the CBS network's Philadelphia affiliate WCAU-TV. When a fire destroyed the Convention Hall in 1953, *Big Top* was temporarily moved to the WCAU studios. But the show's audience of 350 proved too large for that facility to accommodate, so in September *Big Top* moved to the Pennsylvania National Guard Armory at 32nd and Lancaster in Philadelphia.

I was hired to play guitar during *Big Top*'s live commercials for Sealtest. Graham played the xylophone and a very fine musician named Freddy Shimmen played the celeste (and doubled on the calliope in the circus band). As we performed, some of the show's cast sang the sponsor's recurrent jingle: "Get the best, get *Sealtest.*" Each week I was on that show I thanked God that I'd been hired specifically as a musician. I never had to sing that silly ditty! (Believe it or not, in my younger days I was kind of bashful when it came to singing. I used to play a kazoo around the house and my father would tell me, "Take that thing out of your mouth and start singing!" I never had singing *lessons*, but I did learn how to sing.) The leader of the Sealtest circus band was an Italian fellow named Joe Brasile. His stage nickname was Mr. Five-by-Five, and he wore a white uniform, hat and all, while he performed. Up there on the bandstand Joe looked like a cross between the Good Humor ice-cream man and John Philip Sousa!

Quite a few people on *Big Top* experienced national fame. One was Dan Lurie, a weightlifter and bodybuilder from New York who, as "Sealtest Dan, the Muscle Man," lifted real barbells during the commercials. Over time, Danny and I became good friends. The original ringmaster for *Big Top* was Jack Sterling. Six feet tall and sporting a trim mustache, Jack was perfect for the role. As the radio host of CBS' *Jack Sterling Show*, which was heard nationally for 18 years, Sterling was already well known before he began "moonlighting" on *Big Top*. When Jack left the show after seven years, a handsome movie actor named Warren Hull, who had the bluest eyes you ever saw in your life, took his place. (Warren is perhaps best remembered as the host of the TV game show *Strike It Rich*.) There were three clowns on *Big Top*. One, Philadelphian Jack Whitaker, went on to become a great sports announcer for the CBS and ABC networks. Ed McMahon, then a staff announcer for WCAU-TV, employed a large, blinking nose as part of his clown costume. Ed, of course, ended his career as Johnny Carson's sidekick on *The Tonight Show*. The third clown was local radio personality Bill Hart, who was very well known around Philadelphia. Bill was about six foot nine, and from my perspective—still growing to five feet four—he looked like Wilt Chamberlain.

We did *Big Top* every Saturday for about a year and a half. It was a lot of fun, too. Everything was done live in those days, so we came in at six in the morning to run through the commercials. Then, while the circus acts rehearsed, my father, Dan Lurie, Graham Prince, Freddy Shimmen, and I would eat breakfast together. Then we'd meet again for lunch after the show ended at 1 p.m.. Best of all, I received 35 bucks a week for doing those commercials (the same as my dad earned at Stetson), plus all the ice cream I could eat. And when I wasn't playing my guitar, I'd get to sit and watch the rest of the show.

Just before my second record for Cadillac came out, a very significant change occurred in my life, even if I didn't regard it as such at that time. On my first record, Graham had spelled my surname G-R-A-C-I, just the way I had for my first 16 years. Then one day

Graham said to me, "Chahlie, I hope you don't get offended, but I'm gonna have to change your name a little bit."

"You're not changing my name," I protested. "If a guy named 'DiMaggio' could become famous, what's the matter with 'Graci'?"

"No, no, no," Graham explained. "I want to add an 'e' to the end of your name to make it easier to pronounce. It even looks nicer in print."

We'd always used the Americanized pronunciation, "Gracie," as did most other people when they addressed members of my family, even before the "e" was added to my surname. But there were always a few who'd try to pronounce it "GRAH-see," or "GRAH-chi." I thought about it for a while. The more I did, the more I felt Graham might be onto something. "You know," I told him, "that's not a bad idea. Let's go with the 'e.'" So adding the "e" was Graham's idea, and I've been using it ever since.

Sometime in the early summer of 1952, we cut two additional songs for my second release (Cadillac 144). What I remember more than anything else about this session was the stifling heat in that recording studio. If you've ever been inside a recording studio you know it's a soundproofed, tomblike chamber. Fans to move the air, or any type of air conditioning were out, because the premises had to remain absolutely quiet. As the day wore on, I was thankful each time the engineer opened the small window between the studio and the control booth. Whenever he did, we felt a welcome rush of cool air. About seven hours after we'd begun, Graham Prince was satisfied that he had two acceptable song takes for my second Cadillac Records release. I was satisfied just to breathe some fresh air. One tune we cut was another song I'd written, titled "Rockin' 'n' Rollin'." The other was "All Over Town." We used pretty much the same lineup of musicians we had for our first session, except this time, when we did "Rockin' 'n' Rollin'," Graham included a vocal group in the mix. If I remember correctly, he used The Modernaires, best known for their work alongside Glenn Miller in the 1940s. Although well past their peak popularity, The Modernaires remained active in the business.

People who haven't heard "Rockin' 'n' Rollin'" often assume the song is some sort of early reference to rock and roll. But "rock and roll" as a musical genre was still on the cusp of existence when I wrote that song. If you listen to the words, a fellow is singing to his girl about "rockin', rollin', baby back to you." But there was no musical connotation intended on my part when I wrote it.

As with my first Cadillac record, I'm not certain exactly when my second effort for Graham Prince's label was issued. The dates are a blur to me. But if the label number of my second release is synchronized with the label numbers of Cadillac records reviewed by *Billboard*, that second record most likely came out during the fall of 1953, just about the time I began my senior year at Southern. That summer, Cadillac had relocated its headquarters from the Brill Building to West 55th Street in Manhattan. I did my final session for the label some time between then and early 1954. With the help of some fine black female gospel singers, we cut two spirituals. "'T'Ain't No Sin in Rhythm" is a rousing gospel number that, in the sanctified church tradition, really jumps. The more pop-oriented flip side, "Say What You Mean," has a bit slower tempo and contains a fine R&B-like sax-guitar-sax bridge.

If the release dates of my first two records for Cadillac are fuzzy, the date for my third (Cadillac 154) remains a real mystery. Once again, examining the label numbers of Cadillac records reviewed in *Billboard*, my final release may not have hit the retail shops until early 1955. Because of slim sales on my first two records it's possible that Graham Prince, who was always cash-poor, had left those remaining two sides I'd cut for him in the can. In the meantime, I left Cadillac Records. Around March 1955, concurrent with my first record for my new label, Graham may have put those old Cadillac sides out hoping to capitalize on any publicity generated by my latest release.

Although my records for Cadillac didn't sell that well, they did make a hero out of me at Southern High. Most of the fellows knew me and liked me. I was considered a "guys' guy." I was one of them. I never walked around with my nose in the air. I knew if I ever began behaving like somebody special, they surely would have come at me. So I never had any problems. The guys I went to school with always greeted me with a "Hey Charlie, what's up?" During lunch I'd grab my guitar, begin to play, and everyone around me would sing. We had a ball together. There may have been some envy or resentment behind my back—you never can please everybody—but never directly to me.

While at Southern I learned of a not-so-secret admirer, one who lived only blocks away from me—none other than the "Docile Don," Angelo Bruno! I'd already cut a couple of sides for Cadillac and had begun to make a little noise around the neighborhood. One day my dad's cousin Benny—the number writer—came over to the house and announced to my father, "Dixie, somebody wants to talk to you." ("Dixie" was my father's nickname. As an amateur boxer he'd used the name Kid Dixie, which the guys in the neighborhood shortened to Dixie, and it stuck.)

"Who's that?"

"Angelo."

We knew right away who "Angelo" was.

"Talk to me about what?" asked my father.

"About Charlie."

"All right," replied my dad, knowing full well that when Angelo Bruno wanted to see you, there was no other choice. "Let's make an appointment."

He did, and when the time came we walked over to the Bruno's row home on Snyder Avenue. The Don himself greeted us at the door and offered a "God bless you" in Sicilian. My father replied in Sicilian, which, by the way, was the only language spoken the entire time we were there. My dad and I sat down with mixed degrees of anticipation and anxiety racing through our minds.

"Sam, your son's becoming pretty well known around here," said the Don. "We understand he's very talented. What we'd like to do is take over the management of his career. We'll handle Charlie. Whatever he needs—wardrobe, education, anything—will be our responsibility." My father didn't move a muscle. He sat there like a stone and listened as Angelo Bruno, the underworld Boss of all Philadelphia, made his pitch. Eventually the Don ominously dropped the other shoe: "Realize, Sam, whatever we tell your son to do, he'll have to comply."

With that, my father abruptly arose from his chair. With no

inkling of what was about to transpire, I instinctively did the same. Then, looking down at the seated Don, my dad began to speak in a most deliberate yet determined manner: "I appreciate your offer to do all of that for my boy," he told Bruno. "With all due respect, and nothing personal, Charlie's *my* son and he'll do what *I* tell him." Standing next to my dad, I felt my blood run cold. But after what felt like an eternity, Angelo Bruno, perhaps the most feared figure in Philadelphia, gave my father a silent nod of deference. He thanked the Don and we walked out of his house. I never spoke a word the entire time we were there.

During our walk home my father turned to me and said, "Never hang with those people. If you live by the sword you'll die by the sword." I knew my dad *and* my grandfather had always felt that way. They both believed that honesty is the best policy. That philosophy has paid off, too. Nobody in my family has ever been in jail, or even inside a police station for that matter.

I was quite fortunate to have things turn out the way they did with the Don. There never were any repercussions on his part. Had my father not held his ground in that intimidating situation, by the time I eventually hit the big time the mob would've had a stranglehold on me. The only one in our family to feel a bit disappointed was my father's cousin Benny. Benny figured if a deal was cut with the Don that day, he might have received a chunk of the action.

I still wasn't used to being Charlie "Gracie" with that added "e" when it hit me one day: "This is it! I want to be a professional entertainer and recording artist." Seeing how easy and how much fun it had been to make those records for Graham Prince removed any doubt from my mind. After my lengthy initial session for Cadillac I made it a point to study each song before I went in to cut it. That saved quite a bit of time once I got to the studio. I'd lay down one take—on occasion, several—and that was it. There was no overdubbing or other special effects to worry about, and the studio musicians I worked with were solid pros. After hearing a new song once or twice they were ready to go. The happiest guy of all may have been Graham. He never again had to foot the bill for studio overtime.

I only wish I'd kept a few boxes of those Cadillac waxings. Each of those recordings is pretty hard to find today, mostly because we hardly sold any of them when they came out. We *may* have sold up to 1,000 total, or perhaps less. I literally had to give them away when they first came out. I think I gave away more records than Graham Prince sold. Most of the time the reaction was, "Oh I didn't know you made records, Charlie." Today those discs are each worth a couple hundred dollars or more. At least I did have the foresight to salt away one copy of each. I'm a squirrel. I save everything.

5

DOREEN THE TASSEL QUEEN

Sometime around late 1954 or early 1955 19-year-old Charlie Gracie signed a recording contract with Gotham Records. More than likely, Gotham owner Ivin Ballen was captivated by the growing popularity of Bill Haley, who, along with his group, the Comets (nee Saddlemen), were the only white singers successfully marketing uptempo rhythm and blues tunes to a growing white audience. And Haley was doing so from his hometown of Chester, Pennsylvania, right under Ivin Ballen's nose.

Gotham was a regional label—a small-scale operation compared to the majors. It was formed in New York by record wholesaler Sam Goode (Goody) in 1946. Ballen purchased Gotham from Goode in 1948 and moved the company to Philadelphia. In 1951, he relocated his operation to an abandoned church on Federal Street in South Philadelphia. After renovation of the premises, Ballen had his own recording studio, record pressing facilities, and a print shop.

After several years, Ballen looked to expand Gotham's horizons. The niche market of Gospel music that Gotham had cultivated was enough to sustain his revamped "vertically integrated" operation, but it offered little in the way of growth potential.

Ivin Ballen realized he couldn't sustain the national success of a star of Bill Haley's magnitude; it was simply beyond Gotham's capabilities, not to mention the capabilities of Ballen's own wallet. But there were new fields he could till. Down in Memphis, Tennessee a 19-year-old hillbilly implausibly named Elvis Presley had put out a couple of records on a tiny label and was already causing quite a stir throughout the South. Billboard magazine reported that the kid, who sang with a "hillbilly blues beat," had just become a regular on the "Louisiana Hayride." Whether somebody of such a rural bent could ever gain mass acceptance in the urban north was uncertain at that point, but word had it that a few of the major labels already had their eyes on Presley.

Someone like the promising singer from South Philadelphia named Dominick Bello was more within Ivin Ballen's limited realm. The young Bello—now calling himself Freddie Bell—was doing quite well for himself, fronting a dynamite stage act out in Vegas. What is more, Freddie Bell and the Bellboys were said to be on the verge of signing a recording deal with Teen Records, a small Philadelphia label partially owned by Bandstand's Bob Horn.

Freddie Bell's ascendance from the Delaware Valley to the bright lights of Vegas prompted Ivin Ballen to envision another local figure, Charlie Gracie, perhaps hitting the big-time himself. Having pressed and distributed Gracie's records for Cadillac, Ballen was quite familiar with the favorable young singer-guitarist who made them. Charlie's home was not far from Gotham's new digs, and on occasion Charlie had even frequented the Federal Street plant to watch his own recordings emerge from its pressing machines. Ivin Ballen had little to lose by offering the promising fresh singer a recording contract.

I started becoming popular around town because of my records. Not that they sold well, but because their very existence put me, a local guy, in line to appear with Bob Horn on his Philadelphia-based *Bandstand* television show. I must have done Horn's *Bandstand* at least four or five times before it was handed to Dick Clark. As soon as "Boogie Woogie Blues" was issued, I was asked to appear on the show. Bob was a very gracious guy—at least he was to me. Thank God he put me on his show and gave me a chance to promote my first record. At that point in my career it was great exposure.

Horn and his *Bandstand* show were hot and growing even stronger in the Delaware Valley region. Bob, in his mid-thirties, was older than the kids of my generation. He wasn't a bad-looking man, but he seemed to have a perpetual sneer on his face and a sinister look about him, à la Richard Nixon. Let's just say you wouldn't want to buy a used car from the guy. Bob was a heavy smoker, which added an even harsher edge to his persona. During breaks in the show he would hide behind a curtain in the studio and puff away on a cigarette. But Bob was a big name in Philadelphia, one of the *mahoffs*[12] in town. He had been in radio there for many years. My mother used to listen to him all the time.

Despite his somewhat unsavory appearance, Bob had a pretty good rapport with the kids on his show. When the cameras were off and the kids got out of hand, he chastised and admonished them just like a father would—"Hey, sit down there, dammit!" But overall, the kids were pretty loyal to him, and it wasn't too long before *Bandstand* became Philadelphia's hottest local television production. It reached the point where the show could create a hit record in town. (When *Bandstand* went nationwide in 1957 with Dick Clark at the helm, it helped make hit records all across the country.)

Bandstand was broadcast from WFIL-TV's studio, located at 46th and Market Streets, right next to the elevated railroad in West Philadelphia. Each day after school the kids would line up there by the hundreds, and that studio didn't hold many people. A lot of those high-schoolers became "regulars" on the show, eventually growing famous themselves. Perhaps the most widely known of them turned out to be local disc jockey Jerry Blavat, who I've known since he was a little cocker and one of the original dancers on Horn's show. The only contact I had with any of the other *Bandstand* teens was with Arlene Sullivan, who was president of my fan club for a while. Arlene's a lovely woman, who I still see every once in a while when I play a concert in the Philadelphia area.

I was also very friendly with disc jockeys Joe Grady and Ed Hurst, the hosts of a show called the *950 Club* on radio station WPEN. In those days, Grady and Hurst were quite influential in the Philadelphia area; they could make or break you. Most people don't realize that Bob Horn modeled *Bandstand* along the lines of Grady and Hurst's *950 Club*. A lot of neighborhood teens went there to dance, but you couldn't see them as the *950 Club* was broadcast on radio only. (The program received its name for its spot on the AM radio dial.) Grady and Hurst frequently invited guest artists into the WPEN studio to plug their records, and I was on their show numerous times.

I also began to entertain at dances in the Philadelphia area. Disc jockeys such as Bob Horn conducted record hops around town, which would sometimes draw as many as 200 or 300 teens. In those situations, I had an advantage over most of the other young singers. They weren't musicians; they just sang. Rather than lip-sync like those guys did, I'd plug my guitar into my amp and then sing and play live on the spot. As I participated in those record hops and other related activities, I developed a nice rapport with the local music industry people. It was a win-win situation. Everyone was nice to me, and my fan base continued to increase.

As soon as I turned 18 I began to work the nightclubs, although not yet on a steady basis. Beginning in the spring of 1954, I attended high school during the week and, to pick up a few bucks, I'd work the regional clubs on some weekends. "Charlie," the agent would say to me, "I've got a gig for you in Lebanon (Pennsylvania)." I'd toss my guitar in the car, drive some 80 miles to the gig, perform, collect my 20 bucks, drive home—and then pay the agent his $2 commission! From that point on, I considered myself a nightclub entertainer.

I kept telling myself it wasn't about the money; it was about the *experience*. I was getting my feet wet while I made new friends and contacts in various cities on the circuit. Some of those friendships began in a most improbable manner. There's my friend George the bartender, for instance, a guy I met on the road when I was about 18 years old. I was working the Carnival Room in Pittsburgh, just up the street from the old Roosevelt Hotel, where I used to stay when I was in town. Performing one night, I noticed George smiling and winking at me. I didn't know what the hell was going on. I was an innocent, baby-faced kid, trying hard to justify my 150 bucks a week salary. After my final set of what was then the very early morning, George approached me.

"Let's go out and have breakfast," he suggested.

Well, when you're a youngster on the road, you don't pass up anything that's free. I figured, "Hey, if this guy wants to buy me breakfast, I'm gone!" George and I headed to the local diner and slid into a vacant booth. We no sooner had seated ourselves across the table before I felt George's hand on my leg, squeezing it. That's when the light bulb in my head finally went on. "Wait a minute George," I protested. "I don't know what's on your mind. I don't know if I *appear* gay to you, but I'm *not*. I'm straight as an arrow!"

"Oh, I'm so very sorry," he said. "Please forgive me. I thought you were one of us."

If I'd been the type of guy looking to take advantage of someone, after that uncomfortable introduction I could have leveraged anything I wanted from George. But I never abused his generosity (e.g., the offering of his yellow DeSoto convertible for my personal use whenever I played Pittsburgh), and over the years we grew to love each other as friends. One time I'd finished my gig at the Carnival Room and was preparing to fly home to Philadelphia. "Forget about the plane," George said. "Some friends and I are getting ready to drive to Atlantic City. We have to pass through Philadelphia, so come with us. We'll drop you off along the way and you can pocket the airfare."

"Great!" I replied. "I'll call my mom and tell her to have dinner ready for all of us. She's a great cook. I know she won't mind."

When George pulled up to the Roosevelt Hotel to pick me up, his DeSoto was packed with guys and girls. I jumped into the remaining available seat and off we went. When we arrived at my parents' South Philly row home, George parked the DeSoto right out front and I led the parade up the steps to the front door. I made the round of introductions and my mom invited everybody in. As we ate dinner, everyone engaged in innocuous pleasantries. I thought, "Man, this is going even better than I expected!" But no sooner had we finished eating, when my mother got me alone.

"Who *are* those people, Charlie?" she demanded. "Is there something *wrong* with them?"

"No, ma, they're gay."

Once that cat was out of the bag, George and his friends didn't stick around very long. Saying they were eager to continue on to Atlantic City, the group thanked my parents profusely for their hospitality. Then I said my goodbyes. I felt bad for them, considering the way things suddenly ended. They were wonderful, some of the nicest people I'd ever met. Plus, George had saved me a $100 plane fare, which was no small thing. He and I remained friends for a long, long time. Many years after I was married I had George over to meet my wife and kids when I was performing in Pittsburgh.

I graduated from high school in 1954 and became a full-time professional entertainer, prepared to make my living by performing in the clubs. I mentioned earlier the development of my "backbeat" guitar technique. Once I began to work the nightclub circuit it really came in handy. Most of those early joints I worked had a three- or four-piece band to back me. But I often had to play what is known in the business as "the lull," the downtime between the sets of the headlining performer. At that time a typical nightclub bill consisted of a singer, a song-and-dance team, and a comic. Between those acts, or sometimes when they took a break, I'd go on and perform for 20 minutes, singing and playing the guitar. By using my backbeat technique I was able to sound like a couple of pieces, if not a small combo.

Those times I did have a band behind me I'd lay off the backbeat a bit, unless I wanted to accent a particular piece. But many musicians I worked with weren't hip to what I was doing. Most of them played "one and three, swing," which is a big band sound (and a whole different form of music from what I was into). In those cases, I made sure to tell the drummer exactly where I wanted the beat.

Because I recorded for Cadillac Records, Graham Prince became my booking agent by default. He proceeded to book me into venues where I earned anywhere from $150 to $175 a week. Outside the Philly area, I worked in Ohio and a few other nearby states, as well as in the Pittsburgh area. Since Graham once lived in Flint, Michigan he had a lot of connections in the Detroit area. Early on, he booked me into a supper club called the Club Gay Haven (in those days the word "gay" meant "festive"), which was located on West Warren Avenue in nearby Dearborn.[13] The Gay Haven was well known; it used to showcase the very top stars, people such as Frankie Laine, Johnnie Ray, and the Four Lads. I played the Gay Haven twice: the first time as an unknown added attraction, the second after I'd become famous.

I'll never forget what happened to me during my initial gig there. I was thrilled to death to learn Patty Andrews of the Andrews Sisters would be the star of the show I was opening. My God, Patty Andrews! As a kid, I used to see her and her singing siblings in the movies, and I loved all their records. I never thought I'd be working with anybody of Patty's stature.

That night, the Gay Haven program opened with a dance team, after which I did my 20 or 25-minute spot. Patty then closed the show with an hour-long performance. The entire time she was onstage I stood to the side with my mouth hanging open, watching her, trying to learn anything and everything I could. I was so enamored of Patty's stardom that when she finished her performance I was tempted to approach her and say, "Hi, my name's Charlie Gracie. I'm just starting out in this business…" Patty's dressing room was only a few feet away from where I changed my clothes, but we never did get to talk. The woman never spoke a word to me; never even a "hello." But she did speak to the manager of the Gay Haven, who epitomized a mob enforcer—or at least Hollywood's version of one. You know, the type with the crooked nose, who spoke in a gruff voice, as if he was auditioning for a part in a 1930s gangster movie. "Hey, kid, c'mere…"

After the first night's show he came up to me and said with a menacing tone, "We have a little problem, Charlie."

"What? Did I do something wrong?"

"No, kid, you didn't do nothin' wrong. It's just that the star of the show is breakin' my balls. Evidently you're too strong an act for her. She doesn't like it and wants you off the show. She told me, 'If that kid's here tomorrow night I quit!'"

It was as if someone had punched me right in the stomach. "Holy smoke!" I thought. "What a controversy to be involved in." "So what are you gonna do?" I asked the manager. "You want me to go home, I'll go home. I didn't come here to upset anybody."

"No," he told me. "*I'm* runnin' this joint. She won't decide what you do. I will!" Some time later I found out the club's manager liked me a lot and had said to Patty, "Look, you can quit if you want, but that kid's stayin' here. And if you wanna get paid, you'll finish the week out."

Patty fulfilled her commitment, but I was hurt, as well as broken-hearted. I felt I'd been the cause of this brouhaha. Approaching the end of her career, Patty evidently felt threatened, perceiving me, with my guitar and a fresh sound, as the wave of the future. I imagined her thinking, "Who *is* this little snot-nose, creating a hard time for the *real* star of the show?" For the rest of the week, each time I finished performing I'd walk by Patty as she stood there, waiting to go on. Whenever I did, I hung my head down to avert eye contact with her. The fact that a kid as green as I was could intimidate a huge star like Patty Andrews was difficult for me to believe. Later on in my career I realized that kind of thing happens all the time in show business. But despite my problems with Patty, the Gay Haven's clientele were excited over my performances. Each night, after I left the stage, I'd hear people say, "Wow! Who *is* this kid?

Around about that time, I decided to leave Cadillac Records. There really was no one particular reason for doing so, especially now that Graham Prince was booking gigs for me in clubs around the country. We had no problems whatsoever. But I hadn't sold many records with Cadillac, and I figured it was time to move on, that perhaps a change of scenery might give my lackluster recording career a boost.

In a way it was a shame that Graham and I weren't able to make things work. The last time I spoke to him—it must have been in the 1970s—he called me and said, "Chahlie, I'm in some financial straits right now. If you could lend me $400 I'd appreciate it very much."

I sent the money to him, not expecting to ever get it back. And you know what? I never did. But I don't care. I owe everything to that guy. He gave me my start in the business and took a chance on me when I was only 15 years old. I didn't find out until quite recently that Graham died in Los Angeles, California in 1981. He was 77 years old, God rest his soul. Graham Prince was a real gentleman. He just never had the necessary finances to fulfill his expectations.

Near the end of 1954 or the beginning of 1955 I signed a contract with Philadelphia's Gotham Records to record for the company's subsidiary label, 20th Century. It's strange the way things played out: Cadillac's manufacturing and distribution deal with Gotham ultimately caused me to sign with Ivin Ballen's label. Gotham's pressing plant was located at 29th and Tasker Street in South Philly, not very far from where I lived, so on occasion I dropped in to watch my records being pressed. When I did, the company sometimes gave me some copies to pass along to disc jockeys. During those visits to Gotham I saw a lot of Ivin Ballen. It turned out that he had his eye on me for some time. But he made no overtures as long as I was with Cadillac, for fear of jeopardizing the pressing and distribution deal he had with Graham Prince. As soon as Ballen learned I'd terminated my affiliation with Cadillac, he offered me a contract. "I'd like you to record with us, Charlie. What do you say we go into my studio and cut a couple of records?"

"Sure, fine." I replied.

Gotham wasn't an elaborate setup, but they got the job done. I cut a couple of nice records with them. They were recorded at the company's studio, located right next to the pressing plant. We did two sessions for 20th Century, and possibly a third. The records sounded somewhat like Bill Haley-type things, with a pronounced backbeat and rimshots throughout. We used a combo that included a string bass, trumpet, piano, two saxophones, and drums. But those recordings also belied Gotham's shoestring budget. On some of the numbers there's no bass. And it's pretty tough to play quality music with no bass; that's the real bottom of the sound. Also, Mr. Ballen wouldn't spring for a vocal group to back me up. As a result, those recordings sound sort of naked.

The first sides we cut were "My Baby Loves Me," which I wrote, and a tune called "Head Home Honey." The record was released in March or April 1955. I also recorded a version of the venerable

"Frankie and Johnny" at that session, or perhaps at the second one, but that track wasn't released until decades later.

My records for 20th Century were credited to "Charlie Gracie and the Wildcats" but there never was a group called the Wildcats. When we cut those records I didn't have a band. Except for a brief time, much later on in my career, I always worked as a solo artist, both in the studio and on stage. When I walked into the Gotham studio for the first time, I met a combo who'd been hired to record with me. They were a little older than I was and all of them were good musicians, well seasoned from working club dates. After we finished recording, Mr. Ballen said to me, "We gotta come up with a name for this group."

I really didn't care what they were called. They weren't *my* band. The word "wild" happened to be a hip term back then, and I offhandedly remarked: "Call 'em something wild. In fact, why not call them the 'Wildcats'?" And that's what we did.

For my follow-up release we cut two additional songs. I'd written a tune called "Honey Honey," which accounted for one side of the new record. Then we laid down a lively number called "Wildwood Boogie." Conceived with the regional record-buying market in mind, "Wildwood Boogie" made reference to a popular summer getaway spot for Philadelphia-area residents. Ivin Ballen's timing was perfect. He released the record around June 1955,[14] just as the Wildwood crowd was gearing up for another summer of fun and sun down the Jersey shore.

It's funny how your perspective on some things changes over time. I never thought those records I cut for Mr. Ballen were fantastic (although, for their time, I think they were fine). But today I find that my audience really goes for that 20th Century material. Whenever I'm at a gig nowadays, people say to me, "We love those songs, Charlie!" They'd buy them by the thousands if I had them to sell.

Unfortunately, I had limited success with both of my 20th Century records back in the day. As with Cadillac Records and Graham Prince, I never received a nickel from Mr. Ballen. But I was still a young kid then and I really didn't care about royalties. I was working the nightclub circuit pretty steadily and I saw those records as promotional devices. If, once in a while, one of them was played on the radio, that gave me a little boost. It was enough to keep me employed.

When I first started out, running around from radio station to radio station, trying to get my records played, it wasn't anything like today, where you've got to deal with a program manager and all kinds of other people. In those days you walked into a station with your record and actually sat down and talked to the disc jockey. Most likely he'd play your record, if not on the spot, then soon thereafter. After listening to the type of music played by Georgie Woods, Jocko Henderson, Lloyd "Fatman" Smith, and other jocks on Philadelphia's two black radio stations, WHAT and WDAS, a lot of those guys were astonished to see this little *white* boy singing blues. "*You're* Charlie Gracie? Man, we've been playing your record here; we thought you were a black dude."

"No, it's just me," I'd reply.

I began to make a name for myself in the Delaware Valley, not only in Philadelphia, but in nearby cities such as York, Reading, Lancaster, Harrisburg, and Camden, New Jersey. I was now making $175 to $200 a week working the clubs, at a time when my father was still making less than half that amount at Stetson. Since leaving Graham Prince, I'd been sort of freelancing, calling different agents and even lining up various jobs myself. That enabled me to work with numerous agents: Neil Belmont, Happy Burns, and Bernie Landis, to name just a few of them.

Another agent I'd tried to contact several times was Bernie Rothbard. But for one reason or another we were never able to connect. The day Bernie and I finally did meet, I was working a weeklong gig at a strip joint called Carroll's Cafe, located at 52nd and Walnut in West Philadelphia. All the strippers wore these little pasties on their breasts, along with tiny bikini bottoms. That was the first time I'd ever seen a woman almost totally naked. I was the only guy in the show and I thought I'd died and gone to heaven! Led by a dazzler billed as "Doreen the Tassel Queen," the women came out bumping and grinding to music played offstage by a trio of black musicians, one of them a blind piano player: "Dah-dah-DAH-ba-

BOOM, ba-BOOM!" Believe it or not, those guys actually played quite well. Too bad nobody was in the house for *them*—or *me*, for that matter. When my turn came, I'd sing a few songs while Doreen and the other girls took a well-earned break. To this day, whenever I work a nightclub I joke with the audience about my experience at Carroll's. "I didn't make much money there," I tell them. "But my face cleared up in a week." Ba-BOOM!

It's ironic that at the same time I was trying to get in touch with Bernie Rothbard, he'd already heard about me through the grapevine. "I gotta go see this kid," Bernie thought. "Whoever he is, he's makin' some noise."

The film *Broadway Danny Rose* is the story of a touching, small-time talent agent played by Woody Allen. Like Danny Rose, Bernie Rothbard was an agent who never wanted to blow a gig. He'd search high and low for *anything* that he could sell, in order to collect his 10% cut. Over the years, Bernie found work for such oddball acts as a virtuoso who played Mozart on three harmonicas simultaneously and a midget dressed like a leprechaun who played the saxophone and told off-color dwarf jokes. "You want a singing parakeet?" he'd say. "Gimme a day or two!" That was Bernie Rothbard, or "Philadelphia" Bernie, as he came to be known in the business.

Bernie was originally from North Philly. He was in his early forties when I first met him. He'd started out back in the 1930s as an usher at the city's famous Earle Theatre, which was located on the corner of 11th and Market Street. Bernie worked his way up the ladder at the Earle to eventually become treasurer of the famous showplace. (That was *the place* to go back then. My mother and father took me there to see Frank Sinatra when I was seven years old.) One of his jobs was paying the live acts that appeared on stage before the movie was shown. In doing so, Bernie had the opportunity to meet many young entertainers who were just starting out in the business. He also had the gift of gab, which didn't hurt him any. Bernie eventually parlayed the knowledge he'd accrued at the Earle into the theatrical booking business.

As America entered World War II, Bernie was working in the Philadelphia office of the Jolly Joyce Talent Agency. Bernie spent three years overseas with the Eighth Air Force (8 AF) during World War II, at a base in Norwich, England where he booked acts to entertain the troops. After the war, Bernie returned to Jolly Joyce for a brief time. Then, in 1946, he went to work for the Eddie Suez Talent Agency. Operating out of Philly's Shubert Building—the city's equivalent to New York's Brill Building—the Suez Agency booked entertainment for most of the cocktail bars and lounges in the city. In 1952, Bernie became a full-fledged partner with Eddie, and the company's name was changed to the Suez-Rothbard Agency. Bernie was Jewish, Eddie was part Italian and part Lebanese. Eddie was a former boxer, a big, rough-looking guy who resembled Jack Dempsey. But his looks were deceiving. He was an extremely mild-mannered and soft-hearted former dancer. Bernie and Eddie remained partners for many years.

The night I met Bernie at Carroll's I was in the middle of my act when a guy walked in and began to watch me intently. (He wasn't difficult to spot; there were probably no more than 10 or 12 men in the audience.) I had no idea who he was. "What the hell are you doin' in *here*?" he asked me after I left the stage.

"I'm trying to make a living," I told him. "I'm trying to develop my career."

"Well, the name's Bernie Rothbard. I run a talent agency in this town," he responded. "I gotta get you outta this place, kid. You don't belong here. You have too much talent to be doing this. Don't worry, if you're not 21 yet, I got a legal way of getting you out of this. How old are you, anyway?"

"Look, I can't leave," I protested. "I'm making $150 a week here, and most of that goes to my parents to help them out."

Bernie kept insisting he could help *me* out.

"Well, all right," I finally conceded. "If you think I've got so much talent, *you* handle me; *you* book me."

The manager of Carroll's didn't object to me leaving the gig, so Bernie and I shook hands on it and walked out of the joint. Because we didn't really know each other, we later formalized the arrangement by signing a one-year contract. As time went on, Bernie began to book me into joints that were a little bit better, a little classier. After our first year together we never signed another contract, we simply shook hands each year. The way I saw it was: I'm a decent, honest guy. If he's a decent, honest guy, then we don't need a contract. Whatever happens between us, we can always sit down and work things out. And that's just what we did. Bernie and I grew to be more than business associates. He became my friend; I became his. We grew to be pals.

Around 1958 or 1959, Eddie Suez wanted to get out of the talent booking business, so he and Bernie parted ways. I went with the newly formed Bernie Rothbard Theatrical Agency. To say things worked out is an understatement. I stayed with Bernie for 36 years. When I'm onstage performing I often tell the story about how I was working in Carroll's strip joint when I met him. I often add a little more humor by telling the audience: "Every night when I went to work at that joint my father would cry. 'Dad, why are you crying?' I finally asked."

"'Take me *with* you!,' he pleaded."

That's an entertaining "showbiz" story. It also happens to be bullshit. But people love it. They hear it and laugh for several minutes.

I'd been fairly successful moving my career along on my own, lining up a somewhat better gig here, earning a little more money there. With Bernie Rothbard now pulling the strings, I was about to experience the utmost of professional ascensions.

6

BUTTERFLY

Bernie Lowe (Lowenthal) was born in Philadelphia in 1917 to parents of Russian-Lithuanian Jewish heritage. He learned to play the piano at an early age, while both his parents worked long hours to put food on the table. A teenager when the Prohibition Era came to an end in 1933, Lowe honed his skills playing barrelhouse numbers in former speakeasies. He spent much of the 1930s as a pianist on the road with various "society" bands, including those of Meyer Davis, Jan Savitt, and Lester Lanin. During that time Lowe also performed regularly on a radio program broadcast by WPEN in Philadelphia. Just prior to WWII, Lowe and fellow musician Artie Singer landed steady gigs in the house combo of the Walt Whitman Hotel in Camden, New Jersey. After getting married in 1943, Lowe spent the war years in the Navy. When the war ended he rejoined Singer, this time as a member of the studio orchestra of Philadelphia's WIP radio. As the big bands fell by the wayside, Bernie Lowe and Artie Singer, aided by the G.I. Bill, opened their 20th Century Institute of Music in the Center City section of Philadelphia. When Paul Whiteman decided to look for a combo to appear regularly on his TV Teen Club show, he chose Bernie Lowe to put one together, and in 1952 Lowe became musical director of Whiteman's show.

It had been Lowe's desire to get into the record business for some time, but with limited capital, the ever-anxious and perpetually parsimonious musician went no further than to tiptoe around the edges of the industry. He, along with Artie Singer and local musician/ jazz impresario Nat Segal, formed S-L-S (Singer-Lowe-Segal) Records, to no avail. In 1955, Lowe, Segal, and Bandstand emcee Bob Horn created Teen and Sound Records and uncharacteristically scored a national hit with Gloria Mann's "Teen-Age Prayer."

Lowe also began to write songs with a comedy and jingle writer named Kal Mann (Kalman Cohen) and they celebrated their first writing success as a team in 1955, with Nat King Cole's "Take Me Back to Toyland." In 1956, Lowe and Mann signed an exclusive writing deal with the powerful New York-based Hill & Range music publishers, for which they earned $150 apiece each week. The duo was fortunate enough to get one of their songs, "Teddy Bear," placed on Elvis Presley's recording schedule for 1957.[15] But according to Lowe and Mann's contract, if "Teddy Bear" (or any other song they wrote) became a hit, Hill & Range would deduct the money the songwriters were paid as a salary from their royalties. In the meantime, Lowe and Mann wrote another song for which they had high hopes. It was titled "Butterfly." But if Lowe and Mann registered their names as the writers of that potential-packed tune, Hill & Range, and not Lowe and Mann, would own all the rights to the song.

Bernie Lowe was determined to not let that happen. But there was only one way he could get "Butterfly" recorded and released without any writing credits listed on it. He would have to put the song out himself. With that, Lowe borrowed $2,000 from his family and formed Bernard Lowe Enterprises, consisting of Cameo Records and Mayland Music song publishing, in the basement of his tiny suburban North Philadelphia row home.

As it happened, the first five records Lowe put out on Cameo stiffed, and his $2000 bankroll was just about depleted. Bernie Lowe had one last chance to roll the dice, but to do so he desperately needed to find a suitable singer to record "Butterfly."

❖

In 1956 Elvis became a superstar. Boy, what a phenomenon. He joined RCA Victor in the fall of 1955 and within a year sold more than 10 million records, including 5 million-sellers. Elvis alone was responsible for two-thirds of the singles that RCA, the largest recording company in America, sold.

Bill Haley had made an earlier impact on the music industry and for a brief time, especially in Europe, nobody was any hotter than he was. Bill was always bigger in Europe than he was here in America. But his physical appearance proved to be a detriment in his battle with Elvis' smoldering persona. He was kind of stocky and he had a pudgy face. He appeared old, when actually he was still a young man. His downfall was sealed once Elvis and the ensuing teenage idols began to appear. Every record label tried to land its own version of Elvis. It was a highly unlikely feat, but doable. For a time, Capitol Records did just fine with Gene Vincent, and would-be music entrepreneurs—Bernie Lowe included—took notice.

In 1956, Bernie lived in a little row house, with an office in his basement. I'm telling you, the guy was as poor as I was. Bernie was making 125 bucks a week playing the piano in that little orchestra for Paul Whiteman on his *TV Teen Club*. Although I never actually met Bernie, I knew *of* him through the show.

The next time I saw Bernie was in December 1956. He had Bernie Rothbard with him and before I knew what was happening, the two Bernies paid a visit to my parents' house. Bernie Lowe was fighting a bad cold that day. His nose was running and he felt miserable. My mother, who happened to be making chicken soup that afternoon, said, "Sit down Bernie, have a bowl! It'll make you feel better." Meanwhile, I handed him a box of Kleenex.

Bernie Lowe began to tell me about a record company he'd started called Cameo. A few days earlier he'd called my agent and said, "I always thought Charlie had a lot of talent. He's a good singer and he plays the guitar exceptionally well. I'd really like to get him into the studio. I know he hasn't recorded for some time," he added, "but I'd like to give him a shot. Elvis is the hottest thing around at the moment, and I'd like to record someone along those lines, and Charlie's got that sound."

Bernie then relayed that conversation to my dad, who replied. "What kinda deal are we talking about?"

"We'll give him 2¢ a record."

Two cents, 4¢, 10¢, who cared? At that point we were just looking for an "in." Then Bernie Lowe turned to me and said, "Charlie, you're really a great little artist. We're gonna make a lot of money together!"

"Okay, great," I thought. "That's fine with me!"

Bernie Lowe had been looking for a tall, sexy, handsome Presley-type who could sing and play the guitar. But he couldn't find one in Philadelphia so he wound up with all five-feet-four-inches of me! As the two Bernies sat there with me in our little row home on Pierce Street I felt as if we were a kind of family. Yet in another sense we were more like Larry, Curly, and Moe—three guys about to stumble into who knew what?

This was probably Bernie Lowe's last shot before his dwindling bankroll ran out. Behaving like a guy who was down to his final shot, he pulled out all the stops. First, Bernie arranged for time at Philadelphia's top recording studio, Reco-Art, which was located at 12th and Market Streets in the Center City Philadelphia area. Since the early 1940s, that workhorse studio had been noted for its acoustics, particularly for the pristine mono sound it produced by utilizing a makeshift 40-foot-long echo chamber.

The long-time resident sound engineer at Reco-Art was named Emil Korsen. Emil was a great engineer and a perfectionist to boot. Bernie Lowe told Emil what he wanted and Emil got that exact sound. The proof is in those records I cut for Cameo some 55 years ago. They've certainly stood the test of time and they continue to ring as clear as a bell. Bernie cut a deal with Emil Korsen and booked a session there for December 30. In lieu of paying for studio time, Bernie gave the sound engineer a little piece of the action on whichever songs got released from that session.

For my first Cameo release, Bernie Lowe and Kal Mann chose two songs they'd written: "Butterfly" and "Ninety-Nine Ways." Before we entered the studio, Bernie and Kal had me cut demos of both songs, just me singing to my own guitar accompaniment. This gave me a feel for both tunes and a chance for Bernie and Kal to get some kind of balance between the vocals and the music.

Before entering a studio to record any song, I like to live with a tune for a couple of weeks. That way, when it comes time for the actual recording session, I won't make a fool of myself. By the time we went in to record the finished masters, I already knew the melodies, the lyrics, and all the chord changes for both songs. I wouldn't have to read anything because I had it all in my head; I could concentrate on my playing. I always prefer to work that way.

After observing my preparedness, Bernie decided that making further demos was a waste of time—as well as his money. During my two years at Cameo I went directly into the studio and laid down the actual tracks. "Charlie, I never have any trouble with you in the studio," Bernie told me on more than one occasion. "You know what you're doing. All I have to do is get the band to coordinate with you."

If you listen to the demos of "Butterfly" and "Ninety-Nine Ways," you'll notice the words don't completely match those of the finished products.[16] With my help, a few changes on both the lyrics and the music were made before the final takes were recorded. Given my contribution, I should have been credited as one of the cowriters on both songs, but that's not how things worked in the business back then. In all honesty, at that point I didn't give a damn about songwriting credit. I just wanted to sing and play. I didn't realize it then, but later on down the road I could have made a few bucks from writing. I should have gotten involved with it, but I was a victim of my own youth and inexperience. I recently started a publishing company of my own. I suppose it's never too late.

Dave Appell and his group, the Applejacks, backed me in the studio that day, as they would on all my Cameo recordings. Dave and the guys were very fine musicians. They went on to become Cameo's de facto "house orchestra," playing on a lot of things for Bobby Rydell, the Orlons, Dee Dee Sharp, Chubby Checker, and many others. As an instrumental group they also had a few hits of their own in 1958, including a version of "Mexican Hat Rock" and a song written by Dave and Kal Mann called "Rock-a-Conga."

Bernie and Kal were really high on "Butterfly's" prospects, and I thought the recording came out very well. I did all my own guitar work on both songs while Bernie played piano. At Cameo everything was done live with the band—"take seven," "take 11." Bernie sometimes did overdubbing on my recordings after I left the studio or at a later date.

I had recently purchased a new guitar, an electric hollow body Guild Stratford X-350. In fact, I bought two of them at the same time. They cost me about $750 apiece. One was a "sunburst," which had a dark finish with the sun emblazoned in the center of the body. The other had a "blonde" finish. Today you'd pay up to $10,000 for similar Guilds, *if* you could even find one. I bought the two Guilds not only for the different finishes, but also because no two guitars are alike. There might be 50 million guitars in the world, and they each have a different tone and a different feel. My Guild X-350s were handmade in the same year by the Diaz Brothers, from Rhode Island, yet they play differently. The neck might be a centimeter off, or the depth from the string to the neck might vary a bit. You can feel things like that. Incidentally, I used the sunburst Guild in my first Cameo session.

I don't have a whole slew of guitars like some guys do. I've had those same two Guilds, along with a Gibson, all these years. They're the *only* guitars I've used since 1956 (I also have a banjo). By now you might figure somebody at Guild would've said "Charlie, thanks for your loyalty to our product; to show our appreciation, here's one of our guitars as a gift." But for all the years I've been in the business I've never received a guitar—or even a set of strings or a pick—from Guild or from any other company. I know musicians who play other instruments, who don't even play the guitar, yet they've been given 20 or 30 guitars in their lifetime. As for me, my life's always been like that—hidden!

Bernie Lowe produced and arranged my first Cameo session and every subsequent session I did for that label. In the studio, Bernie was the absolute boss. And he knew exactly what he was doing. He understood how to make an artist stand out. Bernie knew how to cut a guy and he also had a great ear. You don't get to play piano for someone of Paul Whiteman's stature if you're a slouch. Whenever piano was needed on one of my sessions, it was Bernie who played it.

Both Bernie and Kal were musically hip. They understood what was happening in the music business. Whether they personally cared for a particular type of music or not, they never hesitated to jump on it if they thought it had potential. I'll give them credit for that. Bernie Lowe was a musical genius. He knew exactly what he wanted with "Butterfly," and we didn't stop until we got it.

Despite the promising start with "Butterfly," we soon realized we had a potential problem on our hands. One night in January 1957, I was playing at the Cadillac Show Bar (no connection to Cadillac Records) up on Broad Street and Roosevelt Boulevard in North Philly around the time that "Butterfly" and "Ninety-Nine Ways" were released. During my break I liked to watch *The Tonight Show*, which was then hosted by comedian/musician Steve Allen. The program aired nightly and featured a stable of "regular" performers that included Steve Lawrence and Eydie Gormé, and a young crooner named Andy Williams. My recording of "Butterfly" had been out a week or so when I flipped on *The Tonight Show* and, lo and behold, there was Andy Williams singing, "You tell me you love me, you say you'll be true..."

"Holy Christ, I'm *dead*, man!" I immediately thought. "That guy's got exposure on national television five nights a week. How am I going to compete with *this*?"

It turned out that Andy Williams wasn't the only singer to cover—or copy—my version of "Butterfly." There must have been 10 or 12 cover records of that sucker![17] The numerous copies of my record weren't as troubling to Bernie Lowe and Kal Mann as they were to me. Both were sitting pretty to cash in on more than just the sales from my records. As the writers and publishers of "Butterfly," they stood to make money from *any and all* versions of their song, no matter who recorded them. But Bernie, a chronic worrier to begin with, was terrified that Andy Williams' copy of "Butterfly" would overshadow the Cameo version, and with it his dream of presiding over a successful record label.

In fact, when Bernie found out that Andy was going to cover "Butterfly," he decided that some pre-emptive action was needed. Bernie immediately turned to his old pal Dick Clark, who he'd known since they worked together on *Paul Whiteman's TV Teen Club* (Dick announced the commercials on that show). Six months before "Butterfly" was released, *Bandstand* original host Bob Horn got into some hot water over his alleged hanky panky with one of the show's young female dancers. Bob was subsequently fired and left town, but his misfortune proved to be a stroke of luck for WFIL. The station looked to a young, fresh-faced Clark, who worked for them on radio, and chose him to fill the void left by Bob's dismissal. He was perfect in that role, and the rest, as they say, is history.

According to transcripts of testimony from the House Subcommittee on Legislative Oversight's hearings into payola in April 1960, less than two weeks after the release of "Butterfly," Bernie Lowe offered his good buddy Clark a 25% share of the song's publishing royalties if Clark would promote my original version of the song to a group of influential disc jockeys across the country.[18]

Dick told Bernie he "would be very happy" if the Cameo owner scored a hit with "Butterfly," and that "it wouldn't make any difference one way or the other" if he received a share of the songs royalties. But, explained Dick, Bernie "insisted that I take a financial interest in the song." According to Clark, he again said that any payment on Bernie's part "was unnecessary and the discussion ended."

Whatever was said or not said between Bernie and Dick, in order to get my record moving in Philadelphia, I was booked to perform "Butterfly" on *Bandstand*. Dick then took the record with him to a meeting in New York of deejays from all across the country. He told that influential gathering that *my* version of "Butterfly" was the one doing well in Philadelphia.[19]

Meanwhile, I was the guy who *really* had a looming problem with all those copycat versions of "Butterfly." As the recording artist, I'd get paid only for the copies sold of my particular version. Like it or not, that's just the way the music business works. After giving it some thought, I decided the picture wasn't so bleak after all. When it came to "Butterfly," not only did we have it "in the groove," we also had Dick Clark behind us—in more ways than I actually understood at the time.

In the pre-*American Bandstand* era (the national version of

Philadelphia's *Bandstand* wouldn't go on the air until that coming August), the Holy Grail for any pop singer with a record to plug was the nationally televised *The Ed Sullivan Show*. Sullivan was a former newspaper columnist with peculiar diction and an awkward stage presence. His show, the granddaddy of TV's variety offerings, was originally titled *Toast of the Town*. It made its debut on the CBS network in 1948. In 1955 it became *The Ed Sullivan Show*. Each Sunday evening, from 8 to 9 p.m., Ed's show offered a hodgepodge of talent: movie and stage actors, comedians, opera and ballet performances, circus and animal acts, and, of course, a singer with a hit record to plug. The show's format was little more than televised vaudeville. It was also the biggest venue on which someone in show business could hope to appear, and a tough nut to crack. To be invited you either had to be an established star, a hot item, or you had to know somebody. Tim Brooks and Earle Marsh wrote in *The Complete Directory to Prime Time Network TV Shows*: "to play Sullivan was to make headlines..."[20]

On March 10, 1957, in front of America's biggest variety show audience, I performed "Butterfly" on *The Ed Sullivan Show*. I didn't consider myself a star by any means; I just happened to have a big hit record. I was thrilled to death to just go there and meet some people I considered to be *real* stars. That night I shared the stage with the renowned actors Henry Fonda and Don Ameche, as well as a big name from the silent film era, Ben Blue. Are you kidding me? I watched those guys on TV and in the movies when I was a kid. It was also a thrill for me to be in the company of one of the greatest basketball players of all time, Wilt Chamberlain. Wilt was so tall that it would have taken a ladder for me to look him directly in the eye. Also on the show that night was one of Ed's frequent guests, Señor Wences, a guy who made a living conversing with a talking face drawn on his hand! If you watched Ed's show during the 1950s you must remember the signature line of the Señor's wigged (and wigged out) hand: "It's all right? All right!"

The Sunday morning of the broadcast I arrived at the theater at 11 o'clock. Talk about being in awe. All I kept thinking was, "My God! I can't believe I'm doing *The Ed Sullivan Show*." Before the actual broadcast, everybody had to partake in two rehearsals *and* a dress rehearsal. We did so many run-throughs that when my time finally came to perform before the nation, it felt the same as doing another rehearsal. But there was one nice thing about those dry-runs: I got to meet Ed, even though he spoke to me for just a few minutes. "Hi Charlie, great to have you on the show. Go out there and do a good job tonight," was about the extent of our conversation.

When Bernie Rothbard found out I was scheduled to close the program he wasn't happy. "Dammit Charlie, that's a bad spot. Sometimes they run out of time and they knock you off the show. Maybe they bring you back to appear on the next week's show, but maybe not." Since I was scheduled to be the last act to go on that night, I took my time backstage. But suddenly, about 10 minutes before airtime I got a knock on my dressing room door: "Mr. Gracie, you're opening the show. You've got five minutes!"

Holy smoke! That hit me like a hammer. "What do you mean, 'five minutes'? I was supposed to close the show."

"No, now you're *opening!*"

Wow! Everything had changed. That's how the Sullivan show—live television—worked. For whatever reason, acts were sometimes moved around at the last minute. In a way I was glad, because now I couldn't possibly be bumped from the program. On the other hand, I knew that a lot of people preparing to watch at home would go to their refrigerator or go to the bathroom before sitting down in front of their television sets. And by that time they might have missed me.

With all honesty, my appearance on *The Ed Sullivan Show* was truly the only time in my life I felt scared to perform. This was the epitome of show business, and because it was done live, I knew if I made a mistake I'd look like a schmuck.

Ed introduced me, saying "Right over here I have a curly-haired young Philadelphian who just cracked the jackpot with his big record...He originated the recording of 'Butterfly.' So let's all join in and give him a terrific hand. His name is Charlie Gracie." I thought, "My God, I'm on!" and immediately suffered a severe case of what they call "dry mouth." Somehow I managed to pull myself together and give a flawless performance, even managing to get through my guitar solo without so much as a hitch. To top off my dream night, I received 5 grand (worth more than *eight times* that amount in today's money!)[21], which was my biggest paycheck up to that point.

Our entire family was thrilled to see me experience that magnitude of success. My Aunt Lena and my cousins from Brooklyn even came to the show that night. I was still feeling pretty good by the time I returned home to South Philadelphia the next day. When I walked through the door, the first thing my grandmother said to me was: "Don't get a big head, Charlie. Don't get a big head."

Getting a "big head" would never be a problem for me, but coping with the aftermath of such a grandiose opportunity would be an eye-opener. I'd always thought that once anybody got a shot on *The Ed Sullivan Show* they were set for life. Boy, was I mistaken.

My version of "Butterfly" appeared on *Billboard's* Top 100 chart for 17 consecutive weeks, from February to the end of May. Things continued to roll as my follow-up hit "Fabulous" joined "Butterfly" on the Top 100 in May and began its own run up the charts. One month later, "Fabulous" reached number 16 on *Billboard's* Best Sellers listing.

Andy Williams' version of "Butterfly" sold heavily on the West Coast, but we killed him across the rest of the country and around the world. It was said that Andy had sold a million copies of the song. Perhaps, but we had the bigger-selling record, there's no question about it. Don't take my word for it. Archie Bleyer himself, the owner of Cadence Records and producer of Andy's version of "Butterfly," admitted that while "Andy's record did very, very well...Charlie Gracie had the bigger version."[22]

Andy was always a class act. Sometime ago he appeared on one of those late-night network talk shows and told the audience: "One of my first big hits was a song called 'Butterfly,' but mine wasn't the original record. An artist named Charlie Gracie recorded it first." How gracious of Andy to acknowledge me. We met quite a few times over the years and, to the day he died (in 2012), Andy continued to give me credit for the original version. God rest his soul.

I could never do a show without including "Butterfly." I still get tons of requests to sing it. And don't forget, I was covered twice on that particular record. The flip side, "Ninety-Nine Ways," was so popular that about a month after it was released, the movie actor Tab Hunter came out with his version of the song. Tab's record became a fairly big seller, which caused a lot of people who hadn't bought "Butterfly" to go out and purchase it for the B-side, and that boosted my sales. Driven by the popularity of two versions of "Ninety-Nine Ways," the song began a run of its own up *Billboard*'s Top 100, eventually reaching number 11.

Those were heady times as "Butterfly" soared up the charts. I felt like I was sitting on top of the world. Later I was to discover just how naïve I'd been while I blissfully reveled in my newfound success. Too bad things couldn't have remained the way they first appeared. But "Butterfly" would not only forever evoke pleasant memories, it would also be a reminder of the sordid behind-the-scenes acts all too common in the pop record business. Although I had absolutely no involvement in—or even any knowledge of—this chicanery, my biggest hit record will be forever linked to shenanigans that surrounded the song's publishing and songwriting royalties.

It wasn't until 1960, during the federal government's hearings on disc jockey payola that I became aware of the disreputable facts. No writing credit was listed on *any* of the numerous versions of "Butterfly" that were eventually released. This, in itself, was highly unusual for the record business. The songwriter's name is almost always listed on the record label, just below the song title. Bernie Lowe and Kal Mann wanted to make certain that Dick Clark, who played a big role in the promotion of my record, would stand to gain financially from the song's success. Obviously, they couldn't overtly list Dick's name on the record as its songwriter, so they didn't credit anyone.

If you flip the recording of "Butterfly" over, you'll see "Anthony September" listed as the writer of "Ninety-Nine Ways." "Anthony September" in reality was the nom de plume of Anthony Septembre Mammarella, Dick's *Bandstand* producer. Given that "credit," a lot of people thought Tony also wrote "Butterfly." But the truth is he didn't write either song. And as a condition of Bernie Lowe's scheme, Tony had to return most of the songwriting royalty money he did receive for "Ninety-Nine Ways" to Bernie.[23]

Eventually it came to light how Bernie managed to transmit that money to Dick Clark. After "Butterfly" soared to the top of the charts, Bernie approached Dick and said he was "very grateful" for the *Bandstand* host's promotion of me and of my recording of "Butterfly," and "wanted to give" Dick $7,000 from the song's publishing royalties. Clark's response is uncertain. He testified at the 1960 disc jockey payola hearings in Washington that he'd again told Bernie that such payment "wasn't necessary." But Bernie testified at the same hearings that Dick's reply to him had been: "Well, OK, if you want to give it to me." Either way, Bernie proceeded to give Dick the $7,000, in the form of a check made out to one of Dick's music companies.[24]

At the time, I paid no attention to all the machinations going on behind the scenes over those writing credits for "Butterfly." As I mentioned earlier, I really didn't give a damn about that stuff. I never had any personal problems with Dick. He was always very cordial. If Bernie and Dick were cutting back-room deals over publishing, I had no knowledge of it. Nor was it any of my business. But it has been said that guys walked into Dick's office carrying briefcases and when they came out, those briefcases were much lighter. I don't know much about that either, but if you consider the situation and the power that Dick commanded in the music business, I don't think it takes too much imagination to see what was going down.

All I cared about was that *my* name was on "Butterfly," that the song was being played heavily on the radio, and that I was selling a ton of records. When I opened up the latest edition of *Billboard* and saw "Charlie Gracie" listed at number 1, what the hell more did I want out of life? Most guys will never get to see that in their lifetime.

If only I'd been paid by Cameo for every record that I sold, I'd have been in great shape. But it didn't take long for me to discover that Bernie Lowe most likely had no intention of paying me the full amount I was due. Today I realize I wasn't the only victim. There were other unfortunates—Frankie Lymon and the Teenagers and hundreds more—who were vulnerable kids unwittingly caught up in that tidal wave of injustice. But in 1957, I had no way of knowing that my time of exploitation had only begun.

7

FABULOUS

Thanks to the emergence of rock and roll, during the mid-1950s America's pop music business began to flex its newfound muscle. RIAA sales figures indicate that in 1955 the industry grossed roughly $227 million. The following year the figure rose to roughly $331 million. Even loftier heights were reached in 1957, when the industry gross increased by a whopping $9 million.[25] Elvis Presley remained the reigning force in the marketplace. By the summer of 1957 he'd turned out three more million-sellers, including the Bernie Lowe–Kal Mann penned "Teddy Bear."[26] Independent record labels such as Cameo accounted for 60% of singles sales that year.[27] Bernie Lowe was an impressive player. By mid-year, sales of "Butterfly" had already topped one million copies, a figure that would more than double by the end of the year. As befitted any record man worth his salt, Bernie Lowe wanted more.

My single "Butterfly" continued to put up big sales numbers. I knew it would take some time for royalties to work their way back to the record company and then on to me. But I still hadn't seen much money from Cameo. Eventually the situation reached the point where I thought the company should have paid me at least a few bucks. I said something about that to Bernie Lowe and he wrote me a check for about five grand. It was the first money I'd ever made from *any* of my records. When I got home, the first thing I did was announce to my family, "I *finally* got a check!"

"What do you wanna do with it?" my father asked.

"Whatever you want, dad. It's up to you."

"Well," he said, "since you were a kid, one of your dreams has always been to buy a Cadillac, so get whatever your heart desires."

That night we visited Scott Smith Cadillac in Philadelphia. As soon as we walked into the showroom I saw a gorgeous white '57 Coupe de Ville displayed on the floor, behind velvet ropes. My God, I stood there bedazzled! We'd driven there in a beat-up '53 Ford.

"How much you want for that car?" I asked the salesman.

"$5,300."

To me, that was astronomical. Most people didn't make that much money in an entire year. Then the salesman began to get cocky with this five-foot-four, baby-faced 21-year-old kid in *his* showroom. As if *I'd* ever be able to afford a Cadillac.

"Don't put your fingerprints on the car, son," he snapped as I admiringly ran my fingers along a front fender.

That was all I had to hear. I looked him right in the eyes. "Wrap it up," I told him. "I'm driving it home!" That Caddy was the first thing I purchased with what I assumed was just the beginning of my forthcoming rewards from Bernie Lowe and Cameo Records.

On April 5, 1957, we went back into Reco-Art to record a follow-up to "Butterfly." Bernie Lowe had released only one other record on Cameo since then, and he couldn't wait on me any longer. "Butterfly" was still doing well on the charts, but Bernie wanted to get my next release going before my first hit dropped off the radar.

Three months earlier I had arrived at Cameo as an unknown commodity. Considering that I now had a million-seller to my credit, you might think my second Cameo session would go down vastly differently than the first. But that wasn't the case at all. I acted no differently this time. I just walked into the studio and said to Dave

Appell and his group, "Hey guys, how ya doin'?"

"Hey, Charlie. Congratulations."

"No, no," I corrected them. "*I* didn't have a hit. You guys were on the record, too. *We* had a hit." Of course, if you read the label of "Butterfly," Dave and the guys received no credit whatsoever for playing on the song. Bernie Lowe gave *himself* credit, but that was the extent of it. So I expressed my thanks to the Applejacks. They were wonderful musicians, an excellent band and great vocalists too.

For most of my tenure at Cameo, Bernie and Kal decided which songs they wanted me to record and I simply went along with their choices. For our second session they'd selected two more songs they'd written, "Plaything" and "Just Lookin'." I knew right away that Bernie and Kal planned to do what most producers of a hit record did: follow it up with a similar-sounding song that reminded people of the hit still playing in their mind. "Plaything" was "Butterfly" inside out. The words were new, but the tempo and arrangement—including the backing chorus and Bernie Lowe's prominent piano bridge—clearly reflected my recent hit.[28]

We completed the master recording of "Plaything" and began to work on "Just Lookin'." I believe Bernie and Kal's desire to build on the Elvis phenomenon caused them to let me stretch out more on my guitar playing during this recording session than I had on my first. Instead of having Bernie up front on piano as they had with "Butterfly," my guitar was more prominent in the final mix. In addition, Bernie relinquished his piano bridge solo to my guitar break. Since we didn't complete "Just Lookin'" in the allotted studio time, we would finish it at the next session, held on April 9.

Evidently Bernie and Kal weren't sold on putting out "Plaything" as my next release, because at that April session they presented me with yet another of their compositions, this one called "Fabulous." "Fabulous" had an arrangement along the lines of "Just Lookin'," including the guitar break, but the song was a bit more laid back. It also contained a chorus that was certain to evoke comparisons to Elvis Presley.

Given those three songs from which to choose, Bernie and Kal decided to forego the "Butterfly" sound and lean more toward Elvis and my guitar. "Fabulous" was to be the A-side, with "Just Lookin'" as the flip. This time there would be no hijinks involved with the songs' writing credits. Since Bernie and Kal were no longer under contract to Hill & Range, their names appeared as the writers of both tunes. Actually, the names "Land" and "Sheldon" appeared on the label as the writers of "Fabulous." Since Kal and Bernie used their own names for songs that were licensed by the American Society of Composers, Artists and Publishers (ASCAP), for legal reasons they needed to use different names for those tunes licensed by Broadcast Music Incorporated (BMI). Bernie used "Land," the maiden name of his wife, while Kal used "Sheldon," which was his son's middle name. While this process is legal and proper within the music business, to an outsider looking in, it conveys a slippery slope to shiftiness.

Despite the lack of any royalty finagling, "Fabulous" did not remain free of contention for long. This time the wrangling involved the song's publishing, and how a significant portion of those rights ended up with Elvis Presley, of all people. I hadn't done an outright impersonation of Elvis when I cut what we all hoped would be my next hit. Yet no one could deny that "Fabulous," arranged in a vein quite similar to Elvis' "Don't Be Cruel"—a big hit for him the previous summer—sounded an awful lot like Elvis himself. Sure enough, when "Fabulous" hit the street a lot of people remarked on its similarity to "Don't Be Cruel." A *Billboard* review in the April 27, 1957 edition even made reference to the song's "highly Presleyesque...performance, material, and vocal backing."

That was valid criticism, but do you think "Don't Be Cruel" wasn't based on some previous song? The British musicologist Bill Millar wrote that when Bernie Lowe was in the process of convincing Kal to become his songwriting partner, he told him, "All we have to do is rewrite somebody else's hit record."[29] Although I never heard Bernie or Kal say anything to that effect, Millar's quote *does* sound like something either of those two might have uttered. Also, "Butterfly" sounds a lot like "Singing the Blues," the Guy Mitchell smash that preceded it. There's a lot of plagiarism in the music business. Songwriters steal everything and anything from each other. Many people are guilty of the same bloody thing. Remember George

Harrison and "My Sweet Lord"? The courts agreed that he lifted that melody from The Chiffons' '63 hit "He's So Fine," and he had to pay them monetary damages. It cost him a fortune. The bottom line is this: there are just seven notes in music. Sooner or later you're bound to trample on some melody already out there.

Bernie and Kal quickly learned through the grapevine that when Elvis heard "Fabulous" for the first time he wasn't upset; in fact, he liked the song so much he wanted to do his own version of it. Talk about vexation! If Elvis had recorded "Fabulous," I would have been buried. Nobody was bigger than the King. We might have sold 200 records, but he would have sold 2 million! When Bernie Lowe got wind that his second bid for a hit might be sabotaged, once again he decided to take action. To get Elvis to lay off "Fabulous," he made a deal with the King's manager, Colonel Parker, and gave them a hunk of the publishing rights. As with "Butterfly," I wasn't privy to, nor was I interested in any of that. Only after the fact did I learn how Elvis ended up with a piece of "Fabulous."

"Fabulous" and "Just Lookin'" were released in April. This time it was another crooner, Steve Lawrence, one of Andy Williams' cohorts from *The Tonight Show*, who covered me on "Fabulous." But Steve's copy didn't do any damage. My version reached number 16 on *Billboard*'s Best Seller list, while his record didn't even register on that chart. On *Billboard*'s Top 100, my record reached number 26 and Steve's stalled at number 71. "No harm done," I thought.

On the strength of my appearance on *The Ed Sullivan Show* I began to work the really big venues, places such as the Copa in Pittsburgh and *The Howard Miller Show* in Chicago. And Bernie Lowe's synchronism was sublime. He'd released "Fabulous" right around the time that I headlined Alan Freed's rocking *Easter Jubilee of Stars* 10-day stage show at the Brooklyn Paramount.

The ancient Paramount Theatre was a true entertainment palace, an ornate testament to the 1930s golden age of cinema, with a monstrous balcony that literally shook when the place got rocking. Alan always filled the joint, and at that point in my budding career he provided me with my largest live audience up to that time. Four thousand screaming teenagers could be an intimidating audience for a young kid, but I wasn't fazed at all. In fact, I was thrilled to death.

Alan was a real sweetheart to me and it was a great honor for me to work for him. I know it gave "Fabulous" a big boost. And what a fantastic lineup of talent. Some of the more notable acts included Buddy Knox and Jimmy Bowen, along with a stellar array of vocal groups, including The Cellos, The Cleftones, The Del-Vikings, The G-Clefs, The Harptones, and The Solitaires.

As if that wasn't enough, Alan also booked his trusted showstopper, the incredible Bo Diddley. Bo parked his green '55 Cadillac right outside the Paramount, and between shows he and the guys in the band would go out and wax it. One time I poked my head out there while he and his buddies were shining it up and yelled, "Hey Bo, I'll bring *my* Caddy around. You can do mine next!" I'll never forget that.

We did four or five shows a day. As far as I was concerned, the only drawback to doing so many performances was that I wasn't on stage long enough to really show my talent. There were numerous acts—15 or 20—so that if each act did, say, a half hour, the show would have turned into a marathon. As it was, each act performed two or three songs, which meant we only had time to run through our hits. For me that became tedious, because I wasn't afforded the opportunity to showcase my extended guitar work, which has always been a big part of my live performances.

Truth be known, the performing aspect of those big rock and roll shows wasn't the highlight of the event for me. The real fun came from socializing with the other artists: Chuck Berry, Eddie Cochran, The Del-Vikings, Bo Diddley, The Everly Brothers, Screamin' Jay Hawkins, Tommy Sands. The frolicking that went on backstage was another show altogether. Oftentimes we'd sit in a dressing room and pass around our guitars, just to get a feel of what it was like to play them.

Some of the artists I worked with were quite pleasant, while others tended to be egocentric. The Everly Brothers and I had a great rapport. We hung out together. I remember one time in Chicago I treated them to lunch. There was always a rivalry between those two. I never saw them bicker or anything of that sort, but whenever we were together I could sense the competitive tension between them.

Tommy Sands was another great kid. Not too long ago I again worked with Tommy, this time in Austria, along with Freddy Cannon. I also did several shows with Chuck Berry, the great poet of rock and roll.

But of all the performers I met during the early part of my career, Eddie Cochran became my closest friend. We first met on tour in Chicago in 1957. At the time, Eddie was promoting "Sittin' in the Balcony," his first single for Liberty Records. We also did a couple of shows together in Washington, D.C. Eddie was the nicest kid you'd ever want to meet—good-looking and talented, yet very humble and respectful. We hit it off from the start and grew to be really close buddies. There was a chemistry between us. I remember the time I was backstage with my guitar and Eddie said, "Hey Charlie, teach me some of those licks."

"Eddie, it's tough to teach those things to anybody," I replied. "Just watch my fingers as I play."

Another time I said, "Eddie, next time you come to Philadelphia, let me know." And sure enough, he did. The first time in town, he called the house and we invited him and his manager Jerry Capehart to have dinner with us. Man, did Eddie love Italian food! My mother cooked up her favorite pasta recipe with the red sauce (or gravy, as we called it), the one with the meatballs, sausage, and braciole; all that great Italian stuff. And Eddie couldn't get enough of it. He was absolutely delighted.

"Mrs. Gracie," he told my mom, "you make the *best* sauce!"

Another time, Eddie and I appeared on a television show, along with the Ames Brothers, Sam Cooke, and The Diamonds. But my biggest thrill that evening was sharing the stage with Jay Silverheels, the Native American actor who played Tonto on *The Lone Ranger* TV show. I couldn't believe it; *Kemo Sabe*! I got to meet Tonto!

Eddie performed in England about two years after I completed my second tour there. During that interim, several other American rockers had already followed in my footsteps. I've done at least a half-dozen tribute concerts in Eddie's honor in England. During one of those times, I visited the site of Eddie's fatal automobile accident on April 17, 1960. That evening, Eddie left the Bristol Hippodrome after having given one of his typically electrifying performances. He was headed for London Airport for a flight home to the States when the limo he was riding in skidded out of control and into a light pole. Gene Vincent, Eddie's costar, was in the vehicle with him and suffered a serious leg injury. Eddie died at St. Martins Hospital in Bath the next day.

When I heard the news it was as if the world had stopped. What a tragedy! Eddie was just 21 years old, too young to die. I don't think he gets enough credit in America for his contribution to early rock and roll. Ironically, the British and the Europeans revere him more than we do.

On May 11, 1957, about a month after I performed on Alan Freed's *Easter Jubilee of Stars*, I appeared on the legendary deejay's ABC-TV *Big Beat* program. This was my second coast-to-coast television spot in as many months, and one that I truly enjoyed doing. It was another big shot for me, too, because in those days a nationwide TV appearance was hard to come by. (Dick Clark's *Bandstand* remained a regional show at that point.)

With me on Alan's show that evening was Jimmy Bowen and Ivory Joe Hunter, a very fine rhythm & blues artist who performed his big hit, "Since I Met You Baby." Also on the bill were singers Eydie Adams (wife of legendary comedian Ernie Kovacs) and Andy Williams. In case you're wondering, Andy did *not* sing "Butterfly" that night.

It remains one of rock history's obscure facts that Alan Freed hosted a network television rock and roll show before Dick Clark did. The downfall of Alan's ABC-TV *Big Beat* came after Frankie Lymon was shown dancing with a white girl. The show's sponsors, particularly those on ABC's affiliated channels in the South, were quick to vilify both Freed and the network for showing what they considered to be an inflammatory scene. When the smoke cleared, ABC cancelled Freed's groundbreaking show just weeks before *American Bandstand* made its debut on August 6, 1957.

With a couple of hit records under my belt, my agent Bernie Rothbard was able to secure additional top bookings and TV shows. I did a lot of television spots around the country similar to *Bandstand*, in major cities such as New York, Chicago, Washington, and Pittsburgh.

I was earning pretty good money working the nightclubs, too. I'd gone from making 150 bucks a week to bringing in anywhere from $1,500 to $2,000—in those very same places. I even had my handprints set in concrete on the sidewalk in front of Skinny D'Amato's famous 500 Club in Atlantic City. I had no idea how long this level of fame was destined to last—10 minutes, 20, maybe? (Years later they removed my section of concrete from the sidewalk and replaced it with Sammy Davis, Jr.'s. So you never know!)

I'd quickly moved into a much higher income tax bracket, too; one in which I was paying about 63¢ on the dollar to Uncle Sam. In addition, I had to pay my lawyers and Bernie Rothbard, so after everyone else received their cut, I was left with about 15%. Even so, it was more money than my family and I had ever seen. Fortunately, I didn't have to rely on royalty money from my record sales to put food on the table. Every once in a while Bernie Lowe paid me a little bit—a couple of grand here, a couple of grand there. But it soon became obvious that the relatively small sum he did shell out was not nearly enough to square us for what were now multimillion sales of "Butterfly." My original contract called for a royalty of 2¢ per record sold. Since we seemed to be doing so well with "Butterfly" *and* "Fabulous," I finally said to Bernie, "You think you could possibly increase my royalty by a penny or two?" I figured that wasn't out of line. I wasn't asking for *his* share. I just wanted my own little piece of the pie, which was miniscule compared to what Cameo was making.

"Well," Bernie replied, "Let me think about it."

If the Cameo boss did, he never said anything more to me on the subject. Meanwhile, I tried my best to rationalize the situation. At least I was getting *some* money from Bernie.

The crowd of 4,000 that I played to at Alan Freed's Brooklyn Paramount show didn't remain my biggest live audience for long. In May 1957 I performed in front of more than 30,000 people at the old Connie Mack Stadium (seven years before the Beatles did their famous "baseball" concert at Shea Stadium in New York), located at North 21st and West Lehigh, in North Philadelphia. Known as Shibe Park until 1953, the stadium, with its French Renaissance façade, was one of the most ornate facilities in all of American sports.

Originally the home of baseball's Athletics of the American League, Connie Mack also became home to the National League's Phillies in 1938. The two teams shared the stadium until the Athletics moved to Kansas City in 1954. (The park was closed in 1970.)

Annually during the baseball season a fundraiser called "Johnny Night," which helped raise money for disabled kids, was held at Connie Mack. On the night of my performance for that benefit I drove to the stadium with my father and Bernie Rothbard. The place was sold out, not only because of "Johnny Night," but because the Phillies, who were off to a great start that year, were set to begin the second game of a double-header against the Pittsburgh Pirates. While my dad looked for a place to park the car, I walked up to the gate through which I was told to enter the stadium.

Easier said than done. I always had a youthful looking face, and I was slightly built. I must have appeared as if I was about 15 years old that night. (I was carded until I was 37, for God's sake!) To make matters worse, I didn't have my guitar with me because my father and Bernie were carrying it. "My name's Charlie Gracie," I told the gate attendant. "I'm performing here tonight. I was told to come in through this entrance."

With barely a glance, the gatekeeper gave me his standard brush-off: "C'mon kid, beat it! You can't get in here."

"But I'm singing here tonight," I protested.

"Look kid, I told you, beat it before I call the cops!"

Lucky for me, the director of "Johnny Night" made a timely appearance at the gate and recognized me. "What's the matter, Charlie?" he asked.

"This guy's giving me a hard time," I explained, pointing to the ticket-taker. "He won't let me through."

"C'mon," he said, "come with me."

"I'm sorry," the gatekeeper apologized as we entered. "But you're about the fourth guy tonight who told me he was Charlie Gracie!"

After the completion of the first game, I strode across the infield to second base, where a stage had been set up. It was quite a thrill to walk out there and stand where guys such as Joe DiMaggio, Robin Roberts and Ted Williams played ball. In fact, it was in that very stadium that Williams, playing in a double-header on the last day of the 1941 season, went six-for-eight to raise his batting average from .399 to .406. No major leaguer has hit .400 since.

I sang "Butterfly" and "Fabulous" that evening, but my performance sounded terrible. Back then, amplified sound in stadiums as cavernous as Connie Mack was horrendous. But despite the poor acoustics, the crowd enthusiastically cheered for me. With that, I quickly got the hell off the platform and went to watch the game. When I arrived home that night I felt as if I'd become part of baseball history myself.

May proved to be a memorable month for me. Not only did I get to play before that huge outdoor crowd at Connie Mack, I received a Gold Record from Cameo Records for selling a million copies of "Butterfly." It was a thrill to have such a prestigious award presented to me on ABC-TV's variety program *Circus Time*, hosted by Paul Winchell, the most popular ventriloquist of the new television era. But it also made me wonder about the substantial amount of money I still had coming from Bernie Lowe and Cameo.

Other performing opportunities came at me quickly and before I realized it, "Fabulous," too, had run its course on the charts. Things weren't going very well for Bernie Lowe and his fledgling enterprise. Since issuing my second record for Cameo, Bernie had released records by just two other artists on that label and both had stiffed. Out of the 12 records Bernie released since forming Cameo, only "Butterfly" and "Fabulous" had made the best-seller charts. If not for those hits, Cameo Records would have been out of business months ago. I wasn't Bernie Lowe's best hope to have another hit, I was most likely his *only* hope.

So it was with a sense of urgency that Bernie booked an evening recording session at Reco-Art for June 26. As with our previous sessions, he and Kal Mann again planned to record three songs, from which they'd select two for my next release. Bernie and Kal had decided to abandon the musical direction of my previous record, backing away from the Elvis-tinged "Fabulous" in favor of the style that had started our success. The first song we did that night, titled "Wanderin' Eyes," had a tempo reminiscent of "Butterfly." And my guitar work was overshadowed by Bernie's piano triplet bridge that sounded an awful lot like the one he played on my first hit.

Then, after completing an update of the old Hilltoppers' hit, "Trying," we began work on a second ballad, the old Floyd Tillman hit from 1948 called "I Love You So Much It Hurts." That song had been a country hit several times over, one I loved the first time I heard it. So when Bernie and Kal suggested I record "I Love You So Much It Hurts," I said, "Let's do it!" (If nothing else, I knew my mom would go for it.)

Not long after that session I headed for a studio in New York City for a recording of a different sort. I was about to appear in a film! Dick Clark, or somebody representing Dick, contacted Bernie Rothbard and asked if I'd be interested in doing a movie. Are you kidding me? Of course! It was an unimaginable opportunity.

The name of the picture, to be released by Warner Brothers, was *Jamboree*.[30] I know Dick had something to do with its production and financing, and If you watch the film you'll notice that he has a larger role than the other deejays who appear in it. Other performers in the film were Frankie Avalon, Count Basie with Joe Williams, Jimmy Bowen, Fats Domino, The Four Coins, Buddy Knox, Jerry Lee Lewis, Lewis Lymon and the Teenchords, Carl Perkins, Jodie Sands, and Slim Whitman—everybody except ZaSu Pitts!

Each artist was given the opportunity to sing one song, which was filmed in a location apart from the movie set and later edited into the film. The song chosen for me was titled "Cool Baby." In what Bernie Lowe believed to be a stroke of marketing genius, he planned to release "Cool Baby" that fall, to coincide with the film's debut. My film performance, along with Jerry Lee's rendition of "Great Balls of Fire," was shot in New York that summer. I don't remember exactly what I was paid for my cameo appearance in the film (sorry for the pun—I just couldn't resist), but it must have been about four or five grand.

Jamboree was only a momentary distraction that kept my mind off Cameo and the accruing amount of money I was owed by Bernie Lowe. Meanwhile, a major diversion from that festering sore spot was about to claim about two months of my life. Sometime in

June I received a call from Bernie Rothbard. British show business impresarios Lew and Leslie Grade were beckoning to bring me over there for a tour. My records continued to sell well overseas and in some cases they fared even better than here in the States. ("Butterfly" reached number 12 on Britain's *New Musical Express* Top 30 in April, and "Fabulous" topped out at number 8.) But when Bernie Rothbard brought up the idea of a British tour to Bernie Lowe, the Cameo owner became quite cool to the suggestion. "That's not such a good idea right now," he told my agent. "I need Charlie here to promote his new record!"

"Charlie's got a chance to make himself $3,000 or $4,000 a week over there, I can't turn that down," replied Bernie Rothbard. "Besides, Great Britain is a new horizon for him. How many chances like this do you think he's gonna get in his lifetime?"

More than a little pissed off by my agent's persistence, the Cameo owner dropped an ominous warning on Bernie: "If I were Charlie," he cautioned, "I wouldn't go there right now."

On one hand, I could understand Bernie Lowe's point: "You're hot at the moment, so stick around and promote your latest record." The strange thing was, Lowe never made that point directly to me. But Bernie Rothbard—who was like a father to me in later years—said, "Charlie, this a hell of an opportunity and the money is spectacular. The records will take care of themselves here. You go to England!"

So the two of us sat down and began to make the necessary plans. As I look back on it now, I think my decision to go to Great Britain over Bernie Lowe's objections was what put the first major crack in our relationship.

8

ENGLAND SWINGS

During the mid-1950s, when black rhythm and blues disguised as "rock and roll" intruded on the turf of staid, conservative pop music moguls, there was great resistance. But America's unreserved society and unbridled capitalism ultimately prevailed and a new era in American popular music was born. An even stronger preservative situation existed in Great Britain where the British Broadcasting Corporation (BBC), which controlled all radio and television in that island nation, did its best to shield the masses from the scourge of American rock and roll. As a result, the development of British rock lagged considerably behind its Yankee forerunner. The imaginative British rock and roll musician-turned-producer Mickie Most, who at one time produced 11 consecutive number 1 hits in his country, had this to say about England's early rock and roll efforts: "Mostly they'd get a song that was going up the American charts, get somebody to send a copy of the record over, and cover it, and 9 times out of 10, the English cover was dreadful....They used to have these musicians who were real jazzers, who thought that playing this rock 'n' roll thing was a bit of a joke, and that was our early rock and roll...pathetic, really."[31]

The beachhead for American rock and roll was established in

Britain in the spring of 1956, when Elvis Presley's "Heartbreak Hotel" became a huge hit there. Even then, jazz-influenced young Brits initially gravitated toward the more "swing style" rock of Bill Haley, who was the first American rock and roller to tour Britain.

Despite the growing number of original American rock and roll recordings that began to penetrate Britain, the country's efforts to rock remained feckless—until 1958, when Cliff Richard's dynamic original composition "Move It" burst forth.[32] It was no coincidence that this seminal British rock and roll record appeared about a year after genuine guitar picker Charlie Gracie took the island empire by storm. "I used to do 'Fabulous' on stage," recalled the since-knighted Sir Cliff, in 2010. "I loved (Charlie's) stuff."[33]

In late July 1957, Bernie Rothbard and I sailed from New York Harbor to Great Britain aboard the Cunard Line steamship RMS *Mauretania* to begin what was originally booked as a six-week tour of that country. I was very excited to be going to Britain.[34] It was the first time I had been abroad, and since I was a history nut—as I still am today—it was like going to the land of my dreams, to see things that have been around for 2,000 years. The *Mauretania* was a 38,000-ton vessel, which was pretty big for those days, but despite its size, I got a bit seasick before the ship even left the dock. Not long after we came aboard I told Bernie, "I don't feel right."

Bernie's worldly advice to me: "Don't think about it."

I never did get very seasick, probably because once the *Mauretania* began her voyage the ocean seemed like a huge lake. Being out there on those calm waters made a beautiful midsummer scene, but after the sun went down the picture changed. It became ominous. When I looked out on the deck I couldn't see anything. It was pitch black out there. Every once in a while I'd see a ship on the horizon, maybe 12, 15 miles away, and I'd think, "Thank god! There are other people out here."

Bernie and I enjoyed first-class treatment during the voyage. My only problem was, the first night out I got lost in the bowels of the ship. When I went to return to my stateroom I couldn't find it. Remember, I'm a South Philly kid. I'd been in rowboats and tiny fishing boats before, but never on a ship the size of the *Mauretania*. What the hell did I know about a ship that size? But once I found my room everything was wonderful. The ship's food was great; it had a swimming pool; it had everything.

I was amazed at the number of passengers on the ship who, because of my hit records, recognized me. One night we sat at the Captain's table—big *mahoff*, you know—and during the course of our dinner he said to me, "Mr. Gracie, it would be nice if you did a show here for the people in first class."

"You know, with all due respect," I replied, "I'd like to do a show for the fellows down in the 'pig and whistle'—the guys that are shoveling coal down below." The captain agreed, so later that evening I grabbed my guitar and headed below. As I descended the *Mauretania*'s labyrinth of narrow, twisting stairways I felt like I was in a scene out of a movie. When I finally reached the coal stokers I could see the coal dust and grime on each of their faces. I did an impromptu show for those guys and they ate it up. They really loved me and looked on me as if I were one of them—a peasant.

With two days left at sea before we docked at Southampton, I felt the adrenaline beginning to build inside me. I couldn't wait to get to England and hit the stage, when suddenly I was given cause to wonder just exactly what I was getting myself into. On the second day of August I received a radio/telephone call from a newspaper reporter from the London *Daily Mail*. He told me one of Britain's best-known singing stars, Dorothy Squires, had just backed out of her commitment to appear on the same London Hippodrome show that I was scheduled to headline. Miss Squires was upset that some American she'd never even heard of was going to receive top billing over her. I was at a loss for words. So Dorothy Squires had never heard of me? Well, I'd never heard of her *either*! As for the Hippodrome show, I had no say about who was to be billed where. I told the reporter as much, and that was the end of our conversation.

On our seventh day out, August 3, we landed in the port city of Le Havre, France and the following morning we docked in Southampton, England. I was the second American rock and roller to perform in Great Britain. (Bill Haley and His Comets had been there in February 1957.) Now it was my turn—the chance of a lifetime—and I intended to make the most of it.

Since I wanted to look my best when I performed overseas, I'd made it my business to do some shopping on South Street before I left Philadelphia. A haberdashery there called Diamonds sold luxurious men's clothing, such as fancy Oppenheimer 3G tailored men's silk suits. In those days, Oppenheimer suits were the crème de la crème, cut in what we called "zoot suit-style," with the big collars and lapels. The pegged pants looked their hippest with a chain draped from one of the pockets. Most people couldn't afford them. They sold roughly for 350 bucks apiece, which was a lot of money for a silk suit back in 1957. But I looked at the cash layout as an investment, and bought four of them to take with me overseas. I still remember the colors: One was a beautiful gray; the others green, blue, and black. I couldn't wait to get up on the stage in Britain and put those suits to good use.

I was booked into the Moss Empire chain of theaters for the duration of my British tour. They were known as "Empires," and were *the* theaters in each town, venues where the *stars* appeared. If you were hot, you worked the "Empires." They were elegant buildings, simply gorgeous structures, most of them dating back to the early 1900s or even earlier. Most of them were a lot larger than our American theaters. It's a shame that many of them are gone now, torn down for new development on the valuable land they occupied.

Moss Empire specialized in variety shows, a form of entertainment that was still in vogue during the 1950s. People flocked to the theaters to see those live shows, each one with seven or eight acts on the bill. (Ed Sullivan really did know what he was doing.) As I prepared for my first overseas gig, I was humbled to discover that I would be at the top of the bill. People were actually coming to see *me*, more so than the rest of the acts, and I was determined not to let them down.

I believe my greatest asset as a performer is the wherewithal I developed early on in my career. I wasn't a cute little kid some talent agent or record company scout discovered sitting on a doorstep. By the time I reached Britain, my years of singing and playing on the nightclub circuit had already made me an accomplished performer.

To some degree I was prepared for what lay ahead of me. Other than my appearance on *The Ed Sullivan* Show, I was never scared or jittery playing before an audience of any type, anywhere. I had the tools: I could sing, I could play, I had confidence in myself, and I knew I could go out and meet the challenge. And I *was* about to be challenged!

I gave my first performance that Sunday evening at Southampton's Gaumont Theater, where I was scheduled to work with Ted Heath's Orchestra. (While in Britain, I always had a band of some sort behind me.) Ted Heath was one of the great British orchestra leaders of all time, considered by many to be the Stan Kenton of Europe. He was a wonderful, very mild-mannered and reserved man who sported a dapper pencil moustache. Ted and I had some nice conversations, but that didn't mean that problems were not forthcoming.

Heath's orchestra consisted of very accomplished jazz musicians, but they couldn't play rock and roll. Nobody in Great Britain could play rock and roll in those days. As I took the stage for my first show I gazed down into the orchestra pit and saw that all the musicians had gray hair (such as I have now). It looked like a Q-tip convention! I was on the stage with my amplifier—which I carried from the States because none was available for me there—and I was loud! But because the orchestra wasn't amplified they couldn't hear *my* beat and had to rely on a conductor. Between the conductor, the drummer, and me playing the backbeat on my guitar, we managed to keep a rhythm and some kind of chord thing going. But it sounded pretty ragged.

Don't misunderstand me, those guys in the orchestra were all very good musicians and they tried their damnedest. But when you have a 10 or 12-piece orchestra—as opposed to a four-piece rock and roll band—you can't go up there and just wing it. You have to have written charts to keep track of things. The guys in the orchestra were playing arrangements I'd brought along that were written for me by one of Tommy Dorsey's former arrangers. Those guys played their asses off, but rock and roll was still a *strange* music to those people, man. They just didn't have the feel for it. Throughout the night the drummer played some sort of two-and-four UMP-chick, UMP-chick, UMP-chick beat, which made the show kind of difficult for me to do. Pit orchestras were contracted to accompany me throughout the tour, but I regarded them as inconsequential and incidental to my music. For the most part, my shows were built around my guitar and the drummer.

Playing *around* an entire orchestra as opposed to playing *with* it was just one of the challenges I faced on my British tour. Another was learning to roll with the punches of those inevitable unexpected moments. The first one came as I waited in the wings of the Southampton Gaumont, decked out in one of my South Philly zoot suits. The stage director took one look at me and said, "You can't go out there like that!"

"What do you mean, I can't go out like that?"

"You look like some Teddy Boy. You can't go out there looking like a Teddy Boy!"

"What's a Teddy Boy?"

"A London hoodlum!"

Well, what the hell did I know about "Teddy Boys?" I found out later that they were British working-class teenagers who represented the vanguard of that nation's emerging youth culture. Like America's teenagers, the Teddy Boys wore clothing intended to shock their parents' generation. Their wardrobe consisted of an over-size Edwardian-style drape jacket, high-waist, narrow "drain pipe" pants, and a high-necked, loose-collared fancy shirt. Their hairstyle of choice also reflected American adolescent culture: they sported heavily greased "D.A.s," or "duck's asses," featuring a pompadour in front, and long sides combed to the back.

"You just can't go out there looking like that," insisted the stage director. "At least take the jacket off. You can't wear the jacket."

So I did the first show with no jacket, just my shirt, slacks, and my guitar. As I mentioned earlier, I was quite thin in those days. I only weighed 112 pounds. And when I turned sideways you might think I'd left the room.

Following my first performance the stage manager rushed over to me and said, "You're too small. They couldn't see you in the back of the theater. Put the jacket back on!" So, for the second show I wore the jacket. Go figure!

For me, that incident was another example of destiny calling. As

I stood there on the stage, with my back to the audience, the curtain parted and I was already playing my guitar—"dump-da-da, dump-da-da." The audience took one look at my outfit and my ducktail, and as I slowly turned to face them I didn't even have to open my mouth. Those kids went bananas! They began to scream, holler, and carry on. By the time I actually began to sing, they weren't even listening. They just screamed louder and louder, making as much noise as they possibly could, as if I were Elvis himself. But I didn't want to be Elvis. I wanted to be me. I laughed inwardly as I thought, "Why are these people screaming for me? They're nuts! I'm not Elvis Presley. I'm not anything *like* him."

Although Elvis never did get to Europe, the kids in that audience clearly needed somebody to fill that void. It could have been *anybody*, but that particular night I happened to be number 1, top of the bill. So I became the new phenomenon in that rock and roll starved country. Not only did I look like the kids' idea of what an American rocker should be, I looked like *them*. I was one of their peers. I could imagine them saying to each other, "Wow, this guy's one of us!"

In all the years I've been in show business I never performed anywhere where I received bad vibes from anyone. Never. Every audience on that British tour thought I was wonderfully entertaining. And since I always try to be accessible to my fans, I never refuse to sign an autograph, so my dressing room was always full of people.

During that tour I received a taste of what it must have been like to be Elvis. Of course, I didn't have that stature that Elvis had. But who did? I was always a diminutive guy, more the Mickey Rooney type. I couldn't walk out from the stage into the audience, because I would have been trampled. I had to leave the theater from different exits each night to avoid fans who tried to pull my clothes off. But I went through the whole schmear. And I must say in all candor and honesty, it never affected my psyche at all. I just took it in stride.

My first night in Britain proved to be really exciting. Just to walk onstage in a strange country, with 3,000 people in the audience, and then receive such an extraordinary ovation was a great thrill. It was like Joe DiMaggio hitting a home run with the bases loaded! Yet who could have imagined that it would be that way for the entire tour, in every theater I played.

I couldn't wait to get to London. We were booked into that city's famed Hippodrome for a two-week, two-shows-a-night stand, the longest stint I'd ever done in one theater. The renowned Hip, located on Leicester Square, right in the center of London, had opened in 1900. It was originally designed to present circus performances, so the premises featured a large tank for aquatic performances. In 1909, to accommodate the increasing popularity of variety shows, the Hippodrome's stage was enlarged.

My performance at the Hippodrome was originally scheduled to begin on August 12, but was moved up a week to keep the iconic showplace open after its traditional summer season ended on August 4. Frankly, I was a bit surprised when I first saw the place. Considering its outsized reputation, the Hippodrome isn't very large. Some of the other British theaters had 2,500 or 3,000 seats. The Hippodrome, with a seating capacity of just 1,340, was quite intimate. I could tell the minute I walked into the place that when I sang, I'd literally be face to face with my audience, which was great. I love performing that way.

I consider myself very fortunate; I was the last in an extremely long line of entertainers over a half century to perform on the Hippodrome's eminent stage. Legends such as Bing Crosby, Judy Garland, and many other show business greats had sung through those same microphones. After my two-week run there ended, the Hippodrome was set to close forever. The famed building was scheduled to undergo major renovations and reopen as a swanky cabaret-type supper club.

It never crossed my mind that I'd make newspaper headlines *before* my performance at the Hip, but that's exactly what happened. Thanks to Dorothy Squires (the performer I first heard about on the *Mauretania*), I ran into some unexpected publicity. I'd since learned that Miss Squires was one of Britain's most lauded singer-entertainers, often referred to as "the Bette Davis of song." What I didn't yet know was that her very public tiff, which was exploited wildly by the British press, amounted to a stroke of extremely good fortune for me.

Dorothy Squires was a charismatic and electrifying stage performer who topped theater bills throughout Great Britain whenever she performed. If that wasn't impressive enough, she was also a prolific recording artist. By the end of the 1940s the blonde-haired and glamorous Miss Squires had developed into one of the most popular performers in Britain. In 1953 she married the up-and-coming actor Roger Moore, several years her junior. The couple lived in America for most of the decade while Moore (a future "James Bond" in film) pursued his acting career in Hollywood. Miss Squires occasionally returned to Britain for television and theater engagements, one of which happened to be at the London Hippodrome in August 1957. When I was later added to the show and Miss Squires was bumped from top billing and replaced by mine, she angrily withdrew from the production.

The British tabloids eagerly picked up on Miss Squires' orchestrated agitation. Most English teenagers already knew who Charlie Gracie was, even if their parents and grandparents didn't. But her melodramatic outbursts only served to enhance my reputation in England. London's *Daily Sketch*, for one, ran the bold headline: "WHO IS CHARLIE GRACIE, ANYWAY?"

Bernie Rothbard was ecstatic. Here was publicity that he couldn't have arranged, even on one of his best days. And it was all free! "Who is Charlie Gracie?" indeed! Many adults who'd never heard of me came to the Hippodrome out of pure curiosity, packing the joint nightly. At one of my performances Princess Margaret was in the audience. (The following year, movie legends Claire Bloom and Vivien Leigh attended a performance.) I'm not sure if she was there to hear my music or to see what all the fuss was about—perhaps both. The bottom line is, I played to a princess that night! I also received remarkable write-ups in the press. I have scrapbooks full of them. I'll admit it. I enjoyed basking in the glow of the spotlight. We all have a bit of an ego.

Dorothy Squires (or her management) evidently had second thoughts over her very public outburst. One night during the tour we showed up at a London nightclub where Miss Squires happened to be performing. She graciously introduced me from the audience, then called me up to the stage and gave me a peck on the cheek, as if to say, "no hard feelings, Charlie." She even asked me if I'd like to do a number, but I politely declined.

Lew and Leslie Grade were the two British entertainment impresarios and booking agents who were instrumental in bringing me to Great Britain. They, along with booking agent Harold Davison, were like the Jewish mob over there. They ran the entertainment business in London. One night during my stand at the Hippodrome the Grade brothers took me out to dinner. One of my favorite dishes is pork chops. No matter where I travel, I always try to order some. But when the waiter came to take our orders that night, I failed to realize two things: The Grade brothers were Jewish and we were in a kosher restaurant. Naturally, pork was not on the menu, but I never looked, I just went ahead and ordered. That was an awkward moment for our waiter, but the Grade brothers were nonplussed; they insisted that somebody go out and find some pork chops and cook them for me. Afterwards, Bernie Rothbard was all over me: "Charlie, how could you order pork chops in a kosher restaurant?"

"Well, why didn't you nudge me or something, Bernie?" I replied. "What do I know about kosher restaurants?"

Generally, I found it pretty tough to get a good meal in Britain. You have to remember, it had been only 12 years since the war ended, and the "Americanization" of Britain had yet to occur. That was especially true when it came to food. Often, I'd be pretty hungry by the time we arrived at a theater. I remember one time in particular when the only food we could get consisted of some little wedge sandwiches with pieces of ham in them, along with a pot of tea. That ham was so gristly I could just about get it down. It was also impossible to find a hamburger in that country. Not a *good* hamburger, *any* hamburger. Today in Britain they have hamburger joints all over the place. They also have a good selection of Italian places. But it sure wasn't that way in 1957.

During that first British tour I always had a driver on call. He'd take me from town to town, and sometimes while traveling a long distance we'd become quite hungry. Aside from pork chops, another food item I consumed a lot of was fish and chips. The English had little trailer-type stands along many of the roads where you could buy fish and chips—sort of like we sell hot dogs and hamburgers in the States. Sometimes I'd have my driver pull over so we could grab some. I really loved that tasty combination, but I could never get used to the way it was served by the British. They'd actually wrap the fish and the French fries—drenched in the oil they used to fry the stuff—in old newspapers. By the time I was finished eating, my hand looked like I'd stuck it in the oil of an engine crankcase! But the slimy mess I had to contend with was well worth the effort; the fish and chips never failed to satisfy. To this day, when I go to Britain I *still* indulge in that greasy delight.

Three weeks after the tour began, my father arrived in England and caught up with Bernie and me. He would have sailed over on the *Mauretania* with us, but when we left home in July, my grandmother, who was terminally ill with colon cancer, had recently undergone an operation and didn't have long to live. Naturally, my dad refused to leave his mother in that condition, so he stayed behind to help care for her until she died. After she passed away, my father sailed to England on the French vessel *Le Liberté* and met us in London.

For a guy who'd been a working stiff all his life, the trip to Britain was quite an experience. One night at the Hippodrome he and Bernie Rothbard sat together in the audience. Thrilled over the success I'd achieved, both were overcome by their emotions and began to cry like babies. For God's sake, who the hell ever thought I'd get the opportunity to headline the London Hippodrome? *I* certainly didn't. Being a kid from a poor working-class family, there were times when I was on the verge of tearing up myself. It felt like a dream. I was afraid my mother was going to wake me and say: "Get up Charlie, it's time for you to go to school!"

During my time in London I also happened to cross paths with a 17-year-old British pin-up girl by the name of June Wilkinson. June was an attractive brunette who I'd liken to Jayne Mansfield or Mamie Van Doren—big chested and voluptuous, built like a brick you-know-what. June was dubbed "the Bosom" by Hugh Hefner, and appeared in *Playboy* magazine in 1958. At the time we met, she worked in a London theater as a topless fan dancer. (Two years later she was acting in grade-B movies.)

Frankly, June Wilkinson wasn't my type. But she was making an appearance at London's swanky Embassy Club, not too far from where we were staying, and Bernie and my father wanted to go and have a look. I went along reluctantly. There must have been five or six people in our entourage that night, including a couple of British talent agents. As we waited for the show to begin, Bernie and my father sat there drinking beer. I'm not a drinker, but as I think back on that night now, perhaps I should have had a few.

June came out wearing a bikini bottom, with her considerable breasts "covered" by those little stripper-style pasties. Immediately, visions of Doreen the Tassel Queen flashed through my head. June then stood behind some type of plexiglass-type enclosure and several men selected from the audience proceeded to shoot little rubber darts—the kind they make for kids to play with—and attempted to hit June's pasties. When all the "shooting" ended some 10 or 15 minutes later, the audience just sat there, somewhat amused and somewhat confused, wondering what was next. But there was no "next." That was it. June had no real talent; at least none that I saw that night. She didn't sing or dance or anything of that sort. Her entire "act" that evening consisted of serving as a target for those toy darts.

Since I was a visiting star from another country, June was directed to our table and introductions were made all around. I was quite surprised when she sat down next to me, after which we talked for a few minutes. Evidently word was passed to the press that I was in the supper club where June was performing. When we finally left, in the wee hours of the morning, the British paparazzi suddenly appeared out of nowhere and began snapping pictures of June and I walking together. As the flash bulbs popped around us, they shouted such inanities as: "Is Charlie getting married?"

It was like one of those typical Hollywood bullshit-type things. Was I getting married? My god, I'd just met the girl! Later, in the sanctuary of my hotel room, I thought about the media trap into which I'd unwittingly walked. You know the Brits and their circus-like tabloids. They try to make mountains out of molehills. You meet somebody, you have a little fun, and you laugh. Then you walk out of the place and they've got you engaged. But it didn't end there.

I was shocked when I got a look at the morning's newspapers. The paparazzi had indeed blown the whole encounter out of proportion. They'd concocted some kind of transatlantic romance between June and me. If you believed the hype, we *were* about to be married. The funny part was, nothing had gone on between us. June seemed like a nice girl and we'd simply spent some brief and extremely public time together. There was really nothing more to it. Certainly, neither of us was in love (at least not with each other). We were simply two young celebrities who'd just struck up a friendship.

I was somewhat perturbed about the entire thing. But "Philadelphia Bernie" Rothbard sure wasn't. Reminding me of the Dorothy Squires press bonanza, Bernie said to me, "Ahh, Charlie, it's publicity. Any kind of PR is good when you get your name and your picture in the papers—even if it's not true!"

As the end of my two-week run at the Hippodrome grew near we hit the road for the British provinces, where I played to capacity crowds. One night Lew and Leslie Grade came to me and said, "Charlie, you're really packing them in. Would you consider extending your tour from 6 weeks to 10?"

At that point I was getting homesick and I really wanted to get back to the States. It was the first time I'd been so far away from home for so long. It was also the first time I'd been apart from the young woman I'd been dating for the past two years. Her name was Joan, and by that point I was missing her even more than I thought I would. In those days it cost something like $25 to make an overseas telephone call of just a few minutes, so instead, I'd send Joan a postcard every once in a while, just to let her know I was still alive and thinking about her. But I'm not much of a writer, and that infrequent phone call turned out to be our only means of communication.

I also missed my mom's Sicilian cooking. I longed for that gravy she made. When you poured it over macaroni, sausage, or braciole, it was simply unbeatable, and I hadn't tasted anything *close* to that since I'd arrived in Great Britain. If you were brave (or foolish) enough to order, say, a spaghetti Bolognese, the meat had a strange odor and a foul taste. It was savage, man!

If I ate once a day during that trip I was a happy guy. But I must confess that I do love my sweets. I also made the silly mistake of letting the media in on that secret passion. The next night—in fact, each and every night for the rest of the tour—when I went into my dressing room I found an assortment of pastries, cakes, and cream puffs, much of it supplied by my fans. There was so much of it waiting for me each day that I had to give most of it away.

I told Bernie how much I missed being home, but he sided with the Grade Brothers. "Where the hell else are you gonna make $4,000 or $5,000 a week, Charlie?" he asked. "Stay here!"

I had to admit, that sure *was* a lot of money in those days, even if I did have to pay taxes on it in Britain, then again in America. In the end, I caved. "Aah," I said to Bernie. "I'll stay."

Before we left London for the provinces I made several television appearances. Not only were variety shows big on the British stage, the public also craved seeing them on television. Perhaps the biggest show of its kind was *Sunday Night at the Palladium*, Britain's equivalent to *The Ed Sullivan Show*. *Everyone* over there watched it. (One of the supporting acts on the Palladium telecast the night I was on was a 20-year-old newcomer from Cardiff, Wales by the name of Shirley Bassey.) Backstage after the show I met Tommy Steele, who, at the time, was sort of the "Elvis of England." Tommy eventually left rock and roll and became a "gentleman" actor who appeared in a lot of West End plays in London and on Broadway. When I happened to meet Tommy again, about 10 years ago, we looked at each other and he said to me in very proper English, "Charlie, you haven't changed at all, you little bahrsted (bastard)."

To which I replied, "*You* certainly have!" I managed to "get" Tommy that time, and he laughed heartily in appreciation.

I also appeared on a television variety show from Blackpool called *Meet the Stars*. But perhaps the most notable TV venue I did was the BBC-TV's Saturday evening *Six-Five Special*, produced by Jack Good and hosted by disc jockey Pete Murray. *Six-Five Special* was Britain's first attempt at a rock and roll program. (It took its name from the time of day it was broadcast—at five minutes past six on Saturday evenings.) On it, my supporting act was a young Petula Clark, already a star in Great Britain although still unknown in the States.

As we motored throughout the provinces, my itinerary called for me to play weeklong Monday through Saturday gigs in several large cities, and then travel to the next city on Sunday. On occasion, we'd do a show on a Sunday in a town or city along the way. Then we'd repeat the cycle in the next city. I particularly enjoyed those weekly bookings because I got to spend five or six days in the same hotel.

We had a fantastic road manager in John Clapson, who saw to everything—limousine, five-star hotels, the whole nine yards. Even so, everyday living was still kind of primitive in Britain compared to the States. For one, the roads were bad; they just didn't have good highways over there. Also, there was no television in the rooms, even at the five-star hotels. Not that the lack of a television was any great loss. What TV they did have was controlled by the government. Besides variety shows and ancient movies, the few other programs they offered seemed to be about dart throwing and things of that sort.

I found that there wasn't much to do while on the road in Britain except eat or sleep. You could go to bed early and listen to the radio but, as was the case with television, there wasn't much variety to choose from. If I got lucky I was able to find Radio Luxembourg, a station that sometimes played American rock and roll. But overall, to fight the boredom of the dull and dry BBC, I took to reading each night. In fact, I read like a fiend when I was over there.

Our first stop was Blackpool, located about 100 miles north of London. At the time, that city on the Irish Sea was Britain's most popular seaside resort. On Sunday, August 18, we did two shows at the ancient Blackpool Opera House (built in 1889). Then we were off to the Midlands, to Coventry, the region's second-largest city after Birmingham. Visiting Coventry proved to be a surprisingly moving experience. I had time to visit the ruins of the twelfth-century Coventry Cathedral, one of the many buildings destroyed in 1940 by a German Luftwaffe bombing raid that devastated that city. The local citizenry decided to leave the bombed-out shell of the old cathedral as a grim remembrance of the war. Among the ruins there was an unexploded Nazi bomb that had been preserved as a kind of memorial. (Four years after I left Coventry a new cathedral was constructed next to the ruins of the original one.) At the Coventry

Theatre I headlined a typical British variety production, doing two shows nightly in a weeklong run.

I enjoyed the performing aspect of my visit to Coventry, as well as the chance to experience a bit of the city's history. I also got a big kick out of an unexpected opportunity that came my way there. As an old high school soccer player, I jumped at the chance to play a bit of what is known as "football" everywhere but in the States. After I'd mentioned in passing to some members of the local team that I'd played soccer in school—center forward and all that jazz—they started to question me about it. Then, to my surprise, they invited me to scrimmage with them at their Highfield Road stadium. I carried no athletic gear of my own with me so the team let me borrow one of their uniforms. All of them were huge guys compared to my bantamweight. The shorts I was given hung down past my knees (I'd be right in style today). And the jersey they gave me was three sizes too large. With borrowed shin guards and soccer shoes, when I ran out onto the field I looked like a penguin! But all the fellows on the Coventry squad were very gracious to me. We scrimmaged for about a half hour, which was a lot of fun. Next, the team included me in one of their tug of war contests, which I enjoyed almost as much as the football. Finally, they initiated me by throwing me into a tub of water.

While we were on the field somebody had evidently tipped the press that a "visiting celebrity" was scrimmaging with the local football team, because a reporter with a camera suddenly appeared and took my picture while I was heading the ball. That photo appeared in the *Coventry Telegraph* the next day. The nightly BBC-TV news reported: "American rock and roll star Charlie Gracie, who used to play English-style football back home, scrimmaged with the Coventry team today." I had a great time in Coventry that day, I really hated to say goodbye.

Next we headed for a weeklong run in the northeast English city of Stockton-on-Tees. On the way there we passed through the seaside resort town of Morecambe (pronounced MORK-em), where we stopped to play a special Sunday concert. Stockton-on-Tees, named for its location on the River Tees, is renowned for its historic market, which dates back to the year 1310. On August 26 I played the city's

Globe Theatre, which, in the years following my departure, hosted some of the most famous rockers in history, including Buddy Holly, the Rolling Stones, and the Beatles (who, incidentally, played there the day President Kennedy was shot in 1963).

When we arrived at Stockton's Globe Theatre we were dismayed to discover—as had been the case in Southampton with Ted Heath—I'd be alone on stage while the orchestra performed in the pit. After working with Heath we'd learned that for us to hear one another I needed to be closer to the other musicians. And after making that adjustment, my two subsequent performances with great jazz orchestras, one led by saxophonist Johnny Dankworth and the other by clarinetist Sid Phillips, turned out fine. But there I was in Stockton, facing the original problem again.

Those musicians gave it their very best, but they couldn't hear me at all and I could just barely hear them. They were so weak in certain spots that I was forced to keep playing rhythm on my guitar. I knew that if I attempted to take the lead the whole damned thing would have fallen apart then and there. Because of that, I was limited to the amount of single-string guitar I could play. Then, to make matters worse, during the first of two performances I broke a string while playing "Guitar Boogie."

While all that was going on, I had no clue that stage manager Bill Lee had one of those newfangled (for 1957, anyway) Grundig TK20 magnetic tape machines and recorded both performances that night. After the second show he came up to me with the reel-to-reel tape and offered it as a memento. I gratefully accepted it and thanked him for the gift. Listening to it today makes quite clear just how incidental those large orchestras were to my performance. Artistically speaking, the Stockton recording is nothing to brag about—the performance sounds very muddied. But despite the inferior sound quality, that recording remains significant for two reasons. First, you're able to hear the rapport between the audience and me. Second, high quality live recordings of 1950s stars in their chart-topping heyday are rare indeed. This is one of only a handful in existence—a piece of rock and roll history! Later on, when electronics became more sophisticated, live recordings became more common.

After I returned home, I placed the tape in a cabinet, where it sat for the next 20 years, until an English fellow named John Beecher somehow found out about it. John called Bernie Rothbard and they worked out an agreement whereby Beecher leased the rights to the recording for 25 years. My Stockton Globe performance was finally released commercially on vinyl in 1983, on his Roller Coaster label. Because of that busted string, I was unable to perform my show-stopper "Guitar Boogie" in the second Stockton show.

Therefore the show heard on side one of Beecher's original vinyl album contains "Guitar Boogie," while the one on side two has a song I was forced to play in its place. The Stockton album was subsequently reissued on compact disc in 1996, along with two unreleased tracks—"Ling Ting Tong" and "Dream"—that I'd recorded with my own group in Philadelphia in 1970.

John Beecher is a great fellow. Over the years he and I became good friends, and we remain so to this day. Thirty-one years have passed since my Stockton recording first came out, and the original lease has been perpetually renewed on a yearly basis.

After leaving Stockton we continued to travel northward. My next weeklong stay was at the Empire Theatre in Glasgow, Scotland, and those Scots proved to be a great audience. We then returned to England for one-week runs in Manchester (at the Palace), Liverpool (the Empire), and finally, Birmingham (the Hippodrome).

It was at the Manchester Palace, during the second week in September, that 15-year-old Graham Nash and his sister were in the audience. After the show they both waited outside the Midland Hotel where I was staying. When I finally showed up there we spoke for a few minutes. During that time they congratulated me on my performance, after which I signed some autographs. When Graham related this encounter to me many years later he pointed out how his sister had scooped up the butt of a cigarette I had discarded and still has it to this day!

Graham's family lived in Manchester during World War II, a city which, being a major industrial center, was subjected to heavy bombing by the Germans. Life there became so perilous that, in 1942, Nash's mother was evacuated to Blackpool so she could safely give birth to her son. After the war, while attending school in Manchester, Graham met a fellow named Allan Clarke. In 1956, just one year before my visit to Graham's home city, he and Allan dubbed themselves "The Two Teens" and began gigging around town. I probably don't have to tell most of you that in 1961 Graham and Allen founded a band they called the Hollies.

During the third week in September, 15-year-old Paul McCartney was in the audience for my concert at the Liverpool Empire. This was shortly after Paul had joined a local skiffle band called the Quarrymen, which was led by a teddy boy named John Lennon. Not long after I returned to the States in 1957, the Quarrymen began to gig in small clubs around Liverpool.

Bernie Rothbard had some business to tend to back in the States, so he returned to America while my father and I finished that first British tour together. After completing my week at the Birmingham Hippodrome, I bid farewell to London with two Sunday shows at the Granada Walthamstow. On Monday, September 30, I returned to Colston Hall in Bristol for my two final shows prior to heading home. The tour was a smashing success. We enjoyed packed houses throughout the United Kingdom. The British booking agent Harold Davison had already received a multitude of offers for a return engagement and was ready to put together a follow-up tour to begin next April.

On the first day of October, my father and I boarded a BOAC Lockheed Constellation at Heathrow Airport and headed for New York. Those workhorse "Connies"—four-engine prop jobs with that distinctive tri-rudder tail—cruised at about 300 miles per hour, so we faced a bloody 14-hour plane trip before touching down. As we winged our way home, my dad and I were already looking forward to our return to Britain.

My tour helped to blaze a trail for American rock and roll. As one of the very first American rockers to appear in Great Britain, I helped establish a pattern of things to come. Along with Paul McCartney and Graham Nash, other future rock stars—Eric Clapton and Joe Cocker among them—saw me perform in their native country. They were just impressionable kids at the time, maybe four, five, or six years younger than I was, and I became a musical inspiration to each of them. Later on, Eddie Cochran and Gene Vincent, followed by a slew of American rockers, carried the torch to Great Britain.

For three decades I remained oblivious to the impact I'd made on those future stars. Who knew back then? The first time I performed overseas I was just tickled to death to be making big money. Never in my wildest imagination did I envision that what I was doing would have an effect on anyone. "This is it," I figured. "I'll take my one shot here and I'll go back home." It wasn't until many years later, when some of those stars began to meet and thank me for doing what I did (a few even offered to perform or record with me), that I began to realize the lasting impact I'd made on them.

When we landed at Idlewild (now JFK International), there were mobs of teenage girls waiting at the terminal gate to greet me. My family was there, too, as was Bernie Rothbard. I was really hoping to see Joan, who was living with her grandparents in West Philadelphia at the time, but as I scanned the crowd she was nowhere in sight. At first I thought she must have gotten caught in the mob, but she never showed that day. When I finally got home and saw Joan, I told her how disappointed I was that she hadn't been waiting for me when I landed. "Why didn't you come to the airport to meet me?" I wanted to know.

"I just didn't think I should be there," Joan replied. "I knew nobody would have known I was your girlfriend. But even so, I thought I might have been in the way. I just didn't think it would have been right." That's Joan for you, always quick to put my considerations before her own.

My tour of Great Britain had been a triumph in every sense of the word. But the good times and the glory were quickly tempered by the uncomfortable reality that I faced back in the States. While I was away I'd been too busy to even notice that sales of my third Cameo record, released back in July as I left for England, had not met everyone's expectations at home.

With "I Love You So Much It Hurts" having been designated as the "hit" side of the record, Bernie Lowe had relied on disc jockeys across the country to plug the first ballad of my career, and one culled from the country genre, no less. Nobody really knew what to expect, but I have to say that, when compared to the success of "Butterfly" and "Fabulous," the results were kind of disappointing. Part of the problem may have stemmed from the fact that disc jockeys were uncertain which side of my record to get behind. Although "I Love You So Much It Hurts" was designated the "plug" side by Cameo, *both sides* of the record received *Billboard*'s coveted Spotlight review.[35] To muddy the waters further, Bernie Lowe took out a full two-page spread in *Billboard* to trumpet what he described as my "third and biggest" record. But by touting the disc as a "sensational two-sider," Bernie may have inadvertently given both songs the kiss of death.[36] It was no secret that most jocks preferred to take one side or the other of a record and run with it.

Whatever the reason, neither side of my "two-sided hit" received a particularly robust push from the nation's deejays. (Elvis was one of the few singers in the business strong enough to cause a two-sided hit.) For a brief time "I Love You So Much It Hurts" and "Wanderin' Eyes" were both heard on American radio, but Dick Clark failed to play either side on *American Bandstand*, and ultimately neither side caught on. "I Love You So Much It Hurts" only managed to struggle to number 71 on *Billboard*'s Top 100, and the flip side, "Wanderin' Eyes," failed to appear on that chart.

Meanwhile, in Britain, *both* sides of the record charted. "Wanderin' Eyes" climbed to number 6, while "I Love You So Much It Hurts" settled at number 14. That wasn't much of a surprise to me, because the heavy airplay I consistently received in Britain meant that most everything I cut fared better there than it did in the States. Also, there's no doubt in my mind that the publicity generated by my presence in Britain as the record was released factored into the popularity of both sides over there. Throughout my British tour I'd say to the audience, "Now I'd like to do one of my new recordings," and inevitably they'd elicit a collective, "Ooooh" as I broke into "I Love You So Much It Hurts." But they also expected to hear "Wanderin' Eyes." All of which led me to think, perhaps Bernie Lowe had been right in wanting me to remain in the States to promote my latest record.

9

CONFRONTATION

Charlie Gracie's exploitive treatment by Cameo Records was nothing out of the ordinary for the cutthroat pop music business. In all but a very few cases recording artists were powerless and expendable. Even so, a fortunate few possessed some sort of "juice," perhaps dynamic star power, a godfather in the business, a respectable string of hit records, or some other leverage against exploitation. The ascendance of Eric Hilliard "Ricky" (later "Rick") Nelson, another talented and good-looking young singer, was concurrent with the rise of Charlie Gracie. But unlike Charlie, Ricky was fortified by multiple doses of "juice." At the time "Butterfly" was on its way to becoming a monster hit, 16-year-old Ricky, a member of the cast of the nationally televised Adventures of Ozzie and Harriet *television show, was every teenage girl's heartthrob. Ricky's dad, Ozzie, one of the slickest and savviest godfathers one could hope to find in the entertainment business, was enthralled and impelled as he watched Elvis sell boxcars of records in 1956. The influential and manipulative manager–dad then approached his son about cutting a record of his own and began to wield his considerable "juice."[37] Each time Ricky was ready to release a new record it was premiered on the family's nationally televised show, which just happened to be watched each week by at least 25 million people, many of them adolescent, record-buying females already ga-ga over Ricky's knock-dead looks.*

There are several solid parallels between the first two chart hits by Charlie and Ricky. First, the debut records of both artists, with Ricky following Charlie by about three months, were two-sided hits of comparable magnitude.[38] Next, their follow-up releases, "Fabulous" and "You're My One and Only Love" (also released about three months apart) reached number 16 and number 14, respectively, on Billboard's Top 100. Third, both artists failed to receive the proper royalties on their first two hits. And finally, both artists threatened legal action to collect the money owed them. (Nelson successfully sued his record company.)

It was here that the careers of Charlie Gracie and Ricky Nelson embarked on opposite trajectories. By August 1957, about the time Charlie defied his record company and left for Great Britain, Ozzie negotiated a blockbuster of a recording contract for Ricky. The new pact included an astounding $1,000 per week payment for five years, against 4.5% royalties, plus full approval over song selection.[39]

No matter where you go or how great a time you have, it's always nice to return home. That's exactly how I felt when I arrived back from Great Britain. Bernie Rothbard had lined up a series of steady bookings for me and I was able to immediately jump right back into the swing of things. For the rest of 1957, I worked the best clubs on the circuit, including Ben Maksik's Town and Country Club in New York, the Casino Royale in Washington, D.C., and the Copa in Pittsburgh. And I worked as often as I liked.

Also, Bernie Lowe was eager to get me back into the recording studio. I think if Bernie had had his way, he would have hustled me off to Reco-Art the moment I stepped off that BOAC Constellation. The Warner Brothers' film *Jamboree*, in which I sang "Cool Baby," was set for a November release. To capitalize on that promotional opportunity, my recording had to be on retail store shelves by the time the film opened. For that to happen, Bernie needed a flip side for "Cool Baby," and he needed it in a hurry.

In a Reco-Art session on October 13 we got a successful take of the medium-tempo Lowe–Mann-penned rocker "(You've Got a) Heart Like a Rock." Bernie rush-released "Cool Baby," placing an ad in the November 4 edition of *Billboard* that touted the song as the music trade magazine's "Spotlight Recording of the Week."

Bernie Lowe may have been in a hurry to get my next record out, but Cameo Records still refused to come across with any more of the royalty money I was owed. I thought that after the two months I'd spent in Britain I'd at least see *some* of those earnings when I returned home. "Butterfly" had sold upwards of 3 million copies worldwide by then, and although my contract with Cameo called for that measly royalty of 2¢ per record, 2 pennies times 3 million added up. In this case it amounted to some $60,000. And that was for "Butterfly" alone. But with my fourth record for Cameo just released, there I was, still waiting to be paid in full for the first one. I'd achieved the formidable goal of earning a number 1 record, but I felt like I wasn't being treated properly. I told Bernie as much, but he was in no mood for accommodation. Bernie remained sore at me for taking those two months to tour England when he thought I should have been in the States promoting his records.

We finally had a couple of discussions about how much I thought I was owed by Cameo. "We had a number 1 record with 'Butterfly,'" I told him. "That thing sold a few million copies." Bernie begged to differ, maintaining that sales of "Butterfly" amounted to only 700,000 records.

I really didn't know exactly how many copies of "Butterfly" had been sold. How the hell could I check? The company kept two sets of books. But I continued to press Bernie. "If it sold only 700,000 copies, then why did you give me a gold record?" I fumed. "And why did you announce in the trade papers that 'Butterfly' had already sold a million copies?"

Bernie brushed it all off as "hype."

Hype? "Butterfly" was a hot seller all over the world, not just in America. My records sold well around the globe, including Belgium,

France, Germany, Holland, and Japan. In Britain I had five Top 20 hits, several of which were covered by European artists. Bernie knew that. As the songwriter, he stood to earn the songwriter money on all of them.

Cameo was playing me for a fool, selling millions of records while paying me for much less than that, and I was ticked off. I knew I was being screwed and the ongoing dispute became a black cloud over my head. Sure, it was nice to hear Bernie tell me what a great artist I was. But how long can you live on flattery? I couldn't live on praise alone. I wanted some *paper* from him. *Pay* me for my talent!

I assessed the situation as best I could. I didn't think Bernie Lowe would want to discourage me from promoting "Cool Baby," especially after the nation's tepid response to my last release. I also tried to factor in Bernie's relationship with Dick Clark. After all, Dick was Bernie's good buddy, if not his benefactor. At that point I was uncertain whether or not Dick actually owned a piece of Cameo records. But I felt fairly confident that *some* sort of business connection existed between the two of them. And if there was, I figured Bernie would want to protect it by keeping me at least *somewhat* content.

Turned out I was right. Near the end of 1957, Clark was in the process of forming Swan Records, a label that, in conjunction with Cameo, would be run as virtually one company. In addition, Dick and Bernie became "silent" investors in a record distributing firm that handled both Cameo and Swan. They also became equal partners in a record-pressing plant. Only later did I (and a lot of other folks) discover just how intertwined were the business dealings of Bernie Lowe and Dick Clark.[40]

It seemed like the right time for me to act. "I'm hot right now," I figured. "Cameo won't dump me." But before taking any action, I wanted to consult with Bernie Rothbard.

"Two pennies, three pennies, four pennies," exclaimed my agent. "What the hell's the difference, Charlie? You know you're not getting all your money anyway. Just be quiet about it."

That may have been okay for Bernie, but not for me. I'm a funny guy. Because I trust most people, I find it hard to accept somebody who's trying to screw me. Maybe I'm a schmuck for being so trustworthy, but that's just the way I'm wired. I hoped all along that things wouldn't come to this, because I don't like confrontation. But I'd grown somewhat belligerent about Bernie Lowe's line of bullshit and, despite Bernie Rothbard's advice to "cool it," I called the Cameo boss on it. "Where's my money?" I demanded. Then we really had it out.

After going around in circles once again and getting nowhere, I figured I had nothing to lose by trying a new tactic. I suggested to Bernie that instead of us continuing to argue over royalties, we could end the stalemate by renegotiating my contract. "Instead of paying me 2¢ a record, give me 4¢," I told him. Now, it may seem peculiar that I was concerned with increasing my royalty rate when I wasn't receiving much money from Cameo to begin with. But I still held a faint (albeit naïve) hope that Bernie would eventually come around and pay up. And if he didn't, I had an ace up my sleeve.

After Bernie first approached me about recording for Cameo and I'd signed my name to a contract, I was still several months shy of my 21st birthday. Not being of legal age, my contract was invalid. I'd kept that information to myself, but if I had to, I was determined to use it.

Accompanied by our attorneys, Bernie and I met in New York, in a spot right off Broadway. It might have been Jack Dempsey's Broadway Restaurant, I really don't remember, but it was one of those joints musicians and other show business people frequented. The lawyer with me that day was not particularly well versed about the workings of the music business. He was a general attorney who'd been introduced to me by one of my uncles. The only reason he was there was for legal advice, because I didn't know anything about law. Going in, I explained my position to the attorney, who assured me: "I'll be there to listen to everything and to protect you."

We all sat down and the conversation began amicably enough. It was Bernie and I having a *tête-à-tête* over the table, with the lawyers in the background. But when I mentioned to Bernie that I'd like a couple more pennies per record, it became obvious that he had no intention of discussing royalties. One thing led to another, and I realized now was the time: "Well, you know what, Bernie?" I calmly stated. "My contract's invalid."

A smirk came over Bernie's face, as if to say, "Yeah, right!"

"He's correct," my lawyer chimed in. "That contract is null and void. My client wasn't yet 21 when he signed it."

You should have seen Bernie's reaction. Caught completely off guard, his face paled in disbelief. Then, confronted with the evidence to back up my claim, the head of Cameo Records began to act as if he was a beaten man. "Okay, Charlie. What do you want?"

"Forget about the age thing," I reassured Bernie. "I don't want out of my contract with you. All I want is a couple pennies more per record. And I *would* like to get paid what I've already earned." With that, we renegotiated my contract, increasing my royalty from 2¢ per record to 4.

Now that I look back on it, the whole thing was a waste of time. Asking for that royalty increase was a matter of principle. But it was really stupid on my part. If Bernie hadn't paid me 2¢ a record, why then would he pay me 4? To make matters worse, I blew $5,000 of my own money to pay my attorney for that day—*plus* his expenses to travel to New York. I thought he would have taken that travel money out of his 5 grand, but he too was just another shyster.

The entire episode between Bernie Lowe and me was really unfortunate. He and I were just beginning to find our way, I as a recording artist and he as a label owner. "Butterfly" was our first hit together. But what *should* have been something positive instead led to the destruction of our relationship. Springing that invalid contract thing on Bernie and then asking for a couple of extra pennies per record was the straw that broke the camel's back, put the crease in the paper. It made Bernie *very* unhappy. He had a right to be upset with me. But by the same token, I had a right to be angry with him. One thing I knew for sure; we had a rocky road ahead of us.

Since my British tour, the ground beneath Bernie Lowe and I had shifted considerably. I was no longer Cameo's "go to" artist in the company's quest for its next hit record. Cameo had since released back-to-back records by other artists and both had become sizeable hits. The first, "Back to School Again," by the 42-year-old civil rights pioneering black comedian Timmie "Oh Yeah!" Rogers, was a timely novelty penned by Kal Mann and Bernie Lowe that any record-buying teenager could identify with. Largely through the efforts of Dick Clark, "Back to School Again" became a popular dance number on ABC-TV's new *American Bandstand* show.[41]

The second of Bernie Lowe's latest successes, "Silhouettes," was a rhythm & blues ballad sung by a young vocal group from Harlem called The Rays. "Silhouettes" was a fantastic gimmick record about a broken-hearted lover who thought he saw silhouettes through a window shade of his girl kissing another guy. But things turned out okay after the heartbroken fellow discovered he was on the wrong block and had been looking at someone else's window. Released in September, "Silhouettes" became Bernie Lowe's first million-selling record since "Butterfly."

The premier of *Jamboree* was held in November, in Wilmington, Delaware. Why that location was chosen, I have no idea. But Wilmington's only about 40 minutes from where I live, so I drove there with my dad. Connie Francis was included in the festivities because she'd overdubbed the vocals for the young actress Freda Holloway, who played the female lead in *Jamboree*. Connie didn't have a ride that day, so my dad and I chauffeured her around the city. I have one of the original theater lobby cards for *Jamboree* hanging in my den. It's in perfect condition and worth about 4 grand. I also have a copy of the Warner Brothers soundtrack recording, which is a pretty rare item. As a matter of fact, only a few thousand promotional copies were pressed. It was never released to the public. What can I say? That's me, saving more stuff.

Cameo released "Cool Baby" on the heels of "Back to School Again" and "Silhouettes." With the song featured in *Jamboree* you'd figure it would have gotten at least *some* airplay. But "Cool Baby" never even scratched *Billboard's* Top 100. By all rights, the song should have at least done that. But there may have been more going on than meets the eye.

During the 1950s, disc jockeys were reluctant to program more than one or two records released on the same label. They didn't want to appear as though they were playing favorites (precisely because many of them were doing just that). With most of the nation's jocks playing "Back to School Again" and "Silhouettes" regularly, they weren't looking to add a third Cameo disc. So any promotional advantage I might have gained by singing "Cool Baby" in *Jamboree* went by the boards. Lending credence to this scenario was the fact that even though my record was dead on arrival at most American radio stations, in Great Britain "Cool Baby" reached number 25 on the pop charts.

I was no longer Bernie Lowe's best hope to turn out a hit record. I wondered, had the Cameo boss purposely released "Cool Baby" on the heels of his two latest hits, knowing that disc jockeys would most likely ignore my record? Was this my "punishment" for having forced Bernie to renegotiate my royalty rate? Stubbornness is a funny thing. All of a sudden, Bernie was starting to cook. He had money coming in from his two current hits and was now entrenched with Dick Clark and God knows how many other people in the record business. Feeling his oats, Bernie may have figured, "That little punk. I'll straighten him out!" It certainly wasn't beyond him to do something like that.

So it's *possible* that Bernie Lowe was willing to cut off his own nose to spite his face. I won't say *absolutely*, because I don't know for sure. The only thing certain was, after my contract renegotiation, we were both stuck with the results. Bernie knew he had to fulfill his obligations to me. But if I didn't sell any records he wouldn't have to pay me anything. He never said a word about it, but he could simply record me until my contract expired. At that point there was nothing either of us could do about it. So we continued on like an estranged married couple living in the same house.

About the time when things began going downhill with Cameo, I was hoping to improve my immediate future, as well as that of my entire family. They'd given me every opportunity in life and I wanted to repay them somehow. But until my success with "Butterfly," I felt I could *never* do that. The thing I wanted most was to get my family the hell out of our cramped row home on South Philly's Pierce Street and become suburbanites. Thanks to the money I was bringing in from my performances, by the beginning of the previous summer I'd managed to save enough for a down payment on a new home. I said to my mother and father, "I want to buy you a house. Let's go look around for one."

The house they finally chose was located on Marilyn Drive, right on top of a hill in Havertown, a suburb just west of Philadelphia. The place was built by Eugene Crown, who'd put up hundreds of his "Crown Homes" throughout the area. This particular model was a brand-new, spacious split-level. It had four bedrooms, two-and-a-half baths, a laundry room, a double garage, and was surrounded by about half an acre of property—the whole schmear. It was just beautiful; a mansion compared to where we'd come from.

I bought that house for my parents, not for me. My name wasn't even on the deed. I said, "Mom, Dad, thanks for all the wonderful years during which you treated me lovingly as your son. This is for you and, of course, for my two younger brothers." With that, I handed them the keys to the place. The entire family moved into that house—my parents, my two younger brothers Frank and Bob, and I. All of us were thrilled.

We didn't arrive as complete strangers on Marilyn Drive because we were right across the road from Bernie Rothbard's house. From the front of our place we could see the back of his. Because of that proximity, Bernie's family and mine grew very close. His wife's name was Grace (although everybody knew her as "Debbie"). She was an Italian girl; her maiden name was Calabrese. Debbie had been a nightclub dancer; she was very personable and very attractive. That's how she and Bernie met in 1948. I knew his entire family, the Italian side and the Jewish side. They were all wonderful people. After we became neighbors and time went on, Debbie and my wife Joan became quite friendly. Occasionally we'd go to Bernie's house for events like Bar Mitzvahs or other family get-togethers, and if Joan and I had, say, a little birthday gathering we'd invite Bernie and Debbie. They eventually had two marvelous sons, Robert and Kevin.

With my trip to Britain looming, we hadn't moved into the place until November. And when we did, my mother was in her glory. She thought she'd died and gone to heaven. I was in my glory, too. "Mom, you can furnish it with anything you want," I told her. Right away she went furniture shopping in Philadelphia at an exclusive place called Rubins—the best in the city. I remember signing the check for everything my mom picked out. It amounted to $12,000, just for furniture!

I also bought my father a Lincoln convertible. Then, although he was only 44 years old, I insisted he retire from Stetson. He'd already spent 33 years in that god-awful place and, as far as I was concerned, that was more than enough. Once we got settled in on Marilyn Drive I began to give my mom a certain amount of money each week to run the household. I also gave my father some spending money and I paid all of the bills. The money I was earning from my performance bookings came to me so fast that I didn't feel any pressure at all from being the sole means of support for my entire family. I was delighted I could fulfill that role. I really thought we were going to live happily ever after in that house.

After the disappointing sales of "Cool Baby," I thought Bernie Lowe would want to get another of my records out pretty fast. But things began to change for the Cameo president; he hadn't spent very much time in the recording studio of late. Bernie had altered his method of operation after purchasing the completed master recording of "Silhouettes" from independent producers Frank Slay and Bob Crewe. After Slay and Crewe's recording sold a million copies, he took to trying to buy another hit for Cameo instead of producing one himself.[42]

To watch Bernie Lowe operate, you'd never imagine the tension that now hung in the air between the two of us. Curiously, the Cameo boss didn't act any differently toward me in the studio than he had when we'd first teamed up. I was always the type of guy who did whatever he wanted, so on November 24 when we finally did return to the Reco-Art studio, I simply said, "What do you have in mind, Bernie? You want to do two songs, three? Whatever you want is fine with me. Let's just do it."

But when we got around to the actual recording process, something did seem out of synch with Bernie: In the past he'd always been a model of efficiency and decisiveness in the recording studio. Now he seemed uncertain. Counting that November session, we logged a total of three recording dates before the end of the year. Yet we were no closer to having even *one* song ready for my next release.

Bernie had always been a chronic worrier. And since he'd failed to come up with a significant hit after issuing "Silhouettes," it's quite possible that he'd lost confidence in his ability to produce. But whatever it was that affected him, I wasn't about to throw in the towel. Whenever I recorded I always did so to the best of my ability, 100%! And despite the widening gulf between Bernie and me, I would never consider intentionally making a bad record. Even so, Bernie chose not to release any of the four songs we recorded during those dates. [43]

It took two recording sessions at Reco-Art in January 1958 plus an additional overdubbing session to finally get the two sides for my fifth Cameo release. They were both uptempo numbers, one titled "Crazy Girl," the other "Dressin' Up." It came as no surprise to me that Bernie and Kal Mann had written both tunes. Except for "Cool Baby" and "I Love You So Much It Hurts," they'd penned all my Cameo releases.

"Crazy Girl" was chosen to be the A-side. Featuring a solid horn arrangement, the song was reminiscent of the recent Larry Williams' hit, "Bony Moronie." When I heard the finished track I thought it might be the best rock and roll record I ever recorded for Cameo—or for anybody. Thanks to Dave Appel and the Applejacks' vocal backing on "Dressin' Up," the song had an exciting gospel feel to it. My guitar work was prominent throughout and the hot licks on the guitar bridge really stood out. I thought both sides were potential hits.

For our next session, held during the middle of January, we changed recording studios. Evidently Bernie had had some kind of problem with the sound engineer Emil Korsen and decided not to use his services. Instead of Reco-Art we went into another studio somewhere nearby. After all these years I'm not certain which one it was, but I remember how tiny it was, just a cubbyhole compared to Reco-Art. It very well could have been the cramped studio in Cameo's original office complex at 140 South Locust Street.

We recorded just one song that evening, a tune called "Love Bird." Instead of using a bass, Bernie brought in a fellow from the Philadelphia Orchestra—"Chick" Musumeci—who played the tuba!

"Love Bird" was a Charleston-era type number, with a "Da-ta, Da-ta" beat. When I listen to that song today, I hear a cute little number. And to have a musician from the Philadelphia Orchestra play on it is unique. But the night we recorded "Love Bird" I had a much different opinion of the song. When I heard the playback I was beside myself. "What are we *doing* here, man?" I protested. "This is *not* rock and roll!"

Considering the number of songs we recorded that remained unreleased after Bernie and I had our dispute, I'm not certain he was ever serious about putting out another record of mine. I believe the only reason Bernie recorded me after that was because he had a contractual obligation to do so. The burlesque "Love Bird" was Bernie's "kiss-off" to me. He *knew* I had to record that noncommercial farce to uphold my end of our agreement. But I refused to offer him any sort of gratification for his antagonistic scheme. I went in and did the song as best I could. As we left the studio late that January evening I had no idea that "Love Bird" would be the last number I would ever record for Cameo.

10

DEPARTURE

Joan Gracie (nee D'Amato) wasn't exactly new in town. Newly returned would be more accurate. Originally from South Philadelphia, Joan and her family had moved to suburban Upper Darby when she was nine. After her parents' divorce several years later, she remained with her mother. "A year and a half later we moved back to South Philly," *she recalled,* "into Charlie's neighborhood. I was 14 years old when I met him, but I looked more mature.*

"One day I was walking down the street with a friend of my mom's. I saw a picture in a storefront window of a guy holding a guitar. 'Oh, who's that?' I asked.

"'I know him,' replied the friend. 'My husband gave him his first guitar lessons when he was younger. He lives right down the street.'

"'Really? Wow!'

"All the guys in the neighborhood used to hang out on the corners back then. On one particular corner there was a soda shop, a kind of luncheonette. Every day my sister and I would walk by, just talking to people we'd see in the neighborhood. I knew a little bit about Charlie making records, because at the

luncheonette the proprietor had a loudspeaker outside and he'd play Charlie's records. And then, finally, one day I saw Charlie standing there and I said to my sister, 'Let's go in and get a Coke.' Then Charlie walked in and we sat down in a booth and started talking. He eventually asked me how old I was. Of course, I lied. I think I said, 'Oh, I'm 16.'

"That was 1955. That's how it started. Then Charlie would take me to his house and we'd sit on the steps with his parents. To us, that was a date. We also did a lot of walking together. We walked to the movies; we walked everywhere. We didn't go for rides in cars in those days. Charlie didn't even own a car. When it became apparent that my family liked him, I finally I told him my real age."

I met Joan in the spring of 1955. I was already out of high school. I was already 18, going on 19, gigging in and around the immediate area and going on the road by myself, working the nightclubs. Of course, in those days I wasn't making much money. Nobody had any money then, so whenever I was home in South Philly I used to hang on the corner. There was a little restaurant and malt shop there, owned by a guy named Tony, who'd grown up with my dad. We'd always hang there in front of Tony's. It was a place to meet, like a watering hole. Then I began to notice that every couple of days during the week a very attractive, very pretty little girl walked down the street. She was always with another girl, who I later found out was her sister Marie. You know how it is for guys 18, 19, 20 years old. They're on the street, the testosterone's flowing, and a pretty girl is bound to catch somebody's eye: "Hey look. Pretty chick over there!" So at first I didn't think anything of it.

Then one day while I was on that corner I met that very pretty girl I'd recently noticed. I found out her name was Joan. I don't remember exactly what we said, but I *do* recall two things: when I asked her out for a date she said yes; and when I asked her how old she was she lied to me. She said she was 16 but she was only 14. Well, in those days the girls looked more mature!

Although at the time "Head Home Honey," my first record for 20th Century, had just been released, I didn't make a big deal about it to Joan. I wasn't that kind of guy. I didn't think I had to behave that way, and in hindsight I was right. Joan still tells me, "Charlie, you were the sharpest guy on the corner." Don't get me wrong. I didn't hang on the corner wearing a jacket and tie or anything like that, especially in the heat of the summer. But I never was the type of guy who liked to lie around in clothes that looked like I'd worn them for three days. My pants were always creased and I wore a nice starched shirt. I always looked like I was ready to perform, and I'm still that way. To this day, if either of my kids happen to be at my house and see me with my hair combed, wearing clean clothes, and looking like I'm getting ready to go out, they'll ask, "Where you going, Dad?"

"I'm not going anywhere," I tell them. "I'm going down to watch TV with your mother!"

All the other guys I hung with back then looked sharp, too. We were very meticulous about our hair; we used to wear that greasy stuff in it. We never wore those characteristic leather jackets, which are nowadays more a Hollywood movie fabrication of the 1950s than anything else. Back then, none of us could afford one.

After Joan and I met we went out a few times and before I realized it, we started to fall in love. Who knew? I didn't have to win over her parents, but since her mom and dad were divorced I did have to meet them separately. Joan's mother was happy with me. Then I met her father, a good, hard-working person, and he, too, seemed satisfied. So everything turned out to be fine. I think both of Joan's parents were thrilled that their daughter was going out with a fellow who they perceived was *somebody*, even though I never thought of myself as anyone special. We had a long courtship that lasted about three years. Then, in 1958, we decided to get married. I was planning on returning to Great Britain in short order, so I figured, "Okay, we'll get married and I'll take Joan with me as my wife." I asked her to marry me, and after she agreed to, I got the blessing from both her parents. The only one in Joan's entire family to give us some trouble was her grandmother, who felt we should wait a little longer so that her granddaughter could get her "hope chest" straightened out. Back then, that older generation was quite concerned about such things: "Oh, you must get the sheets, the pillowcases, the china" and all that other stuff.

If only things had gone so well with my own family. When I told my mom and dad that Joan and I intended to get married I was caught off guard by their response. "If you get married you're going to ruin your career!" my mother blurted out. The reaction by both of them was unbelievable. They gave me an impassioned anti-marriage argument, which forced me to do some quick thinking.

Pop singer Pat Boone, host of a brand-new weekly network television musical variety show at the time, was one of the fastest-rising stars in show business. And he happened to have the number 1 hit record on the charts with "April Love." "How about Pat Boone?" I said to them. "He's married. He's already got kids. How did that affect *his* career? It certainly hasn't hurt it any." Convinced that marriage might not be a bad career move after all, my parents gave Joan and me their blessings.

Speaking of Pat Boone's latest recording, Bernie Lowe released my next record, "Crazy Girl" and "Dressin' Up," in January 1958, taking a full-page ad for it in *Billboard*. ("Charlie's Newest and Greatest.")[44] But once again, by releasing two quality songs on the same record, Bernie Lowe may have hurt the chances of both. "Crazy Girl" was made the A-side, but worrywart Bernie, anticipating the sales potential of "Dressin' Up," hedged his bet. While the other five records in Cameo's *Billboard* ad mentioned the A-sides only, both my songs received equal billing. Never one to pay much attention to any of the printed media hype for my records, I never imagined that Bernie Lowe's indistinct *Billboard* ad would be the last promotion I'd ever receive from Cameo.

In March 1958, *Billboard* published its annual list of million-selling records of the previous year. And there it was: "Charlie Gracie—'Butterfly.'" (Andy Williams' version was not listed.)[45] Bernie Lowe had finally admitted—although not to me personally—that "Butterfly" had sold *at least* one million copies. Not that he'd ever pay me in full for that achievement. Oh, Bernie did give me a few additional royalty checks along the way, a couple of thousand dollars here, a couple of thousand there. But that was a pittance compared to what I was still owed. At the time, I was supporting five people in my family, and Joan would become the sixth after we were married. And the bills never stopped. My work in the clubs was a godsend, but I really could have used more of that money owed me by Cameo.

Always anticipating that next hit record, I remained unconcerned of a looming problem. My heavy schedule of club appearances was predicated on my high show business profile. And it was my hit records (whether I was paid for them or not) that sustained that level of popularity. If the hits dried up, my bookings would surely tail off to some degree. But I wasn't thinking about any of that, even though Bernie Lowe had—aside from those infrequent royalty checks—pretty much taken to disregarding me in every way possible. I don't know if he kept his anger toward me under his hat for the rest of his life, but there was no visible turmoil between us at that time. In conversation, Bernie never referred to my upcoming return to Britain. Not that I even cared. I sensed it was just about over for me at Cameo, and I really didn't think what I did or didn't do made any difference to the label boss.

As my situation with Cameo deteriorated day by day, I looked at my second overseas tour as an opportunity to build a second home of sorts—a refuge, if you will, across the sea. They say fame is where you find it. If my career in the States happened to suffer, I figured I might at least be fortunate enough to become famous in another part of world.

On February 15, 1958, as my latest Cameo release languished in the nether world of uncharted records, Joan and I were married in St. Callistus Church, her home parish in West Philadelphia. One of the quirky things I still recall about our wedding ceremony was that the name of the priest who conducted the Mass was Father McKenzie, a name later immortalized by the Beatles in "Eleanor Rigby." The reception was very intimate. I never cared for those affairs done in large halls and certainly didn't want anything that extravagant for Joan and myself. We kept it local and invited immediate family only. Since the Gracie clan wasn't large to begin with, it was a nice, small family celebration, one we were all happy with.

When we emerged from St. Callistus on our wedding day, it was snowing heavily. I wasn't that concerned because we'd made reservations to spend the night at the Walnut Park Plaza Hotel, which was only two or three miles from the church. We were scheduled to fly to Miami the next day, and we managed to get to the hotel by pushing the car halfway there through the snow. As a result, I came down with the flu—or something close to it. I was sicker than a dog, man. At one point I had a fever of 102. I couldn't shake it for three or four days. On top of that, because of the weather, many of the guests at the Walnut Plaza hadn't checked out, so the only room available to us was one with a Murphy bed—one of those things that folded down out of the wall. I figured we'd just make the best of it and be off the next morning, but every time I so much as touched that bed, the thing squeaked like hell. "Oh Jesus!" I thought to myself. "This is how we're going to spend our wedding night?"

Meanwhile, the snow continued to pile up. When we awoke the next morning there was more than 16 inches of the stuff on the ground, and we were unable to get out of town. We stayed at the Walnut Plaza a second night, and the following day we *still* were stranded. By that time, things had devolved into a terrible situation; Joan and I stuck there in that room and me thinking I'd blown the whole thing. I saw only one way to get out of that mess: Our honeymoon would have to wait until April, when I was scheduled to tour Great Britain again. "You know what?" I said to Joan. "Let's go home and enjoy some good hot soup!"

A year after my first overseas tour, some guilt over what I'd subjected Joan to while I was away for those 10 weeks still remained. Now that she was my wife I wanted to make it all up to her by seeing that she had a great experience when we traveled overseas as husband and wife come the spring. But before I could make that possible, I had to deal with a vexing problem from an unexpected source—my own parents.

I should have expected as much, because during the past six months anytime somebody in the family brought up my first trip to Britain it was done very gingerly. Of course, it all stemmed from the infamous June Wilkinson incident, which Joan had learned of as soon

as I'd returned from Britain. I couldn't have kept it from her even if
I'd wanted to, because it was spread throughout the scrapbooks of
press clippings I'd brought back with me. Unfortunately, even during
those times when nothing provocative is happening, some women—
even my own mother—imagine things. When my mom saw all those
sensational press clippings about June Wilkinson she wondered what
the heck had gone on over there. Then she started in on me: "You
lettin' Joanie see that stuff?" All I could do was reassure her *and* Joan
that there really was nothing to the whole thing. It was harmless—all
publicity and hype.

But whenever Bernie Rothbard and my father made the
unpardonable mistake of reminiscing about the night in London when
we went to see June Wilkinson's "act," my mother became overcome
by agita. In her mind, perhaps there had been some hanky panky
going on. I think a big cause of my mother's suspicion was that when
my father returned from England he acted as if he'd developed his
own fan club there. In a teasing sort of way he'd brag to my mother
about the women he'd met: "They thought I was young-looking; they
loved my Philadelphia accent," things of that sort.

My mother became more annoyed each time my father said
things like that, and I understood why. He was 44 when he went to
Britain, still a relatively young man, and he didn't even look *that* old.
People always thought he was 10 or 15 years younger than his actual
age. My father also remained as ruggedly handsome as ever. To top
things off, that was the first (and only) time my dad had been away
from my mother since they were married.

Of course, my father saw things from a totally different perspective.
After I'd taken him with me to Britain the first time, he figured: "I'll
go with Charlie again, to keep him company. I'll be his chaperone, his
bodyguard"; stuff like that. He should have realized that I was now in
love with Joan the same way he'd fallen in love with my mother. This
time I wanted to take my wife, not my father, with me. But I knew he
was really set on going with me again, so I'd put off telling him as long
as possible that it just wasn't going to happen.

Then, one night, Bernie Rothbard came over to our house to
discuss my upcoming trip. As he and I sat and talked, my father—as

he usually did—kept a close ear to our conversation. He still had no idea he wasn't going back to Britain with me. Meanwhile, Bernie went on and on with all kinds of details about the trip: "Blah, blah, blah, blah. And since you'll be taking Joan…"

"What!" The instant my father heard that, he flew into a fit. He'd convinced himself that he should be the one there with me; that I needed him more than I needed my wife with me. "What do you mean, you're taking Joan? What's *she* gonna do in England? It's not easy over there, you know. She won't be able to keep up with that pace." On and on and on it went. I think he and Bernie argued back and forth for about three hours.

When my mother learned of my intentions to take Joan—and not my father—she really liked the idea of her husband remaining home with her. She began telling Joan, "Oh yes, *you* should go with Charlie. *You* should be with your husband. *You* deserve it, especially since your honeymoon was ruined by that snow storm." And every once in a while she'd turn to my father and say to him, "You let Charlie go there with his wife this time!"

I finally had enough with my father. Every guy who's ever been in love knows the feeling. You forget about your mother, you forget about your father, and you forget about your friends. All you think is, "I want my sweetheart with me!" I finally told him, "I love you dad and I always *will* love you. But you've been to England with me. This time I'm taking Joan. You're not going, dad. I'm taking my *wife.*" Eventually my father calmed down and accepted my decision. He wasn't angry, but he *was* disappointed. He really did want to come with me.

On Thursday, April 3, Joan and I boarded a BOAC flight at New York City's LaGuardia field, bound for London's Heathrow airport. We didn't know it beforehand, but Pat Boone and his wife Shirley were booked on the same flight. We first saw them at the airport terminal, standing on the opposite side of the ticket counter from us. That's when we discovered we'd be flying together. But we never got the chance to speak at that moment. Pat had a large entourage with him—his manager, his conductor, and several other people, plus all their wives. I think that was Pat's first trip to Britain. He was booked for just one show, and would be there for only three or four days.

There were other entertainers besides Pat and myself on the plane, including the Hilltoppers vocal group, set to appear on one of the same television shows on which I was booked. Not long after we took off Joan nudged me. "Charlie, see that lady across the aisle? She's *somebody*, but for the life of me I can't remember who." Well, carrying a huge fur coat, and with an infant being cared for by a nanny, the woman in question certainly *looked* as if she was a "somebody." Joan kept glancing over and glancing over until finally it dawned on her: "Patricia Neal. That's the actress Patricia Neal!" I'm sure other passengers also recognized Miss Neal, but nobody outwardly paid any attention.

It was a great flight, everything was first-class. Pat Boone and his wife were in a special section in which they were able to pull a curtain across their sleeping bunks. Those old Constellations had only two seats on each side of the aisle. The seats were wide, and you could tilt them back. Not at all the way they squeeze you in today, like sardines in a can. Those old propeller-driven planes took something like 12 hours to fly to England, and perhaps 14 hours on the return trip, so all that space really was a comfort.

We arrived in London on April 4. It was 3:30 in the afternoon, hundreds of fans were yelling and screaming behind police barricades, and the London press was out in full force. That didn't affect me so much, but I was worried over how they'd treat Joan. As we stepped off the plane and onto the portable steps leading down to the tarmac, the photographers began snapping pictures. It wasn't until then that we had our first opportunity to speak to Pat Boone and his wife. Things grew a bit tense as flash bulbs popped all around us. They were so bright and there were so many of them that we couldn't see the people in front of us. "Oh my God," I exclaimed, "this kind of pandemonium is more than I expected!"

The authorities quickly hustled us, along with Pat Boone's entourage, into a nearby hangar, where an impromptu press conference was held. Joan wore high heels, which made her appear a bit taller than me. That only fueled the paparazzi, who loved to play up the fact that I'm only 5' 4". Joan was only 17 at the time and she thought the press might try to make something of that, so she told them she was 19. (In hindsight, I'm glad we avoided anything like the notorious, press-driven Jerry Lee Lewis incident involving his 13-year-old bride that took place in Britain only weeks after Joan and I left the country.) I shouldn't have been caught off guard when June Wilkinson's name came up, but I was. Nobody in Britain knew I was now married, so the press, in a scene designed for their own benefit, went into some kind of self-created frenzy when I introduced Joan as my wife. "Charlie's married, but not to June!" one reporter shouted. "Charlie's married to Joan, not to June!" yelled another. And so it went.

The next morning, the same "Charlie and June" nonsense made headlines. *The New Musical Express* reported that my current tour had "hastened" my marriage to Joan because I "didn't want to leave her behind." And, of course, they couldn't avoid asking: "And what happened to June Wilkinson?"

Those guys felt free to write whatever suited their needs, whether it was truth or fiction. Seeing it all in print, especially with Joan there at my side, was pretty upsetting. I took one look at a rack of the mudslinging tabloids and thought, "Ah, here they go again."

My second British tour covered pretty much the same ground as the first, except it was quite a bit shorter than the previous one. My itinerary consisted of five one-week engagements, with a few individual dates thrown in along the way. We returned to most of the venues I'd played in 1957, since I'd packed them before and would most likely do so again. On April 5, Easter Eve, I appeared on Val Parnell's *Saturday Spectacular* (ITV) television show along with fellow American artists June Christy and the Hilltoppers. On Easter Sunday, in front of more than 2,000 avid followers, I played a return engagement at Bristol's Colston Hall. Then we drove up to Liverpool for a week's run at the Empire Theatre. On April 12, I made a BBC-TV appearance. Following the telecast we then headed for Britain's east coast, to the city of Hull. It was in Hull that I experienced the extreme fanatical devotion of some of my followers.

It began after the second of my two Sunday performances at Hull's Regal Cinema. As Joan and I headed for the waiting limo, we were mobbed at the stage door. I began to navigate our way through the enthusiastic throng as fans clutched furiously at my jacket, my shirt, and my tie—anything they could get their hands on. I was determined they wouldn't get my jacket (and they didn't), but at some point I realized one fan would return home with my tie as a trophy. No big deal, I thought, as Joan and I took refuge inside the limo; I could easily replace a tie for my next gig. It wasn't until we were under way and Joan asked me for the time, that I realized that another "fan" was going home with my wristwatch! Boy, did my heart sink. I really treasured that watch, not for its monetary value, although it must have set her back a significant amount, but as a personal memento from my loving wife. Joan had given me that timepiece—a stylish Bulova with a personal inscription—as a Christmas gift a year earlier. And now it was gone!

My road manager happened to be in the limo with us as I bemoaned my situation. "No need to worry yet, Charlie," he reassured me. "I'll tell the press what happened and explain to them just how much that watch means to you. We'll offer a reward for its return, no questions asked, and hope for the best. The reporters are certain to play it up big."

Having been raised on the rough streets of South Philly, I wasn't too optimistic about ever seeing that watch again. Then again, plan B was to simply kiss my cherished timepiece goodbye. "What the hell," I said. "Let's give it a try." And wouldn't you know it? Several days later my watch was returned. I gladly paid the reward—no questions asked.

Episodes of overzealous adulation, such as that in Hull, occurred quite frequently during both my British tours, so I wasn't surprised by this latest one. Today I view them with a seasoned veteran's perspective, as a kind of occupational hazard—one far preferable to a performer's ego than exiting a venue to the stony silence of indifference. I've never become comfortable with those tumultuous rituals, but at least I learned to remove my wristwatch before subjecting myself to them.

After leaving Hull, we drove south again. I had a week of performances lined up at the Birmingham Hippodrome, followed by two Sunday gigs at St. Georges Hall in the city of Bradford, which is located just west of Leeds. Then we took a motor trip back down to the Finsbury Park district of London, for a week at the Finsbury Empire. Sunday, April 27 was a particularly busy day. We did two shows at the Granada Theatre in the East Ham district of London, after which I became the first leading American artist to appear on that evening's *Top Tune Time* BBC-TV show. We then made the long drive north to Scotland for a one-week return engagement at the Empire Theatre in Glasgow.

Then it was on to one of England's oldest cities, York, where, on Sunday, May 4, we did two shows at the Rialto Theatre. After leaving York we headed for our last weeklong booking, in the northeastern coastal city of Newcastle. We finished up with two Sunday concerts on May 11 at the Granada Woolwich, on the River Thames, in the eastern part of London.

Before the tour began, I wondered how my female fans would react to Joan as my wife. I have to say they were simply lovely to her and treated her with respect wherever we went. They regularly brought her flowers, candy, and little homemade gifts. As the tour began to wind down I realized I'd developed a deeper appreciation of my overseas followers.

Before we bid goodbye to England I experienced one of those serendipitous delights that, if you're lucky, jump into your life every so often. Joan and I were having dinner after taking in one of London's West End shows. There was nobody else in the restaurant when who the hell walks in but the iconic actor Charles Laughton and his wife, Elsa Lanchester. Holy Moses! I couldn't believe it. What a thrill that was. I was in total awe. Visions of me as a kid, paying 10¢ to see Charles Laughton in the movies, flashed through my head as the maître d' proceeded to seat the famous couple only a few tables away from us. "My God!" I thought. "I can't believe I'm in the same room with this guy."

"Go get his autograph, Charlie," Joan kept urging me. "Have him sign something."

"Go get his autograph? I can't move!" And I really couldn't. I was frozen.

Joan and I flew back to the States on May 12. I immediately began to work the nightclubs and the theaters again, but not having had a hit record in almost a year now began to take its toll on the quality of my bookings. I pretty much took whatever gigs I could get.

While I was still in Britain, Bernie Lowe had released my sixth record for Cameo. That was somewhat of a surprise, considering I hadn't recorded anything for the company in four months. But my contract required Bernie to release another record by me, and evidently this was it. When I discovered which of my songs Bernie had released, *that* was no surprise. The first time I heard the playback of the tuba driven "Love Bird," I said to Bernie, "You know, you've got some other things in the can. Why don't you put one of them out and leave this one where it is?" Although Bernie never said anything to me at the time, he had honored my wish—until now. But in the interim he'd slipped back into the studio to overdub a chirping "Betty Boop"-style "do-wacka-do-wacka-do" female chorus onto that "Roaring Twenties" flavored travesty. Then, against my wishes, he unleashed the doctored "Love Bird" on the public.

For the record's B-side, Bernie overdubbed a female backing voice onto my recording of the Hilltoppers' 1952 ballad hit "Trying," another of my recordings confined to the can when it was recorded at the "Wanderin' Eyes" session, almost a year ago.

Because I'd been in Britain at the time, I had no idea of Bernie's latest machinations. But it's pretty obvious that he was trying to stick it to me one last time. Bernie made no effort at all to promote "Love Bird"; not even a cursory mention in *Billboard*, not so much as a nickel on any advertising. It was as if my record was released underneath a mattress. Try and find it! *Billboard* actually reviewed the thing, but the trade paper's less-than-ringing endorsement didn't help any. "Love Bird" was described as a "Charleston," with me accompanied by "a little girl group." Aimed at "fan listening but questionable for dancing," advised *Billboard*. "Trying," although "nicely handled" by me, was said to have "limited potential" in the market.[46] Ouch!

Bernie Lowe now exhibited classic passive-aggressive behavior. After having the chutzpah to release "Love Bird," he pretended everything was fine between us. But his strategy was beginning to wear me down. Forget about my receiving only limited airplay. Now I got none at all. That's when things began to get really rocky, when everything started to fall apart.

I'd slowly come to the realization that Bernie had written me off. There would be no future recordings and no additional payments for all those records I'd sold. Bernie was just stringing me along until my contract expired. But I was prepared to end everything then and there. I shared those thoughts with Bernie Rothbard. "Charlie, I'd think about that twice if I was you," he counseled. "I don't believe that's a wise decision. So they're screwing you; you're getting robbed. So what? Just keep your mouth shut and continue to work even if you don't get paid. If you somehow manage to get a few more hits down the line, you won't need Bernie Lowe and Cameo."

I'm a principled person, and my position wasn't so much about the money as it was that Bernie Lowe was giving me the shaft. I'm the type of guy who wouldn't steal a dime from anybody, and by the same token, I don't want a dime stolen from me. That may have been a noble attitude, but in hindsight it also was stupid. Ardently following your principles sometimes leads to stubbornness and that can cause you to cut off your nose to spite your face. Which is what I did. I decided to stand up for a principle. Unfortunately, I was in an unprincipled business.

Despite Bernie Rothbard's warning, I went ahead and confronted Bernie Lowe one last time. We met in New York and I again told him I didn't think I was being treated fairly. Bernie gave me his old familiar line: "Look Charlie, let's not argue about this. Let's let our lawyers handle it." When I heard that, I saw red. We'd gone the lawyer route once before, and what had *that* gotten me? I had a phony increase written on *paper* and nothing more. I was finished with lawyers. "Forget about it," I thought. "This guy will *never* pay me!"

Once again destiny came into play as I made a fateful decision. I looked Bernie straight in the eye and said with all the resolve I could muster: "Bernie, I'm going to have to sue your company for the money you owe me." As I spoke those words, a voice inside my head told me, "Charlie, this is something you really don't want to do."

Let me say right here that my dad was partly instrumental in my decision to sue Cameo. You know, there's a peculiar side to my life. I've always been sort of the loner type. I never had a close buddy to hang out with, and my brothers and I were born so far apart that I didn't pal around with them either. Don't misunderstand me. I've been happy living that lifestyle. I have many friends. But where a lot of people can say, "This is my *best friend*, man," I never had a best friend—except for my father. He was my best friend. We were like pals; I used to take him with me to my gigs. He was like a brother. That's what happens when you're raised in that closed Sicilian environment. Many Sicilian families have that same problem. My dad was very protective of me, to the extent that, in this case, his custodial instinct overcame his sensibilities.

In another way, my entire family was fortunate that "bad advice" was my father's only contribution to my problem with Bernie Lowe. My father had a gun and he wanted to shoot Bernie. "I'll kill that son of a bitch!" he told me on more than one occasion. "Dad, no dad," I pleaded. "That's all I need is for *you* to go to jail. It isn't worth it. We'll find a way out." I understood my father's rage, but I never knew whether or not he was serious.

All my dad could think of was, "Bernie's screwin' my kid! Charlie helped him make a lot of money, and now my son's gettin' the shaft." My father walked around the house muttering, "Bernie Lowe. That son of a bitch!" Then he'd say to me, "It's *your* money. You earned it. If he won't pay you, sue him!"

When my father urged me to sue Cameo he meant well; he was trying to act as my manager. But he had no experience at all in that field. He was a laborer. He didn't know the first thing about the music business. So although it was unintentional, my father gave me some very bad advice. And because my father was my best friend, my "buddy," I listened to him.

When Bernie Lowe heard the word "lawsuit," he turned whiter than he had after I'd told him I'd been underage when I signed my original contract with Cameo. Still, he maintained his rigid stance about having the lawyers decide everything. "Look Charlie," he said, "this can be worked out. Just let your lawyer talk to my lawyer."

I'm not sure why, but at that moment I finally realized that Bernie, a classic pessimistic worrywart, was fearful that if he did make a decision to pay me, he'd forever fret that he'd offered me too much. Bernie was truly incapable of settling this dispute himself. I thought, "You know what? Let's just end this thing so I can get on with my life and find a record company that will appreciate me."

"Okay Bernie, fine," I replied. "We'll give the lawyers one last shot at averting a lawsuit. If they determine that you owe me back royalties, you can just write me a check."

So after all we'd been through, all of the battles we'd fought, in the end it came to a mutual decision between Bernie and me. Our lawyers began to discuss the end game of what was supposed to have been a great deal for both of us. They eventually reached an agreement whereby we didn't have to wait for my contract to expire. A settlement figure in the amount of $50,000 was decided on, which Bernie agreed to pay in monthly installments. I was free to walk away from Cameo. And so we parted company. Bernie proceeded to send me a check in the amount of $1,500 a month until he paid me the 50 grand (almost $400,000 in 2012, adjusted for inflation).[47] When I received such a significant amount of money at that point in my young life, I thought I was rich. After I received the last check from him, Bernie Lowe was out of my life. Or so I thought.

No longer such a hot name, I pressed on. In November 1958, after I'd finally broken from Cameo, I signed with Coral Records, a subsidiary of Decca, which was then one of the top five recording companies in the world. Paul Cohen, the executive who ran Coral, had been with Decca since that American arm of the British parent company was formed here in the States in 1934. In 1945, Cohen was named head of Decca's Country division and went on to become one of the movers and shakers largely responsible for Nashville's emergence as the capital of country music. About seven months before I landed at Coral, Cohen had assumed the post of A&R director.

I don't remember exactly how I signed with Coral. The music director there was a New Yorker named Dick Jacobs, who'd been with the company since 1953. Coral was pretty much a pop label, and Jacobs and his orchestra backed all of its top artists, including two of its biggest stars, Teresa Brewer and The McGuire Sisters.

Coral had only one rock and roll artist. But if you could select just one, Buddy Holly would be an outstanding choice. Ever since Buddy Holly and The Crickets signed with Decca in 1957, Norman Petty had produced their music, the bulk of it in Clovis, New Mexico. (The Crickets' records were released on the subsidiary label Brunswick.) About the time that I arrived at Coral, Buddy split from The Crickets to go out on his own. Norman Petty continued to work with The Crickets, and Buddy moved to New York City to work with Dick Jacobs.

When I signed with Coral I really thought I was on my way. Besides joining the home of Buddy Holly and The Crickets, I was impressed by Dick Jacobs. He was one of the first major figures involved in the mainstream pop music business to take rock and roll seriously. Dick had already worked with Bobby Darin and Jackie Wilson. When it came to bridging the gap between pop music and rock and roll, nobody was more adept at it than Coral's music director.

Dick was also one of the most respected arrangers in the business. The guy was at least as talented and knowledgeable as Bernie Lowe, perhaps more so. When I first met Dick, he told me, "Charlie, you're an excellent artist. We consider it a significant opportunity to have you on the label. It's going to be great. We're going to have hit after hit together."

"Gee, Dick, that sounds great to me," I said. "I'm excited, too."

With Dick in charge of my first Coral session, I went in and cut some nice records. The first tune we did was called "Doodlebug," a mid-tempo thing with a backing chorus and a musical bridge of pronounced piano triplets. I'd be lying if I said the song didn't evoke thoughts of "Butterfly." "Hurry Up, Buttercup," which was selected for the B-side of the record, was the second tune we recorded. It had a "Chalypso" beat (combining the cha-cha with calypso), which, at the time, was a hot dance among teenagers.

Released in January 1959, both sides of the record received strong reviews from *Billboard*. Both were said to be "cute rockers," and Coral "could get some action on either one."[48] It's always nice to receive a positive review, but after reading *Billboard*'s opinions, my first thought was, "Here we go again with the two-sided 'kiss of death.' C'mon guys, choose one side or the other and get behind it!"

Just weeks after the record was released, Buddy Holly was killed in that infamous plane crash. My God, what a shock that was. I couldn't believe it. I also felt bad for the other two performers with him, Ritchie Valens and J. P. Richardson, known professionally as "The Big Bopper." I'd never met Buddy but I sure loved his music and the way he performed. He didn't have a great voice and he wasn't a grand guitar player either, but he had that certain sound. Buddy had a unique musical style and a creative musical mind. He was quite innovative, having just begun to incorporate strings and such into his music. I'm quite certain, had Buddy lived, he would have continued to be an innovative force in pop music.

Almost immediately after Buddy's tragic death, most of Coral's current projects came to a screeching halt. The label was focused on getting as much of the doomed artist's music as possible onto the market in a timely manner. As a result, neither side of my record received much airplay. In the scheme of things, it was just one of several Coral releases that fell by the wayside, orphaned by the very company that created it.

Then again, when Buddy was killed, destiny once again came into play. Just before "Doodlebug" was released, Coral had undergone a departmental shake-up. Paul Cohen abruptly left the company and Dick Jacobs was named to succeed him as the head of the label. Dick said to me, "Charlie, unfortunately, Buddy's gone. I'm deeply sorry he was killed, but this is the perfect opportunity for you to fill the void that we have. It seems as if you came into this company at just the right time." But when "Angel of Love" and "I'm a Fool That's Why," my second record for the label, was issued that May, it didn't fare any better than my first Coral release.

For whatever reason I just couldn't get radio airplay anymore. Oh, I received *some*, but nothing like I did when I had my hits with Cameo. One problem with recording for a big company such as Decca is that they release numerous records at the same time. When that happens, you don't get the narrow concentration of promotional work on your project that you would if you were with a smaller company. With so many records to promote, they can't concentrate on a select few. Decca's philosophy seemed to be, "put out records on everybody, and we'll go with whoever comes up with a hit." But I never came up with that first hit.

The guys at Coral and Decca had been around a long time, and they knew how to cut records. The ones I made were good; I never cut a bad record with them. I was happy with the results, but I think the material they gave me wasn't as strong as it could have been.

On the other hand, the underlying reason for my lack of airplay may have had nothing to do with the type of material I recorded, or the size of the record company. Perhaps my affliction was none other than Bernie Lowe. I don't recall exactly when Bernie Rothbard told me this, it could have been when I was with Coral, or it could have been later. But one day he said to me, "Charlie, you're not gonna like what I'm about to tell you. I just happened to cross paths with your old pal Bernie Lowe and I mentioned to him that you'd landed on your feet and were recording again. Lowe then said to me, 'Bernie, your boy will never have another hit again as long as he lives. We'll see to that.'"

Whoah! Hearing those words, I had to sit down for a minute. "Bernie said *what*?"

"He told me you'd never have another hit as long as you live."

Right away, visions of *American Bandstand* flashed across my mind. Once I left Bernie Lowe, I was finished with Dick Clark, too. Dick was no longer inclined to play my records, because there'd be no "reward" forthcoming from Bernie. With Dick and Bernie being extremely close friends as well as partners in several music-related enterprises, it's not hard to imagine Bernie telling Dick, "You see what that Gracie kid did to me? He tried to sue me. I don't want that little son of a bitch appearing on your show, Dick!"

There's one final matter to consider: I may not have been the only one to experience the bitter taste of Bernie Lowe's retribution. Except for Len Barry of The Dovells, none of the artists who successfully recorded for Bernie ever had another major hit after they left the company—none of them!

1935. My parents, Sam and Mary Graci, as newlyweds.

1936. My first year of life as the firstborn son of Sam and Mary Graci.

1946. My grandfather and namesake, Calogero Graci. He was, and still is, my hero.

1944. Yours truly at age 8.

1948. Age 12 with my first guitar, a $15 Harmony, outside our South Philly row house at 735 Pierce Street.

1955. Just out of high school at age 19, I had already been making records (since 1951) and working as a musician and entertainer at clubs and ballrooms in the Philadelphia area.

1957. Me and my father at the Reco-Art Studio in Philadelphia, where I recorded Cameo Record's first hits.

1957. Ready to rock the United Kingdom. My first tour was a resounding success and was extended from five weeks to ten by agents Lew and Leslie Grade.

August 1957. I had the distinct honor of being the last headliner before the famed London Hippodrome closed and was converted to a cabaret and supper club. In 1983, the Hippodrome reverted back to its original name, and it operates today as a casino and entertainment venue.

1957. The spoils of success. I paid $5,300 cash for my first car, a 1957 Cadillac Coupe deVille.

1957. Proud papa! My dad sailed over to the U.K. to join me for the second half of my extended tour. The British press found his personality and thick Philly accent entrancing.

1957. Mary Poppins meets rock & roll! Laughing it up with the "charwomen" (house cleaners) at the London Hippodrome. The British press published photos of me similar to this numerous times.

March 25, 1957. A dream comes true. "Butterfly" not only reached the No. 1 position in America but sold extremely well in at least a dozen other countries.

1957. With my dear and late, great friend Eddie Cochran after a concert in Washington, D.C.

May 1957. Receiving my gold record for "Butterfly" on Circus Time, a national ABC-TV program hosted by comedian and ventriloquist, Paul Winchell. My manager, Bernie Rothbard, is on the left. I introduced my follow-up hit, "Fabulous," on the same show.

April 1957. Headlining the Brooklyn Paramount for Alan Freed was a great honor. I admired Alan, and we were very friendly.

June 1957. Rehearsals for the Howard Miller Show at the Chicago Opera House. Left to right: the Everly Brothers; unknown male; singer and pro golfer, Don Cherry; unknown female; yours truly; and Eddie Cochran. The concert, which included Chuck Berry, Brenda Lee, and Tab Hunter, was sold out!

1957. On stage at the Bolero Club in Wildwood, New Jersey. Today, the street in front of the Bolero Resort has been renamed in my honor to commemorate the many summers I played at that island haven.

Veteran singing star DOROTHY SQUIRES refused second billing to GRACIE at the HIPPODROME in LONDON. Her "walk out" made headlines across the United Kingdom. MS. SQUIRES was married to movie actor ROGER MORE of "James Bond" fame at that time.

'WHO IS CHARLIE GRACIE, ANYWAY?'

Here's the man Dorothy didn't know

This is Charlie Gracie, 21-year-old American rock 'n roll disc star who tops the bill—above, Britain's Dorothy Squires.

He tops the pop parade

American singer Charlie Gracie bovey arrived at outhampton yesterday, after topping the merican hit parade ith "Butterfly" nd now he's topping e bill at the London ppodrome.

And right is British singer rothy Squires who walked t of the show asking: he is this Charlie Gracie. Miss Squires was dropped hit down the bill to make y for Charlie and his tar—so she left.

GLASGOW Daily Record

AND DOROTHY DROPS OUT

MISS SQUIRES IS WRONG, SAYS CHARLIE

WHEN Charlie Gracie heard Dorothy's views he said: "Miss Squires is absolutely and indubitably wrong in saying I am unknown.

"I made the big time when my recording of 'Butterfly' sold over 1,000,000 copies in the States. It sold well here too. In the first ten days my disc 'Fabulous' has sold 500,000 copies.

"I have made a movie and I've topped the bill in music halls all over the States.

LONDON HIPPODROME
6.15 Monday SAT. 8.45
August 5th
Telephone: GER. 3272
The Young American Singing Star
CHARLIE GRACIE
DOROTHY SQUIRES

The Young American Singing Star
CHARLIE GRACIE
DOROTHY SQUIRES

News Chronicle
2nd August 1957

Dorothy 'Squires quits after a —billing row

SINGER Dorothy Squires declared last night that she had walked out of the London Hippodrome show, due to open Monday, because of the way she was billed. She was to have appeared on the same bill as Charlie Gracie, young American singer who recently made several successful records.

She said she was promised "equal billing" with Gracie. "And what happens? I find that I'm just a first featured artist."

Daily Sketch Reporter

AMERICAN singing sensation Charlie Gracie is "sorry" for British singer Dorothy Squires, who stormed out yesterday from a new West End show.

She walked out because she did not like her first-featured billing for the London Hippodrome show. She had expected to share top billing with 21-year-old Gracie.

● I'M NOT CATTY...

He has shot to the top of the U.S. Hit Parade with his record of "Butterfly." His "Fabulous" is having a big sale.

But last night, at her home in Bexleyheath, Kent, 35-year-old Miss Squires exploded with: "Who is this Charlie Gracie, anyway?"

Charlie Gracie will get more than £1,000 for singing at the Hippodrome.

Gracie's pride was injured when I phoned him two days out from Southampton in the Mauretania last night.

"What did you say he name is? I've never heard of her, either," he said.

"Miss Squires told me it's disgraceful that British star should be treated in this way. I've been in America for you years, starred in Los Angeles and never hear of this Mr. Gracie. And I'm no being catty."

Her 31-year-old actor husband Roger More comforted her as she explained: "I accept the shared top billing because that is the only way a British star can get into the West End these day

"Now I find I've bee stuck at the bottom. I just saw red and had to wal principle."

"This is a matter of principle."

"Mr. Gracie came back over the radio telephone "Gee, I'm terribly sorry."

PAGING CHARLIE GRACIE ★
THE LITTLE ROCK 'N ROLL ☆
IMPORT WHO UPSET ☆
DOROTHY SQUIRES ★

By PHILIP PURSER

ON to the stage of the London Hippodrome last night whirred the young man who kept Dorothy Squires off it. If she hadn't heard of Charlie Gracie before—that's what she said — Miss Squires will be hearing plenty now.

Charlie, the latest Rock 'n' Roll import, is 21 and only 5ft. 4in.

But what he lacks in inches he makes up in ergs, the yardstick of energy.

He uses about a million a performance. While he sings the veins on his temple stand up like mountain ranges on a relief map.

He strums a shiny guitar linked to an amplifier. Last night a string snapped with a twang.

Undisturbed, he skipped an instrumental solo and threw in an extra song.

1957. I received massive press coverage throughout the U.K. when veteran singing star Dorothy Squires refused to accept second billing to me at the London Hippodrome.

August 1957. Yours truly captured by the British press outside the London Hippodrome.

July 1957. In front of the legendary 500 Club in Atlantic City, New Jersey. Watching me place my signature into fresh cement are (left to right): 500 Club owner, Paul "Skinny" D'Amato; my father, Sam Gracie; my manager, Bernie Rothbard; and president of Cameo Records, Bernie Lowe.

1957. Teen adulation came with success and in Britain it often got out of hand. I never thought of myself as a teen idol but as a musician and showman first. Trying to maintain order behind me is my manager Bernie Rothbard.

November 1957. The premiere of the movie Jamboree *in Wilmington, Delaware. Yours truly at center next to songstress Connie Francis, flanked by actors Paul Carr and Freda Holloway (left), and singer Andy Martin (right).*

November 1957. The Stanton Theater hosts the Philadelphia premiere of Jamboree Front row, left to right: president of Chancellor Records, Bob Marcucci; yours truly; Dick Clark; songstress Jodie Sands. My parents and two younger brothers, Bob and Frank, are to the right in the back rows.

1957. Surrounded by fans after performing at the Casino Royal in Washington, D.C.

1958. Gazing into the future? Between 1957 and 1958, I scored three U.S. hits and a total of five in the U.K. Two years later, I was struggling to keep my career intact and a roof over my head.

February 15, 1958. Joan and I got married at St. Callistus Roman Catholic Church, her home parish at that time, in the Overbrook section of Philadelphia. We've been inseparable ever since.

1958. Family portrait taken by one of the Philadelphia papers in the living quarters of the Havertown, Pennsylvania home I purchased for my parents. Left to right: My father, Sam; my mother, Mary; my youngest brother, Bobby; Joan; and me.

April 1958. Joan and I arrive with Pat Boone and his wife, Shirley, at the London Heathrow Airport where British police had to restrain several hundred fans.

1958. My second U.K. tour began with a national television appearance on Val Parnell's Saturday Spectacular *with the Hilltoppers and June Christy.*

1960. Me and Perry Como. Perry was a sweet man and a true superstar. I was honored to meet and work with him.

1965. After The Beatles hit in 1964, it wasn't long before I formed my own quartet.

*1997. With Dick Clark, celebrating the
40th anniversary of* American Bandstand.

*1999. Me and Sir Paul McCartney
backstage at the Hammersmith, Odeon
in London. Sir Paul threw a party to
celebrate the release of his album* Run
Devil Run, *which included a cover of
my hit "Fabulous."*

*2000. Backstage with two great artists, Stephen Stills (left) and Graham Nash
(right). Graham and I recorded duets on two of my albums:* For the Love of
Charlie *and* I'm All Right!

2003. Me and Andy Williams. Andy was as talented and classy as they come. His cover of my hit "Butterfly" reached the No. 1 position on the Billboard chart as well. Andy graciously appeared in the PBS-TV documentary Charlie Gracie: Fabulous! He was a good friend and I miss him.

2006. Van Morrison proudly holds his Charlie Gracie t-shirt and a copy of my PBS-TV documentary. I was honored beyond words when he asked me to tour with him.

January 2000. I was Van Morrison's special guest performer at the Wiltern Theater in Los Angeles, California.

2010. With my middle brother, Frank (left), and younger brother, Robert (right). Sadly, we lost Robert in 2012.

2011. Celebrating my 75th birthday (left to right): son, Charlie, Jr.; Joan; Gail Barsky; my daughter-in-law, Kim; me; and my daughter Angela.

2012. Chubby Checker and I rocking out to "Shake, Rattle and Roll" at Wildwood, New Jersey's 100th anniversary concert. Chubby has always shown me great respect, and the feeling is mutual!

June 2014. Wrapping up a recording session with Dee Dee Sharp at Lanark Studios in Lancaster, Pennsylvania. Charlie, Jr. is to the left.

2014. Headlining the 26th annual Blues to Bop Festival in Lugano, Switzerland.

September 2014. Stage side in Wildwood, New Jersey with my two trusted companions, Joan and my Guild X-350.

11

ESTRANGEMENT

As Charlie Gracie's career hit a wall, the inconspicuous alliance between Bernie Lowe and Dick Clark continued to benefit both parties. In 1958, with Cameo Records now a successful company possessing a bright future, Bernie Lowe made two significant business decisions. First he formed a new record company called Parkway Records. Then he bought out several minority investors in Cameo and merged the two companies to form Cameo-Parkway Records.

But in November 1959, the staunch affiliation of Bernie Lowe and Dick Clark fractured. Due mainly to the large number of independent record companies located in Philadelphia by the early 1950s, that city had acquired a reputation within the pop music industry as a wide-open town for disc jockey payola. With the concurrent rise of rock and roll and American Bandstand, Philadelphia continued to lead the way in payola notoriety.[49]

Although rumors of payola continued to abound, no proof of any of the allegations had as yet come to light. But as the federal government's formal investigation into bribery in the pop music business began in November 1959, the nefarious practice's web of secrecy and innuendo began to unravel. In one particular instance,

Edward D. Cohn, the owner of leading Philadelphia record distributor Lesco Distributors, revealed to federal investigators for the House of Representatives how it cost him thousands of dollars to get his records played on local radio stations. "This city has a reputation of being the worst place in the country for payola," he declared.[50]

Among the considerable occurrences of payola in Philadelphia that began to surface was the fact that Bernard Lowe Enterprises, since its inception in 1956, had made promotional payments to disc jockeys, and Chips Distributing (of whom Lowe and Dick Clark were "silent" partners) had made similar payments.[51]

A s 1958 drew to a close I gained a new record company and a whole lot more. On December 12, my son Charlie, Jr. was born. (In case you're wondering, he was named after my grandfather, not me.) You might think the addition of another mouth to feed put added burden on me as the sole support of my extended family, but I'd never felt that kind of pressure before my son was born and I didn't feel any after he arrived.

At that point in my career I still thought I was on top of the world. My ongoing work in the clubs kept me well known in the business, and I was still able to pull in more than $1,000 a week. I put that money into the bank and took it out only as it was needed. What's more, I'd finally negotiated my freedom from Cameo Records and had recently signed with Decca/Coral, a major company that was ready to release my first record. Although I was reassured by the grip I now thought I had on my professional career, I was about to be blindsided by circumstances in my personal life that would bring me to my knees.

It's the rare married couple that doesn't experience an array of pitfalls over the years. Unfortunately, Joan and I weren't in that exclusive group. The problem wasn't between us, we were happy together and very much in love. The difficulty we encountered stemmed from the increasingly strained relationship that began to develop between my parents and Joan.

My mom and dad seemed to like Joan when they first met her. Before we were married I'd bring Joan over to the house and we'd sit on the front steps with my parents and talk for hours. In those days parents expected their sons to marry a virgin, and my mom and dad would have been opposed to any girl whom they thought didn't meet that requirement which, of course, she did. And once my parents got to know Joan they realized she was a "nice" girl and never doubted her character. So once I managed to diffuse their "marriage as a career-killer" argument, the prospects for Joan and I looked rosy. Joan was an Italian girl, so you'd think my parents would have readily accepted her. But that wasn't the case. Although Joan was Italian, she wasn't Sicilian. Once she became part of the Gracie family, my mom and dad began to treat her as an outsider. And nothing—not even marriage—could change that.

My parents weren't unusual in viewing any non-Sicilian as some kind of an "outsider." Sicilians are a peculiar lot. Their families are extremely close-knit. And believe me, it's tough when you come from a family where everything's glued so tightly together. I suppose if you haven't been raised in such a manner it's a difficult concept to understand. To tell you the truth, I think it's kind of foolish, myself.

As a young boy growing up in that environment, it was tough for me to recognize what was happening. I was my parents' first-born and they loved me to death. My mom and dad both were filled with love, and our household always reflected that warmth. Now don't get me wrong, love is a wonderful thing. But when you smother someone with it, that's not healthy. Things eventually reached a point where my parents' love for me became somewhat obsessive—a fixation that didn't allow any room for others. I didn't realize that at first, because I was a part of the "tribe." But as I became a young adult I began to understand the issue at hand. My parents needed to ease up on the reins a little, but that wasn't about to happen. There were times when I thought, "Mom, Dad, I love you. If you need me, I'm always here. But stop smothering me!"

A mother and daughter-in-law relationship can be a complicated thing. To a certain extent, a mother is always afraid that her daughter-in-law will overshadow the relationship with her son. Even so, the two women usually manage to get along fine, if not wonderfully. Unfortunately that wasn't the case between my wife and my mom. From the very start of my marriage, my mother seemed to harbor a grudge against Joan. Each time she saw my wife she thought, "You're taking my son away from me." And when my mother saw me she now imagined, "You're taking your love from me and giving it to *her*." Once Joan and I were married I certainly didn't love my parents any less. I simply spread my love around a bit more. But my mother and my wife—two adult women living under the same roof—soon became a cause of bitter resentment within our family. Whenever I agreed with Joan and not my mother, my mom would say, "Charlie, you've changed since you got married."

I'd tell her, "Ma, you don't know what you're talking about!"

Faced with the reality of our marriage, my mom and dad did accept Joan to a limited extent. Still, because my wife wasn't "blood," she was always the "stranger," ever the "outsider." And my parents would come right out and tell her, "You're not a Sicilian. You're an Abruzzese and a Neapolitana!"

We soon realized that the problem was more than a case of dissimilar bloodlines. Joan was regarded by my parents—especially my mother—as some kind of threat. All the while, Joan did everything she possibly could to be accepted and to fit in. She watched my mother cook, all the better to learn how to prepare the Italian food our family loved so much. But even when Joan made a particularly great meal, my wife never received a compliment from my mother—not one. My mom was a "needler," who somehow always managed to be that thorn in your finger. For instance, she'd declare, "Not bad, Joan, but my gravy's still better." Joan carefully observed my mother clean the house and then did it in the same meticulous manner. But in my mom's eyes, Joan could never do *anything* as well as she did. I'd say to my mom. "Joan's my wife. You're my mother. Don't compete with Joan. There's no competition here." But it was always, da-da ZING, da-da ZING. "Mine is better than yours!"

The fact that my family and I often spoke Sicilian in our house—a language that Joan didn't understand—made this difficult situation even worse. She naturally thought, "They're talking about me. Why else would they be speaking that way?"

Joan knew I was on her side, so she tried to let my mother's antics roll off her back as best she could. Sometimes we'd even manage to laugh about it, but I know it was annoying for my wife to hear that kind of derogatory talk all the time.

If you're wondering what, if any, part my father played in this domestic turmoil that engulfed us, I think he really liked Joan. The two of them usually got along quite well. My wife and I would tease him and joke with him about all sorts of things, and he'd laugh. I really think my father wanted to compliment Joan, but he was afraid to do so because of my mother. As wonderful and lovable as my mother could be, she was a tough woman and very headstrong, and my father just went along with whatever she said and did because he didn't want to hurt her feelings.

As the months went by, relations didn't improve one bit between Joan and my parents. By the time we returned home from England the pattern of behavior had grown depressingly predictable. Whenever I defended my wife, my parents' response was: "How dare you speak to us like that? What's happened to you since you got married? You never used to talk that way to us." I never raised my voice to them, let alone yell or scream, but I have to admit there were occasions when I should have been more supportive of Joan. I realized none of the friction with my parents was her fault, but there were occasions when I did put some of the blame on my wife. She sometimes agreed with me, saying, "Well, maybe it *was* my fault." Her response quickly brought me to my senses and I reassured her, "Don't be crazy. You never did anything to cause trouble."

Joan eventually came to believe that if she outwardly accepted that my parents came first, she'd at least be tolerated by them. "I'll just stay out of their way," she reasoned. "Whatever they say, they're the bosses." But even that wasn't enough. Many of the problems with my parents were figments of their imagination and, as such, unsolvable. For example, after Joan moved into the house I'd bought in Havertown, my parents believed my wife's goal was to appropriate the house for herself. Forget the fact that the deed to the house was in my parents' name, not mine. My wife *never* would have considered something like that. It would've been the last thing on her mind. But none of that mattered to my parents. I really don't know what the hell they were thinking at the time. They just imagined all kinds of things.

The fact that my mom and dad had few friends didn't make things any easier on us. They didn't socialize easily with other people. Anything and everything they did involved only our family. And on the rare occasion when a member of Joan's family visited us, my parents acted as if they resented them being there. My mom and dad also felt they should be included whenever Joan and I had friends come to visit. One evening, just after Joan and I had enjoyed coffee with some friends in the kitchen, my mother confronted us and voiced her disapproval: "Oh, so now you don't even ask us to join you when you're with your friends!"

Another aspect of our domestic strife stemmed from the fact that I was often away from home. Because my record sales had fallen off, I began to work the nightclub circuit more frequently. It kept our heads above water financially, but while I was on the road Joan had to endure my parents' injurious behavior in virtual isolation. You have to remember she was just 17 or 18 years old at the time, just a kid, for God's sake. She was mature for her age, but somewhat timid. While I was away, my mom and dad tried to keep her isolated—even from her own family. Joan really didn't see anybody else except my mom and dad. They didn't want any "outsiders" to intrude, even on the telephone. "What do *they* want?" my parents would demand if anyone in my wife's family so much as called to see how she was. Joan confided in me that while I was away she often felt like Cinderella.

Things became so unbearable for Joan that on one occasion when I was on the road she called a cab late one night and quietly left the house to stay with her mother in South Philadelphia. When she returned the next day, my parents cornered her in a bedroom and started browbeating her. They actually told her she was crazy. "There's something wrong with you, girl." When I retuned home they informed me, "Your wife is sick!"

As Joan and I endured this abuse on a daily basis, the tension grew to an unbearable level. I was caught between a rock and a hard place. I didn't want to hurt my parents, and I didn't want to hurt Joan. I realized I had to stand on my own two feet or risk the possibility of a divorce. But when I defended my wife and admonished my parents about their behavior, instead of considering my perspective, they resented it.

After Charlie, Jr. was born, a new source of conflict arose. After we moved to Havertown we switched family doctors and began consulting a local pediatrician who'd been recommended by Joan's gynecologist. My parents' reaction was predictable. "Oh, no," they insisted. "You should take the baby to our doctor in South Philadelphia!" We didn't agree, and so each time our new pediatrician offered his opinion, my mother would say, "Don't listen to him!"

Joan had to swallow pretty hard, but we held our ground. There were times when Charlie, Jr. became ill and the pediatrician had to come to our house. (Remember those days when doctors made *house calls*?) The first time that happened, my mother and father actually tried to tell the doctor what to do! Instead, he scolded them and told them to stop interfering. Even so, they wouldn't back off an inch. One night, just before Joan's birthday, my parents started with the doctor business again, insisting he was the wrong pediatrician to use. "Dad, Mom, this doctor's *great*," I told them. "He's thorough and dedicated. We like him and we're *not* switching."

The next morning, when I saw my parents they told me Joan had snubbed them as she came downstairs to make breakfast. "Your wife didn't even say hello to us this morning, Charlie." As their voices rose and they proceeded to have it out with me, Joan appeared. I thought to myself, "This is some birthday present for my wife." That particular flare-up didn't amount to much, but I knew it was just a matter of time before the next incident occurred, and I'd lose my temper and put my parents in their place again.

After a year and a half of the humiliating treatment at the hands of my parents, our domestic situation continued to throb like a festering blister. It was near impossible for Joan to remain under the same roof with them. Then, on that fateful day in August 1959, the blister finally burst.

The specific reason for this final cataclysmic confrontation has faded from my memory. Suffice it to say, once again my parents had claimed that my wife failed to show them the respect they believed they deserved. But this time would be different. During my mother's ensuing rant she appeared on the verge of completely losing control. I couldn't remember ever seeing her in such a catatonic state. She became a real "screaming Mimi" as she raged at Joan and me: "You know what? Get out of here. Both of you leave this house—right now!"

I was stunned. Thoughts flew through my head too quickly for me to even begin to sort them out, let alone react in a rational manner. For some reason, the words of my Aunt Josephine jumped to the fore. "Charlie," she'd told me on many occasions, "be a man and stand up to your parents. Don't allow them to treat you and Joan this way. I know them all too well, especially my brother. You've got to be a man. Stand up to them, Charlie. Stand up to them!"

I'd never taken Aunt Josie's advice—at least not to the extent I should have. But at that moment I stood up and gave no ground. "Okay. That's it," I blurted out. "I can't stay here any longer. I gotta get out of this place. I *am* leaving!"

Then it was my mother's turn to be shocked. As a look of disbelief came over her she stammered, "No, no, Charlie. Stay here. I'm sorry I told you to leave the house."

But in my mind I'd not only reached the point of no return, I'd crossed it. "No, Mom, that's it," I replied. "This no longer has anything to do with *me*. I bought this home for you and Dad. But I finally see that you and Joan just can't live in the same house. So you do what *you* want to do." Then I turned to Joan, who'd been standing there in silence. "Get out of the house," I told her. "Get out of the house now!"

With that, Joan ran across the road and headed for Bernie Rothbard's place, determined never to return to the emotional caldron she'd just fled. I then grabbed Charlie, Jr., who sat nearby wearing only his diaper, and gently placed him in my Caddy. And before another word was said, "Boom!" I was gone. I can't begin to explain the mood I felt during those dreadful moments, other than to say it was a kind of emotional frenzy. As angry as I was, I was also broken-hearted. As I stopped at Bernie's to get Joan (Bernie was at his office), my eyes were filled with tears.

"I'm never going back there!" Joan screamed when she saw me. "Don't worry about it," I assured her. "We're not going back." Then I drove off.

All I had in the car at the time was my guitar and amplifier. "Holy shit!" I thought as I roared aimlessly down the street. "Where am I going?" I had no idea, either literally or figuratively. As I sped on, my tears made it difficult for me to see. If I'd been some kind of a nut, and we'd come upon a bridge, I probably would have driven off it and killed us all. That's how anguished I felt.

I later found out that my kid brother Bob had overheard my mother and I arguing, and had called my Aunt Josie. "There's a big argument going on here," he told her. "You'd better get down here and see if you can help settle it." My aunt, along with my Uncle Jim, jumped into their car and made the 15-minute drive from West Philly.

During that dark moment I happened to meet my aunt and uncle driving in the opposite direction. We saw each other, tires screeched, and both cars came to a stop.

"What happened, Charlie?" Aunt Josie wanted to know. "What are you doing? Where are you going?"

"We had a fight," I explained. "Joan and I are moving out."

"Oh my God!" she exclaimed. "You can't just 'go away.' You have no clothes, no money. You don't have anything. C'mon over to my house. You can stay there for the time being."

My Aunt Josie was right. If I hadn't met her and her husband I don't know where the hell I'd have gone that day. Joan, the baby, and I really did have nothing but the clothes on our backs. We drove to my aunt and uncle's house and they got us settled down. Then Aunt Josie went back to my parents' place to get some clothes for Joan and Charlie, Jr. I later returned to retrieve some of my own things.

We stayed at my aunt and uncle's for a few weeks, until we managed to find an apartment. By then, at least my father had time to think things through. Just as I did, he felt terrible about everything that had happened. But that made no difference to Joan. She kept repeating, "I'm not going back there again, Charlie. I won't go back to that misery!"

I knew Joan was right. What slight relationship there had been between her and my mother had been totally destroyed. When Joan and I got married I thought my family would all live together harmoniously. What could I do now? There's an old saying: "A son is a son till he takes a wife, a daughter's a daughter all of her life." It had taken some time—probably too much time—but I'd finally realized that I needed to follow that age-old advice. The devil never sleeps. Joan and I could never go back to living with my parents. It was time to make my own life with Joan and our son.

As if that period of turmoil and readjustment wasn't enough of a burden, in September 1959 my career took another turn for the worse. The slump began right after my third record for Coral had been released. The A-side, a mid-tempo pop tune called "Because I Love You So," was one of the few songs that I actually had a hand in writing. I cowrote that particular number with a good friend of mine named Teddy Lass, who lived on Flatbush Avenue in Brooklyn, New York. Teddy and I would spend hours writing songs. We penned three or four songs together in that manner. Unfortunately, the telephone company made more money from those songs than Teddy or I did.

The flip side of the record was a cha-cha called "Oh-Well-A," which I thought sounded at least as good as the plug side, maybe even a bit better. But despite Coral's promotion—I *assume* they promoted me—I drew very few radio plays. My latest effort for the label met the same fate as my first two. Neither side managed to make a dent in the charts.

By that time, I knew my tenure with Decca/Coral had reached its end. It's a shame the way things didn't work out with Coral, because I cut some quality records for them. But my departure was simply company protocol. When an artist signs with a major company like Decca/Coral, they afford you several shots at a hit and if nothing happens they drop you. And you can't really blame them for doing so. While a smaller outfit such as Cameo depends on just a few artists, a company as big as Decca/Coral has a larger stable of talent to pull from. If a particular artist can't cut it, the company simply moves on to someone else. In my case, there was no animosity on either side. It was purely a case of: "Nothing clicked; your contract's up. Next!"

So there was destiny at work again. My life to that point had been too good to be true. But once Decca/Coral cut me loose the roof began to fall in. With diminished airplay, my name was no longer in the public eye. The salary I once commanded for my live performances began to dwindle. As new recording stars emerged on the scene, record buyers began to forget about me.

While professionally I was up to my eyebrows in horseshit, the alienation I experienced from my parents was much more devastating. It was far worse than not having another hit record. I could handle the career decline, but what happened with my parents was a nightmare. That problem with my own flesh and blood caused my whole world to fall apart. I was *shocked* that such a thing could happen to me. There are no words to express what I went through during that period. It was like being kicked in the groin. To this day, when I think about it my heart still aches. Long after it was over, Bernie Rothbard said to me, "Charlie, considering what you went through, most guys would have blown their brains out."

Around the time my contract with Coral expired, Joan, Charlie, Jr., and I moved into a duplex unit in a small apartment complex in a neighborhood called Llanerch Hills (that's a Welsh name, pronounced LANN-ark), located about 10 minutes away from where we'd lived in Havertown. I was pretty lucky to find such a place. It was brand-new—never lived in—with two bedrooms, so Charlie, Jr. was able to have his own room. Aside from his crib, we didn't have many household possessions when we moved in. We bought an inexpensive sofa and some other accessories, and my Aunt Josie truly helped out by giving us some additional furniture, including a kitchen set. Unlike Havertown, the apartment was located in a middle-class neighborhood. But we were happy just to be there by ourselves. (For my part, I could have lived in a cardboard box and it wouldn't have bothered me.) We felt that freedom of not having to answer to anyone. It was like being unchained!

Joan and I settled in, and before long my routine became similar to the routines of my neighbors. I trudged along, making a living and paying the bills. My rent was 90 bucks a month, which, in those days, was pretty steep. But most important to me, I was able to make the payments and keep performing. The big difference was, instead of working the Chicago Opera House or the London Palladium, I now worked in bars and cafes *next door* to elegant showplaces like that. Even so, I was still well known locally. While we paid rent just as everybody else did, most people thought I owned the entire apartment complex. Because this was such a humiliating point in my life I didn't deny it.

"You own the whole row, right Charlie?"

"Yeah, the whole row."

Despite such an optimistic start, our first year or so at Llanerch Hills turned out to be really terrible. Being nearly estranged from my parents was very difficult for me, and my mother continued to resent Joan. I had more contact with my father. He hadn't worked since I'd told him to quit his job at Stetson. That was fine when we all lived together in Havertown and I handled the finances, but when Joan and I left, my bank account was pretty low—$800 low, to be exact. Even so, I felt I couldn't leave my father without anything. "Dad," I said to him, "I've got 800 bucks. Here's 400 for you."

Since then, I'd barely had the means to support my own family. We Gracies always believed that when faced with adversity you swallowed your pride and did what you had to do. At that point, my father realized what he had to do. Unfortunately, he had only one skill—making hats—so the poor guy had to return to Stetson, where he earned $90 a week. Believe me, that wasn't easy for him, especially after telling his coworkers two years earlier: "See ya. I'm done! My kid's gonna take care of me now. I'll be working for him."

My dad had to eat crow. You know how people can be; his coworkers taunted him unmercifully. "Hey, what happened, Sam? Where's your son now?" They were rotten that way, and my father had no choice but to take it. I felt terrible for him because he was still my father, so whatever they did to him, they did to me. That really broke my heart. I cried many a night for him.

My father's plight wasn't the only reason for tears. After he went back to work, my mother tried to take it out on Joan. She actually had the nerve to call my wife one day. "You've got to go to work!" she snapped. "Charlie left us flat here."

Joan couldn't believe it. "Go back to work?" she said. "I already work. I have a little baby and a household to take care of."

"Well, you've got to go to work and help us out!"

"How can I get an outside job and take care of the baby?"

"I'll watch the baby," my mother told her. "You have to go to work and help us!"

Can you believe it? I got my mother on the phone and really had it out with her.

Joan didn't talk to my mother or father again for several months. "You know what?" she told me, "I don't think I ever want to *see* those people again!"

Thankfully, one good thing did come out of that episode. My father worked at Stetson for only a short time before he was able to escape from that place once and for all. My brother Frank's father-in-law was a painter and he managed to get my dad into the industrial painting business. My father didn't have the $100 necessary to join the painter's union so he asked me for the money. I gladly gave to him, relieved that my father was able to find a new trade. And he made a good living from it for the rest of his life.

After I parted ways with Decca/Coral, I was without a record deal for some months. Even so, my two British tours had been so successful that I was asked to return there. But how could I travel to England for five or six weeks and leave Joan with the baby when she wasn't even talking to my parents? I couldn't abandon them for that period of time. I just couldn't do that. I was always there for my wife and son, to shop, take them to the doctor, whatever had to be done. Besides, I didn't even have enough money to leave Joan and Charlie, Jr. while I was gone. You also have to consider the emotional state Joan and I were in. Yes, it was very tough for her. On the other hand, that was *my* flesh and blood I left in that house in Havertown. I can't emphasize enough how extremely gut-wrenching that decision had been for me. Lastly, I didn't think it was a sensible business strategy for me to travel all the way to Britain at that time. The trip wouldn't have done anything to increase my record sales (especially now that I was without a label again). So I said I just wasn't interested.

I think my decision disappointed the agents in Britain. I was still a sizeable name over there, and the promoters would have made money with me in 1959. But within a year's time their interest in me waned, and I began to realize I'd blown a good opportunity. Even so, in the States there was an ongoing interest within the industry to record me, so I remained optimistic that I'd soon sign with another company.

Meanwhile—as if I needed one—I was given a reminder of my recent tribulations with Cameo Records. During the fall of 1959, in a joint venture by Dick Clark and Bernie Lowe, Swan Records released its first 12-inch long-playing album. It was a compilation of 12 of the biggest hits from the Cameo and Swan labels titled *Treasure Chest of Hits*.[52] Of course, "Butterfly" was one of the songs included on the album. But due to my settlement with Cameo I didn't receive any royalties from the sales of that LP. Some things never change.

Not long after the release of Swan's *Treasure Chest of Hits* I was flabbergasted to wake up one November morning and see an 8-by-10 picture of me in the *Philadelphia Bulletin*. Ordinarily somebody would have to commit murder to get a photo that large in the newspaper! It was an old photo, taken when I was 16 years old, wearing a white confirmation jacket—the same photo Bernie Lowe had used on the cover of the sheet music for "Butterfly." Along with my photo was a big story by the *Bulletin's* notable columnist Frank Brookhouser about the breaking music business payola accusations.

My first thought was, "Why in hell are they using *my* picture in a story about disc jockeys and payola?" It was just horrible! Evidently someone "dropped a dime" on the alleged bribers, and with Brookhouser using my picture in his column, a lot of people thought I was the culprit. It also didn't help that my name was so strongly connected to "Butterfly." That photo was great for a day's worth of publicity, but coupled with the payola story it drove a nail into the coffin of what lingering hopes I had for a career comeback.

So help me God, I had nothing to do with those payola revelations. Remember, I was born and raised in Southwark, an area where you were taught to keep your mouth shut, no matter what. You *never* squealed on anyone. Except for the time when I went face to face with Bernie Lowe and demanded my royalties, I never blew the whistle on anyone. Besides, I didn't know what the hell was going on behind the scenes. I didn't find out about Dick Clark's involvement with Cameo and Bernie Lowe until 1960, when Congress investigated and brought it to light.

Knowing what I know today, I think anyone who denied taking money during that time is a liar. I think a lot of industry folks were on the take. That's just the way the independent labels and the record distributors operated. When I started out in the business, some of the promo guys took me along with them when they made their rounds to meet certain disc jockeys. We went to York, Reading, Lancaster— all the little out-of-the-way stations in Pennsylvania. Ten or 20 bucks usually got your record played. It wasn't like in the larger cities where you had to come up with a few hundred a week to get the job done. I'll tell you this: if someone at Decca/Coral had used a little grease to get *my* records played, a few of those singles may well have charted. Payola still goes on today although, thanks to the internet and the digital recording process, the record companies' stranglehold on the industry has been broken. But it's *always* about money. Love of money is truly the root of all things evil. Many people continue to sell their souls for it.

For a year or so after the breakup of my family I went through a lot of mental anguish. My career was shot and I was reduced to living in that Llanerch Hills apartment with my wife and Charlie, Jr. During the fall of 1959 I began to take my son to visit my parents at their home in Havertown, but Joan refused to go along. "I'm just not comfortable being in their company," she'd remind me.

When Christmas Day came, Joan's mother finally said to her, "Oh, for Charlie's sake you should forgive them and go over there as a family." So Joan gave in and went with us that Christmas Day. It came as no surprise that my parents were really cool toward her. Things continued that way, but at least we didn't have any more arguments.

In a matter of just two years, I'd gone from rags to riches to rags again, and there was very little money coming in. After I'd left Cameo, my booking agent Bernie Rothbard said to me, "Charlie, we made a bad move, but don't sweat it. You have talent. We'll keep you working. You'll always make a living." Fortunately, Bernie was right about the work. My personal appearances had always been where I made the bulk of my income. But there was one big change Bernie failed to mention.

While I was on top I made anywhere from 1,500 to 2,000 bucks a week. When you're hot, you're hot. Chart success brings national recognition. Conversely, when the hits stop, your bookings get thinner. After my short and unproductive tenure with Decca/Coral I was without a record company again. I hadn't had a hit record in the States in almost two years and things had become pretty quiet. "Uh, Charlie Gracie. Well, we booked him for $1,500 when he was hot. Now? We'll give him $375." That's a helluva drop. Even more worrisome, the gigs grew more infrequent.

I was really up against the wall and was forced to take whatever they offered. I couldn't let my recent success become a distraction. I had to dismiss it from my mind, swallow hard, and go forward.

We were about to celebrate Charlie, Jr.'s second birthday. At the very least, we wanted to offer some cake and refreshments to our families. But after just paying the rent, we didn't have enough money left to have even a small celebration. I felt like I had to do something, so I cashed in some empty soda and beer bottles and we used the deposit money to buy a birthday cake. Joan prepared some of her homemade pizza, and we bought frozen juices and brewed some coffee for the adults. Even my parents showed up for the occasion and to our great relief, no one ever found out what we had to do to pull it off.

That very same weekend we went through the ordeal of cashing in those soda bottles I finally landed a gig. I don't remember what it paid, probably about $125, but whatever the amount, we regarded it as money sent from heaven. God was good to us in that particular instance and, as we would eventually discover, in other ways. As bad as things were, somehow we always managed to get what we needed to sustain ourselves.

In 1960, after eight months without a recording contract, I finally signed with another big outfit, Roulette Records in New York City. My good friend Al Gallico ran Shapiro, Bernstein & Co., a company that had published a couple of my songs for Decca/Coral. I'd met Al because Shapiro Bernstein's offices were located right across from one of the studios used by Decca/Coral. He was quite a nice guy—brilliant, I thought—and was beloved in the music industry. Al was a fellow Italian-American, a *paesano* from New York who'd come up the hard way. The two of us hit it off really well and kept in touch for many years.

While I was still with Decca/Coral, Al had offered me a contract for $50,000 a year to write songs for the Shapiro Bernstein publishing outfit. But back then, very few people—myself included—knew or even cared about songwriting royalties, and I declined Al's offer. "I'm a performer," I told him. "I can't sit in a room all day long and write songs."

When Al learned I was no longer with Decca/Coral, he said to me, "Charlie, if you're interested, I can put you with Roulette Records."

Roulette! Every music industry insider knew Roulette was the label owned and operated by the sinister Morris "Moishe" Levy. Moishe allegedly had connections to the New York-based Genovese crime family. If his artists dared to ask for royalties, Moishe would respond: "You want royalty? Go to fuckin' England!" Levy was the kind of guy whose idea of persuasion (or dissuasion) was to dangle some unfortunate soul by his feet out a window 10 stories above the street below until the inverted mortal saw things the boss' way.

Roulette's premier hit maker was Jimmie Rodgers, a 26-year-old pop-folk singer/guitarist from Camas, Washington, who, since his debut in the fall of 1957, had racked up a dozen Top 40 hits for Moishe. How Jimmy fared with the royalty department is anybody's guess. But when his contract with Roulette expired he returned to the West Coast to find a new record company. For this I'd demanded that Bernie Lowe cut me loose?

"Hey Charlie, we're gonna cut in Nashville," Al Gallico said when it came time for me to record. As things turned out, I cut all my records for Roulette in Nashville. Of course, that was before Nashville became *the* place to make records, before it was branded "Music City." When we went down there in April or May of 1960, Al had already arranged session time at Nashville's top studio, which was owned and operated by Harold and Owen Bradley. Bradley's, which had opened in 1954, was the first studio built on what came to be known as Nashville's famed Music Row. In 1958, Owen Bradley became vice-president of Decca's Nashville division and went on to produce hits for country greats Red Foley, Ernest Tubb, and Kitty Wells, among others. Meanwhile, the Bradleys rounded up the best studio musicians in Nashville, a group that came to be known in the business as The A-Team.

When I arrived in Nashville, most of that A-Team was waiting for me inside the studio. I recall the guitar picker; his name was Grady Martin. Oh my God, talk about brilliant guitar players. Grady Martin played on *everybody's* records. I'm not certain about the rest of the musicians who played at my session, but most likely they included Boots Randolph on sax, Bob Moore on bass, and Buddy Harman on drums. After introductions all around, plus the usual small talk, the producer handed me the music for the first song we were about to cut and said, "Okay Charlie, sing it through once." I'd barely finished singing when the producer called out: "Okay, take one."

"What? Take one? How about the musicians," I wondered. "Aren't we going to run this thing down together at least once?" No, we weren't. We did one take and, to my surprise, it was perfect. I was thrilled to death. Once again, I thought I'd hit a home run. As I turned away in jubilation, I was stunned to be standing face to face with the legendary country artist Eddie Arnold. I almost dropped dead on the spot.

"Oooh, son," Eddie said to me, "that sounded *so* good!"

I was speechless. All I could muster was a stammering Jackie Gleason "omi-na, omi-na, omi-na." Finally, I managed to say to Eddie, "My mother loves you. My father loves you. I love you!"

Some wonderful recordings came out of those sessions for Roulette. The production and musical accompaniment was absolutely top notch, once again infusing me with a sense of optimism. A mid-tempo rocker called "The Race," which featured Boots Randolph's wailing sax, was selected for my first release. I remember thinking that the flip side, "I Looked for You," written by an aspiring young songwriter, was also a pretty hip tune. "Great song!" I exclaimed when I first heard it. "Who's this writer Burt Bacharach?" Of course, nobody knew who Burt Bacharach was back then. (In 2008 a collection of songs written by Burt and recorded by other artists, was released.[53] I'm proud to say I'm included on that CD, singing "I Looked for You.")

After *Billboard,* in its May 1960 edition, gave "The Race" a four-star rating ("very strong sales potential") noting that "Gracie turns in (an) exciting performance,"[54] the tune looked like a fine choice to be my lead single. Talented musicians, expert studio production, a well-reviewed vocal performance, top sound quality, and a favorable trade paper review—what more could I ask for? Well, how about some airplay? It was the same old story. You can go in and cut a great record but if no one hears it, who's going to buy it?

I think the people at Roulette were more disappointed than I was, because they waited a full *seven months* before releasing my follow-up record, a country-tinged ballad I'd cowritten, called "Sorry for You." When that song also bombed, I added Roulette to the growing list of labels that had taken a chance on me only to be burned. At the same time, I counted my blessings: at least I'd been spared a confrontation with Moishe Levy over potential royalties.

In May 1960, my parents sold their house in Havertown and bought a more modest one in southern New Jersey. That was all well and good with me. It was their home. If I'd been looking to make money on that house I would have put my name on the deed. "God bless them," I thought. I was happy to see them settled.

The move was good for Joan, too, because it put a little distance between her and my mother. My parents *still* refused to fully accept Joan. Occasionally they'd come to see me perform when I worked one of the nearby clubs, but they became irritated if Joan was there with me. They still considered her presence to be some kind of intrusion. They mockingly referred to her as "the tail," as in, "Oh, he had to bring 'the tail' with him!"

My downward spiral in show business continued into 1961. Everything I touched turned to *dreck,* as they say in Yiddish. My club gigs dwindled to the point where there was almost no work. That was disheartening, but if I'd been able to continue—even at that pathetic level—things would've been bearable. But it grew worse. There were long stretches where I had absolutely *no* work. "What do

I do now?" I wondered. "Start selling encyclopedias?"

But I kept at it and surely enough in the waning days of summer I had an opportunity to record again. The one-off session was produced by a grand old man of the Philadelphia record business, Harry Chipetz. Harry had gotten his start in the business back in the mid-1940s, working for a local jukebox/record distributor. In the early 1950s Harry had operated the Philadelphia branch of Marnel Record Distributors before moving on to a distributor called Cosnat. In 1957 Harry Chipetz became president and manager of Chips Distributing Corporation.

One day, out of the blue, Harry said to me, "Let's go into the studio, Charlie, I want to cut you." It was the same story once again. Everybody wanted to record me. All I can say is that once again my talent became my salvation. Why else, given my dismal track record, would other labels continue to show an interest in me?

What the hell, I figured. At that point I had nothing to lose. I knew Harry was the president and manager of Chips. What I (and a lot of others) didn't know was that Harry originally had two silent partners: Bernie Lowe and Dick Clark. When the payola scandal broke in 1959, the ABC network had forced Dick to divest himself of the numerous music-related companies in which he had a stake. Dick sold his share of Chips to Harry and Bernie.

Over the years, I've been asked if I would have made that record with Harry if I'd known at the time he was a business partner with Bernie (and formerly with Dick). That's hard for me to answer at this point. I always liked Harry. He was a nice guy and I never had any issues with him. When he asked to record me in 1961, I thought he really had faith in me. On the other hand, knowing what I know now, why would Harry want to spite Bernie and Dick by cutting me? I still don't understand that.

When Harry brought me into the studio he wanted to recapture the sound I had on my hits with Cameo. Late that summer we headed back to the familiar Reco-Art studio to record with Emil Korsen again. Utilizing the studio and the engineer responsible for my most successful recordings, I began to think if I got lucky it might happen again.

After we'd done an acceptable Buddy Holly style take on

"Makin' Whoopee," the Eddie Cantor standard from the Roaring Twenties, we turned our attention to the flip side. Harry had a song titled "W-Wow" picked out, but for some reason we struggled to get an acceptable take on it. After numerous attempts I thought I'd break up the monotony. I began horsing around with the song in my best Porky Pig imitation. I began it with "De-DEE, de-DEE-ya, dit, dit, dit," after which I ran down the first verse of the tune. Before I realized what was happening, the musicians had created a funky beat to go along with my silly performance. To everyone's surprise, Emil told Harry, "That's great! Let's cut it like that."

Harry also thought the novelty effect just might work. "In fact," he added, "I think we got ourselves a hit record here!"

Honestly, after hearing the playback of "W-Wow" I felt like a schmuck. But I had to admit the song *did* sound kind of cute. "Who knows?" I thought. One thing was certain: I couldn't sell any *fewer* records than I'd sold the past three years. "All right, Harry. If that's what you want, let's do it. I'd rather sing it straight, but if you want me to do Porky Pig..." He did, and we proceeded to cut "W-Wow," "pig-style."

"What do we do with it now?" I wondered.

"Well, are you a man?" Harry asked me. "You got any guts?"

"You're damned right I've got guts."

"Would you go see Dick Clark with the record?"

"Yeah," I told him without hesitating. "I'll go see Dick Clark."

Well, the day I did go to see Dick I must have sat in his office for two hours. It reached a point where I didn't think he ever intended to see me in the first place. But Dick eventually came around. When he did, I wondered if he was thinking, "Let me get rid of this guy."

We talked and, to my surprise, Dick played the entire record. Then he said to me, "I think you did a great job on that, Charlie. There's only one problem. I'd be afraid to play something like that on *American Bandstand* because it makes fun of people who stutter."

As whimsical and cheeky as I was in those days, I came back at him—not in a cocky manner, but snappy: "Excuse me Dick. You know Porky Pig's been a big star for years. He's never been accused of making fun of anybody. Yet when I imitate him you tell me it's making fun of people?"

"Well, you know, Charlie, that's the way I feel about it."

"You know what," I thought, "let me get the hell out of here before I lose my temper and say something I'll regret."

"Okay, Dick," I replied. "Thanks for your time. Thank you very much." With that, I stood up and walked out of his office. I didn't see Dick again until 1997, when I attended the Fortieth Anniversary reunion of *American Bandstand* in Philadelphia.

Harry Chipetz's attempt to recapture the sound I got on my Cameo recordings was a noble gesture, but we both knew my latest recordings would never appear on that label. When the record was released in September it was done so by Felsted, a subsidiary label of London Records. I'll be damned if I remember how Harry hooked up with Felsted. Who knows? Maybe he figured, "Charlie's still famous in England, I could sell records there." I really don't know what his motivation was.

Felsted touted "Makin' Whoopee" as the A-side of the record. I thought "W-Wow" could have been a hit as well, and *Billboard* agreed. The music trade magazine gave both sides its highest rating: a Spotlight Single of the Week ("strongest sales potential of all records reviewed this week"). The reviewer noted that this was my "strongest wax here in a long time....Both sides can go."[55]

Believe me, I did my utmost to make either side "go." But this time it was Felsted that didn't have the muscle to give my record a fighting chance. Once again, I received minimal airplay and miniscule sales. No matter whom I recorded for—Coral, Roulette, Felsted, any of them—I always went out and promoted my records as best I could. Although I still managed to get a little play here and there throughout the country, it was very difficult to crack the Top 40 stations. And they were the big guys. Without their concentrated airplay you couldn't have a significant hit. It also came as no surprise that the biggest guy of all, Dick Clark, never played either side of my Felsted record. His fear of airing "W-Wow" aside, Clark certainly could have played "Makin' Whoopee," because that also was a good record. But guys like Clark always had an excuse. If they wanted to play your record they played it, and if they didn't, they'd find any excuse not to.

12

THE WILDERNESS

During the summer of 1963 Bernie Lowe moved to consolidate his fiefdom. A year earlier he'd hired Harry Chipetz to be Cameo-Parkway's general manager. Now Cameo-Parkway purchased from Chipetz what amounted to a controlling interest in Chips Distributing. Then, toward the end of 1963, Cameo-Parkway moved to newer and larger facilities in a spacious three-floor building located at the corner of Broad and Spruce Streets in the heart of Philadelphia. Despite those moves, cracks began to show in Bernie Lowe's empire. Cameo-Parkway was still in the black, but the company's net income for 1963 fell almost one-third from the previous year.[56]

In 1964, Bernie Lowe's world continued to grow darker. First he lost his neighborhood promotional venue when his pal Dick Clark fled Philadelphia for television-land in California. At the same time, Motown's "Sound of Young America" began to come alive. Philadelphia disc jockey Hy Lit recalled the time he was in Lowe's office as the label owner anxiously paced the floor, lamenting, "Look at this Motown, starting to come on with unbelievable records!"[57]

Adding to Lowe's woes, the first wave of the "British Invasion" hit America's shores in 1964. During one crucial weekend that February, American Bandstand made its debut in Hollywood and Ed Sullivan introduced The Beatles to America. One month later, Cameo-Parkway produced its final Top 40 hit under Bernie Lowe's stewardship (Chubby Checker's "Hey, Bobba Needle"). By year's end, the company had lost almost a half million dollars,[58] and Lowe was so beside himself that he contemplated calling Charlie Gracie to help right the ship.

History books recall the early years of the '60s as an era of optimism for America. The nation's youthful president John F. Kennedy had successfully heralded his vision of a New Frontier—a program, he claimed, designed to "get the country moving again." Well, I sure would have welcomed a boost from JFK's New Frontier to get my career moving again. It was as if somebody had pulled the plug. My phone stopped ringing and domestic squabbling continued to dog me. Reduced to a bit player in a nightmarish scenario, I continued to fall by the wayside.

Meeting the needs of an ever-growing family continued to be a challenge. Ever since our daughter Angela (a "Christmas Eve" baby, born December 24, 1961) arrived, she and Charlie, Jr. had to share a back bedroom of the duplex where we lived. As the kids grew older and more active, our living space became more cramped. There was no way I could afford to get a bigger place, and the only thing I seemed to be getting was older. There were times when I just wanted to crawl under a rock. But as bad as things seemed at that point in my life, I was determined to slog on. "What the hell," I thought. "I've got nothing more to lose."

I realized that one of the most valuable things I possessed—which no one could take away from me—was the experience I'd gained from all my years as an entertainer. Taking whatever gigs I could get, I was man enough to perform in all kinds of joints. And some of them were really toilets. I frequently played five sets a night, six nights a week, "sawing wood," as they say in our business. That was often discouraging, yet I managed survive.

I almost got off the ground in 1962 with a sort of twist-inspired song I'd written called "Night and Day, U.S.A." That August I signed with President Records, a tiny label that was a part of the giant London American Group. President's artist and repertoire man, Marv Holtzman, was the type of guy I'd call a music industry "lifer." He was a pretty sharp fellow who'd gotten his start in the business during the early 1950s, working with singers such as Roy Hamilton and Brook Benton. So much time has passed that I can't even remember how Marv and I actually met, but when I finally got to speak with him in New York he said to me, "Charlie, you're still a viable artist. Let's go in and try a couple of things."

The contract I signed with President was little more than a distribution deal. The company paid for the actual manufacture and distribution of my record, but I was responsible for the cost of everything else. That included securing the musicians (in this case, Billy Mure and His Combo), writing the arrangements for each song, and producing the session (the only one I ever produced). Fortunately, I was somehow able to convince four or five fellows to put up the money to back the project, or else it would have died then and there.

As I recall, we cut five or six songs for President. I believe every record I ever made throughout my career was at least decent. Many were quite good and a few were excellent. But during the session for President, I did make one record whose style—although I'm not ashamed of it—just wasn't for me. At one point while we were in the studio, Marv handed me the words and music for an Italian song he wanted me to do called "Just Like Us (Come Noi)." I could tell right away that particular number called for a semi-operatic voice. It was a vocal mismatch for me, but when I told Marv I didn't want to record the song, he slammed the hammer down.

"Charlie, you *have* to do it!"

How was I to know that one of the composers of "Just Like Us" was none other than Billy Mure, the bandleader I'd hired for session. God only knows what promises were made to whom, but to this day I strongly suspect that Billy's writing "Just Like Us" was why Marv insisted that I record it. Such is life in the pop music business. Besides, had "Night and Day, U.S.A." become a hit, I would have made out in the royalty department, too. When the record came out in September the flip side was a tune *I'd* written, called "Pretty Baby."

WIBG's Hy Lit, one of Philadelphia's leading disc jockeys, actually began to play "Night and Day, U.S.A." Soon, a few other jockeys began to get behind it. Man, that song *almost* got off the ground! ("Night and Day, U.S.A." actually *charted* in Philadelphia.) But eventually I ran out of "incentive" money and couldn't afford to pay anyone else. If only I had another couple of thousand dollars to throw around, I still believe it would have caught on in other cities.

Things could have been worse. At least the operatic "Just Like Us" wasn't chosen as the flip side for the record. I thought, with any luck at all, that embarrassment of a recording might remain in the can forever. But I should have known better. When my second President disc, "Count to Three," was released, "Just Like Us" appeared on the flip side. Fortunately for me, not many (if any) people went out and bought "Count to Three." Still, I cringe whenever I hear "Just Like Us."

Another song I recorded for President that day was a tune I'd been inspired to write after the birth of my daughter Angela, who was named after my paternal grandmother. To this day, I wish President had decided to release "Angela" instead of "Just Like Us." Sad to say, "Angela" was never issued, and nowadays I don't know if the master tape of that particular recording even exists. Some years after I cut "Angela" I did make a private tape recording of the song. But then somebody burglarized our house and stole not only my tape recorder, but also my home recording of "Angela." It was quite a nice tune and I'd love to hear it again. I can recollect parts of "Angela," but for the life of me I can't remember the entire song. Every now and then I imagine how great it would be to one day have someone call and say, "Hey Charlie, we came across one of your lost recordings. It's called 'Angela'..."

There were gaps between my numerous recording contracts, some of which lasted much too long. But sooner or later somebody always thought it was worth the time and the money to take me on. The company to do so after President was New York City's Diamond

Records. Joe Kolsky and Phil Kahl, brothers who'd helped Morris Levy start Roulette Records back in 1957, formed Diamond in 1961. The label's biggest hit maker was Baltimore's own Ronnie Dove, who, during his career, was responsible for 11 Top 40 hits.

I don't remember exactly how I got started with Diamond, but I do know the record producer Jerry Ross had a hand in it. Jerry and I had crossed paths from time to time, both of us being active in the Philadelphia music industry. He'd gotten his start in the music business as a WFIL radio disc jockey in 1956, not long after Dick Clark became host of *Bandstand*. From there, Jerry went into record promotion and then graduated to songwriting and record production. He became A&R director for Mercury Records for a time and enjoyed great success writing and producing hits for artists such as Jerry Butler, Bobby Hebb, and Spanky and Our Gang. But before Jerry's success at Mercury, he produced my record for Diamond.

In January 1965 I signed a guaranteed single release deal with Diamond, along with a five-year binder option to be activated at the company's behest. Our lone session, at which Jerry Ross was assisted by his young hotshot Philly arranger Joe Renzetti, was done in New York City. Things went surprisingly well that day, with both tunes— "He'll Never Love You Like I Do" and "Keep My Love Next to Your Heart"—cut in less time than anticipated. Because we'd paid for three hours of studio time, I began racking my brain for an additional tune to record. We finally decided to do an updated version of the Buddy Holly classic "That'll Be the Day," which they never released.

The Diamond single came out in February. *Billboard* never reviewed either side, which was a real kick in the head. Do I have to tell you what happened next? If you guessed no radio plays—*and* no five-year recording deal—you're right on the money.

But the pop music business often takes quirky twists and turns. "He'll Never Love You Like I Do" eventually became an underground hit in Britain. I was completely unaware of that until about two or three years ago, when I took part in a program at a blues club in Center City, Philadelphia. A busload of British blues aficionados who happened to be in town was there and as I walked out on stage they gave me a standing ovation. I had no idea why. Then one of the organizers of the show said to me, "'He'll Never Love You Like I Do' is a big 'Northern Soul' hit in Britain, Charlie." That really surprised me, because I'd never once heard the bloody thing played on the radio. What didn't surprise me was that I never saw a penny from the song.

In retrospect, my record for Diamond and all the things I cut for Coral, Roulette, and Felsted, were probably doomed from the start. Because of the Cameo debacle, airplay was next to impossible for me to obtain. Bernie Lowe's cross-country network of people—including the all-important *American Bandstand* connection—commanded that much respect. The network controlled things to the point where someone such as Bernie Lowe was able to guarantee that most any artist could be shut out.

But not everyone in Bernie Lowe's network of accomplices abandoned me. Although Kal Mann continued to write and work with Bernie, Kal and I always maintained a good relationship. Kal often called me, and each time I'd pick up the phone he'd say: "Charlie, this is Kal Mann. *I* didn't take your money." Then he'd laugh.

"Come on Kal," I'd protest. "Why do you keep bringing that up? Forget about that. Let's do something. Let's get a hit!"

Kal was a prolific songwriter who was always on the lookout for other artists to record his material. For a number of years he had me record demos of songs he'd written. Kal would then use those dubs to try to interest other artists in recording them. After I left Bernie Lowe I did about a dozen of those demos. I also recorded a couple of Kal's songs myself. Needless to say, we didn't have any luck with them. But through thick and thin, Kal and I remained friends until the day he died.

Despite my extended contact with Kal, I never imagined I'd ever speak with Bernie Lowe again. As a matter of fact, Bernie and I hadn't spoken for several years after I left Cameo. Then one night I received a telephone call.

"Hey Charlie, it's Bernie Lowe. How're you doing?"

I was flabbergasted. Bernie acted as if nothing negative had ever happened between us. I've always been the kind of guy who, if you're my friend, I'll be with you all the way. If you're not my friend, I'd just as soon not associate with you in any way, shape, or form. But there I was, speaking with a guy who by all rights was dead—at least in *my* mind.

It may be hard to believe, but despite all the strife Bernie and I'd been through business-wise at Cameo, I'd always liked him as a person. What had happened between us was really a pity. Bernie was a brilliant pianist and arranger. He had an ability to capture the exact sound that he wanted in the studio. Combined with my talent, I thought we had a nice thing going. Everything seemed *perfect*; our dispute should never have happened. I never wanted to leave Bernie or Cameo Records. I liken our split to a divorce. We had a good marriage until Bernie started to get greedy and didn't want to pay me.

I really can't explain it any further than that. But at that moment when Bernie called, I had absolutely no animosity toward him. "Hey Bernie," I matter-of-factly replied. "What can I do for you?"

"Charlie, listen, I've been thinking about everything that happened between us. I'm hoping we can let bygones be bygones."

"I'm willing to do that," I replied, wondering what was coming next.

"You know I always thought you were a great talent. I'd like to cut you again. What do you say we go back into the studio? I think we can get another hit."

I almost fell through the floor. Not only did Bernie have the *chutzpah* to feed me that "great talent" line once more, he actually wanted to *record* me again! It was no secret that, by then, Cameo's fortunes had begun to wane. Popular music continued to change and younger people—the record buyers—traditionally gravitated to whatever was current. Yet Bernie had remained static to the point where his vision of "current" had become passé. He'd lost his touch and Cameo-Parkway's pool of hit records had dried up. Bernie was fading away, grabbing at straws, and I was one of the last straws he happened to reach for.

"I'd like to cut you in the style of a Johnny Rivers, with a more bluesy, heavier rock style than we used before," Bernie explained. "You could knock that stuff out easily, Charlie. I know you could."

I was between labels at the time and pretty desperate myself. "Yeah, fine," I told Bernie. "Let's give it a shot."

But it wasn't meant to be. Bernie never called back and that was the last I'd ever heard from him. In hindsight, it was probably just as well. I could envision the same shit all over again. That seemed to be my karma. I felt like I was stuck in quicksand. No matter how hard I tried to move, I just keep sinking.

In June 1965, not long after Bernie called me that last time, he sold Cameo-Parkway to a consortium of Texas businessmen and retired a millionaire.[59] During the later part of Bernie's life he became chronically ill, plagued by psychological issues as well as his physical ailments. His wife Rosalyn, who cared for him at their home for many years, later revealed that her husband suffered from "depression."[60] (It has been said that Bernie would watch two or three television sets simultaneously, or just sit and stare at his money piled on a table, scared to death he might lose it all.) He spent his final years in some sort of mental health facility.

Bernie may have died a wealthy man, but accumulating all that money didn't bring him any joy or happiness. Not that I ever wished anything of the sort that actually happened on him. I believe Bernie was already paying for what he'd done, not only to me, but to others as well. At least he and I had a reconciliation of sorts. There's truly no malice in my heart toward him. May God rest Bernie's soul.

"Viva Las Vegas" sang Elvis in 1964. It was a time when many an entertainer headed to Vegas to work the lounges and make a name for him or herself. My parents used to tell me over and over, "You've got to go to Las Vegas, Charlie. You're not going to get anywhere by staying around here. You've got to go on the road. It's okay to leave your wife and kids for a while."

In one respect I know my parents meant well, but they really didn't know the first thing about show business. "Viva Las Vegas" and all that crap. I felt like I was headed for oblivion, and the last thing I wanted at the time was to leave my family for *that* place!

As my popularity waned and my name continued to fade, I set aside both my chase for more hit records and my dreams of another breakthrough. Fortunately I had the mental discipline and fortitude to go out there and work as a musician every night. I was able to develop the mindset of a "journeyman" performer. But despite my eagerness to work, Bernie Rothbard found it more and more difficult to secure national bookings for me. There was always some other entertainer on the rise, eager to grab the spotlight that I once commanded. Fortunately, Bernie did manage to keep me alive within the Philadelphia tri-state area. Since I lived there and continuously worked that territory, my name remained relatively strong. But the big money was gone. I was lucky if I made $300—less Bernie's commission of 10%—for a full week's work.

On a typical gig I'd sing and play the guitar from nine at night 'til two in the morning, just grinding it out. Man, that was a tough way to make a buck. My distinctive guitar style, which sounded like two or three instruments playing, proved to be a lifesaver. I'd do five 40-minute sets each night, as the people danced just as they would have to a full band. They loved me when I played in that manner, and so did the owner of whatever joint I happened to be working. Instead of footing the bill for an entire combo, he had only *me* to pay!

I frequently worked the local dive I mentioned earlier called Hoagie Joe's. Every town has at least one place like it; bar on one side, pizzeria on the other. At Hoagie Joe's I performed while sitting on a little stage on top of the piano. And every so often I had to endure the humiliation of some liquored-up wise guy who thought he'd impress his friends by getting on my case: "Hey *star*, what are you doin' in a place like *this*?"

It was really humiliating, really tough. I was often tempted to punch a few of them right in the mouth. But most of the time I kept my cool. "Better to 'have been' than 'never was,'" I'd usually retort. But there were occasions when the mortification managed to get the best of me. "What did you pay for your beer anyway pal, $2?" I'd ask the heckler. "If you don't like my act, I'll give you back your $2 and you can get the hell out of here." It took some time, but from bar to cafe, I eventually won them over. "I may be down at the moment," I'd admit, "but I'll come back up again."

Oh, I worked some real joints all right, frequently in the city of Chester, Pennsylvania, which happened to be Bill Haley's home base. I did many a gig at Chester's El Rancho Club, where I shared the bill with regional entertainers such as Steve Gibson and the Red

Caps and Mike Pedicin. I also played regularly at Chester's Ukrainian Club, where I shared the stage with a very funny rubber-faced, Jewish comedian by the name of Joey Talbot. One time I did a record hop at a Chester drive-in theater, where the roof of the concession shack served as the stage. As the kids twisted in the dirt below us, I mused about the distance (both literally and figuratively) between that drive-in rooftop and the Brooklyn Paramount.

At one point, in an attempt to secure some additional bookings, I even put my own band together. I'd done my single act for years, but during the 1960s the business began to change. The bar scene grew very popular and small bands began to push the single acts aside. I suppose you could credit the Beatles' sudden and stunning popularity for much of that change. But whatever the reason, most of the bars and clubs began to feature a band that would perform up to five hours a night. Sometimes they'd have two bands. To survive, I figured I'd better get a little unit together. Bernie Rothbard was all for it. "Yeah, Charlie," he told me. "That sounds like a great idea!"

Guitar, bass, and drums were the backbone of the kind of music that I played, so I began to work with a trio. It was during my attempt to diversify that I taught my brother Frank to be a musician. He'd recently gotten married and needed an additional job, so I said, "Why don't you come and play bass with me." In the beginning, Frank needed time to learn all the songs in my repertoire, so I'd sing and play as I called out the changes for him. In time, Frank not only mastered the bass, he stayed with me for about 10 years.

I always tried to keep my combo as small as possible. By going with a trio instead of a quartet, each of my guys stood to make more "paper." Occasionally I'd add a sax or a piano to the band, which gave me a break from playing lead all the time. Using that formula, I was able to successfully work the club circuit. I managed to make a living that way for more than 25 years.

But no formula's perfect, especially when it comes to the unpredictable world of entertainment. Although I had the combo, there still were times when gigs were sparse and I was forced to go out and do a single. One of those gigs Bernie Rothbard lined up for me called for what was known in the business as a "strolling troubadour." I'd walk among the patrons in a restaurant, singing and playing my guitar. There also were times when I'd go into a cocktail lounge and just sit on a stool with my guitar and sing for an hour or an hour and a half. Anything it took to make a living.

In 1964, if you resided in Delaware County, just west of Philadelphia, you might have celebrated New Year's Eve with the Charlie Gracie Quartette. That would have been at the Broomall Inn's Carnival Room ("Beautiful Go-Go Girls featured Tuesdays and Thursdays"), out on McDade Boulevard in the town of Holmes. I also worked the Carnival Room with the Irish-American character actor and comedian Mickey Shaughnessy (who sometimes worked as "O'Shaughnessy," depending on the number of Irish within traveling distance). Mickey made his bones on the Catskill Mountains tourist resort circuit in New York State. He managed to enjoy a brush with the big-time when he appeared in the film *From Here to Eternity* with Burt Lancaster and Frank Sinatra. He also served as Elvis Presley's "cellmate"/musical mentor in the film *Jailhouse Rock*.

A couple of miles to the north of the Carnival Room, close to our Llanerch Hills apartment, I had steady gigs lasting almost a year at places like Richettis' and the Alpine Inn. Both venues, which featured dining and dancing into the wee small hours, were located on Baltimore Pike in Springfield, Pennsylvania. A few miles to the west, in a city called Media, I frequently performed at a great little showplace called the Log Cabin Inn. North of Philly, in the suburb of Hatboro, I worked the Blair Mill Inn. Hey, it was a gig. And it was only about an hour's drive from my home.

Most of the joints I worked were fairly nondescript; one looked pretty much like the next. (Almost all of them are gone now, replaced by car dealers and computer outlets.) But occasionally I performed at a few rather unique venues. One of the most peculiar was a place up on Route 1 in Penndel, which is located northeast of Philadelphia. It was there that Jim Flannery owned a club and restaurant called the Constellation Lounge. Try to imagine performing inside the actual fuselage of a decommissioned Constellation airliner, propped up 10 or 15 feet in mid-air! Flannery's newspaper advertisements for 1977 boasted that during our nightly "flights" I kept the musical pace "light and lively" on the bandstand.

That's only a small sampling of the many places where I used to grind out as many as 30 sets a week. During that time, I never seriously contemplated putting down my guitar and getting some sort of nine-to-five job. Whenever such thoughts entered my mind I'd tell myself, "No. I'm a performer. Singing and playing my guitar is what I do, and I'm going to continue with it no matter what."

I wouldn't allow Joan to go to work, either. During our really low points she'd say, "Well, maybe I should help by going out and getting a job."

"No. I'm the male; I'm the breadwinner," I told her. "We'll make it somehow." To be perfectly honest, there were weeks when I wasn't so sure we *would* make it. But that's the way I was raised, and in my heart I knew show business was the only way I could ever make a living. Somehow I *had* to make it work.

To have Bernie Rothbard by my side after all those years together helped more than I can say. There were times when I was reduced to working for $75 a night. After the gig I'd visit Bernie, and when I put his 10% commission on the table he refused to take it.

In show business you're up and down all the time, and somehow you manage to get through the rough stretches. But *this* was really bad. We never actually went hungry, which I considered to be a blessing, but there were many times I didn't have enough money to pay the rent. I can recall days when I was down to my last dime. As the dry period dragged on, I began to have doubts as to whether I'd be able to see it through. All I could think was, "God, you have to help me."

During such challenging times, a person has to have faith; has to have trust. I never lost my faith, and sure enough, somehow I always found a way to pay the bills. Every once in a while I got lucky and landed a nice venue that paid 200 or 300 bucks a week. In those days you could live on such a puny amount, and that kept us afloat. It wasn't *fun*, but I did that for many years.

We were never in danger of being evicted and no one ever came to take away my TV. Still, there were a couple of occasions when I absolutely had to borrow money from other people. For instance, there was the time our health insurance payment came due and I was tapped out. Being self-employed, I had to foot that bill myself, and I thought, "My God! How am I going to pay this?"

It so happened that a couple we'd become close friends with noticed that I hadn't gigged for quite some time and figured—correctly—that we had to be struggling financially. Since they'd been married a long while and didn't have any children, money was no object for them. One night they just came right out and said it: "Charlie, we know you and Joan are going through a rough time right now." Then they offered us a blank check, saying, "Whatever you need, just fill in the amount." I hated the idea of borrowing money from anyone, but we were really up against a wall. So I took it, knowing that if I could just get through the next couple of months I'd be able to pay them back. No one else ever knew about that loan, and a couple of months later I was able to pay it back.

I looked at those "down" years as a test from God: "Charlie, I'm going to see if you can get through this. Let me see how much you really believe in me." He was trying to teach me some kind of lesson about faith, and I think I learned it well. God never let me down. He always kept the door open just enough to enable my family and I to survive. Thanks to Him, we got through those difficult times.

It had been about 10 years since the rift with my parents occurred. So as to remain as close as possible, I'd spend time with them whenever I could. My efforts paid off, too. The relationship between Joan and my parents actually improved somewhat. We were never able to patch things up completely, but at least we progressed to where we could speak to one another in a civil manner. We even reached a point where all of us would go to my parents' place on Sundays for the family meal. But those little breakthroughs aside, as both the son and the husband, I remained caught in the middle of that very painful experience. Some kind of wedge remained there, always that little cog in the wheel, that off-kilter "clump, clump, clump."

Christ Almighty, I went through hell with that. I didn't have any vices to fall back on, but my faith in God, along with the comforting presence of Joan and my kids, were my saving grace. When I wasn't performing, I was at home with my family as much as possible. And when I did have to hit the road for a few days, I took Joan and the kids with me whenever possible. I always kept them close.

By 1969 I thought I'd given up chasing another hit record. But early that year I headed back into the recording studio, thanks to Harry Chipetz, who'd produced my recordings for Felsted back in 1961. After Bernie Lowe had sold Cameo-Parkway, Harry continued to bounce around the local music scene he knew so well. Now he'd cooked up a recording deal with probably the only guy in town with more experience in the business than Harry himself, Nat Segall. Nat was no stranger to me; I'd known him for many years. He owned most of Sock & Soul Records. Jerry Blavat, a local deejay known as "the Geator with the Heater," owned a small piece of the label. (It was no coincidence that Nat also served as Blavat's manager.) It had been four years since I'd cut my last record, and I was very grateful to Harry and Nat for this opportunity.

My arrangement with Sock & Soul was strictly a one-off, but I'm pretty sure if the new record had sold reasonably well, Harry and Nat would have given me another shot. The session was produced by Philadelphia musician/arranger Vince Montana, who, at the time, played the vibes in Kenny Gamble and Leon Huff's renowned Philadelphia Soul house combo (soon to be dubbed "MFSB"). We cut two songs that night, "Walk with Me Girl" and "Tenderness," the latter penned by the exceptional writer and good friend Bud Ross. It was the first time in my career that I had a chance to try my hand at some blue-eyed soul. Working with talented musicians and a veteran studio crew, the session went down like clockwork.

I left the studio quite satisfied that I'd nailed both recordings. They sounded great. I had a gig lined up for later that evening, and by the time I arrived home from it and prepared for some sleep it was already 4 a.m. I was dead asleep when my phone rang at about 9 that morning.

"Hello Cholly," Nat said in his heavy Jewish accent. "You ready for this? Ve gotta double hit, Cholly. Ve gotta double hit!"

"Nat, I worked a gig until 3 o'clock in the morning," I mumbled. "I'm going back to sleep. When the royalty checks start rolling in, *then* you can wake me!"

"Walk with Me Girl" / "Tenderness" turned out to be anything but a "double-sided" hit. It *was* a damn good record, but nobody played the thing, not even Jerry Blavat!

Following my latest recording disappointment I had one try left in me. Sometime in 1970 I took my own group into Frank Virtue's studio up on North Broad Street and recorded the old Five Keys hit "Ling, Ting, Tong," along with the 1940s ballad "Dream." But I was unable to find a label to take them on. (Those songs finally saw the light of day in 1996, when both tunes were added as bonus tracks to the CD release of my 1957 Stockton Concert.) It would be 10 long years before I'd record anything that was released to the public.

For years, Joan and I had wanted to buy a house. But, as 1970 began, I still hadn't saved enough money to do so. We continued to live month-to-month, just getting by. After making our rent payment there was hardly anything left to put aside. Each day I'd think, "I have a wife and two kids and we've long since outgrown this cramped apartment." I wanted to look for a bigger place, but a larger apartment meant higher rent.

Meanwhile, Joan and I refused to abandon our dream. It so happened that a good friend named Joe Gillespie was in real estate, and Joan and I took to cruising around, looking at houses with him. We searched and searched, until one day I finally faced the grim reality. "How are we going to buy a house?" I said to Joan. "We don't even have enough money for the down payment." The situation seemed hopeless; it was a very lonely moment for us. But as we sat there in our distress, God saw our anguish and heard our plea.

Within a matter of days I got a phone call from Bernie Rothbard: "I've got a great summer gig for you, Charlie. It's a joint called Jack's Place, down the Jersey shore in the town of Avalon."

Avalon is a resort area located just 15 miles south of Atlantic City. The booking Bernie secured for me was by far the strongest gig I'd had in quite some time.

Oh, wow, man! I hung up the phone, I got down on my knees, and I thanked God. I still refer to that experience as the "miracle of my life."

I'd been working down the shore for a few summers by then, so I knew the drill. When school got out we'd grab the kids and head for the ocean. I worked hard and made exceptionally good money that particular summer, and after I paid all of my bills I came home with about 1,600 bucks. It was just enough to—at long last—enable Joan and me to seriously look for a house. And it came at just the right time.

One day in the spring of 1971, our landlord said, "Charlie, my mother wants to sell her house, so we need to move her into the apartment you've been living in.

"Okay, we're out," I told him. "But I need time to find another place. You've got to give me 60 to 90 days."

"Take three months, Charlie," he replied. "I really hope you find what you need."

We reconnected with Joe Gillespie and soon found a little home that suited us. The funny thing was, Joe must have passed by that house three or four times before Joan finally asked him, "What about that house there?"

"Oh, that one?" Joe replied. "I didn't think you'd be interested in that one."

The house was located in Drexel Hill, which is a lovely suburban neighborhood lined with brick and stone colonials, just west of the Philadelphia city line. In 1955, a contractor built the home plus an identical one side by side—one for him, the other for his son. The houses even had a shared driveway. (Many years later, in an ironic twist, Charlie, Jr. and his lovely bride Kim purchased that home next door.)

After the down payment and the settlement (the latter paid for with the earnings from another great gig at the shore in the summer of 1971), I didn't have 10¢ left in my pockets. But for the first time in our 13 years of marriage, Joan and I had our very own place. Compared to where I came from, our new home was a mansion. I think our mortgage payment—taxes included—was about $400 a month. I made the payments every month for 25 years without missing one. After that, it was ours, free and clear. I've lived in four houses in my entire life. After residing there for 40-plus years, I'm happy as can be. If I came into a million dollars tomorrow I'd just as soon stay where I am.

Joan and I still marvel about how we had *exactly* the minimum amount needed to get into the place. "It's as if God arranged it," I said to Joan. "I am a believer. I know the Good Lord had His hands on it. There's no question about it in my mind." We both agreed that it was a small miracle. I got down on my hands and knees again, and thanked Him!

At long last, things were beginning to look up. When I reflect back on those difficult times I thank God He gave me the strength to make it through. I'd say the roughest years for me were between 1959 into the early to mid-1960s. During all those years as a journeyman musician I often thought, "You know what? You have to maintain a stiff upper lip, as the British say. Just go out there and do what you have to do. Whatever it takes." Sure enough, by the late 1960s, with my little combo intact, I began to work more frequently. Although my gigs remained spotty throughout the 1970s, overall, I managed to work on a fairly steady basis and earned a decent buck.

One of my more memorable gigs back then was the local "Tournament of Stars" golf benefit for disabled children, which was held each September at the Llanerch Country Club in nearby Havertown. In 1973, the celebrity golf star of that event was none other than Bob Hope. A skilled golfer, Hope deftly quipped his way through a round that Saturday afternoon. I was supplying the day's entertainment when the renowned comedian, surrounded by his entourage, completed his round and headed for the "nineteenth" hole. As Hope neared the clubhouse, he spied me playing my guitar and said to the fawning crowd around him, "Who's that up there? Tiny Tim?" Over the outburst of laughter that ensued, I began to sing and play "Hello Dolly." However, in honor of the featured guest I changed the lyric to "Hello Robert." Then I went into my best version of Bob's memorable theme song, "Thanks for the Memories."

Wrapping up the festivities that evening, a huge banquet attended by 500 guests was held. Several entertainers were on the bill, including a few legendary personalities, among them Hope and Jimmy Durante.

For some reason—perhaps to allow the big celebrities an opportunity to slip away unnoticed—it was decided that I would close the show. When they told me, I thought, "You've got to be kidding. I have to follow all those stars? No one will want to watch *me* after they've seen the likes of Hope, Durante, Al Martino, Buddy Greco, and Howard Keel."

As the night's festivities drew to a close, I was, according to plan, on stage, singing and playing. All of a sudden, Durante got up to leave. "Oh shit," I said to myself. "That's it. The whole joint's going to walk out with him and I'll be up here singing to myself like a schmuck!"

But on his way out, Jimmy purposefully walked around behind me, put his hand on my neck and said, "Hey folks, ain't this kid great?" As the audience gave me a warm ovation, Durante then walked out of the room—by himself. The *great* Jimmy Durante. What a classy guy. I'll never forget that as long as I live. He saved my ass that night!

Many of us live our lives vaguely aware of some life-altering event we know we'll someday be forced to confront. We each tuck it away in a corner of our mind and we live with it, because there's absolutely nothing we can do about it until it occurs. That day came for me in 1977. Some time earlier, around 1969, during a routine physical examination, my father learned he had a spot on his lung. "It's probably because you had pneumonia as a child," the doctors told him. "Just continue to come back and have it checked every so often." Well, my dad never went back.

Years later I received a call from my mother. Right away I could tell from the tone of her voice that something was wrong. She said my father was having great difficulty breathing. I told her to dial 911 and then headed over to my parents' house as fast as possible. Before I got there, the paramedics had put my father on oxygen and taken him to the hospital in an ambulance. The next day I went to see his doctor.

"Charlie," he said, "I wish I could give you some good news. Your father has an upper respiratory cancer and we can't operate. I'm afraid he's terminal."

"Holy Christ!" I said to myself. I had flashbacks of my dad, a heavy smoker, working in that Stetson hat factory, each day inhaling toxic fumes from raw chemicals. Then I broke down and wept like a baby.

My father didn't last long, maybe six weeks or so. It was a very trying time. To complicate things, my gigs suddenly dried up and I entered another one of those "desert" spells. Then, while working a one-nighter at the Drexelbrook Country Club, I received a call informing me that my father had taken a turn for the worse. The doctors thought he would probably die that evening. But when I explained my circumstances to the boss, he insisted that I stay and complete the gig. After receiving the devastating news about my dad, I was simply unable to play any longer. The owner of the club wasn't pleased, but what could he do? I just walked out and headed right to the hospital.

My father made it through the night, but I knew he wasn't going to survive much longer. It's funny how things sometimes work out. Because of my dad's terminal condition I wanted to be with him every day I could. Ordinarily, my work would have prevented that. But now, because I didn't have any work, Joan and I could come and go as we wanted. To be by his side in the hospital, we made the trek to New Jersey every day for six weeks. I wore out my Cadillac driving back and forth, but it was a great comfort to be with my father during his last days.

He had always been a rugged man, built like an ox. It was a shame to see him wither away like that, but I was right there to hold his hand when he took his last breath. As I sat there watching him, many thoughts raced through my head. Naturally, I thought about the divide that had come between us and how I would have gladly forgone all of my success in exchange for eliminating that rift from our lives. But when my father died he knew how much I loved him. The day was September 9, 1977. It was about three weeks after Elvis Presley had passed. In fact, my father had been in the hospital when he heard about Elvis' death. "Ah, that poor kid," he remarked. And then my dad proceeded to follow him. He was 64 when he died, still a relatively young man. Each of us has his or her own time, and that was his. It was a tough time for me, man, very tough. But I managed to keep my composure and handle the situation well.

At that point God was really working in my life. About a year before my father's death, Joan and I had begun to attend charismatic prayer meetings, part of an ecumenical movement that was going on within the Catholic Church during the '70s. A couple we knew had invited us to a prayer gathering at their house, where we'd met a group of people that included not only Catholics, but also members of other Christian denominations. Joan and I thought perhaps my parents would get something out of it, so before my father became very ill we actually took them to a couple of the meetings.

"When's this going to be over?" my father asked the first night there. "We're Catholic. We're not changing our religion!"

"Dad, we're not changing our religion," I reassured him. "We're Catholic, too!"

Joan and I began attending church regularly—Sunday Mass, prayer meetings, and other faith-based activities—when my gigs began to taper off again. After having experienced so many setbacks, and now experiencing the death of my father, it wasn't easy for me to keep the faith. "I'm getting closer to the Lord and look what's happening!" I exclaimed to Joan. "Why is God doing this to me?" But there's always a reason for everything that happens.

13

ENGLAND SWINGS...AGAIN

Growing up and living life as the son of Charlie Gracie has proven intriguing, to say the least. For all my father's accomplishments, numerous American recording stars have far eclipsed his chart success. But I'd bet that few of them have come close to his life of achievement.

While it's up to each of us to carve out a life worth living, not everyone is fortunate enough to accomplish something that will ultimately render them happy and satisfied. In that respect, Charlie Gracie, Sr. soars high above all the chart toppers. He also continues to thrive as a full-time working musician, in a career now in its sixth decade (a feat that's eluded many hit makers). The love and devotion my father receives from his global fan base and from his family is a great testament to his success as a performing and recording artist and as a man.

When my sister Angela and I were in grammar school we never gave a second thought to what our father did for a living. For as long as we could remember, he was a musician and an entertainer—that's what he did! However, his occupation seemed a little unusual for our schoolmates and neighborhood chums to fathom. Performers work nights, and our dad (and mom) were always home with us during the day. But when evening arrived, our friends often saw our father leave the house dressed in a spiffy suit or tux, climb into his Cadillac (dad always had one, new or used), and drive off to his gig. We chuckle now when we think of how, on more than one occasion, our friends would ask, "Are you sure your dad's not in the mafia?"

My sister and I learned there were fringe benefits to having a dad in show business. Whenever possible, we went on the road with our parents. I can still recall those exciting journeys to cities such as Shreveport, Louisiana and Pittsburgh, as well as to some of the mountain resorts in upstate Pennsylvania and New York. Our summers were often spent at the New Jersey beach towns where dad performed.

Angela and I also received a kind of "education" our friends back home could never imagine. It was a heady experience for us youngsters to hang out in a world of musicians, singers, comedians, and agents—most of them colorful characters in their own right.

While we were too young to remember the dark period immediately following dad's "blacklisting," we did become aware of the serious financial challenges our parents faced during those lean years. When circumstances got rough, it took the faith and courage of our parents to keep our family together. That only increased our love and admiration of them. As I grew older I also began to fully understand the bad hand dad was dealt. He'd truly paid his dues—and was still paying them!

By the 1970s, a wave of '50s nostalgia swept the nation and dad's early chart hits were categorized as "golden oldies." Although I never aspired to a career in music (I teach at-risk youths), I became utterly fascinated by those pioneering artists who'd created rock and roll. Furthermore, I began to notice that whenever the media reviewed the names of those who laid the groundwork for this genre of music, the name "Charlie Gracie" was seldom included. This was especially true in Philadelphia, of all places. Apparently, the long shadow cast by my dad's lawsuit against Cameo, and the ensuing fallout with Bernie Lowe and Dick Clark, had reached well into the 1970s. This was unacceptable and it was time for me to take some action.

Dad was never one to toot his own horn. But who better to have as an advocate than one's own son? Next to my mother and Angela, who appreciated his underdog status more than I? Don't get me wrong, Bernie Rothbard and others continued to do a marvelous job managing the business end of dad's career. But once I left high school for college, I took it upon myself to become his de facto press agent.

At first the biggest challenge was to reintroduce dad's musical history to the world. My efforts to connect with the mass media— newspaper columnists, magazine writers, radio, and television— led to numerous Charlie Gracie exposés. Philly's first rock and roll star was finally getting his props! Dad's overseas resurgence and new revelations from the likes of (the late) George Harrison, Paul McCartney, Van Morrison, and Graham Nash extolling his guitar virtuosity didn't hurt either!

Now, as I reflect back on my father's long and winding musical journey, through the changing trends, the victories, the defeats, and "resurgences," he has remained essentially the same unassuming fellow. Yet, whenever he takes to the stage it's as if a supernatural transformation takes place. Call it poetry, call it art. It's undeniably a thing of beauty to witness a man fulfilling his God-given mission: creating happiness through entertainment. Dad possesses the inherent gift of enabling his fans to become part of his calling. It's more about them and less about him. And therein lies the key to his success as a family man and as a showman!

–Charlie Gracie, Jr.

Toward the end of 1975, a Canadian fan named Richard Grows entered the picture. Richard had grown up outside of Chicago where, as a teenager, he became a big fan of my music. He contacted me by phone and with great enthusiasm said, "Charlie, I'd like to put out all your early recordings—those things on Cadillac and 20th Century—on an album designed for record collectors. Most people are not aware of those early recordings and I think there'd be a great interest in them." Richard said he was planning a trip to Pennsylvania during the Christmas holidays and hoped to meet me and discuss releasing the album. I told him I'd look forward to it.

Joan wasn't so sure. "Who is this guy, coming all the way from Canada?" she asked. "We don't know him from Adam. How do we know he's on the level?"

Richard and his wife Penny arrived at our house as scheduled. We talked over lunch and he turned out to be a knowledgeable and personable fellow. Richard then spent *days* with me, inquiring about my career. "How much do you want for the rights to those recordings?" he finally asked.

I told Richard I didn't own the rights to any of that music. He then explained how those songs were already part of the public domain overseas because Europe's copyright laws are less stringent than they are here in America. Richard went on to say he could release them there without violating any copyright laws. After hearing Richard out I gave him my blessing. "I don't want anything," I told him.

Richard was quite surprised by my response. I think he finally gave me about $60, just to make the deal legal. I signed the papers and told him, "Do what you want with 'em."

After Richard left, Joan and I agreed it was great that those old and somewhat obscure records would again see the light of day. Of course, neither of us had any reason to think anything significant would come of the album's release. "He's making it available for collectors," we thought. "It's no big deal."

Richard released the album on his own Revival label in September 1976, and his plan to do so in Great Britain and Europe rather than in America proved to be the correct move. The first 10,000 copies of *Charlie Gracie's Early Recordings* sold out almost immediately, and a second run of 10,000 went off the shelves almost as fast. I'd made a powerful impact throughout the United Kingdom during my two late '50s tours and apparently much of my fan base was still there. I had more hits over there than I had in America. And, as I would later discover, many of those British artists who emerged in the 1960s looked up to me as one of their musical influences. Even so, a lot of those fans in Britain who snapped up Richard Grows' album were surprised; they thought I had passed on. As Mark Twain once stated about his own "obituary," "The report of my death has been greatly exaggerated!"

Looking back, I can say emphatically that the album released by Richard Grows marked the beginning of my international comeback. Its brisk sales didn't go unnoticed by British Decca, which, in 1978, put out an album of its own, titled *Charlie Gracie—Cameo-Parkway Sessions*. That collection contained most of my Cameo Recordings, plus the two sides I cut for Sock & Soul, as well as "How Many Times" and "Remember You're Mine," the two unreleased demos I recorded in 1971. British Decca pressed 25,000 copies of that album on its London label, and that run sold out almost immediately. Once my dormant fan base realized I was still alive and actively performing, things began to happen I never could have imagined.

I won't forget that freezing cold January night in 1979 when I received a phone call from Bernie Rothbard, who seemed pretty excited. "Charlie," he exclaimed, "I was just contacted by London Decca Records. They told me they'd released an album of your old Cameo-Parkway songs a year ago and it sold like hotcakes. Evidently your following over there is still quite strong. London Decca is wondering if you'd consider doing a promotional tour."

"What?" I thought. "Fans were actually clamoring for my records again?" That hadn't been the case for 20 years! Still, I didn't get overly excited. At that point, the concept of renewed interest in my career seemed more like a fairy tale. I had no idea of the musical trends developing in Great Britain; I hadn't been there since 1958. But Bernie's call did spark a glimmer of hope. I was determined to not let this opportunity pass me by.

"You know what?" Bernie said, "I'm going to make a trip to Britain and check things out. I want to size up exactly what's going on over there."

In America and across the Atlantic, the decade of the 1970s had given rise to a wave of 1950s nostalgia, which manifested itself in films such as *Let the Good Times Roll* (1973), television programs such as *Happy Days* (1974), and recorded music such as John Lennon's retro-rock album *Rock 'n' Roll* (1975). In Great Britain, unlike the States, they'd never really gotten over 1950s-style American rock and roll. By the mid-1970s, London had become the base for a primitive mix of basic rock and roll and rhythm and blues called "pub rock," and a British neo-rockabilly movement had also begun to take shape.

Spearheaded by a thriving Teddy Boy culture, almost every British city and town had its own rock and roll "club" or "society" (e.g., Leeds Rock 'n' Roll Club, Leicester R 'N' R Society, Coventry Rockabilly Club, Bradford Rock 'n' Roll Club, York Rock 'N' Roll Appreciation Society, Sheffield Vintage Rock 'n' Roll Society, and so on), which promoted regularly scheduled get-togethers and dances. Society members championed throwback rock and roll and neo-rockabilly acts such as Crazy Cavan and the Rhythm Rockers, the Flash Cats, the Rockabilly Rebs, the Riot Rockers, the Tennessee Rebels, and Johnny and the Jailbirds. This underground phenomenon eventually found its way back to those in the know in America. Then an American '50s-devoted musical trio called the Stray Cats, who couldn't get arrested in their home country, moved to England and began selling records by the millions.

Bernie Rothbard flew to England and met with three British promoters. When he returned, he told me about the rockabilly revival that was in full swing over there and how people in the business wanted me to perform as part of it. "I met several bookers while I was over there," Bernie reported. "The agent we're gonna go with is a fellow named Paul Barrett, who's based in Wales. Paul's the guy I trust the most. He's one of the 'honchos' of the British rock revival; currently the manager of Crazy Cavan and Shakin' Stevens—and Shakin' Stevens is one of the biggest success stories of the entire revival movement. I didn't even have to sell Paul on you, Charlie. He's known about you since British Decca put out that compilation of your Cameo recordings last year. Paul will bring you over to Britain and represent you while you're there."

"Whatever you say, Bernie!"

We decided Bernie would accompany me on the tour. As a cost-saving measure, Joan would stay behind. It was tough for me to make that trip without her, but she was more comfortable with it than I was. She reassured me the arrangement was fine with her. Joan understood that the upcoming trip was a business matter and that it was Bernie who should be there with me. (As things worked out,

Bernie came with me on my first four return tours overseas. On the fifth trip, Joan started accompanying me.)

Joan and the two kids—aided and abetted by Bernie—even planned a little surprise, a *bon voyage* party for me before Bernie and I left for Britain. "You have to go over to Bernie's house," she said to me the night before we left. "He told me he needs to sort out a few matters with you before the trip." As I walked out the door, Joan and the kids sprang into action and began to get things ready for the party. Meanwhile, Bernie played his part perfectly. When I got to his place he stalled for as much time as possible. Then, after he ran out of credible excuses to keep me there any longer he concocted some reason for him to return with me to my place. When we got there and walked inside, about 60 guests greeted me with: "SURPRISE!"

The urging of London Decca, and Bernie Rothbard's encouraging scouting expedition aside, as we prepared for my return to Britain for a 15-city tour in September 1979, we still weren't totally certain what to expect. My 21-year absence most likely would have created a degree of apprehension from some of my fan base. Because of that, the tour was relatively brief, a little more than two weeks. From our standpoint, we considered it an opportunity for me to get my foot back in the door.

When Bernie and I arrived in London I encountered a fan base (young and old) steeped in 1950s culture and enamored with the music of artists both deceased (Elvis, Eddie Cochran, Gene Vincent, Buddy Holly) and alive. Much to my amazement, the latter group included me! At that moment it became obvious that Richard Grows had done his homework back in 1975. I was amazed to discover what Richard had detected years earlier: 1950s-based music had never really disappeared in Great Britain. That core of fans was there from the start and it's still there today. I was also tickled to death that after not visiting Britain for 21 years its people still remembered me. "My God," I thought. "I'm still alive here!"

At the airport, a gentleman named Bob Dick (now deceased), who eventually became a very close friend of mine, was there to greet us. Bob had entered the picture through the recommendation of an old friend of Bernie's. It turned out that this friend had show business connections in Britain and when he heard that I was going there to perform, he told Bernie about Bob. As a result, Bernie arranged for Bob to coordinate the tour.

Bob was a Scotsman and an extremely wealthy entrepreneur. At the time, he resided in a beautiful apartment in the Knightsbridge district of London, which I'd say is the equivalent of a posh brownstone neighborhood in Manhattan. I suppose it was fitting that Bob arrived at the airport in his chauffeured Silver Cloud Rolls Royce. But as we drove through London to our hotel, the Rolls suddenly stalled in the middle of the street. We had to get the disabled car over to the curb, so Bernie and I jumped out to help the chauffeur push it. You have to visualize that scene for a moment: When I got off the plane in London I was dressed in a flamingo pink suit and white shoes. I looked like a bird! "Geez, how unlucky can a guy be," I said to Bernie as we struggled to push the stalled Rolls to the curb. "One minute a driver picks me up in a $600,000 Rolls Royce and a few minutes later I'm pushing it through London, dressed in a flamingo suit."

The chauffer of the Rolls eventually managed to guide it to the curb, and we jumped into a cab to complete the journey to our hotel. After we checked in and went to dinner, Bob and I got to know each other a bit. Among the many interests he was involved with was a stage production of a musical revue called *Bubbling Brown Sugar.* The show, which starred the multi-talented TV, nightclub, and motion picture entertainer Billy Daniels, had opened on London's West End in 1977. (*Bubbling Brown Sugar*, after debuting off Broadway in New York, moved to Broadway in 1976–77.) I was surprised to learn that Bob had arranged for me to meet Billy in London.

"Charlie, great to see you!" said the renowned entertainer.

"My God," I stumbled, awestruck by such a legendary performer. "I'm such a fan of yours." We talked for a while, and Billy was just wonderful, a real classy gentleman. (About a year later I was working at Palumbo's supper club in Philadelphia and, lo and behold, who the hell's starring there but Mr. "That Old Black Magic" himself. I was booked to open for Billy! Isn't that something? We meet in London and a year later I'm sharing the stage with him in South Philly.)

Paul Barrett had booked two weeks of ballroom and theater

appearances for me on that initial 1979 tour, beginning in his native Wales. Paul lives near Cardiff, which is the capital of Wales. Since 1979 he's continued to bring me over to Britain, as well as to numerous European countries where I never thought I'd ever get to play. Over the years, Paul, his wife (who served 12 years as a representative in the Welsh Assembly), and his family have become close friends with Joan and me. He's represented me for almost 35 years now and during that entire time he's always been an honest, steady, and straight-shooting broker. Those are rare qualities in this business and I'm most fortunate to have Paul in my corner.

After my appearance in Wales we made the short journey to England. One of my performances there occurred at the St. Helier Arms in the southwestern London suburb of Carshalton. The St. Helier was a huge tavern-style showplace originally built as a community center in the 1930s. By the time I arrived it had become a noted rock and roll and rockabilly venue. The St. Helier was a hot gathering spot for the Teddy Boys, who came to drink, carouse, and be entertained by neophyte rockers such as Crazy Cavan and American originals including Sonny Fisher and Jack Scott. Of course, with me having been out of the picture for so long, the audience wasn't sure what to expect. I was determined to not leave any doubt in their minds. When I was introduced I strode onstage with my trustworthy Guild guitar and rocked straight into some vintage The Treniers R&B stompers: "Rockin' Is Our Business," "Rock-a-Beatin' Boogie," "Cool It, Baby," and a string of others. As the Teddy Boys stomped, screamed, and waved their bottles of brown ale about, it was as if I'd never left the country. Following my performance, British music connoisseur and writer Bill Millar effervesced in print over my "immaculate set." He described my performance as " tight and generous, with an endearing emphasis on songs which aren't actually about anything except rock and roll itself."[61]

My backing band on that '79 tour was the Bad River Band, led by the English singer-guitarist Dave Travis. Dave had started out with country music. His first album, released in 1968, consisted of Hank Williams songs and was followed by several more country collections. But Dave had another musical interest as well—American rock and roll. That attraction manifested itself in two 1971 music collections: the first, a German cassette titled *This Is Rock and Roll,* and the second, a U.K. album called *Rock 'n' Roll Spectacular.* The year before we met, Dave contributed to the British neo-rockabilly scene with his album *Rockabilly Fever.* On it he paid tribute to seminal artists such as Buddy Holly ("I'm Changing All Those Changes"), Roy Orbison ("Ooby Dooby"), Carl Perkins ("Dixie Fried"), and Jack Scott ("Leroy"). I couldn't imagine it at the time, but Dave Travis would play a significant role in my musical comeback.

At one point during the tour, Bob Dick asked me if I'd be interested in recording a couple of songs for him. Bob explained to me how he was involved in the making of a documentary film about two retired boxers who'd been out of the ring for years. They were "has-beens" who wanted one more shot in the ring. I told Bob I'd love to make those recordings for him, and we went into the studio to cut two songs that were written specifically for the film. One was called "Box On" (also the film's title) and the other "Hold On." The entire session took about 90 minutes.

I thought the songs came out really great, but you have to see the film to appreciate their total effect. If you heard either number without seeing the film, you wouldn't even know they were about fighters. They sound like love songs. Yet both songs fit the film perfectly. During its course, the fighters are seen talking about life in and out of the boxing ring. When they're shown training, I'm heard singing "Box On," which is an appropriate uptempo number. During the actual fight I sing "Hold On," which is a ballad. Neither of those songs was ever released commercially. They were used only in that film (and both won music awards at the Cannes Film Festival), so no one in America has ever heard them. I'm fortunate to have both songs on tape.

I experienced true culture shock after my return to Britain in 1979. It seemed as if *everything* there had changed over the previous two decades; the country had become very much like America. In fact, I think in many cases they now have better quality items in British stores than we have here. Their supermarkets are plentiful, too. So whenever I'm in Great Britain I do eat well. Not like in the old days!

Every venue I played in Britain in '79 was sold out. Of course, they weren't the 2,000 or 3,000-seat arenas I'd played as a major star in 1957 and 1958. Before the tour began, no one was sure if I had the power to fill the larger rooms, so I was booked into venues that held 200, 300, maybe 500 people. But even 500 isn't really that small a draw—unless compared to the 3,000 I performed for in theaters back in the 1950s. Today, many of those old venues are no longer standing. (Two notable exceptions are the Liverpool Empire and Bristol's Colston Hall.) The few others that did manage to escape the wrecking ball became bingo parlors. It really is a shame how television killed much of the theater circuit.

Occasionally, when I go to overseas now I play some of the bigger venues—say those with 2,000 or 3,000 seats. But I have no objection to working the smaller places. I always tell Paul Barrett: "Whatever gig you can get, get it. I'd rather work than just sit around."

My initial tour in 1979 lasted two weeks and it couldn't have been more successful. It was interesting to discover that in the minds of my fans there, I was now looked upon as a legend; the audiences loved me. The long absence from Britain only added to my mystique. The promoters loved me, too. They wanted to know when I could return.

News of my "comeback" success spread quickly. After returning home, Bernie Rothbard and I hardly had time to unpack our suitcases. A week later we were off to Belgium and Holland for a brief tour of those countries. One of the fondest memories of all my travels occurred as we were leaving the States for that one. At Philly International Airport we crossed paths with Pope John Paul II, who was about to begin a two-day visit as part of his historic pilgrimage to America. The date was October 3, 1979, and the airport security and runway detail were prepared for his arrival. Philadelphia Mayor Frank Rizzo and several regional politicians and dignitaries were gathered on the tarmac, waiting to greet His Holiness. While I didn't exactly head overseas with the blessing of the Pope, had it been just a few seconds later, we would have departed without witnessing his arrival. Amazing how that worked out.

My reception in Belgium and Holland was similar to what I'd experienced in Britain just a few weeks earlier. The audiences were large and enthusiastic. While in those countries I had the pleasure of once again working with Buddy Knox, another of rock and roll's early stars. Buddy, a good-looking Texan and a very talented performer, was about three years older than me. It was kind of fitting that Buddy became the first '50s rock star I worked with in more than two decades. For a time, our careers seemed to be on an eerie parallel. The first time we'd performed together was on Alan Freed's stage show at the Brooklyn Paramount back in April 1957. That same year, Buddy's first and second records, "Party Doll" and "Rock Your Little Baby to Sleep," hit the charts exactly one week after "Butterfly" and "Fabulous" did, respectively. Not long after that, Buddy and I journeyed to New York (although not together) to shoot our musical performances for the movie *Jamboree*. And like I'd done, Buddy was prepared to make an overseas tour in 1957. Uncle Sam killed any prospects of that, however, by sending Buddy a draft notice for the army. (The label credit on one of his subsequent singles was credited to "Lieutenant" Buddy Knox.)

After working together in Belgium and Holland, Buddy and I later performed on several package tours in England and several other countries. I always enjoyed Buddy's company; he was a very sweet guy. Sadly, he passed away in 1999.

While performing in Belgium in 1979 I was approached by a fellow named Raoul Reniers, who told me he was in the process of forming a company called Blackjack Records. He asked if I'd be interested in recording an album. What Raoul had in mind was for me to re-record my biggest hits, along with some additional material. Throughout my career, whenever someone expressed an interest in getting me into the recording studio, I always obliged. I figured, why should this be any different? Besides, despite the large amount of recording I'd done over the years, I had never recorded an entire album. Inspired by the success of my recent British tour, as well as from the one I was currently engaged in, I agreed. But I had no idea that my recording experience with Raoul Reniers would be unlike any I had during almost 30 years in the business—and not in a positive way. No matter. At that point in my career, it seemed as if God had given me another chance. My name and my music were now resurrected overseas. In Great Britain, Belgium, Holland, and who knows how many other countries, the "Charlie Gracie" renaissance was underway, and it felt exhilarating.

In 1958, I looked upon Great Britain as a possible savior for my career should anything crippling happen to me in America. It's strange, in retrospect, how insightful my vision proved to be. In the wake of my successful return to Britain and Europe, Bernie Rothbard and I realized how lucrative a market there was overseas, not only for 1950s-era rock and roll, but for me in particular. We decided then and there to make such a tour an annual event. In fact, Bernie felt so strongly about going back to Britain that he didn't want to wait a full year. "Charlie," he told me, "You're hotter over there than we ever could have imagined. Why wait? The people there want to see you." Bernie and Paul Barrett arranged a return trip to Britain for the spring of 1980.

Bernie's timing couldn't have been better. When we arrived in Britain this time, Bob Dick asked me if I'd be interested in recording some additional songs for him. Bob was then involved with a British production called *American Heroes*, a historical musical that touched on the lives of Harry Truman, Joe DiMaggio, Marilyn Monroe, and several other American icons. "Charlie," Bob said to me, "I have a songwriter friend named Barry Mason who's written many hits in his career, most notably for Tom Jones ('Delilah') and Engelbert Humperdinck ('Winter World of Love,' 'The Last Waltz'). He and his partner, Gilbert Johnson, have written some songs for a show they plan to stage in London's West End. They're looking for a guy with a voice, but can't seem to find one. They asked me if I knew anyone who might record the songs as demos, which could then be shopped around. I told them about you. Barry's having a get-together at his apartment tonight, right here in London. If you like, we'll go over there and I'll introduce you."

That night we went to Barry's apartment. When we arrived, it was like walking onto a movie set. A group of girls and guys, maybe 15 or 20 people, were sitting around a piano, singing and talking. A few were even dancing. "Ladies and gentlemen, fellas and girls, meet Charlie Gracie," Bob announced. "You all remember him; he had the big hit 'Butterfly.'"

"Hey, Charlie, how are you doing," a few responded. Others simply nodded acknowledgment. They probably didn't know who the hell I was. But Barry Mason knew.

"Let's run down these couple of things," he said.

Somebody handed me a piece of paper with lyrics written on it and then began to play the piano. I started to sing and one of the guys near me exclaimed, "Holy shit! That's great, Charlie! Your voice is perfect for what we need." That was nice to hear, and I wish my unknown admirer had left it at that. But he proceeded to sting me with a backhanded sort of compliment if ever I've heard one. "You can still sing after all these years," he assured me.

"Well," I politely replied, "I've been an active performer all my life. I may have dropped out of the sight of most people, but I never stopped performing. Last fall was my first time in England in years, but I'm back now!"

When Barry Mason said to me: "Let's go into the studio tomorrow and I'll record some things with you," that gave me about four hours to learn those songs. But I was up to the task. The next day we went into the studio and cut five or six numbers, Broadway-type show tunes. They're beautiful songs, just *dynamite*. They're some of the *best* things I ever cut in my life, and a part of me nobody's ever heard before. None of those songs were ever released, but if you had the opportunity to listen to them they'd make your hair stand on end. Mason and Johnson were tickled to death. They told me, "If this thing ever goes on stage we'd like you to play a part in it."

"Anything you want, pal," I thought. Spending at least a year in London, working five or six nights a week, was fine with me.

The day I was in the recording studio a guy with silver-gray hair, dressed in a sharp-looking tailored suit, happened to walk in. He looked like an undertaker! I found out later it was John DeLorean, the automobile tycoon who designed that stainless steel DMC-12 sports car with the gull-wing doors (the one featured in the film *Back to the Future*). Someone said to me, "Charlie, he's going to put up £0.5 million (about $750,000 at the time) to produce *American Heroes*."

"This is great, man," I thought. "My luck's changing. Everything's going my way. Destiny's about to take a fortunate turn."

But for whatever reason, within 8 or 10 weeks, DeLorean pulled out of the deal. There'd be no money forthcoming for Mason and Johnson's show. Absolutely none. The whole arrangement just fell apart. I don't know the intricacies of DeLorean's business dealings, but I do know that his DeLorean Motor Company was scheduled to begin manufacturing cars in 1981, and it's possible he needed all his cash on hand to get that enterprise off the ground. If, indeed, that were the case, DeLorean might have been wiser to invest his money in *American Heroes*. His ill-fated automobile company fell into receivership and was shut down by the end of 1982.

So there I was, once again in familiar territory. I'd spent most of the last two decades either on the verge of success or on the precipice of disaster (take your pick), trying to grab the brass ring. But each time I had the prize within my grasp it had fallen to the ground. Here was another disappointment, coming right on the verge of a breakout. Singing Broadway-type material written by Barry Mason and Gilbert Johnson would have showcased my talent in an entirely different light. Instead, destiny once again proved to be a dead-end for me. Was this to be the story of my life?

Mason and Johnson never were able to secure enough money to get their production off the ground, and to this day everything about it—those songs I cut included—lies dormant. But I still have those tapes, and every time I hear them they give me chills. I wonder if Barry Mason thinks those songs are worthy of release in today's music market. After all, they're only dubs, done with just guitar, piano, bass, and drum accompaniment. But I think they're good enough to put out just the way they are. If that's not the case, I know what could be done with those songs by applying today's technology. They could enhance those tracks to make them sound as if André Kostelanetz and his orchestra were playing.

I think there's still a market for that type of music. Every once in a while, even in the midst of the rock era, a tune of that sort sneaks in. It happened with Al Martino's "Spanish Eyes," and Louis Armstrong had huge hits with "Hello Dolly" and "Wonderful World" during the Beatles' heyday. If I had the power to have those songs played on the radio for about a month, I think they'd be big sellers. And I'm not saying that because of my singing. The songs themselves are just tremendous. If I had to, I'd change my name to get one of them played on the air. Then, after it became a hit, I'd say, "It's really me, folks!"

During my follow-up tour of Great Britain in March 1980, the crowds were even bigger than the year before. This time around, my fans there knew what to expect. It's amazing what word of mouth alone can do. Much like Bernie Rothbard and I'd done the previous fall, after the 1980 tour we returned home for a brief spell before packing our bags again. This time Bernie and I were set to explore new territory and really expand our horizons. We headed to Finland!

Although my stage career never did get off the ground, my overseas return resulted in a more familiar style of recording activity—although not exactly in the manner I expected. It seems Blackjack Records' Raoul Reniers had his own peculiar idea of how to patch together a record album. And "patching together" are the perfect words to describe his methodology. After getting the okay in 1979 to record me, Reniers had contracted Graham Baker to produce the sessions. Baker, who worked for London Decca, had been impressed by the brisk sales of the 1978 release of my Cameo-Parkway sessions. Now, with Baker on the verge of leaving British Decca, Reniers recognized an opportunity to exploit my revitalized overseas popularity. But by the time Baker agreed to Raoul Reniers' offer I'd already returned to America.

That was no deterrent to Graham Baker. To begin with, he added a trumpet, a trombone, and a steel guitar to the standard lineup of piano, bass, sax, and drums. Then, at studios in London and Belgium, he recorded about 20 instrumental tracks done in the neo-rockabilly vein so popular overseas at the time. Heard today, those backing tracks are—to put it kindly—minimalistic.

The tracks Baker recorded in London were done with my soon-to-be friend Freddie "Fingers" Lee on piano. Freddie was a great boogie-woogie piano player with whom I later recorded a few additional tracks. Freddie was a notable figure on the British rock and roll scene for many years. He and I were very close; he was the kind of friend who'd do anything for you. It just broke my heart when I learned the news of his passing in early 2014.

Along with Bill Haley and His Comets, I toured England, Holland, Belgium, and France with Freddie. As you might suspect, there were moments of humor on such tours. The flashy pianist, who had just one eye and wore an eye-patch, was chauffeuring us on that tour. All the while, we incessantly implored him to "Keep an eye on the road, Fred!"

Another time, Bernie Rothbard and I were preparing to fly from England to a gig in Finland. Bernie and I had boarded one of those smaller-type jets that might have held 100 people at the most. We were sitting next to each other as the last of the passengers entered the cabin. All of a sudden a huge man appeared, weighing about 300 pounds. Inside that cramped airline cabin and wearing a huge 10-gallon cowboy hat, he looked like he was seven feet tall (actually 6' 7"). As the fellow made his way down the aisle Bernie turned to me and said, "Holy shit, Charlie, I thought the damned plane was going to tip over when that guy got on!" That large cowboy turned out to be none other than the rockabilly/country singer Sleepy LaBeef. He, too, was headed to a gig in Finland. Sleepy and I got to know each other that day and we've been friends ever since. He's quite a talented guy and a great fellow. I call him the "gentle giant."

During the spring of 1981 I performed in Finland again. Once again, Bernie accompanied me. Neither he nor I spoke any Finnish, which happens to be a very difficult language to comprehend. In Finland none of the television programs are broadcast in English, as they are in some of the other European countries. So it was tough sitting in our hotel room, staring at the tube and not understanding a bloody word. The first night we arrived there, Bernie and I were really looking forward to going out to dinner. We left our room, hearing nothing but Finnish spoken all around us, and stepped into the elevator. With that, a fellow exclaimed, "Holy smoke, is that Charlie Gracie?"

"What the hell?" I thought, as I whirled around. "What's going on?"

It was the voice of the late Tim Hauser of The Manhattan Transfer. As it turned out, the quartet was performing in Finland, too. "My God, Charlie," exclaimed Tim, "The last time I saw you was over 20 years ago in Asbury Park, New Jersey. I waited in line for two hours to see you perform."

We both had a good laugh over that. "Geez," I told him. "You had to travel all the way to Finland to see me again. Life sure is funny, man!"

When Graham Baker produced those neo-rockabilly recordings for Raoul Reniers he really didn't want a sound that was too polished, and within that context he achieved his goal. But the results were uneven to say the least. Some of those backing tracks sounded quite good, while others were pretty raw, even bordering on semi-amateurish. After Baker brought those tracks back over to the States he had me overdub my voice and guitar at the Phoenix 413 Studios in Camden, New Jersey, just across the river from Philadelphia.

I did the best I could with those tracks, but I wasn't as concerned with their overall quality as I was with their potential to reintroduce me to the current recording scene. And they certainly did that. The Baker-produced sessions culminated in my first record album of new material, a 10-inch, 10-song platter titled *Rockin' Philadelphia*. But instead of coming out on Raoul Reniers' Blackjack label, the album was released by a French company on Big Beat Records in 1980. Today that album is so obscure that most of my fans probably are not aware of it.

After Reniers cut a deal to have those 10 tracks put out on Big Beat, he wasn't about to let my other recordings go to waste. In March 1981, Blackjack Records released *The Fabulous Charlie Gracie*, which contained the balance of the Graham Baker tracks. (It also included several duplications from the *Rockin' Philadelphia* album.) Two of the songs, the old Bobby Lee Trammell rocker "You Mostest Girl" and "Rockin' the Boogie," were spun off the album as a single.

I never knew how many copies those Graham Baker albums sold, but I do know that I never received a penny for either of them. What's more, after Baker received his production money from Raoul Reniers, I never heard from nor saw him again. Musically speaking, neither of those albums was anything to brag about, but at least they thrust me back in the recording game—and at just the right time. In the fall of 1981, I was about to begin my fifth "comeback" trip overseas, with stops in—among other places—Cardiff in Wales, London, and several English towns along the North Sea coast. While in London I also booked some studio time to work on my next album.

Dave Travis and I had become quite friendly after working together during my 1979 tour. He was now eager to step in and produce an album the proper way. Backed by Dave and his Bad River Band, I recorded a high-quality album, which Dave chose to call *Amazing Gracie*. I'm extremely proud to claim this as my first "legitimate" long player. The LP contained 12 tracks of all new material, running the gamut from rock and roll to rhythm and blues to rockabilly, which we cut in London in just one week. *Amazing Gracie* is one hell of an album and certainly a cut above the two previous piecemeal collections that were produced by Graham Baker. In February 1982, it was released on a French label called Charley Records and widely distributed throughout Europe. Surprisingly, *Amazing Gracie* has never been re-released on compact disc.

Talk about destiny and good fortune; over the years Dave Travis and I not only developed a strong friendship that continues to this day, we established a firm business relationship as well. (Things got off to a promising start when Dave actually paid me in advance for the *Amazing Gracie* album.) Dave's a wonderful fellow and very talented. Not only does he sing and play the bass, he was smart enough to get into the publishing aspect of the music business. As a result, Dave has quite a song catalog under his belt, and also owns the Cotton Town Jubilee label.

Several years after making *Amazing Gracie*, Dave called and told me he was coming to America. He was aware that throughout my career I always kept one pristine copy of all my original 45 RPM recordings. "Charlie," he informed me, "I'd like to re-release all the stuff you did from Cadillac in 1952 through 1958 when you left Cameo."

"Be my guest," I told him.

Dave subsequently put those recordings, along with some alternate takes and previously unreleased live recordings I'd made, onto a compact disc. Then (to conform to copyright regulations) he released the collection outside of the United States on his Cotton Town Jubilee label. If you ever come across that particular CD, there's a picture of me on the front cover taken when I was 16 years old!

When I returned to Britain in 1979 after a two-decade hiatus, Bernie Rothbard's modest goal had been for me to get my foot in the door. To my surprise, we accomplished that and much, much more. Things worked out better than either Bernie or I could have imagined. The first several times I'd gone back overseas it had been necessary for Bernie to lay all the groundwork. But after a while, the routine became pretty much established and Paul Barrett was able to handle everything that needed to be done from his side of the pond. Besides, Bernie had his agency to run, and each time he accompanied me meant leaving his business unattended. It was in 1981, after Bernie and I returned from our fourth "comeback" tour, that he told me, "Charlie, it's no longer necessary for me to go along with you on these trips. I know you don't like to travel alone, so why don't you start taking Joan along." No doubt about it, those nights overseas when I had no one to go home to certainly took its emotional toll. But since that time, Joan has accompanied me on every tour, making those trips much more enjoyable.

When my overseas "comeback" began in 1979, those tours lasted an average of two to three weeks. The crowds were large enough for the promoters to make a good profit and I was making a couple of bucks, too. Everybody—my fans, the promoters, Joan, and I—was extremely happy. If I hadn't filled those seats during the first two or three tours in '79 and '80 I wouldn't have been invited back. But the outlook overseas continued to brighten as my re-energized fan base went about unreservedly spreading the news: "Hey, Charlie Gracie's back in town!" On subsequent tours I now played to packed houses.

14

WILDWOOD BOOGIE

Wildwood, situated on an island near the southern tip of the New Jersey coast, is comprised of several associated cities, among them North Wildwood, Wildwood Crest, and the City of Wildwood. The area has long been the summer playground of Philadelphians. The first documented visitors to the island were the Native American Lenni-Lenape, drawn to the Atlantic Ocean's cooling breezes and bountiful striped bass. Each summer, the Lenni-Lenape continued to gather on the island they called "five miles of health and happiness." In 1664, when the English assumed control of the sandbank of tangled trees, vines, and flowers from the Dutch, they called it Wildwood.

During the last quarter of the nineteenth century, Philadelphia-area residents began to frequent Wildwood's shores after doctors claimed the island's salt and sea to be an elixir for their ailments. In 1874, a railroad was laid from Cape May to the south and a more adventuresome sort of visitor began to appear: the summer vacationer. With that influx, a new community called Holly Beach took shape in the untouched wilderness of sand dunes and thickets just south of the initial Wildwood settlement of Anglesea.

The birth of tourism in the Wildwoods officially began on

Decoration Day 1890, with the opening of the island's first grand hotel. A carousel and other amusements began to appear on the beach in the 1890s, and in 1904 the first raised wooden boardwalk was constructed. Holly Beach eventually became Wildwood Crest and Anglesea was renamed North Wildwood. In the early years of the twentieth century, the boardwalk, thick with amusements, stretched from North Wildwood to Wildwood Crest. By the 1930s, Wildwood's reputation as an exciting tourist destination was firmly established.

Then, during the post-World War II years, the entire Jersey shore faced a crisis. Prior to the war, the region's traditional resort lifestyle depended on railroads to transport landlocked vacationers for weeklong seaside stays. With that captive audience on hand, the ocean resort areas developed a healthy nightlife. But with the war's end came a rising popularity of the family automobile, along with a plethora of highway construction. The Jersey shore's new breed of "day-trippers" arrived not by rail, but by auto. Rather than stick around for a week and patronize the hotels and nightclubs, they departed that very same day. By the dawn of the 1950s, most of the shore's grand hotels, humble cottages, and once-animated boardwalks were in decline.

Thanks to a quirk in geographical location, Wildwood continued to enjoy a period of sustained prosperity. Situated about 70 miles from the Philadelphia and Camden, New Jersey areas, the famous boardwalk city was a bit too far away for the day-tripping set. Consequently, most families and young adults who vacationed there stayed for at least a weekend, if not longer. Soon, loud and colorful motels, replete with angular architecture and garish neon lights—all the better to attract their hedonistic clientele—replaced Wildwood's outdated hotels and rooming houses. The resort city's stylishly modern space-age accommodations also supported a flourishing nightlife where well-known entertainers honed their skills before moving on to Vegas casinos. With the likes of Tony Bennett, Joey Bishop, Sammy Davis, Jr., and other major stars appearing nightly, Wildwood began to be promoted as the "Las Vegas of the East" and "Little Las Vegas."

During the 1950s, everything in Wildwood seemed new, especially the music. Just over a month after recording "Rock

Around the Clock," on Memorial Day Weekend 1954, Bill Haley and His Comets debuted their soon-to-be anthem at Wildwood's Hofbrau Hotel. In 1957, Dick Clark, then a local disc jockey on the verge of becoming the nation's Pied Piper of rock and roll, spun records on the boardwalk at Wildwood's Starlight Ballroom. By the late 1950s, up to two dozen hip nightclubs attracted thousands of young people by playing host to rock and roll hit makers such as Chubby Checker, Sam Cooke, Danny and the Juniors, Fats Domino, and Charlie Gracie.

Back in America, my career continued on the upswing. By the end of the 1970s, high-profile gigs had once again become more or less a routine for me. I'm still reminded of my opening for the popular comedian Pat Cooper at Palumbo's, the well-known South Philly nightspot. (If I remember correctly, that particular gig occurred around Christmas time, when "Santa Claus" also made a timely appearance at Palumbos'—although I assure you, not as part of my performance.)

The first real break I'd caught since the 1950s, one that elevated me from the Hoagie Joe's circuit, occurred when I started to secure bookings down at the Jersey shore. That began in 1967, with a summer-long gig in Wildwood. Wildwood has roughly 5,500 year-round residents, but during the summer the population swells to 250,000, with everyone seeking fun and entertainment. I soon realized two things: First, the Wildwood vacationers loved me, and second, my working the shore could be a recurring thing. We retained our duplex in Llanerch Hills and, in addition, I was fortunate enough to rent a house in Wildwood for the entire summer. That meant Joan, the kids, and I could be together throughout my extended residency. For the first time in quite a while everything seemed good.

Although I later managed to land lucrative summer gigs in the seaside resort towns of Avalon, Longport, and others, Wildwood—where I performed most frequently—became my salvation. I likened myself to a migrant worker who picked crops all summer and then lived off that money during the winter. Of course, I performed during the winter, too, but the money I earned at Wildwood became the bulk of my annual income. Over the years, I was booked there at six or seven different clubs, each for a 13- or 14-week season. I worked the largest club in Wildwood, Ben Martin's Bolero Club, and also performed at the Beach Comber, the Hurricane, and the Diamond Beach. After many years I became a fixture in that mecca of summer fun, to the extent that the Chamber of Commerce elected to name a street after me. "Charlie Gracie Avenue" is located right off Atlantic Avenue, a major thoroughfare running the length of the Wildwoods. Today, the Bolero Resort Hotel occupies the corner where the signpost displaying my name is located. In times past, the original Bolero Club stood right there.

I'd actually done my first Wildwood gig back in 1957, when I was hot with "Butterfly" and "Fabulous." That was at Club Avalon, then owned by Bernie Rothbard's partner, Eddie Suez. After headlining the Avalon for 10 days, I embarked on my initial tour of Great Britain. When I returned to the States, I went back to Wildwood and headlined the Bolero. Everyone from Tony Bennett to Johnnie Ray to The Platters worked the Bolero. I performed there with The Treniers, a rocking R&B group, who were absolutely sensational showmen and tremendous musicians. Then, as my recording career began to fade in the early 1960s, so did my appearances at the prestigious clubs, not only in Wildwood, but everywhere else.

Fast-forward to 1979, the year of my triumphant return to England. It was then that I landed probably the best gig of my entire career, at a place called Moore's Inlet, which overlooked the ocean in North Wildwood. At the time, I happened to be working Club Avalon, which, by then, was owned by Cozy Morley, the ingenious South Philly musician and comedian. Cozy and I went way back. Not only did I know him from the old neighborhood, I also knew his parents and his brothers.

During the 1950s, Cozy was the "resident" entertainer at the Avalon. Then, in 1959 he purchased the club from Eddie Suez. The Avalon was huge; it held 1,200 people. Man, what a joint—a dilapidated wood-frame structure that must have been built during the 1920s. It had a wooden boardwalk-like floor and a ceiling covered with burlap. Built into the club's walls was the "air conditioning" of the day—giant fans that rarely worked. Since the Avalon was close to the ocean, whenever a storm hit the area, seawater would rush into the place. I think that was the only time the joint ever got washed!

Cozy never spent a dime to improve the ramshackle Avalon, but it was certainly a fun place to be. The club's owner was a master at what he termed "corn cob" humor. Like Jack Benny, Cozy played on his reputation of being cheap. As emcee and entertainer, he relentlessly poked fun at the run-down surroundings. To Cozy, the Avalon was a "toilet," and when someone headed for the actual ladies' room during his act he'd warn them: "Hey hon, there might not be any paper in there. You might want to take this with you." Cozy then proceeded to toss a roll to the flustered woman as the crowd roared. He would also appear onstage with one of those long-handled money-collection baskets that were familiar to many patrons because of their use during the offertory in the Catholic churches. He'd extend the basket into the audience, which always drew far more laughs than cash.

Whether it was emceeing, doing standup, or singing with his orchestra between featured acts, Cozy simply loved to entertain. If you went to Wildwood you had to go see at least one show at Club Avalon. Cozy brought some of the biggest stars in the world there, including Joey Bishop, Don Cornell, Dennis Day, The Four Aces, Julius LaRosa, and one of my show business idols, the great Johnnie Ray. (I'd first met Johnnie in London in 1957. Then we met once more in the mid-1980s when he played the Avalon and I had a booking directly across the street at a different venue. Johnnie passed away in 1990, and I consider myself extremely fortunate to have had the opportunity to meet up with him one last time.)

Cozy Morley would do two shows a night and then come out to the bar with his banjo and hang out with the customers until closing time. The crowd just loved it. On a weeknight Cozy sometimes drew 400 or 500 people—which wasn't bad—but on Fridays and Saturdays you couldn't get into the place.

I often worked matinees at the Avalon, six days a week in the Bulkhead Room. Then I played nights in Cozy's top room, which was the nightclub itself. We must have performed together a thousand times. If I had to, I could do his entire act!

Cozy was known in the business as a regional celebrity. He was a superstar throughout the Philadelphia area and in South Jersey, yet largely unknown outside that sphere. Later dubbed "Mr. Wildwood," Cozy, who passed away in 2013, lived long enough to see a $60,000 bronze statue of his likeness erected on the grounds of the old Club Avalon.

Working at Cozy Morley's Club Avalon was a delightful experience, but I truly made my bones in Wildwood at Moore's Inlet. Moore's was located on Spruce Street at New Jersey Avenue in North Wildwood, just across the street from the old Avalon. Back in 1912, Robert Moore, another South Philly guy, decided to open a tavern in a vacant building adjacent to a channel of water that led to the Atlantic Ocean. He named it Moore's Inlet. The place survived the Prohibition era, as did countless other watering holes, by selling illegal "hooch." With Moore's situated right on the beach, it was relatively easy for the prohibition "rumrunners" to deliver their bootleg liquor from cargo ships anchored beyond the three-mile limit in the Atlantic. In 1957 Moore's burned to the ground (faulty wiring, they said) and was quickly rebuilt. The seaside business then gradually expanded into a hotel, restaurant, and popular nightspot, which the Moore family eventually sold to outsiders.

By 1979, Moore's was owned by Mike Guadagno and Joe Carideo. After catching one of my performances at the Avalon, Mike and Joe approached me and said, "My God, Charlie, we'd love to have you at our place. You're playing rock and roll music; you've got personality and great stage presence. You'd be perfect for us!" I decided to give it a try, and things went well; so well that in 1981 Mike and Joe booked me for the entire summer season. Joe Bilbee, who was the deejay at Moore's, played records at night, and I did the Saturday and Sunday afternoon matinees on the club's open deck overlooking the Atlantic. Thanks to my lifelong experience performing before diverse audiences, the place was mobbed every weekend. We drew between 300 and 500 patrons each day, which just goes to prove, if you know how to entertain them, people *will* flock to see you on a regional level—whether you have a hit record or not.

Moore's turned out to be my reclamation. Although my work schedule had improved during the 1970s, I never had a guarantee that any of those gigs would automatically be there in the future. Beginning in 1981, I worked Moore's for 25 consecutive summers. (After a decade or so I began to tell the crowds, "We not only play the oldies; we *are* the oldies!") Mike and Joe treated me well, they paid me handsomely, and I had no complaints whatsoever. I made a good living there all those years and while doing so I was able to build a whole new audience within a 200-mile radius. In fact, my following at Moore's grew so large that other club owners in the area didn't hesitate to book me.

I had a great run at Moore's Inlet, and hiring me proved to be a good move for Mike Guadagno and Joe Carideo, as well. They took in millions of dollars during the years I performed there. Then, in 2005, Mike and Joe sold the property to real estate developers for $6.5 million. That area remains a beautiful spot overlooking the Atlantic, but if you should happen to visit Wildwood today, don't bother looking for Moore's. It was demolished and replaced by condominiums.

Sadly, Mike Guadagno died in 2010, God rest his soul. I felt very bad when I heard the news. Mike and I always maintained a good relationship. While the poor fellow had only a few years to enjoy the fruits of his labor, I believe everybody has his or her day picked out, and there's nothing we can do about it. That's why it's important to keep the faith.

I try to live my life one day at a time, feeling content and blessed for each one. And every so often, a day that's truly special touches me. One such occasion occurred in 1986, the year I turned 50. Joan and the kids gave me a big surprise birthday party held at a nearby Catholic Charities facility, the Don Guanella Village for mentally challenged boys and men. (Chris Burke, a television actor with Down Syndrome, who starred in the ABC-TV series *Life Goes On*, is the school's most famous graduate.) At the time, my son worked as a teacher at the facility and I regularly performed there for the students.

Once again, my family was aided and abetted by Bernie Rothbard, who called me on my birthday and said, "C'mon over, Charlie, I need to discuss some business with you." I drove over to Bernie's place as I'd done a hundred times before. "Sit down," he said when I arrived, fidgeting and appearing not quite sure what to say next. In hindsight, Bernie was stalling, aware that as we spoke he was providing Joan and kids additional time to put the finishing touches on my surprise party.

When I finally returned home Joan said to me, "Charlie, we've been invited over to Don Guanella for dinner tonight."

Since we were frequent dinner guests of the Catholic brothers and priests who ran the school, I didn't think twice about it. "All right, c'mon," I said to Joan. "It's already late and I am getting kind of hungry."

When we arrived at Don Guanella I was still in the dark, so to speak. But as we walked into the main room the lights suddenly went on and I was greeted by a loud and enthusiastic: "HAPPY BIRTHDAY, Charlie!" There must have been at least 75 or more people there. Besides family, several musicians and show business colleagues attended the affair.

The evening turned out to be a fantastic surprise (when it comes to things like that I often take the bait). But overall, 1986 proved to be a bittersweet year in my life. A few months after that milestone celebration, Bernie Rothbard suffered an incapacitating stroke while working at his home office. His son Kevin had gone out for the day, so all that time Bernie lay there on the floor, unattended. When Kevin finally returned home he found that his dad was unable to speak and his entire right side was paralyzed.

Bernie survived the initial stroke, but he required hospitalization, followed by extensive rehabilitation at a suburban Philadelphia facility. After Bernie was placed in rehab he grew extremely depressed. I could tell he was also quite angry. He became very stubborn and would just lie there in bed, refusing to participate in any therapy whatsoever.

Bernie's wife Debbie had died of cancer in 1972 and he'd never remarried. Consequently, during the next 15 years or so, Bernie and I had grown very close. After his stroke, I tried my best to make him feel relevant. Each week, when I visited him I made sure to hand him an envelope that contained his commission from my gigs. "You're still my agent, Bernie," I'd assure him. He tried to thank me, but because of his paralysis, he had great difficulty speaking.

While the poor fellow remained bedridden, his friends and business associates eventually stopped coming to see him. Aside from me, the only visitor Bernie had was his son Kevin. (His older son Robert was living in Hollywood, pursuing a career that eventually led to film directing.)

Sadly, Bernie lingered in a nursing facility for almost eight years. I was playing at Moore's Inlet in July of 1994 when he died. I couldn't even attend the funeral because I was unable to get out of that commitment. All through my performance that day, the words I knew Bernie would have repeated to me echoed through my mind: "Go to work, Charlie. Go to work." That's just the type of guy he was.

After Bernie passed, Kevin ran the booking agency for some time. Kevin tried his best, but he just didn't have the moxie for it and eventually terminated the business. Bernie and I always had a great relationship. He was a father figure to me, an honest guy who I trusted completely. In return, he kept me working for all those years. I'd stuck with him to the very end. Now it was time for me to go out on my own.

In October 1987 I took part in a ceremony and concert that launched the Philadelphia Music Alliance. The events were staged at the historic Academy of Music, located on South Broad Street, in the heart of the city. The program honored the initial inductees onto Philadelphia's Walk of Fame. (A tribute I was fortunate to receive in 2008.) Afterwards, the concert included a virtual "Who's Who" of Philadelphia's best-known recording stars. Even with each artist limited to singing only one or two songs, the marathon performance seemingly went on for hours.

At the end of the day, as I sat in a backstage room with Frankie Avalon and Fabian—the "Golden Boys of Bandstand"—along with Bobby Rydell and other local recording luminaries, Chubby Checker bounced in. He strode past everyone else, put his arms around me and exclaimed, "Charlie Gracie! If it wasn't for you, I'd still be plucking chickens!"

Chubby was referring to the fact that I gave Cameo-Parkway

their first hits with "Butterfly" and "Fabulous." If those songs hadn't made money in 1957, Cameo most likely would have gone under. Perhaps some other artist would have earned the distinction of saving Bernie Lowe's bacon, but I was the guy who did.

After the initial burst of recording I'd done in the early 1980s, things quieted down considerably. So when my good friend Jamie Rounds approached me in 1989 about a recording project, I didn't hesitate to take him up on it. Jamie was a former Philadelphian whose musical aspirations led him to Nashville. He was a very talented guy who sang and played guitar and electric bass. Jamie worked with some big talents, too, from John Lee Hooker to John Fogerty. I thought he was a splendid songwriter as well. In fact, I recorded two or three of Jamie's compositions, including "A Little Too Soon to Tell," a tune on which Graham Nash and I sang harmony. That song was included on my 2001 CD *I'm All Right*. Unfortunately, Jamie passed away suddenly in 2013. We'd grown very close and his premature death really hit me hard. Had he lived, I surely would have recorded more of his material.

Another of those songs Jamie wrote for me in 1989 was called "Go Man Go." He had enough faith in me to foot the entire bill for the recording date, including the backing musicians and the producer. I cut "Go Man Go" in New York with former Brill Building songwriter Richard Gottehrer, who was a hot producer at the time (Blondie and the Go-Go's). The backing musicians included Rob Stoner (bass) and Howie Wyeth (drums), both veteran musicians who recorded with Bob Dylan and Robert Gordon. (The voices of the legendary Jordanaires were later overdubbed.) My daughter Angela happened to be visiting our cousins in New York at the time, and I arranged for them to be in the studio that day. It was an experience they enjoyed tremendously.

"Go Man Go" sounded great then and it still holds up today. There was only one problem: no one could place the damned thing. I made a few phone calls, the first one to Al Gallico in Nashville. Al gave "Go Man Go" a listen before telling me, "Charlie, you have a hit record there. But my brother's gravely ill right now. He's got cancer, and I just don't have time to work with you on this. I'm afraid you'll have to do it on your own."

I then called record producer Jimmy Bowen, who I'd known since 1957, when he and Buddy Knox were touring with their group The Rhythm Orchids. Jimmy, too, listened to "Go Man Go." "Charlie, you've got a great song here," he said. "The thing is, I'm inundated with projects right now. I just don't have any time to devote to it. But if you can place it with the right people you've got a hit, man!"

"I got a hit, I got a hit, I got a hit." It was the same old story. Once again, my record (released on the tiny Comstock label) garnered little airplay. While the lack of interest in "Go Man Go" came as no surprise, the experience was still frustrating. While I continued to make great records, very few people ever got to hear them.

I'm always amazed whenever a British rock star tells me he's been influenced by my music and is "thrilled" to meet me. That kind of recognition's been going on for the last 20 years now. Brian May, guitarist, vocalist, and songwriter for the rock group Queen, might have been the first. I originally met Brian (who is also a Doctor of astrophysics!) in May 1996, at a star-studded charity event in England called the Rats Ball. Everybody who was *anybody* in the entertainment business was there that night. At one point someone introduced Brian to me.

"Charlie Gracie!" he gasped.

It was obvious from Brian's reverential reaction that he was familiar with my history and seemed delighted to meet me. To be honest, I wasn't all that familiar with Queen's music and I wasn't all that certain who Brian was. Still, I was flattered that he'd even heard of me. (When I'd toured Great Britain in the late '50s, Brian— the eventual member of one of that country's true supergroups—was not yet a teenager.) As the festivities continued that evening, I was astounded to meet a lot of other wonderful entertainers, all of whom remembered me.

Another British star that often claims me as an influence is the singer Cliff Richard (who in 1995 was knighted by the Queen). A few years ago, while I was doing a radio show, the host asked me if I knew Cliff. "No," I replied. "But I certainly know *of* him. He's extremely talented; he possesses great charisma on stage; and he's sold as many records in Europe as anyone, including Elvis. I think he's just wonderful."

"Well, I have two tickets for Cliff's show tomorrow night, Charlie. If you're free you can come and see him."

"Terrific," I said. "My wife and I would love to."

"Oh, by the way," the radio host added, "Cliff's got all your records on his jukebox."

When I heard that, I figured the guy was pulling my chain. But the next night, after Cliff Richard gave a spectacular performance, Joan and I were fortunate enough to meet him after the show. And I was floored when, during the course of our conversation, Cliff said: "Charlie, I have *all* your records on my jukebox!"

Cliff has often included my recording of "Fabulous" on his all-time Top 10 list. And in the fall of 2013 he released a '50s tribute CD titled *The Fabulous Rock 'n' Roll Songbook*. It was no accident that Cliff used the word "fabulous" in the title, either. His own splendid version of "Fabulous" was included on that CD. What's more, to promote the album, Cliff was gracious enough to appear on a weekly radio program in the States hosted by me and by Charlie, Jr.

Graham Nash, who enjoyed his first taste of success with the Hollies back in the '60s, is another artist who regards me as an important influence on his career. Accompanied by a friend who knew him fairly well, I went to see one of Graham's concerts a few years back. After the show, my friend said, "Charlie, let's go backstage and say hello." We did, and Graham put his arm around me and began to reminisce about our meeting at the Manchester Empire back in 1957. He then thanked me for inspiring him to begin playing music. In fact, Graham later told my son that when he wrote "Teach Your Children Well" he was thinking of me. Imagine how great that made me feel!

About 10 years ago, Graham said to me, "I understand you're cutting a new CD, Charlie. If it weren't for guys like you, chaps like me would never have gotten rich. Well, it's 'payback' time. If you'd agree, I'd love to do something with you on the album." As it turned out, Graham subsequently recorded a duet with me for the *I'm All Right* CD. He's a tremendously creative talent in his own right, yet very humble. I'm honored that after so many years I can still call Graham a good friend.

I first met Van Morrison in the early 1990s, in Newport, South Wales. A friend of Van's named "Mac" McElroy owned The King's Hotel there, where I often stayed while on tour. One evening Joan and I were sitting in the hotel restaurant with our little entourage. Elvis' original drummer D.J. Fontana, who backed me on that tour, was with us at the time. As we spoke, every now and then out of the corner of my eye I saw a fellow wearing a well-worn leather bomber jacket pacing nearby. It seemed like he was hanging back, interested in what was going on with our group, yet too shy to come any closer. I had no idea who he was. I thought perhaps he worked at the hotel. Finally I asked Mac, "Who *is* that guy over there?"

"That's Van Morrison, Charlie! He's a big fan of yours."

"Well, why don't you have him come over and join us," I replied. The way I see it, if you're a fellow musician, I'll sit down and talk music with you as an *equal*. That'll be our common base for discussion.

"Oh, he's very shy," explained Mac. "He won't come over."

"Okay, fine," I thought. "If the guy wants to keep his distance, let him." Still, I wondered how a celebrity of Van's magnitude could be intimidated by *me*, instead of the reverse.

Eventually our get-together at the hotel restaurant ended and Joan and I returned to our room. Not long after, I got a call from Mac. "Charlie, could you come back down now? Van would really like to speak with you."

Mac had been right on the money. Van wasn't comfortable approaching me with a crowd around and a lot of chatter going on. What he really wanted was to sit and talk one-on-one. So he'd waited until everyone left. Evidently Van doesn't readily take to many people. He's been described at various times as "reclusive," "notoriously difficult," and "eccentric." The way I see it, Van has his idiosyncrasies, but so does everyone else. So I went downstairs. He and I talked a bit while I sipped some coffee (which I don't even like). Van, on the wagon at the time, also had coffee. We hit it off right from the start, perhaps because I've always been a straightforward kind of guy. I had a performance the next day, so our first encounter didn't last long. But Van and I would meet again.

There was a club inside The King's Hotel, where Mac showcased various entertainers. (Jerry Lee Lewis is one I particularly recall seeing there.) I performed at The King's Hotel myself on occasion, and who'd pop in while I was onstage but Van Morrison. He'd finish a gig somewhere, say in Ireland or Liverpool, and then fly to Wales in his own small plane to see my show. Gradually, Van and I grew friendlier. I won't say we hung out together, but one night we did sit until four in the morning, bullshitting about rock and roll and the good old days.

As we spoke, Van began to pick my brain. I soon discovered we came from similar working-class backgrounds and had quite a few things in common. For instance, when Van was 11 his father bought him his first guitar. He formed a skiffle group when he was just 12, and then another one two years later. Along the way he learned to play the harmonica and the saxophone. Van left school at age 15 to become a window washer, but his interest in music continued to intensify. Still in his teens, he joined an Irish show band—the equivalent of an American bar or "cover" band—which played current hit songs. He then went on the road at age 17 to play five sets a night in steamy clubs and U.S. Army bases in England, Scotland, and Germany. I certainly related to that.

Although the rest of the world learned of Van Morrison by way of his '60s rock group called Them, he particularly loves the music of the '50s era. In Van's mind, that's when it all began. He was very curious about American rock and roll back then: "Who'd you work with in those days, Charlie?" he wanted to know. "What was it like when you were just starting out?"

Van wasn't that far behind me in terms of rock and roll's development. But you have to remember, at that time performers such as I were just beginning to introduce rock and roll to Great Britain. And when it came to technology and amplification we were still living in the Dark Ages. My God, the sound was raw—really raw! As you probably can tell from listening to my Stockton concert, there was absolutely no fidelity to most recordings of live music from that era. In fact, the amplifier I used at the time didn't even have a reverb unit. It produced what was termed a "flat" guitar sound. That was the Stone Age of live rock and roll compared to what Van would later experience. Today it's an entirely different ballgame.

Toward the end of 1999, a couple of years after Van and I first became acquainted, I was at home, upstairs shaving, getting ready for a gig, when the phone rang. Joan answered it.

"Charlie," she called up to me, "it's Van Morrison!"

"What?" I thought. "Van Morrison? He's on the telephone? You got to be kidding me." I ran downstairs, grabbed the phone and was greeted by his Irish accent: "Hello, *Chaaarlie!*"

"Hey Van, how you doing?"

"How are *you* doing?" he replied. "Listen, I'm in the U. K. right now, but I'm going to the West Coast in a couple of weeks to do a few shows."

"Great," I told him. "Break a leg!"

"Well, I was just wondering if you'd like to open for me?"

I couldn't believe what I'd just heard. Van Morrison wanted me to open for him? He certainly didn't need *me*. But apparently Van saw something in my performances that inspired him to invite me.

"Are you kidding me?" I stammered into the phone. "Of course. I'd love to open for you, Van." I was so excited that I never even asked him about money or anything else for that matter.

"Great, Charlie. My agent in New York will call you in the next half hour. He'll take care of all the arrangements. Oh, and one other thing, I want you to bring your own band."

"Nah, that's not necessary," I replied. "I can work with your group."

"No," Van insisted. "I want you to bring your own band. You play heavier rock than I do. If you use my band you'll burn them out!"

Well, I wasn't about to argue with Van Morrison over the details of *his* tour. Not only was I paid extremely well for that 10-day affair in January of 2000, Van also gave Joan and I the royal treatment. We had a chauffeur at our disposal 24 hours a day and several times we joined Van for breakfast and lunch.

Before we opened at the Reno Hilton in Nevada, Van said to me, "Charlie, give me a strong half hour! That's what I want." I had no intention of exceeding my limit by even a mere second, so the first night I did exactly 29 minutes, and that was it. As I exited the stage the audience gave me a standing ovation.

"Great set, Charlie!" Van exclaimed as he caught up with me.

"Thanks, Van. But those people didn't come to see me. They came for *you*."

"Yeah, Charlie," he exclaimed. "I know that. But you've still got it, man!"

After completing my set I went downstairs to my dressing room to put my guitar away. When I came back up I wiped the sweat off my face and then stood in the wings to watch Van perform. I thought I was finished for the night, but I was wrong. All of a sudden I heard him shout from the stage, "Where's Charlie, Where's Charlie? Tell Charlie to come out here. I wanna play some rock and roll!"

That really caught me by surprise; I never imagined Van would call me out there! I quickly returned to my dressing room and grabbed my guitar. As I ran out to join Van I stumbled over one of the wires lying onstage and almost "slid into second base," right in front of the crowd! Fortunately for me, I was able to maintain my balance and remain upright. Then, with no rehearsal, Van and I jumped into a medley of early rock and roll hits, which included Buddy Holly's "That'll Be the Day," Carl Perkins' "Boppin' the Blues," and Big Joe Turner's "Shake, Rattle and Roll." We closed the set with a rousing duet of the Ray Charles R&B classic "What'd I Say." It was wonderful; a real thrill for me!

That unexpected set with Van confirmed what I'd known all along: rock and roll is timeless. I'd been one of the first to play that kind of music, even before the phrase "rock and roll" was coined, but I wasn't the only one. There were other artists playing what could have been considered rock and roll back then—Louis Jordan, Louis Prima, and Joe Turner, to name a few. Indeed, rock and roll *is* timeless. It makes no difference if you're 17 or 70. You're never too old to rock. There was no way for me to foresee it at the time, but I was destined to prove that very point. In just over a decade, I'd find myself back on the charts with another hit record!

After a few days in Reno we moved on to Los Angeles for two days at the Wiltern Theatre. Joan and I stayed at the Chateau Marmont Hotel, a beautiful place, absolutely exquisite, located on Sunset Boulevard in West Hollywood. The structure is actually a great castle on a hill, modeled after a royal residence in France, while the suites inside are designed to look like large apartments, not hotel rooms. The Marmont was certainly elite, a real playground for the stars. Everyone from Greta Garbo to the Doors' Jim Morrison stayed there at one time or another. John Belushi spent his last night on earth at the Marmont.

Our accommodations were fabulous, but I don't usually make it a habit to stay at $500 a night suites. In all honesty, I would have been satisfied staying with the band at the Beverly Hilton.

Joan and I wanted to walk around and see some of the action, but the Chateau Marmont is in a rather secluded area of West Hollywood. Our chauffeur was prepared to drive us wherever we desired, so we had him take us a couple of miles east to "downtown" Hollywood, tipped him 50 bucks, and said: "Go take your wife out to lunch. We want to take in some of the local color." Joan and I later met up with my second cousin, Mary Ellen DiPrisco, who was a television producer for the likes of Rosie O'Donnell and Regis Philbin. Mary then gave us a personalized tour of the surrounding area.

As you'd expect, there were numerous celebrities in the audience for Van's opening night in Los Angeles. In fact, the entire front row was full of television and movie stars, including Tony Danza, Angelica Huston, and Jack Nicholson. After the show, Angelica and Tony popped into our dressing rooms to compliment us on our performances. Then it was back to Nevada, this time to Las Vegas, where, first, we did two shows at the Hard Rock Cafe. Between performances, Louis Prima's legendary sax player Sam Butera found time to visit backstage to say hello. What an honor that was to be sought out by one of my boyhood idols! The tour concluded about a mile down South Las Vegas Boulevard, at the House of Blues, located in the Mandalay Bay Resort and Casino. A third show—a matinee—was added, which proceeded to sell out in 20 minutes. Overall, the brief tour proved to be a great success. Van seemed elated, and so were we.

I next saw Van when he visited Philadelphia in 2006. He called just as I was preparing for a gig in Wildwood. "Charlie, I'm here at the Four Seasons Hotel. Can you come on down for a visit? I'd like to see you."

It turned out that we had some time to spare, so on our way down to Wildwood Joan and I, along with Charlie, Jr. and his wife Kim, and our daughter Angela, stopped in to see Van. During conversation over a few beers Van said, "I have a show at the Spectrum tomorrow and I'd like you to come and do a couple of songs with me, the way we did in Vegas."

I wanted to say yes in the worst way, but I was then in the midst of a summer-long gig at Westy's in Wildwood. I felt a sense of loyalty, not only to the management at Westy's, but also to my ardent fans, many who traveled great distances to see me. "I hate to say no, Van, but I just can't do it," I reluctantly told him. "I have a show already booked tomorrow at the Jersey shore."

"Shit!" exclaimed Van in disappointment.

Fortunately our paths were destined to cross again. During the summer of 2008, Van returned for a performance in Philadelphia. This time it was his road manager who contacted us and said there would be four front-row tickets to one of Van's shows waiting at the Tower Theater box office. We didn't have much time to chat that evening because after the show Van had to depart almost immediately for Boston, his next stop on the tour. Even so, it was great that he took the time to visit with us once again. There are few artists who have the privilege of sharing the stage with Van Morrison. It was a rare experience that I'll never forget.

Of all the famous musicians who've acknowledged a debt to me, there's probably none bigger than Paul McCartney. I first met Paul in the autumn of 1999, just before I did the concerts with Van Morrison. I was beginning a tour of England and Switzerland, and had already landed in London. After a day or so, my agent Paul Barrett said to me, "You know, Charlie, Paul McCartney has recently mentioned you in several interviews over here."

"Wow! Get outta here!"

"No, he's a big fan of yours," Barrett insisted. "In fact, he'd like to meet you. Paul just performed your hit 'Fabulous' live at the Cavern Club and he's going to release a studio version of the song on a special compact disc single in conjunction with his new *Run Devil Run* album."

Few people get the opportunity to meet Sir Paul McCartney, but I quickly discovered that when he wants to see you, arrangements are made to fit *his* schedule, not yours. To kick off the release of McCartney's new album, a press conference and party was held at the Odeon Cinema at Leicester Square, located in London's West End. Since I was booked to do a show later that evening about an hour's drive from there, Paul Barrett and I knew we'd be cutting it close. But when McCartney beckons, you go!

When Joan, I, and Paul Barrett arrived at the Odeon there were several hundred people in attendance. But McCartney was nowhere to be seen. We were told he was preoccupied at the moment, so we waited. Then we waited some more. Still, there was no sign of Sir Paul.

Finally Paul Barrett warned me, "Charlie, if he doesn't see you soon we're going to have to leave. We've got 1,500 people waiting to see *you*."

"We're this close," I replied. "Let's wait another 10 or 15 minutes."

Then, just after Joan had gone to the ladies room, McCartney's manager suddenly appeared. (It's amazing how these things sometimes happen at just the wrong moment.) He grabbed me by my hand and began to pull me through the crowd.

"Wait!" I protested. "My wife…"

"No. *Now*!" he insisted. "You have to see him *now*."

What could I do? As McCartney's manager continued to pull me along, we navigated a little turn in the room and were confronted by two huge bodyguards sporting tinted glasses and earphones. The guards let us pass and as I turned the corner there was Paul McCartney standing directly in front of me. He looked at me, put his arms around me, and gave me a hug.

"Charlie Gracie!" he exclaimed. "I came to see you at the Liverpool Empire when I was 16 years old. I'll never forget when you played 'Guitar Boogie.'"

I wanted to melt into my shoes. I was dumbstruck; I didn't know what to say. "Oh, uh…thank you, Paul," was about all I could muster.

"Gee, Charlie, you look great."

"You too, Paul." I replied. His wife Linda had passed away the previous April, so I took the occasion to extend my deepest condolences. He thanked me and we conversed for about 20 minutes.

"I've always loved your song 'Fabulous,' Charlie," said Paul. "In fact, I just recorded it."

He then asked me if I'd written "Fabulous," and I'll never forget his response when I told him I hadn't.

"Shit!" he exclaimed. "You could have made some money."

"That would have been nice, Paul" I replied. "But at this point, it doesn't really matter. I was only famous for 15 minutes. You and the other lads were famous for three hours."

Paul laughed, but it's true. He'd come along at just the right time. At the height of my fame, first-generation rock and rollers averaged, say, $1,000 a week. A thousand for an entire week! Today artists can make $100,000 a night. For a complete tour they might come away with a couple million. Man, have times changed!

Then Paul threw me a curve: "Charlie, tell me, how do you keep so fit? Sex, drugs, and rock and roll, right?"

I laughed out loud at that. "Well Paul, I don't know about the sex part. I've been married to the same woman for 41 years. As for drugs, I've never done them. So I'd say it has to be the rock and roll."

Paul chuckled. "Yes Charlie, of course." Then he took the time to introduce me to one of his daughters and a few of his grandchildren. After that, a professional photographer took some photos of Paul and I standing together, which I cherish to this day.

Then it was time for goodbyes. "Keep on rockin', Paul," I told him.

"You too, Charlie; so great to see you!"

I'm truly grateful for my musical career and where it has taken me thus far. As it turned out, Paul McCartney wasn't the only Beatle to acknowledge me as a musical influence. In the March 9, 1996 issue of *Billboard*, George Harrison described my guitar technique as "brilliant." Just imagine if my big-time success had continued for five or six years. I might have had the honor of sharing the bill with the Beatles, as Del Shannon did in the early '60s.

There are several other British rock stars who've told me how much of an inspiration I'd been, among them Joe Cocker, The Kinks' Dave Davies, and Hilton Valentine of The Animals. To have someone say, "You're great" is one thing. But to hear a famous recording artist say, "You inspired me. If not for you I might not be in the position I'm in," is something else altogether. It's not an ego trip for me, but after the ups and downs I've experienced it's certainly gratifying to know that I've been a motivating force for so many artists.

In May 2004 I received the Philadelphia Music Alliance's Lifetime Achievement Award. My good friend, musician and filmmaker George Manney, helped orchestrate the ceremony. The award was presented to me by Chubby Checker, Philadelphia favorite "oldies" deejay Harvey Holiday, and my wife Joan. Graham Nash and Van Morrison each sent video tributes and Paul McCartney sent an audio clip from a BBC radio program he'd hosted. Paul recounted how, after first hearing my recording of "Fabulous," it became one of his favorite tunes. He then played my version on the BBC program. It brought to mind that elite talents remember who started the music and who opened the gates for them. I'd been there at the beginning of rock and roll, and I *am* in the history books. It was—and still is—gratifying for me to know I've left a legacy of sorts for the Gracie family.

It certainly was a proud moment and a great honor to receive the PMA's Lifetime Achievement Award. Sadly, the distinction came so late in my career that my parents were no longer around to share the honor. My father, as I mentioned earlier, passed away in 1977. After his death, my mother remained in New Jersey, residing in a lovely apartment of her own, near my brother Bob. Mom survived my dad by 25 years and during that time we visited her at least every other week. When she passed away in 2002, I was there to hold her hand during that arduous moment. In spite of all the hurt between us, we knew our relationship was one of love and devotion to the end.

Regretfully, I was unable to attend my mother's funeral, which was to be held five days later. Joan and I were scheduled to leave for a month-long tour of Germany and England a few days before that. I hated to go, but the venues were booked many months in advance. I agonized over the issue with my brothers Frank and Bob. Both agreed I should honor those dates; that mom would have understood the obligations of my business. My brothers took charge and gave her a beautiful send-off, and I had the comfort of knowing I'd been there when my mother took her last breath. She had a good life of 86 years, God bless her soul.

The last time I saw Dick Clark was in August of 1997, when he attended the *American Bandstand* 40th Anniversary Reunion. The festivities were held in the old WFIL-TV building, home of the original *Bandstand* studio at 46th and Market Streets. Today, the facility has been refurbished and houses the Philadelphia Enterprise Center, an organization dedicated to the promotion of neighborhood entrepreneurs. Pennsylvania Governor Tom Ridge and Philadelphia Mayor Ed Rendell were on hand at the 40th Anniversary Reunion to designate the facility a state historical landmark. Also in attendance were many of the artists who performed regularly on *American Bandstand*. Among them were Chubby Checker, Danny and the Juniors, The Dovells, Fabian, Connie Francis, and Bobby Rydell. As we reminisced and kibbitzed about the "good old days," Chubby suddenly put one hand on my shoulder and bellowed out his own rendition of "Butterfly" as he mimicked the flight of the insect with the other. For a moment, I was transported back to the Brooklyn Paramount.

I had no reservations at all about seeing Dick Clark face to face again. I hadn't learned about the incestuous relationship between he and Bernie Lowe until years after the fact, and there had never really been any direct confrontation between Dick and me. If anybody carried any guilt, he had to be the one, not me. Accompanied by Charlie, Jr., I entered the building with complete confidence. But I'd be lying if I said I knew what to expect.

Dick's wife Carrie was there, too. When we walked in, the two of them were sitting behind a desk in a tiny office. Dick appeared to be signing a stack of programs. I stuck my head in the room and sharply announced myself: "Hey, Dick, Charlie Gracie!"

He looked up at me and without missing a beat, replied, "Hey Charlie, you look great! You haven't changed a bit."

"Look who's talking, the eternal teenager!"

"What have you been up to, Charlie?"

"Busy as ever. I just returned from a tour of Britain and Austria. You'll never guess who I ran into over there, Freddy Cannon."

"Freddy, really?"

"Yeah, we were on the same bill. It's always a trip to work with Freddy; we have a lot of fun together."

Then my son showed him an old photo he'd brought along of Dick and I standing side by side at the Philadelphia premier of the movie *Jamboree*.

"Gee!" exclaimed the former *Bandstand* host, who also happened to be a self-professed pack rat. "I don't have that one."

"Well I have two copies," Charlie, Jr. told him. "This one's for you. I'd like you to sign the other one for me."

"Sure!" replied Dick.

"Okay," said my son as Dick signed the photo, "can we get a few pictures of you two guys together?"

"Yeah, absolutely!" said Dick.

I didn't know it then, but those would be the last photos I'd ever take with him. All told, Dick and I spent about 15 minutes chatting and not a word was said about the past. I certainly had no intention of bringing up anything at that point. Obviously, Dick didn't care to discuss it either. Better to let sleeping dogs lie. Deep down, Dick, who had the power to make or break a performer, knew very well what had transpired. Many insiders also knew what happened. Yet that day (and afterwards) we all pretended as if none of it had ever taken place.

Given what occurred all those years ago, I could've carried the bitterness with me. But I chose not to. It's all history now. I'm including it in this memoir so that the public will know the truth.

Late in his life, Dick endured a prolonged period of serious health issues before he passed away in April 2012. Believe me, I wouldn't wish that on *anybody*. Still, I sometimes think of the old expression: "What goes around, comes around."

15

I'M ALL RIGHT

"Most people don't know that the Beatles loved those old Cameo masters," said Thom Bell, one of the primary architects of the Philadelphia Soul genre and who worked at Cameo-Parkway during the time Bernie Lowe sold the company. "In 1967, Allen Klein, who then represented the Beatles, offered Cameo-Parkway a deal to buy everything. That's how he got the masters."[62]

Under Klein, who, at various times, has been described as tenacious, blunt, predatory, and aggressive (those being the complimentary comments), Cameo-Parkway became ABKCO. During the early 1970s ABKCO sporadically reissued a handful of Cameo-Parkway masters, including "Butterfly" and "Fabulous."[63] Charlie Gracie, of course, received no royalties from the sales of those songs. After that, the Cameo-Parkway masters lay in a vault for three decades while the existing vinyl was bootlegged over and over around the world.

Meanwhile, Allen Klein's health began to deteriorate,[64] and his son Jody took over as ABKCO's controller. In 2002, Jody oversaw the remastering of the Rolling Stones' albums that had been recorded during the 1960s and he subsequently received much acclaim for the quality of those reissues. In 2005, ABKCO finally began to issue compact discs of remastered Cameo-Parkway recordings.

If my dad hadn't bought me my first guitar back in 1946, I really can't imagine what I'd be doing today. Yet it comes as a great surprise to most people when they discover that I seldom pick up my guitar at home. I'm a showman; I want to entertain! Like every other performer, I need an audience. If I wasn't performing professionally you'd probably find me out there singing gratuitously at senior centers and retirement facilities simply because it brings me great joy and a deep sense of personal satisfaction. (I also try to remain creative. As I lie in bed at night waiting to fall asleep, potential tunes sometime flash through my mind. And once in a while I'll come up with an idea for a new song.) I honestly don't do anything special to prepare for a performance. I just go out there and begin to sing and play. Of course, at my age, it takes a song or two until my fingers loosen up, but they still function fine. Many performers will work with a set list and play exactly what's on there, whether or not it's to the audience's liking. Not me. I simply play whatever comes into my mind. The musicians who regularly back me understand this. Whenever I use my own guys, it's just, "B-flat, fellas." Then I begin to play and they jump right in. The only time I'll use a prepared set list is with a band that's not familiar with my extemporaneous nature. For example, when I go overseas, it's necessary for me to have one.

After three or four songs, I can feel my audience. Whatever the mood calls for is what I'll do. I can sense whether the people want to dance or if they want to sing along with me. If I perceive they want a few more slow tunes, I'll stick with the ballads. But generally speaking, I like to play "up" for my audience. I'm there to create excitement. Some guys will get out there and do four ballads in a row. Excuse me? Where did *you* learn show business pal? If you sing four ballads in a row you'll put your audience to sleep. Wake 'em up!

My personality is also a crucial aspect of my act. A performer needs to know how to touch the people. As I progress through an evening and get my repertoire going, I *feed* off the audience and at a certain point I really begin to cook. When that occurs, when I'm playing and singing well, when the guys behind me are playing great and the people are eating it up, I don't want to get off the stage. That's what show business is all about. I'm there for my audience. I sing and play my heart out because I want them to enjoy themselves. I hope they go home and say, "We went to see Charlie Gracie last night and, man, we had a helluva time!"

Over the years I've been blessed to work with some of the greatest entertainers in show business and I've always made it my business to pay attention, to watch those people who came before me. That's how you learn your trade. On one particular occasion I went into the Latin Casino in Cherry Hill, New Jersey for what was supposed to have been a two-week gig. Instead, I stayed there for a year and a half! And between shows I observed many of the all-time greats: Milton Berle, Myron Cohen, Van Johnson, Joe E. Lewis, Sophie Tucker, Henny Youngman, the list goes on. I learned something from each one of them. Another consummate pro I went to school on was Britain's Max Bygraves. Not only an actor and a crooner, Max was at one time the United Kingdom's top comic. How many other guys can say they worked with such a prodigious entertainer?

Giving heed to these iconic performers enabled me to develop the ability and the confidence to handle any situation on the stage. I was once booked to do a show outdoors at New York City's Lincoln Center before 5,000 people. When I arrived that afternoon, the agent said to me, "Charlie, would you do me a favor? I've got about 1,500 people already sitting in a park nearby. Could you go over there and do a couple of numbers for them before the show?"

I didn't even say "yes." I simply said, "Do you have a microphone and an amplifier? That's all I need." Then I went out there, plugged in my guitar, and did an hour and a half. I sang, I did some comedy, and I had the people falling out of their chairs. After all my years in the business, watching comedians work, I *know* how to tell a funny story. It's all in the timing. And sometimes it can really save your bacon.

Like the time I performed at a Roots of Rock/Doo-Wop Concert held at Southern Connecticut State University. Two numbers into my set—in front of 1,200 people—a string popped on my Guild. The guitar went completely out of tune and needed repairs before I could continue. Another guitarist in the backing band was kind enough to take my instrument backstage to restring it, but I knew that process would take about 20 minutes. So without skipping a beat, I began to tell the audience some of those colorful stories from my early days in show business that you're now familiar with if you've been paying attention. Before long, I had those people in a state of rip-roaring laughter. In fact, things went so well that I began to wonder if they remembered I was supposed to sing and play for them! I eventually was able to complete my musical performance, after which I received a prolonged standing ovation and callbacks for two encores.

"My God, Charlie," the show's promoter exclaimed after I left the stage. "I never saw anything like that in all my life!"

Some people might consider a performance like that to be amazing (the following day I received phone calls and e-mails from many who'd seen the show, asking if the "broken guitar string" episode was part of my act), but to me it's run of the mill. "I've been doing this since I was 10 years old," I told that promoter. "That person you saw out there isn't just *me*. It's *all* the people I've drawn from over a lifetime." I'm not saying I've been sent here by God to entertain people. There are plenty of guys out there who can sing or play better than I can. (They might even be better looking—and possibly smarter!) But *whatever* I do, whatever magnetism I project, it has worked well for more than 60 years. Don't even ask me to define it; I just do what I do.

One thing for sure, I've always kept my act clean and free of sexual innuendos. I could have added some kind of sexual edge and probably gone a long way with it. But as I mentioned earlier, I never wanted to be an "Elvis." I was happy being Charlie Gracie. I believe one of the reasons my fans have respect for me is because I've been married to the same woman for more than 56 years. Whenever I do a show in Britain I tell my audience, "Ladies and gentlemen, my bride's with me tonight. There's my wife Joan sitting out there among you." I go on to remind them, "We spent our honeymoon here in 1958," and ask Joan to stand up and be acknowledged, and they love it. Fifty-six years married to the same woman? That's unheard of in show business; sometimes I can't believe it myself. Joan has her own set of groupies over there, and she even signs autographs for them. She's amazing!

Another edge I have on my contemporaries is that I appear younger than my actual age. It's not because of anything special that I do. It's simply a case of genetics, which I owe to my mother and father. One time, a fellow I knew years ago from South Philly came up to me and said, "Charlie, don't you ever change? You look exactly like you did when you were a kid. Your hair may be gray, and you may have put on a little weight, but your face hasn't changed."

"C'mon now, cut it out," I replied. "You're making me feel *too* good. I'll have to buy you dinner!"

Although I might appear young for my age, there's no denying one particular flaw—my inability to remember someone's name. That fault continues to make me crazy. I'm a gregarious sort of guy and I encounter a lot of people, many whom I haven't seen for a number of years. Naturally, the physical appearance of some of those individuals has changed drastically, and I don't recognize them. Inevitably a guy will yell out to me, "Hey Charlie, how ya doin'?"

"Uh, do I know you?"

"Charlie, we went to school together!"

"When?"

"About 60 years ago."

"Holy smoke, gimme a break!"

Actually, it's hard for me to believe I'm 78 years old and still going strong. I'm very blessed to still have my family *and* my health. I do get a few little aches and pains every once in a while, but nothing drastic. I'm not incapacitated in any way. I don't know many guys my age that have the mindset and the energy I possess. Whenever I perform, I often overhear younger guys in the backing band let out a "phew." I'll say to them, "Yo! We're doing two shows tonight, and you're tired already? In the early days I often did *five* shows a night— by myself. So let's go pal, it's time to rock and roll!"

In the fall of 1991, Joan and my daughter Angela accompanied me while I did a string of performances in Bologna, Italy and Germany. It was during this tour that I cut my *Rockin' Italy* album at Cesena

Studios near Bologna. For that session I was backed by a fine regional rockabilly swing band called The Jumpin' Shoes (who now go by the name The Good Fellas). The Shoes was a six-piece at the time, featuring Piero Balleggi, one of the best rock and roll and boogie-woogie pianists in Italy, and on double bass my good friend, "Lucky the Slapper" Lachini. On *Rockin' Italy* I reprised my big Cameo hits, while also paying homage to classic jive artists such as Joe Turner ("Flip, Flop and Fly"), Louis Jordan ("Caldonia"), Lou Monte ("Darktown Strutters' Ball/The Sheik of Araby"), and Louis Prima "Just a Gigolo/I Ain't Got Nobody"). *Rockin' Italy* is a *hell* of an album. But what happened next was all too familiar. The recording sold fairly well among collectors and to my overseas fan base, but once again it failed to reach the masses due to a lack of airplay. (Nevertheless, in 2011 I performed a 20-year reunion concert held in Bologna to commemorate the release of the *Rockin' Italy* album. As soon as I walked onstage and opened my mouth the people loved me because I spoke their native tongue.)

In 1999, accompanied by Joan, I was delighted to return to Italy. During that tour, we were fortunate to have enough time off to visit Sicily. Since this was my first visit to the "old country," it made me very aware of my roots, and was something I'll never forget. As our flight from Rome touched down on the island of my ancestors, the hairs on my arms actually rose up and I felt chills. When we arrived at my grandparents' town of Sant'Anna, which is located on top of a mountain, I came face to face for the first time with my second cousins and their families. Thank God I was able to speak Sicilian, because they didn't understand a word of English. My cousins own several homes in Sant'Anna, and since one of them happened to be vacant at the time, we had the use of it while we were there. During our week's stay, we traveled by automobile to other neighboring towns for a bit of shopping and managed to get in some sightseeing along the way.

By far the most moving experience of our stay in Sicily involved a visit to the family burial plot. You can imagine what an emotional event it was for me, walking the land of my grandparents and seeing about 20 tombstones with the same name as mine on each one of them.

Ever since then, when I visit the cemetery in Philadelphia where my grandparents are buried and I look at my grandfather's tombstone to see my own name of Calogero, I "speak" to my ancestors in Sicilian and tears actually well up in my eyes.

Our visit to Italy proved to be unforgettable. As well as performing in the homeland of my ancestors, I was afforded the opportunity to play in the neighboring countries of Austria and Switzerland. And since my resurgence overseas I've also been fortunate to perform in Belgium, France, Holland, and Ireland.

Besides *Rockin' Italy* and the many other full-length albums I've recorded, some really unique recordings of mine continue to survive. Take the two live performances I made with The Lennerockers, a hard-driving five-piece neo-rockabilly band from Hagen, Germany. One track is a gospel medley of "Just a Closer Walk with Thee/How Great Thou Art," and the other "Rockin' Pneumonia and the Boogie Woogie Flu." Both were recorded live in Hagen, Germany in 1991. I didn't realize it at the time, but those performances were also caught on videotape, and both can currently be viewed on the internet.[65] There are also the 20 songs I cut in 1996 in the Netherlands, backed by neo-rockabilly singer Phil Friendly and the Bellhops. Among them—complete with bass fiddle and steel guitar—are some true country classics, such as "Hey Good Lookin'" and "Just Because." All of those numbers can be found on the Dutch CD titled *Rock 'n' Roll Legends—Vol. 1 Charlie Gracie with Phil Friendly.* Finally, a number of distinct tracks I've done here and there exist on various compilation albums and CDs, while bootleg recordings of other songs I've done seem to surface on a regular basis.

I've cut LPs all over the world, but it wasn't until 2001 that I finally made an album completely on American soil. That was the year I recorded *I'm All Right* for Lanark Records, a Lancaster, Pennsylvania company owned by Quentin Jones. After learning of my strong track record, Quentin called to see if I'd be interested in recording for him. We got together and talked, and the more I learned about Lanark, the more I felt that company would be a good fit for everybody involved. "Okay," I finally told him, "let's go into the studio and make some music!"

Quentin is someone I would call a multifaceted talent. In addition to producing *I'm All Right*, he also played some guitar and bass on the recording. A single taken from that album was a duet I sang with Graham Nash called "A Little Too Soon to Tell." The album's title song "I'm All Right" is dedicated to Eddie Cochran, whose name I continue to mention whenever I get the opportunity. I consider that Lanark CD to be a wonderful tribute to a dear friend we lost way too soon. Shortly after recording it, in April 2000, I had the honor of headlining the 40th Anniversary Tribute Concert to Eddie, held in England at Bristol's Colston Hall. (That particular performance was recorded and later released on DVD.)

I've been touring and performing throughout Great Britain for so many years that many overseas gigs tend to blur one into another. But two particular tours, both involving Eddie Cochran, will always stand out in my mind. The first included the aforementioned 40th anniversary tribute and the second occurred in September 2006. The latter included a pilgrimage to Rowdon Hill, the site of Eddie's fatal limo crash near the town of Chippenham, and to the hospital in Bath where Eddie spent his final hours. There, in the Eddie Cochran Memorial Garden, the planners of the annual festival, led by Gwen Hale (a long-time devotee of Eddie and myself), unveiled a six-foot-high black granite monument of Eddie. The marker portrayed one of rock's early icons in a classic pose, singing and playing his Gretch guitar, and it was a great honor to be selected to unveil it. It's hard for me to believe Eddie's now been gone for more than half a century. He was just two years younger than me and had a promising future ahead of him. Talk about destiny.

It never ceases to amaze me that ever since my 1980 "comeback," people continue to offer me the opportunity to record. It happened again in 2004, when I was contacted by a producer who said, "I've been a fan of yours for a long time, Charlie. I'd like to cut some music with you."

"Let's go," I replied, and that fall in Berlin we recorded the album titled *Just Hangin' Around*. Unfortunately, *Just Hangin' Around* was also an unintentionally apt description of the album content: a relatively unexciting collection of pop-rock songs previously recorded by other artists. Nevertheless, in 2007 I recorded *Gracie Swings Again* for the same German outfit. This time I was backed by some of Europe's finest neo-rockabilly musicians. What's more, to capture a '50s sound we recorded everything live—complete takes, no overdubs—with genuine 1950s equipment. And to top things off, the session was done on a vintage mono tape recorder from that era. Given those circumstances, it wasn't surprising that *Gracie Swings Again* turned out to be a far cry from its unexceptional predecessor.

You never know what to expect once you sign a recording agreement. And any potential surprise doesn't necessarily stem from the quality of music that is produced. I once made a record that I quickly forgot about after it disappeared without a trace. Then one day I received a knock on my door from the fellow who'd made the recording. "I sold one copy of your record, Charlie," he told me in all seriousness. "I want to pay you for it. Here's the money." Can you imagine wanting to pay me for one record? I tell you, some guys are truly goofy!

Fortunately, at this late stage in my career, I've become involved with a stable recording company that is run in an efficient, business-like manner: ABKCO Music and Records. Nearly four decades ago, Allen Klein purchased the Cameo-Parkway master recordings and, except for a brief period of time, kept them locked in a vault. Neither I nor anyone else knew exactly why. I never did meet Klein, but in 2004 I was introduced to his son Jody. "Charlie," he said, "we're going to put out a box set of four compact discs comprising the history of the Cameo and Parkway labels. Since you started the company off with two big hits, we intend to include them in the set.

"Wonderful," I replied.

Jody and I then had a nice chat, during which he asked me, "What kind of financial arrangement would you be interested in?"

"Listen Jody," I told him. "I've been through this process a thousand times in my life. At this point I've signed contracts with a dozen or more different recording companies. Monetarily speaking, what we're talking about here is insignificant to me. But if the product sells and you want to pay me, I'd truly appreciate it." And that's how I left things.

ABKCO released the *Cameo-Parkway 1957–1967* box set in 2005, and shortly after that Jody Klein came to see me perform at a hot rockabilly venue in New York City called the Rodeo Bar and Grill. "My God, Charlie, I've *never* seen anybody perform like you do," he said after the show. "I had no idea you sang and played that well. And you have such tremendous stage presence and command of what you're doing."

"Well, I've only been doing it for 50 years," I quipped.

"The Cameo-Parkway box sold very well," Jody went on to say. "Our next project will be to release individual compact discs on Cameo-Parkway's major artists. We intend to put out *The Best of Charlie Gracie 1956–1958*, which will also include some previously unreleased tracks."

"Fantastic," I thought. "After so many years, high-quality copies of my Cameo recordings will finally be available to my fans worldwide." After listening to the *Best of* compact disc it was obvious that the production expertise of the team led by Teri Landi (who later shared a "Best Historical Album" Grammy Award for the Rolling Stones' *Charlie Is My Darling—Ireland 1965* CD) had paid off. Musically speaking, those recordings are a testament to the perfect marriage Bernie Lowe and I had at Cameo. There's not one bad recording on that CD. Not one. ABKCO did such a remarkable job on the package that I immediately offered to help with the promotional campaign, making myself available for a series of coast-to-coast radio interviews with Jody Klein and Teri Landi.

Believe it or not, the treatment I received from Jody and his team at ABKCO—which included Joe Parker, with Tracey Jordan, Michael Kirk Allen, and Teri—has been superlative. I offer additional praise to Jody because he proved to be a man of his word. ABKCO sent me royalty statements and actually *paid* me. After the first check arrived, I said to Joan, "I'm not cashing this; it has to be a mistake!" I held the check for a week. Then, for good measure, I held it for another week. Lo and behold, when I finally deposited the check it went through. I was stunned. This was a far cry from the way Cameo treated me. I called Jody, who's well aware of my history with Bernie Lowe, and thanked the man.

"Charlie, you deserve it!" he exclaimed.

Now, here's the real kicker: I made nearly as much money from the sales of my "Best of" ABKCO CD as I did from selling 3 million copies of "Butterfly" in 1957. True story! Somewhere Bernie Lowe is probably demanding, "Where's *my* cut?" As I said earlier, "What goes around comes around."

In 2005, Philadelphia-based film producer Shawn Swords contacted me to ask if I'd be interested in working with him on a documentary of my life. "I first saw and heard you perform at Moore's Inlet some years back and I was very impressed by the incredible rapport you have with your audience," Shawn explained. "After conducting some follow-up research I think you have a compelling story to tell."

I was kind of surprised. Given the usual "bad boy" bios that make it to the screen these days, I thought perhaps my life lacked the sensationalism that most people have come to expect in those things. But Shawn and his team convinced me that my life was indeed one people could identify with. "Well, okay," I told him. "If you believe there's a story there, let's do it!"

Within a matter of weeks Shawn and his crew set to work on the project. Initially they shot some interview footage at my home. Then I took them on a little tour of my old South Philly neighborhood, back to those row homes on Pierce Street where I spent my childhood. One of Shawn's associates traveled to England to film me performing at the weeklong Eddie Cochran Tribute Festival in Chippenham, where I shared the stage with Little Richard and a host of other original '50s rockers. When I saw the final cut I thought Shawn did an excellent job. I was also honored to see show business luminaries Graham Nash, Peter Noone (Herman's Hermits), Tommy James, Andy Williams, Chubby Checker, Frankie Avalon, and a slew of others, who appear in the program to recognize my contributions as a musician and performer. The DVD, titled *Charlie Gracie: Fabulous!*, was released in 2007. An updated and expanded edition followed in 2011 and was shown on 500 public television stations around the United States.

Good things continued to happen as I rocked on through the new millennium. In 2011 I was contacted by Bill Kenwright, a British entrepreneur who's a big '50s music fan. He's also the majority owner of Liverpool's Everton Football Club, a soccer team founded in 1878. Bill has his own radio program on the BBC and he was in the process of creating a "concert they never gave," in which various actors portray famous American rock and roll stars who in reality never actually played together. To close the first half of the show, Bill didn't want an actor; he wanted a genuine artist from that bygone era. With that in mind, he contacted Paul Barrett, my agent in Britain. Paul then explained the idea behind Kenwright's show to me. "Charlie, this is a nice shot for you. You'll spend a week in Liverpool and Bill will pay you handsomely." (What's more, the show was to be staged at the Empire, the very same theater where Paul McCartney came to see me perform in the late 1950s.)

I accepted Bill's offer, and Joan and I were off to Britain once again. I did one performance each weeknight and two on Saturday and Sunday. It was the easiest role I ever had—I played "Charlie Gracie!" It was a wonderful experience and Bill treated us extremely well. One night, after viewing the performance, he told me, "Charlie, you're as great as ever. You haven't diminished one iota in all these years. Earlier today I was at a meeting with the composer Andrew Lloyd Webber. Did you know he's also a big fan of yours? He asked me to say 'hello' and convey his best wishes to you." Wow! Andrew Lloyd Webber, one of my fans—who could have guessed?

Later in 2011, I put the finishing touches on my latest CD, again collaborating with Lanark Records and Quentin Jones. We originally planned to have the renowned musician/songwriter/producer Al Kooper play on a couple of tracks. But after Al's participation he told Quentin, "I've long admired Charlie and I haven't had this much fun in years. If you want me to, I'll produce his entire CD."

Bob Dylan, Jimi Hendrix, and The Rolling Stones are just a few of the stars Al Kooper has worked with. As far as I was concerned, anyone with Al's track record has earned the right to exercise his creative talent. "If he'd like to produce, be my guest," I told Quentin. (As it turned out, Al and Quentin co-produced the album.) To back me, Al then put together a crack unit led by Jimmy Vivino, guitarist for *The Tonight Show*'s house band and *Late Night with Conan*

O'Brien. To have a supporting cast of such talented, high-profile professionals was very flattering.

After hearing the completed CD, Jody Klein was so impressed that he offered to have ABKCO release it. How reassuring to know that ABKCO had enough faith in my talent to make that investment. As well as having issued my Cameo-Parkway *Best of* CD in 2006, the folks at ABKCO have also seen me perform. They believe I still have the moxie. And the CD's title, *For the Love of Charlie* (suggested by Teri Landi), shows a high regard for my professional integrity.

For the Love of Charlie offers a diverse collection of songs: a little rock, pop, country, and blues. Graham Nash returns for another guest performance on a song I wrote called "Rock 'n' Roll Heaven," and Peter Noone (Herman's Hermits) can be heard on another of my compositions, "All I Wanna Do Is Love You." It's funny how some things come about. At one of my New York performances I'd spotted Peter in the audience and offhandedly began to sing, "I'm 'Enery the Eighth, I Am..." After the show he came up to me, gave me a big hug and said, "Charlie, I've been a fan of yours for a long time. If you ever need an additional vocalist on one of your recordings I'd be happy to contribute." Once we began to record the CD I recalled Peter's offer and invited him on board.

My favorite track on *For the Love of Charlie* is a gospel-tinged number penned by Quentin Jones. It's a country song called "And Now I Win" done in a Johnny Cash vein, and it's quite moving. It could have been released as a single. I've always had an affinity for gospel music. You may recall that earlier in my career I recorded two such numbers for Cadillac Records. Considering how green I was at the time, I thought those tracks came out pretty well. Now, near the back end of my career, I finally have an opportunity to do an entire gospel album. Once again, Quentin Jones is at the production helm. As a matter of fact, Dee Dee Sharp, the former Cameo recording star who began her career as a gospel singer, is collaborating on the album. Dee Dee sounds better than ever, and if everything goes according to plan it should be out in the near future.

I've often been asked, "Charlie, if you could have one 'do-over' in your life, what would it be?" My first reaction to that query is that

I have no regrets whatsoever. I've made a good living for myself and for my family. That's what's most important to me. My home is paid for, my son and daughter are grown, and I can relax a bit. I've never been a materialistic person so I don't need *things* to make me happy. If I wanted to put a Rolls-Royce or a Bentley in my driveway, I could do that tomorrow. But what purpose would that serve, to *impress* others? I'm at peace with myself. But to leave things there would be to duck the "do-over" question. And I did say in the opening chapter of this book that I was prepared to reveal everything about my life. So I suppose I'm not quite finished here.

I do realize some of the detrimental things that occurred over the years were partly my own fault. I acted imprudently in ways that certainly came back to haunt me. For instance, it still hurts that I was unable to prevent the contentious atmosphere that existed between my mother and Joan. Yet I'm not sure I could have done things differently, in a way that would have prevented all that unpleasantness. It was my dream to see our entire family live harmoniously under one roof. But sometimes, despite our best intentions, things just don't work out the way we plan. Not every story can end "happily ever after."

I also believe everything that happened to me did so for a reason—even the Cameo Records debacle. Who knows what I might have attained if I hadn't been blackballed by Bernie Lowe and his cohorts? In hindsight, I should have kept my mouth shut. I liken myself to Marlon Brando in the film *On the Waterfront*, when he refused to throw a boxing match for the mob. Had Brando taken that dive he would have gone on to become more successful in the fight game. Likewise, had I taken the dive for Bernie Lowe over royalties, I, too, "coulda been a contender." Instead, I got *crushed*.

But I can't pin it all on Bernie Lowe. My dad also had a hand in the tragedy. He never expressed any regrets for insisting that I demand a proper accounting from Cameo. That was something we just never discussed. (I realize my dad had my best interests at heart, even though his council turned out to be ill advised.)

Ultimately, I have myself to blame. I was a naïve and inexperienced young kid with no business sense. What the hell did I know? Bernie Rothbard was right. I should have heeded his advice and played by their rules. But when Bernie said, "Don't go there, Charlie," my obstinacy got the best of me and I suffered the consequences.

I hope I don't sound too egotistical when I say–barring that setback with Cameo—I could have been one of rock and roll history's household names. Yet when weighing my talent against those considered to be the greats of rock and roll, I believe I'm just as good as a lot of them, and even better than some. During the lean years, that was a bitter pill to swallow, but over time I've learned to accept it.

I'm not a bitter person and I don't hold any animosity toward the people who held me back. Many talented artists go through life and never catch that big break. At least I had my 15 minutes of fame and I'm tickled to death to have experienced that. At the same time, my difficulties with Bernie Lowe taught me that being principled doesn't guarantee justice in this world. So when I look at my situation from a worldly perspective, perhaps I did blow it. But when I view things in regards to eternal life, I can honestly say I didn't make a mistake; I chose the correct road. I believe strength, purpose, and true faith are often found through adversity. This life is only a passing thing. As the prophet sayeth, "All the rest is vanity."

With regard to both my family and the business that I love, I believe it's the Good Lord who's kept me alive, sane, and successful. When adversity arose, I didn't rely on a crutch such as drugs or alcohol, I prayed. And He was there for me. I'll state it right here: God doesn't owe me a thing. It certainly wasn't easy, but I've learned that with His help—and in His time—things will work out for those who trust in His word.

At this advanced stage of my career, I largely attribute my capabilities in the recording studio to my years of performing live. With music, like most everything else, it's "use it or lose it." Throughout my life I continued to hone my profession. I kept the knife sharpened. And I reassured myself: "If ever a hit record should come my way again, I'd still be able to get up onstage and deliver the goods." So when musician/producer/promoter Gary Lefkowith contacted me just about the time ABKCO was preparing to release *For the Love of Charlie* in 2011, I was ready.

I'd recently met Gary at a performance where I opened for

Chubby Checker. After I finished my segment of the show, Gary, who's been Chubby's musical director for many years, approached me and said with a sense of urgency, "Charlie, Chubby's in a jam. His regular guitar player didn't show tonight and Chubby wants to know if you'd mind sitting in for him."

"Why not?" I told Gary as I unpacked my guitar for a second time that evening. Chubby's a gentleman who's always treated me with respect, and I consider him to be a true friend. I backed him on his 45-minute set, after which he thanked me profusely. "It's my pleasure," I told him. "I love you, man!"

Not long after that, a very excited Gary Lefkowith called me. "Charlie, I have a song for you!" he exclaimed. "It's an uptempo number called "[Be My] Baby Doll." I think you'd knock it out of the ballpark."

"Gee, that's great news," I told him, "but I think cutting a single with you at this particular time might conflict with my new CD. ABKCO's treated me very well and the last thing I want is to create any conflict with them."

"Don't worry about that," Gary explained. "This will be a separate entity aimed at an entirely different market. It won't affect your new CD in any way. The song I have in mind won't even sound remotely like anything on it." Considering things from that standpoint I figured, "Well, why not. What the hell do I have to lose?" I agreed to record "Baby Doll."

After all the sessions I've done my career, there's still something magical about going into a recording studio. To give a great live performance is certainly a thrill; when I'm onstage and that spotlight's on me, *I'm* the one who takes the rap. Still, no matter how great the performance, once it's over it's gone—vanished. But a recording is permanent. You can grasp it in your hand; you can share it with others. A recording offers, if not the probability of success, at least the *possibility*. It enables you to dream!

Gary stopped by my home to give me the lyrics and the music for "Baby Doll." I studied the song for a day or two, which, in most cases is really not long enough. But "Baby Doll" came easy for me.

"We'll cut it at your house," said Gary.

"What do you mean, 'cut it at my house?' You going to use a tape recorder?"

"No," replied Gary. "There's a new recording process available now. Without getting too technical on you, I'll call it a 'little black box.' Professionally it's known as an Mbox. We use it with Pro Tools software to create a sort of portable recording studio. All you do is plug the microphone and guitar into it, then just sing and play the chords—the rhythm—to back yourself up. Don't worry, my partner Mike Rogers will take care of all the technical stuff. He's a whiz at it."

I have to say, I was somewhat skeptical. Who ever heard of making a professional-quality song in your own den! But after we cut "Baby Doll" and Gary played it back he exclaimed: "That sounds great, Charlie!"

I couldn't believe the results myself. "My God, that does sound incredible," I seconded. "What do we do now?"

"I'm going to mix this thing properly," replied Gary. "I want to boost the sound. I'll get back to you in a couple of weeks."

Gary then took my recording of "Baby Doll" into the studio and enhanced the ambience of the overall production with an additional guitar as well as drums. The lead guitarist on the song is a fellow named Richie Scarlet. Dubbed "The Emperor of Rock 'n' Roll," Scarlet is best known for his blazing guitar work with Frehley's Comet, the band of former Kiss guitarist Ace Frehley. When I got a chance to speak with Richie he told me that despite cutting his teeth on the British Invasion and guys like Jeff Beck, Jimi Hendrix, and David Bowie, he was also an admirer of Eddie Cochran—and of yours truly! Things like that really embarrass me. "You have to be crazy," I told him. "You outplay me two-to-one!"

Richie did a fantastic solo on "Baby Doll." After hearing the finished product, I thought the record resounded with the roar of a rumbling freight train. But my wife and son didn't share my enthusiasm. "Perhaps it's a little too raucous for you at this point in your career," they both told me. "It sounds like it's aimed at a much younger audience."

"You're crazy," I protested. "It's knock-'em-dead rock and roll. What's the difference how old I am, or what age group hears it?"

Still, Gary and I knew we did face one particular problem. Although I'd continued to record throughout my career, during that entire time span the public essentially heard just the three or four songs that were hits for me back in the '50s. It came as no surprise then, when Gary and I walked into one particular radio station with "Baby Doll," the immediate reaction from the program director was: "Well, this guy's last hit was 50 years ago. He must be some kind of 'has-been.'" Fortunately for us, the program director listened to my record. "Wow!" he exclaimed to one of his coworkers. "I have to admit, this guy still has it!"

Of course, I know I still have what it takes, but you won't find me bragging about it. Fortunately, other radio stations had the same positive reaction to "Baby Doll." Soon after its release, the song began to draw a little play here and a little play there. Then, like a brush fire after a match has ignited it, the flames began to spread. "Baby Doll" caught on as listeners called in and asked to hear the song. I began to receive requests for it at my gigs and, before I knew it, "Baby Doll" started to sell. As 2012 began, my new hot single was being played in many areas around the country and I was booked on a series of promotional events. Sensing a story, the *Philadelphia Inquirer* published a front-page article: "Charlie Gracie Bounces Back." All I could think was, "With headlines of the U. S. presidential primaries dominating the front pages," there I was! The *Inquirer* article focused on the airplay that Dan Reed and WXPN were giving the single and CD sales, which, according to *Billboard's* weekly Nielsen Soundscan report, put the song at number 1 in the Philadelphia region. Nationwide, "Baby Doll" was number 88 on the Pop charts, due in large part to Kid Kelly, who was playing the record on Sirius XM's pop station 20 on 20. In New York we were getting support and airplay from Rita Houston at WFUV and Rob Lipshutz at WXPK. To top things off, the BBC added "Baby Doll" to its playlist, affording me my first British airplay of a current recording in 50 years. (Michael Bainbrook, Jeff Smith, and Mark Hagen helped make that happen.) As you've probably realized by now, I'm usually not at a loss for words. But this unexpected development in my career left me speechless.

Sometimes in life it's strange how things unfold. Gary Lefkowith came out of nowhere and, just as he predicted, "Baby Doll" didn't conflict with the sales of For the Love of Charlie. In fact, I believe "Baby Doll" actually drew greater attention to my ABKCO CD. With its amped-up rockabilly sound, the song not only reconnected me to some of my older fans who may have lost track, but it also introduced me to a whole new generation. For example, shortly thereafter I was booked into The Bitter End in New York City's Greenwich Village, where the sold-out audience was a cross-section of ages. My program that evening consisted of several tunes from For the Love of Charlie along with "Baby Doll." Fittingly, Gary Lefkowith put together my backing band for that show. That group included Richie Scarlet who came out to play the guitar solo on "Baby Doll' just as he had done on the record. It was truly a spectacular evening, which drew several standing ovations. To top things off, in attendance were Jody Klein and his entire executive team.

I've always maintained to those closest to me that I'd be tickled to death to make the charts once again before I leave this world. That was a nice thought, but although I said it, I never really believed it would happen. Before "Baby Doll" hit I thought I was busy enough, but since that time it has been a challenge for me to honor the many requests for personal appearances. The "Baby Doll" experience has been a real shot in the arm.

There are probably a thousand things I've left out of this book simply because I can't remember them all. And, truth be known, I've grown weary talking about myself. My wife Joan has asked me on numerous occasions, "Charlie, aren't you sick of telling those same stories over and over again?"

But what am I supposed to do? I can't make up a new story every time I discuss my career. I strive to tell the truth so that no one will ever be able to say, "Charlie Gracie said he was in such-and-such a place on a certain night. Well, I was there and I know for a fact that he wasn't." The way I see things, if I get caught in a lie, I'm finished. People will think I exaggerated about my entire career.

At this point in my life I've fulfilled my destiny. Only God knows how much time I have left in this world. But I can honestly say that I'm enjoying this chapter—no pun intended—more than I have any other. Periodically some individual or organization honors me with an award for this or for that: I recently had the privilege of playing for the late Commander Scott Carpenter, one of NASA's seven original astronauts, at the Fiftieth Anniversary Celebration of being the second American to orbit the earth. Or a Shawn Swords comes along and offers to do a video documentary on my life. I'm truly grateful for all those honors, but in the end the most important tribute I can receive is the admiration of my fans. To me, my audience is everything. When I go out in front of the people my goal is to insure that they have a good time. My hope is that they love me as much as I love them. That's what my entire life's been about. Whoever I'm playing to—be it an audience of 200, 2,000, or 20,000—if I can satisfy them and they offer me a standing ovation then I know I've done my job, and I'm a proud and happy man.

"There's a story here that neither of us knew.
Much more than meets the eye..."

–Charlie Gracie,
lyric from "Baby Doll"

CHARLIE GRACIE'S RECORDING DISCOGRAPHY

**Unknown Studio, New York City
(Possibly Late 1951 to Early 1952)**

"Boogie Woogie Blues"* (Cadillac 141-A) *original labels contain erroneous title: "Boogie Boogie Blues" (Revival LP 0001 *Charlie Gracie's Early Recordings*) 1976 (UK Revival LP/CD 3016 *Boogie Woogie Blues and Other Rarities*) 1990 (LP/CD 3016 released on CD, retitled *The Very Best of Charlie Gracie—Vol. 2*) 1993 (GVC CD 1001 *Cool Baby; The Singles and More: 1951 to 1957*) May 2008

"I'm Gonna Sit Right Down and Write Myself a Letter" (Cadillac 141-B); both sides credit Charlie Graci; possibly c. June 1953 (Revival LP 0001) 1976 (UK Revival LP/CD 3016) (GVC CD 1001)

ABC-TV Studio, Philadelphia (July 1952)

"Rock the Joint" [live, *Paul Whiteman's TV Teen Club*; previously unreleased] (GVC CD 1001)

**Unknown Studio, New York City
(Possibly Spring or Summer 1953)**

"All Over Town" [mx: A 6060] (Cadillac 144-A) (Revival LP 0001)

1976 (UK Revival LP/CD 3016) (GVC CD 1001)

"Rockin' and Rollin'" [mx: B 6061] (Cadillac 144-B) released possibly c. October 1953 (Revival LP 0001) 1976 (UK Revival LP/CD 3016) (GVC CD 1001)

Unknown Studio, New York City
(Possibly Summer 1953 to Early 1954)

"T'Ain't No Sin in Rhythm" (Cadillac 154-A) (Revival LP 0001) 1976 (UK Revival LP/CD 3016) (GVC CD 1001)

"Say What You Mean" (Cadillac 154-B) released probably 1954, possibly early 1955 (Revival LP 0001) 1976 (UK Revival LP/CD 3016) (GVC CD 1001)

Gotham Recording Studio, South Philadelphia
(Probably Early 1955)

"My Baby Loves Me" [mx: 7CG 1] (20th Century 5033-A) (Revival LP 0001) 1976 (UK Revival LP 3005 *The Very Best of Charlie Gracie*) October 1988 (UK Revival CD 3005) 1993 (GVC CD 1001)

"Head Home Honey" [mx: 7CG 2] (20th Century 5033-B) released c. March or April 1955 (Revival LP 0001) 1976 (UK Revival LP/CD 3016) (GVC CD 1001)

"Frankie and Johnny" [mx: 7CG 3] (unreleased) recorded at this session or the following one (Revival LP 0001) (UK LP/CD Revival 3005) 1976 (GVC CD 1001)

Gotham Recording Studio, South Philadelphia
(Probably Spring 1955)

"Honey Honey" [mx: 7CG 4] (20th Century 5035-A) (Revival LP 0001) 1976 (UK Revival LP/CD 3016) (GVC CD 1001)

"Wildwood Boogie" [mx: 7CG 5] (20th Century 5035-B) released c. May or June 1955 (Revival LP 0001) 1976 (UK Revival LP/CD 3016) (GVC CD 1001)

Reco-Art Studio Sound Recording, 12th &
Market Streets, Philadelphia (December 30, 1956)

"Butterfly" [mx: 7X105A] (Cameo 105-A) (UK Parlophone R 4020-A) (UK Parlophone GEP 8630) 1957 (Swan LP 501 *Treasure Chest of Hits*) fall 1959 (ABKCO 4012-A) 1972 (UK London LP HAU 8513 *The Cameo- Parkway Sessions*) 1978 (UK Revival LP/CD 3005) (ABKCO CD 92382 *The Best of Charlie Gracie*) 2006 (GVC CD 1001)

"Ninety-Nine Ways" [mx: 7X105-B] (Cameo 105-B) (UK Parlophone R 4020-B) April 1957 (UK Parlophone GEP 8630) 1957 (UK London LP HAU 8513) 1978 (UK Revival LP/CD 3005) (ABKCO CD 92382) (GVC CD 1001)

Reco-Art (April 5, 1957)

"Just Lookin'" [partial] (Cameo 107-B)

"Plaything" [unreleased] (UK LP HAU 8513) 1978 (UK Revival LP/CD 3005) (ABKCO CD 92382) (GVC CD 1001)

Reco-Art (April 9, 1957)

"Fabulous" [mx: 7X107A] (Cameo 107-A) (UK Parlophone R 4313-A) (UK Parlophone GEP 8630) 1957 (ABKCO 4012-B) 1972 (UK London LP HAU 8513) 1978 (UK London EP HLU 10563-A) December 1978 (UK Revival LP/CD 3005) (ABKCO CD 92382) (GVC CD 1001)

"Just Lookin'" [completion] (Cameo 107-B) (UK Parlophone R 4313-B) June 1957 (UK Parlophone GEP 8630) 1957 (UK London LP HAU 8513) 1978 (UK Revival LP/CD 3005) (ABKCO CD 92382)

Reco-Art (June 26, 1957)

"Wanderin' Eyes" (Cameo 111-B) (UK London 8467-B) August 1957 (French EP London REU 1001) 1958 (UK London LP HAU 8513) 1978 (UK Revival LP/CD 3005) (ABKCO CD 92382) (GVC CD 1001)

"Wanderin' Eyes" [alternate take] (GVC CD 1001)

"I Love You So Much It Hurts" [partial] (Cameo 111-A)

Reco-Art (June 26, 1957)

"I Love You So Much It Hurts" [completion] (Cameo 111-A) (UK London HLU 8467-A) (French EP London REU 1001) 1958 (UK London LP HAU 8513) 1978 (UK Revival LP/CD 3005) (ABKCO CD

92382)(GVC CD 1001)

"Trying"* [mx: J90W 4343] (Cameo 141-B) (UK LP HAU 8513)
1978 (UK Revival LP/CD 3005) (ABKCO CD 92382) *Vocal overdub
recorded January 20, 1958

Unknown Studio, New York City (June 1957)

"Cool Baby" (Cameo 118-A) (UK London 8521-A) (French EP London
REU 1001) 1958 (UK London LP HAU 8513) 1978 (UK Revival LP/CD
3005) (ABKCO CD 92382) (GVC CD 1001)

"Cool Baby" [alternate take] (GVC CD 1001)

"Cool Baby" [alternate version; featured in the film *Jamboree*] (Warner
Brothers LP *Jamboree* soundtrack, promotional copies only) 1957 (GVC
CD 1001)

BBC-TV Studio, London, England (1957)

(All with Don Kang and His Frantic Five)

"Tutti Frutti" [live, *Six-Five Special* TV program] (GVC CD 1001)

"I Love You So Much It Hurts" [live, *Six-Five Special*] (GVC CD 1001)

"Guitar Boogie" [live, *Six-Five Special*] (GVC CD 1001)

"Fabulous" [live, *Six-Five Special*] (GVC CD 1001)

Stockton Globe, Stockton, England (August 26, 1957)

"Ko Ko Mo" (Rollercoaster LP 2005 *Charlie Gracie Live at the
Stockton Globe—August 26, 1957*) May 1983 (School Kids CD 1547)
March 1996

"Long Tall Sally" (LP 2005) (CD 1547)

"Trying" (LP 2005) (CD 1547)

"Tutti Frutti" (LP 2005) (CD 1547)

"Flip Flop and Fly" (LP 2005) (CD 1547)

"Sway" (LP 2005) (CD 1547)

"Hound Dog" (LP 2005) (CD 1547)

"Guitar Boogie" (LP 2005) (CD 1547)

"Butterfly" (LP 2005) (CD 1547)

"Ninety-Nine Ways" (LP 2005) (CD 1547)

"I Love You So Much It Hurts" (LP 2005) (CD 1547)

"Fabulous" (LP 2005) (CD 1547)

Reco-Art (October 13, 1957)

"(You Got) a Heart Like a Rock" (Cameo 118-B) (UK London HLU 8521) January 1958 (French EP London REU 1001) 1958 (UK London LP HAU 8513) 1978 (UK Revival LP/CD 3005) (ABKCO CD 92382) (GVC CD 1001)

"Baby You've Changed" [originally unreleased] (UK LP HAU 8513) 1978 (UK Revival LP/CD 3005) (ABKCO CD 92382)

Reco-Art (November 24, 1957)

"Snuggle Up Baby" [originally unreleased] (UK LP HAU 8513) 1978 (UK Revival LP/CD 3005) (ABKCO D 92382)

"Tootsie" [originally unreleased] (UK LP HAU 8513) 1978 (UK Revival LP/CD 3005) (ABKCO CD 92382)

Reco-Art (December 1, 1957)

"Yea, Yea (I'm in Love with You)" [originally unreleased] (ABKCO CD 92382)

Unknown Studio, New York City (1957 or 1958)

"I'm So Glad It's You" [unreleased] (ABKCO CD 92382)

Reco-Art (January 6, 1958)

"Dressin' Up" [partial] (Cameo 127-B) (UK London 8596-B)

Reco-Art (January 10, 1958)

"Dressin' Up" [completion] (Cameo 127-B) (UK London HLU 8596) April 1958 (UK LP HAU 8513) 1978 (UK Revival LP/CD 3005) (ABKCO CD 92382)

"Crazy Girl"* (Cameo 127-A) January 1958 (UK London 8596-A) (UK London LP HAU 8513) 1978 (UK Revival LP/CD 3005)(ABKCO CD 92382) *Bernie Lowe piano overdub recorded January 12, 1958

Possibly Cameo Studio, Philadelphia (January 1958)

"Love Bird"* [mx: J90W 4344] (Cameo 141-A) May 1958 (UK LP HAU 8513) 1978 (UK Revival LP/CD 3005) (ABKCO CD 92382) *Vocal overdub at Reco-Art Sound Recording, January 20, 1958

Decca Recording Studio, New York City (c. Fall 1958)

"Doodlebug" [mx: 106227] (Coral 62073-A) January 1959 (UK Coral Q 72362-A) February 1959 (UK Revival LP 3016)

"Hurry Up, Buttercup" [mx: 106228] (Coral 62073-B) January 1959 (UK Coral Q 72362-B) February 1959 (UK Revival LP/CD 3016)

Decca Recording Studio, New York City
(c. March or April 1959)

"Angel of Love" [mx: 106819] (Coral 62115-A) c. May 1959 (UK Coral Q 72373) July 1959 (UK Revival LP/CD 3005)

"I'm a Fool That's Why" [mx: 106820] (Coral 62115-B) (UK Coral Q 72373-B) (UK Revival LP/CD 3005)

Decca Recording Studio, New York City (Summer 1959)

"Oh-Well-A" [mx: 107778] (Coral 62141-A) September 1959 (UK Coral Q 72381-A) November 1959 (UK Revival LP 3016)

"Because I Love You So" [mx: 107779] (Coral 62141-B) September 1959 (UK Coral Q 72381) (UK Revival LP/CD 3016)

Bradley's Barn, Nashville (c. April 1960)

"The Race" [mx: 5C 14976] (Roulette 4255-A) May 1960 (UK Columbia DBHL 4477-A) 1960 (UK Revival LP/CD 3016)

"I Look for You" [mx:5C 14977] (Roulette 4255-B) (UK Columbia DBHL 4477-B) (UK Revival LP/CD 3016)

"Sorry for You" (Roulette 4312-A) c. December 1960

"Scenery" (Roulette 4312-B)

Reco-Art, Philadelphia (Late Summer 1961)
(Produced by Harry Chipetz)

"W-Wow" [mx: FD 417] (Felsted 8629-A) c. September 1961 (UK London HLU 10563) December 1978 (UK Revival LP/CD 3016)

"Makin' Whoopee" [mx: FD 418] (Felsted 8629-B) (UK London EP HLU 10563) December 1978 (UK Revival LP/CD 3016)

Reco-Art, Philadelphia (Summer 1962)
(Produced by Charlie Gracie for Llanerch Productions)

"Night and Day U.S.A. " (President 825-A) August 1962 (UK London HLU 9603-A) 1962 (UK Revival LP/CD 3016)

"Pretty Baby" [mx: 5034] (President 825-B) (UK London HLU 9603-B) (UK Revival LP/CD 3016)

"Count to Three" (President 828-A) fall 1962

"Just Like Us (Come Noi)" [mx: PR 5046] (President 828-B)

"Angela" [unreleased]

Unknown Studio, New York City (February 1965)
(Produced by Jerry Ross, arranged by Joe Renzetti)

"He'll Never Love You Like I Do" [mx: KR 4501] (Diamond 178-A) Winter 1965 (UK Stateside 55402-A) 1965

"Keep My Love Next to Your Heart" [mx: KR 4502] (Diamond 178) (UK Stateside 55402-B)

"That'll Be the Day" [unreleased]

Sigma Sound Studio, Philadelphia (1969)
(Produced by Vince Montana)

"Walk with Me Girl" [mx: H 102A] (Sock and Soul 102-A) 1969 (UK London LP HAU 8513) 1978 (UK Revival LP/CD 3016)

"Tenderness" [mx: H 102B] (Sock and Soul 102-B) (UK London LP HAU 8513) 1978 (UK Revival LP/CD 3016)

Frankfort & Wayne Studio, Philadelphia (Probably 1970)

"How Many Times" [originally unreleased] (UK London LP HAU 8513) 1978

"Remember You're Mine" [originally unreleased] (UK London LP HAU 8513) 1978

Frank Virtue's Studio, North Broad Street, Philadelphia (1970)

"Ling Ting Tong" [originally unreleased] (School Kids CD 1547 *Live at the Stockton Globe*) March 1996

"Dream" [originally unreleased] (School Kids CD 1547 *Live at the Stockton Globe*) March 1996

Phoenix 413 Studios, Camden, New Jersey (1980)

(Charlie Gracie guitar, vocal overdubs; recorded at Phoenix 413 Studios, Camden, NJ, by Kevin Zacheo and Mark Rosche)

(Backing musicians: Freddy "Fingers" Lee—piano; Rover Cover—bass; John Tuck—drums; M. Reinig—sax; Art Hunt, Jr. —trumpet; B.J. Cole—steel guitar; Mark Rosche—trombone. Backing tracks recorded at Airport Studios, London by Keith Gooden and Allan Jones, and at M.D. Studios, Ougree, Belgium recorded by Michael Dickenscheid.)

"Butterfly" (Belgium Blackjack LP NRL 1940 *The Fabulous Charlie Gracie*)

"Corner Shop Rock" (Belgium Blackjack LP NPR 1940)

"Dirty Dog" (French Big Beat 10" LP 0009 *Rocking Philadelphia*) (UK Magnum Force 10" LP MFM 004 *Rocking Philadelphia*)

"Fabulous" (LP 0009) (UK LP MFM 004) (Belgium Blackjack LP NRL 1940) March 1981

"Guitar Boogie" (Belgium Blackjack LP NPR 1940)

"Heart Like a Rock" (LP BBR 0009) 1980 (LP MFM 004) July 1982

"I Love You So Much It Hurts" (Belgium Blackjack LP NPR 1940)

"I'm Movin' On" (Belgium Blackjack LP NRL 1940)

"Little John's Gone" (LP 0009) (UK LP MFM 004)

"Love Doll" (LP 0009) (UK LP MFM 004)

"Love Is Like a Butterfly" (Belgium Blackjack LP NRL 1940)

"My Baby Loves Me" (LP 0009) (UK LP MFM 004)

"Rockabilly Rock" (Belgium Blackjack LP NRL 1940)

"Rockin' Is Our Business" (Belgium Blackjack LP NPR 1940)

"Rockin' the Boogie" (LP 0009) (UK LP MFM 004) (Belgium Blackjack NR4028-B) (Belgium Blackjack LP NRL 1940)

"Too Much Monkey Business" (LP 0009) (UK LP MFM 004)

"Train Down to Hell" (LP 0009) (UK LP MFM 004) (Belgium Blackjack LP NPR 1940)

"Wanderin' Eyes (Belgium Blackjack LP NRL 1940)

"You Mostest Girl" (LP 0009) (UK LP MFM 004) (Belgium Blackjack NR4028-A) 1981

Meridian Studios, London (Fall 1981)

(With: Dave Travis—acoustic guitar, Eddie Jones—guitar, Joe Gillingham—piano, Terry Nicholson—bass, Howard Tibble—drums)

SIDE A: "All Change"/"Lightnin' Across the Sky"/"It Must Be Love"/"I Get the Message"/"Charlie's Whim"/"Buddy's Song"/"Too Much Rock 'n' Roll Music"//SIDE B: "Jean, Jean, the Rocking Machine"/"Starlight, Starbright"/"Don't You Hurt My Baby"/"Blue Levi Jeans"/"Boogie Woogie Blues No. 2"/"This Time I'm Falling in Love"/"I'm Gonna Love You" (French Charly LP CR 30211 *Amazing Gracie*) February 1982

Unknown Studio, New York City (1989)

(Produced by Richard Gottehrer)

"Go Man Go"* (Comstock NR7932) 1989 (Comstock 1935) 1989
*with The Jordanaires overdubbed

Tower Studios, Cesena, Italy (September and October 1991)

"Had a Call"/"Medley: Dark Town Strutters Ball—Sheik of Araby"/"Fabulous"/"Cotton Fields"/"Flip, Flop and Fly"/"Wanderin' Eyes"/"Sh-Boom"/"Caldonia"/"Heart Like a Rock"/"Baby You've Changed"/"I Love You So Much It Hurts Me"/"Lonesome Me"/"Butterfly"/"Medley: Just a Gigolo—I Ain't Got Nobody"/"Head Home Honey" (Italian YEOB LP 003 *Charlie Gracie and the Jumpin' Shoes: Rockin' Italy*) 1991 (Netherlands Rockhouse LP 9413) 1994 (Netherlands Rockhouse CD) December 2004

Hagen, Germany (1992)

"Just a Closer Walk with Thee," "How Great Thou Art," "Rockin' Pneumonia and the Boogie Woogie Flu," "Oh Freedom" [Charlie does beginning recital] (Gema LR-92192 *The Lennerockers and Friends—Volume 1*) 1992

"Now and Then" (UK Translux EP SRT 935-3645) 1993

"It's Fabulous—It's Charlie Gracie" (Cotton Town Jubilee CTJCD 2) May 1995 (UK CD CTCD 2 Stomper Time)

(Compilation and outtakes)

"Honey Honey"/"(You Got) a Heart Like a Rock"/"Butterfly"/"Head Home Honey"/"Cool Baby"/"Ninety-Nine Ways"/"I Love You So Much It Hurts Me"/"Just Lookin'"/"Wildwood Boogie"/"Wanderin' Eyes"/"Fabulous"/"My Baby Loves Me"/Crazy Girl"/"Cool Baby" [alternate take No. 5]/"I'm So Glad It's You"/"Frankie and Johnny"/"Wanderin' Eyes" [alternate take No. 13]/"Boogie Woogie Blues"/"Rockin' 'n' Rollin'"/"Trying"/"Dressing Up"/"T'Aint No Sin in Rhythm"/"All Over Town"/"Say What You Mean"/"I'm Gonna Sit Right Down and Write Myself a Letter"/"Tutti-Frutti" [live]/"I Love You So Much It Hurts Me" [live]/"Guitar Boogie" [live]/"Fabulous" [live]/"Rock the Joint" [live]/"Butterfly" [original unreleased demo]/"Ninety Nine Ways" [original unreleased demo]

Session Sound Studio, Rosmalen, Netherlands (1996)

(New recordings, 20 tracks; other artists: The Bellhops/Phil Friendly)

(Rarity CD192538 *Rock & Roll Giants—Volume 1: Charlie Gracie*) 1997

Unknown Studio, Netherlands (c. 1997)

(Some tracks from this CD were released in U.S.A.)

"Movin' Down Country"/"Hey, Good Lookin'"/"I Fell Apart"/"My Babe"/"Gotta Travel On"/"Hello Josephine"/"Cool Baby"/"You're Sixteen"/"Dressin' Up"/"Nickel and a Dime"/"Just Because"/"Guitar Rag (Steel Guitar Rag)" (Self-released CD *Movin' Down Country*) June 2008

Suzie's New Star Bar (The Lansdown), Clifton, Bristol, England (January 11, 1998)

"Introduction"/"Sh-Boom"/"Boogie Woogie Blues"/"Oh, Boy!"/"I'm In the Mood for Love"/"My Babe"/"Head Home Honey"/"Wanderin' Eyes"/"Medley: All Shook Up—Teddy Bear—Don't Be Cruel"/"Mama Look a Boo Boo"/"Medley: Blueberry Hill—Be-Bop-A-Lula"/"Chantilly Lace"/"Medley: Johnny B. Goode—Too Much Monkey Business— Maybelline—Sweet Little Sixteen"/"Just a Gigolo—I Ain't Got Nobody"/"Medley: I Walk the Line—Folsom Prison Blues—Dang Me—Ring of Fire—Hold Tight"/"Butterfly"/"Fabulous"/"Holy Smoke" [instrumental]/"Let the Good Times Roll"/"White Sport Coat"/"Slippin' and Slidin'—Long Tall Sally"/"Ninety-Nine Ways"/"What'd I Say"/"Shake, Rattle and Roll"/"Whole Lotta Shakin' Goin' On"/"Great Balls of Fire"/"That'll Be the Day—Shake, Rattle and Roll"/At the Hop—Rock 'n' Roll Is Here to Stay"/"Closing Dialogue"/"Butterfly" [reprise] [23 solo tracks + 7 with Bwa Bula and Chene Beck] (Rockstar CD 20 *An Evening with...Charlie Gracie*) April 2002

"Fabulous Charlie Gracie" (Park 561 CD) 1998.

Sound Cage Studio, Lancaster, Pennsylvania (2001)

"Tootsie"/"I'm All Right"/"Let the Good Times Roll"/"Kaw-Liga"/"A Little Too Soon to Tell" [with Graham Nash]/"Lover Boy"/"Crying Over You"/"Gotta Travel On"/"I'm Gonna Love You"/"Still Nineteen"/"I'm Confessing"/"Go Man, Go"/"Times Are Changing"/"Get Back" (Lanark Records/Sunset Records CD 76 *I'm All Right*) September 2001

Lightning Recording Service, Berlin, Germany (September 21–23, 2004)

(Backed by various roots/rockabilly musicians including Ike and the Capers and Jesse Al Tuscan and the Roundup Boys; recorded live on 1950s equipment and taped on a 1962 tape recorder in mono!)

"Baby I Got You"/"When I Was a Young Man"/"Head Home Honey"/"Hey Watcha Gonna Do"/"You Can't Take It With You"/"High Heel Sneakers"/"Just Hangin' Around"/"Love What You Do"/"Oh Babe"/"Please Don't Leave Me"/"Rock-A-Beatin' Boogie"/"Taking a Trip to Dreamland"/"Turn on the Heat"/"Just Hangin' Around" [alternate take] (German Rhythm Bomb CD 5632 *Just Hangin' Around*) April 2006

Lightning Recording Service, Berlin, Germany (2007)

"A White Sport Coat"/"Flat Foot Floosy"/"Georgia on My Mind"/"Pennsylvania 6-5-0-0-0"/"Anytime"/"A Big Bouquet of Roses"/"My Blue Heaven"/"Dance with a Dolly"/"It All Depends on You"/"Jamaica Farewell"/"Jambalaya"/"Mary Ann"/"Sentimental Journey"/"Party Doll" (German Rhythm Bomb CD 5655 *Gracie Swings Again*) October 2007

Lancaster, Pennsylvania (2009–2011)

(Produced by Al Kooper, Quentin Jones, Tom "T-Bone" Edmonds)

"All I Wanna Do Is Love You" [with Peter Noone]/"My Hummingbird"/"Back to Philadelphia"/"Sweet Marie"/"And Now I Win"/"School Days"/"I Don't Know Why"/"Dance My Blues Away"/"On the Way to Cape May"/"Everybody Rockin' [Knockin' Themselves Out]"/"Rock 'n' Roll Heaven" [with Graham Nash]/"Rock 'n' Roll Party" (ABKCO CD *For the Love of Gracie*) fall 2011

Drexel Hill, Pennsylvania (Fall 2011)

(Produced by Gary Lefkowith)

"[Be My] Baby Doll" (Generic Records MP3 Single)

NOTES

1   Broven, John. *Record Makers and Breakers: Voices of the Independent Rock 'n' Roll Pioneers.* Urbana: University of Illinois Press, 2009, p. 426.

2   Jackson, John A. Telephone interview with Kal Mann. January 30, 1993.

3   For anthropological information concerning Sicily's ancestral population, see Wade, Nicholas. *Before the Dawn: Recovering the Lost History of Our Ancestors.* New York: Penguin, 2006, pp. 1, 2–3, 8, 9, 51–52, 64. For early Sicily see: "Agrigento, Sicily," *http://en.wikipedia. org/wiki/Agrigento*; "Origin of Sicilian Language," *http://www.dieli. net/SicilyPage/SicilianLanguage/OriginEssay.html*; Rudolph, Laura C. "Sicilian Americans" *www.everyculture.com/multi/Pa-Sp/Sicilian-Americans.html*; Salerno, Vincent. "Sicilian Peoples: The Sicels," *http:// www.bestofsicily.com/mag/art147.htm*; "Sicilian Chronology," *http:// www.dieli.net/SicilyPage/History/SicilianHist.html - 5Sikels.*

4   Di Giacomo, Donna J. D. *Images of America: Italians of Philadelphia.* Charleston: Arcadic Publishing, 2007; Dubin, Murray. *South Philadelphia: Mummers, Memories, and the Melrose Diner.* Philadelphia: Temple University Press, 1996; Rudolph, Laura C. "Sicilian Americans," *www.everyculture.com/multi/Pa-Sp/Sicilian-Americans.html*; Sitarski, Steven M. "From Weccacoe to South Philadelphia, The Changing Face of a Neighborhood." Pennsylvania Legacies 7, no. 2, November 2007;

Sitarski, Steven M. "Timeline: From Weccacoe to South Philadelphia" *www.philaplace.org/resources/South%20Philadephia%20Timeline. pdf.*

5   In 1957 Sam Gracie revealed he was "determined to make a star" of Charlie, after having "made up" his son's career "even before" his birth. Norris, Floyd. "A Star Was Made by Charlie's Dad." *Daily Sketch,* London, U.K., August 6, 1957.

6   It is uncertain who was on stage with Haley that afternoon. A circa 1951 advertisement by the Saddlemen's management/recording company touts a lineup of Haley—rhythm guitar; Billy Williamson—steel guitar; Johnny Grande—accordion and piano; Marshall Lytle—string bass. The ad bills the Saddlemen as a "cowboy jive band," boasting a repertoire of "popular, hillbilly, jive, cowboy" music. What makes Charlie's account of Haley's performance at Sleepy Hollow so intriguing is his memory of a drummer with the Saddlemen. The group never used a drummer on any of their recordings. Only after Haley changed the name to the Comets in late 1952 did he hire session drummer Billy Gussack to play on their recordings. Whoever Charlie witnessed banging on the drums remains a mystery. But his account of that day's performance suggests that Haley's decision to add a drum to his band's sound was not impulsive, but rather a well-rehearsed experiment. (Information concerning the Saddlemen taken from Haley, John W., and John von Hoelle. *Sound and Glory: The Incredible Story of Bill Haley, the Father of Rock 'n' Roll and the Music That Shook the World.* Wilmington: Dyne-American Publishing, 1990, p. 72; and Komorowski, Adam. Liner notes to *Bill Haley: From Western Swing to Rock.* Properbox CD 118, 2007.)

7   Prown, Peter, and H.P. Newquist. *Legends of Rock Guitar: The Essential Reference of Rock's Greatest Guitar Artists.* Milwaukee: Hal Leonard Corp. 1997, p. 12.

8   Ruth Casey, with the Graham Prince Ensemble, performing "Cry" and "Hold Me Just a Little Bit Longer" (Cadillac 103) was released in September 1951.

9   The Brill was one of two famous buildings (1650 Broadway being the other) that served as the core of the pop music industry in those days.

10 "Boogie Woogie Blues" (incorrectly titled "Boogie Boogie Blues" on the original Cadillac labels) is a remarkable recording for its time. Not

quite rockabilly, it edges provocatively close, until an intrusive soprano sax break temporarily reduces the sound to a more subdued country boogie. Other than Bill Haley, no white man in 1952 rocked harder than Gracie does here. If not for that unfortunate 12-second sax break, original copies of "Boogie Woogie Blues" would easily fetch hundreds of dollars among vintage rockabilly connoisseurs. It's on Charlie's breezy version of "I'm Gonna Sit Right Down and Write Myself a Letter" and "Say What You Mean" that he most elicits comparison to Johnnie Ray.

11 The exact release date for Cadillac 141 remains uncertain. None of Charlie's Cadillac releases were reviewed in *Billboard* and no verifiable release-date information for them has been discovered.

12 "Mahoff" is a local Philadelphian term meaning "big shot."

13 *Billboard's* first mention of Charlie appeared in the May 29, 1954 edition, "Acts and Attractions" column, p. 26: "Charlie Gracie (on Cadillac Records) will get his first café date at Detroit's Gay Haven Supper Club coincidental with the release of his 'Boogie Woogie Blues.' Reason for the hold-back was his coming of age, making him old enough to work night clubs."

"Boogie Woogie Blues" had been released long before then, and in all probability, so had Charlie's second record. The *Billboard* item was almost certainly submitted by Graham Prince, so it is puzzling why the release date for "Boogie Woogie Blues" is so inaccurate. Charlie maintains that he occasionally did club dates before he turned 18. Perhaps this was an effort by Prince to cover his tracks for the times he did book his under-age performer.

14 A review of both songs appeared in *Billboard's* July 9, 1955 edition.

15 Broven, John. *Record Makers and Breakers: Voices of the Independent Rock 'n' Roll Pioneers*. Urbana: University of Illinois Press, 2009, p. 425.

16 The demos for "Butterfly" and "Ninety-Nine Ways" appear on *The Best of Charlie Gracie: Cameo-Parkway 1956–1958* (ABKCO CD 92382), 2006.

17 Along with Andy Williams, the 1957 "Butterfly" copiers include Bill Allen and the Keynotes, Bob Carroll, Betty Johnson, Billy Williams, British rocker Tommy Steele, and many others.

18 U.S. House of Representatives, *Responsibilities of Broadcasting Licensees and Station Personnel: Hearings Before a Subcommittee of the Committee on Interstate and Foreign Commerce, 86th Congress, 2nd Session on Payola and Other Deceptive Practices in the Broadcasting Field. Part II.* April 27, 28, 29, May 2, 3, August 30, 31, 1960 (Washington, D.C., Government Printing Office, 1960). All quotations regarding song royalties are from Lowe's testimony, April 28, pp. 1113–1144, and Clark's testimony, April 29, pp. 1177, 1178.

19 The National Council of Disc Jockeys for Public Service, Inc., based in New York City, was a nonprofit membership corporation formed in December 1956. Clark was listed as one of the regional directors of this organization. Advertisement in *Billboard*, January 26, 1957, p. 71.

20 Brooks, Tim, and Earle Marsh. *The Complete Directory to Prime Time Network TV Shows*, 5th edition. New York: Ballantine Books, 1992, p. 262.

21 "The Inflation Calculator" *http://www.westegg.com/inflation.*

22 Bleyer, Archie. "The Cadence Era: 'Canadian Sunset' Brightens Andy's Disk Career," Andy Williams 52-page "Spotlight Section." *Billboard*, November 11, 1967, p. AW 20.

23 For a detailed account of Horn's *Bandstand* firing and the transition to Clark as the show's host, see: Jackson, John A. *American Bandstand: Dick Clark and the Making of a Rock and Roll Empire.* New York: Oxford University Press, 1997. Mammarella's late widow, Agnes, said, "It looked like we had gotten all this money from Bernie, which we did not get....All the money (we received as royalties from 'Butterfly') was given to Bernie Lowe." She also said her husband's deal with Lowe to have Mammarella's name put on "Butterfly" and "Ninety-Nine Ways" "was Anthony just being a nice guy—and being stupid." (Jackson, John A. Telephone interview. November 18, 1992.)

24 Clark first instructed Lowe to make the check payable to the *Bandstand* host's mother-in-law. But 10 days later, that money plus $5 "interest" was returned to Lowe (Clark called it a loan "re-payment."). Three days after that, as per Clark's instruction, Lowe issued a check in the amount of $7,000 to "Click Corporation," which was owned by Clark. (U.S. House of Representatives, *Op. cit.*, pp. 1116–1124.)

25 In 1955 the industry grossed roughly $227 million. The Recording

Industry Association of America (RIAA) figures were later revised upward. Sanjek, Russell and David Sanjek. *American Popular Music Business in the 20th Century.* New York: Oxford University Press, 1991, p. 137.

26 The others were "Too Much" and "All Shook Up."

27 Sanjek and Sanjek, *Op. cit.*

28 "Plaything" can be found on *The Best of Charlie Gracie: Cameo-Parkway 1956–1958* (ABKCO CD 92382), 2006.

29 Millar, Bill, "A Fifties Star Who's Back in the Spotlight," *Melody Maker,* October 20, 1979, p. 34.

30 The 71-minute film, directed by Roy Lockwood and produced by Vanguard Productions, was originally to be titled *The Big Record* (*Billboard,* July 8, 1957, p. 57) or *The Hit Record* (*Billboard,* July 15, 1957, p. 95). It was retitled *Jamboree* for domestic release and *Disc Jockey Jamboree* for overseas distribution.

31 Tobler, John, and Stuart Grundy. *The Record Producers.* London: British Broadcasting Corp., 1982, pp. 125, 126.

32 "Move It" (UK Columbia 4178) was released in September 1958. Britain's second legitimate rock and roll hit, Johnny Kidd and the Pirates' "Please Don't Touch" (UK HMV Pop 615) was released in June 1959.

33 "Stuart Jones Talks to Sir Cliff Richard," RadioWey.co.uk, November 24, 2010.

34 Great Britain is the largest island of the United Kingdom. It includes England, Scotland, and Wales.

35 *Billboard,* July 15, 1957, p. 88.

36 Cameo ad, *Billboard,* July 22, 1957, pp. 38, 39.

37 Ricky's first session took place on March 26, 1957 at Master Recorders, Hollywood. Three songs were recorded: "I'm Walking," "A Teenager's Romance," and "You're My One and Only Love."

38 Ricky's first record, "A Teenager's Romance" and "I'm Walking," was released in April 1957. "A Teenager's Romance" reached number 2 on *Billboard*'s Best Selling chart; "Walking" hit number 4; Charlie's version of "Butterfly" made number 3.

39 Two years after the lawsuit, the courts ordered Ricky's former record company to pay him $38,000 in back royalties. All information on Nelson is from Selvin, Joel. *Ricky Nelson: Idol for a Generation.* Chicago: Contemporary Books, 1990, pp. 63–67, 73–76.

40 While Clark's involvement with Cameo Records remains indistinct, he was definitely involved with Lowe in other music-business ventures. In December 1957, not long after *American Bandstand* became the most powerful record-promotion venue in America, Clark formed Swan Records, going to great lengths to keep his name from being publicly linked to that company. But Clark, who quietly owned one-third of Swan, was the real clout behind that record label. And since Clark proceeded to give Swan's new releases an exorbitant amount of airplay on *American Bandstand*, he most certainly had good reason to maintain his low profile with that record company. (The precise number of *American Bandstand* plays Clark gave to Swan's records is documented in U.S. House of Representatives, *Op. cit.*, pp.1504–1519.)

To say that Cameo and Swan were run as one and the same company would be an understatement. David Steinberg, Sr. was Lowe's personal attorney in 1957–58. In 1958 his son, David, Jr., joined his father's practice and was put in charge of Cameo's legal matters. The younger Steinberg, whose firm also represented Swan, stated that "there were so many different handshake arrangements between the people who ran both companies," that he "may not have been privy" to all of them. Steinberg described Swan as a "partnership corporation" owned by Clark and Lowe. The attorney also recalled that Clark's partners in Swan— Anthony Septembre Mammarella and Bernie Binnick—"may have owned" their Swan stock "through Dick Clark." The two record labels shared the same office floor at 140 South Locust Street in Philadelphia and were run by the same sales manager. "You're talking about an office with 10 people in it, being run for all the different companies by the same people at the same time," said Steinberg. "They may have been doing something for Swan under the name of Cameo, and vice-versa." (For instance, both labels frequently printed joint advertisements in the music trade magazines.) All quotes from John A. Jackson interview with David Steinberg, Esq., Conshohocken, Pennsylvania, October 8, 2001.

In addition to Clark and Lowe's Swan dealings, in December 1957 the pair became "silent" partners in a new Philadelphia-based record distributorship called Chips Distributing. Clark and Lowe were each given a one-third interest in the company by Chips' ostensible owner, veteran record man Harry Chipetz. Chips subsequently became the Philadelphia distributor for Cameo and Swan Records. Also, in May 1958, Clark and Lowe became equal partners in Mallard, a record pressing company.

For his part, Clark strove to conceal his tangled business dealings with Bernie Lowe. While he swore under oath before the 1960 House Subcommittee investigating payola that he knew about Bernard Lowe Enterprises, he cryptically insisted that he was "not free to answer questions as to the details of that business" (U.S. House of Representatives, *Op. cit.*, p.1246). For Chips, see Chipetz's testimony, U.S. House of Representatives, *Op. cit.*, pp. 1155–1173; for Mallard, see Lowe's testimony, U.S. House of Representatives, *Op. cit.*, p. 1114.)

41 Lowe cut Clark in on half of the publishing royalties for "Back to School Again," which may have helped increase Clark's fondness for the song.

42 Following Lowe's release of "Silhouettes," five of the eight records subsequently issued on Cameo were purchased master recordings.

43 At the November 24 Reco-Art session, Lowe cut "Snuggle Up Baby" and "Tootsie." A December 1 session at the same studio produced "Yea, Yea (I'm in Love with You)." At an unknown New York City studio in late 1957 or early 1958, the ballad "I'm So Glad It's You" was recorded. All these unreleased tracks are available on ABKCO CD 92382.

44 *Billboard*, January 13, 1958, p. 73.

45 *Billboard* described the list as "single recordings that sold a million copies or more as of March 15, 1958. Research on this was carried out via direct contact with the record manufacturers, who have verified the eligibility of each listing." *Billboard*, March 24, 1958, p. 20.

46 *Billboard*, May 12, 1958, p. 40.

47 According to S. Morgan Friedman's "Inflation Calculator" *www.westegg.com/inflation/* the exact amount is $383,492. According to *www.measuringworth.com/uscompare/relativevalue.php* the amount is $389,000.

48 *Billboard*, January 19, 1959.

49 "Philly Wide-Open Town for Disc Jocks among Indie Labels." *Variety*, November 5, 1952, p. 37; "How Big the Payola In Records?" *Broadcasting*, August 31, 1959, pp 35, 36.

50 "Payola Rocks Philly Jocks." *Variety*, November 25, 1959, pp. 55–56.

51 U.S. House of Representatives, *Op. cit.*, pp. 1128, 1131.

52 *Treasure Chest of Hits* (Swan LP 501).

53 *Always Something There: A Burt Bacharach Collectors' Anthology 1952–1969.*

54 *Billboard*, May 30, 1960, p. 41.

55 *Billboard* review, September 25, 1961, p. 35.

56 "Cameo-Parkway Nets $1.10 versus $1.57." *Philadelphia Bulletin*, February 26, 1964.

57 Lowe's "Motown" quote from John A. Jackson interview with Hy Lit, Philadelphia, Pa., September 9, 1992.

58 "Cameo Records Shows $499,319 Loss for '64." *Philadelphia Bulletin*, March 12, 1965.

59 Lowe received $1,165,000 for his controlling interest in Cameo-Parkway.

60 Lowe died in 1993 at age 75. His wife's "depression" quote is from Tamarkin, Jeff. "Cameo Parkway Story." Liner notes to *Cameo-Parkway 1957–1967*, ABKCO CD 18771-92232, 2005, p. 16.

61 Millar, Bill. "Back from the Cold: Bill Millar Meets Charlie Gracie Back in Britain after a Twenty-Year Absence." *Melody Maker*, October 29, 1979, p. 34.

62 John A. Jackson telephone interview with Bell, October 4, 2001.

63 ABKCO 4012, in 1972.

64 Allen Klein died from complications from Alzheimer's in 2009.

65 For "Rockin' Pneumonia and the Boogie Woogie Flu" go to *youtube. com/watch?v=G7WrWmGdyWw*; for "Just a Closer Walk with Thee/ How Great Thou Art" go to *youtube.com/watch?v=c1t70Asi99M*.

INDEX

A

ABKCO, 236, "Cameo-Parkway 1957–1967" CD box set; Klein, Allen, 235, 243; Klein, Jody, 235, 243–245, 247, 253; Landi, Teri, 244, 247. *See also* Gracie, Charlie, recording companies

Abruzzo, Benny (father's cousin), 17, 49, 50

Agrigento Province. *See* Sicily

Alberts, Al, 37, 38, 40. *See also* Four Aces

"American Bandstand," 38, 55, 74, 88, 115, 123, 147, 149, 169, 172, 176, 232, 233, 272n; "Golden Boys of Bandstand," 219; 40th Anniversary Reunion, 170, 232. *See also* "Bandstand" (Philadelphia)

Andrews, Patty, 59, 60

"Angela" (song). *See* Gracie, Charlie, recordings

Appell, Dave, xvi, 82, and Applejacks, 71, 83, 127

Arnold, Eddie, 27, 32, 166

Atlantic City, 12, 57, 58, 89; Skinny D'Amato's 500 Club, 89

Avalon, Frankie, 37, 40, 92, 219, 245

B

D

Gottehrer, Richard, 220

Gracie, Angela (daughter), 131, 172, 174, 183, 184, 186, 191–191, 197, 213, 217, 218, 220, 228, 239, 248

Gracie, Angela Olivieri (grandmother), 7–12, 14, 22, 24, 26, 77, 105, 174, 240, 241

Gracie, Charlie, Jr. (son), 131, 150, 155–159, 161, 163, 164, 172, 183, 184, 186, 191–193, 197, 213, 217, 218, 222, 228, 232, 233, 248, 251

Gracie, Charlie, Sr., backing combo, 180, 181, 187; birth, 12, 13; blackballed, 2, 3, 147, 167–170, 175, 176, 192, 233, 248; British record popularity charts, 93, 115, 120, 124; Cadillac automobiles, 2, 82, 86, 156, 189, 192; and Clark, Dick, 74, 79, 115, 147, 163, 169, 170, 192, 232, 233; "comeback," 195, 197, 200–204, 208, 210, 213, 214, 241, 242; conflict with parents, 2, 3, 150–161, 163, 172, 183, 189, 231, 248; demos, recording, 70, 71, 176, 195, 203–206, 269n; gold record, 91, 94, 119;

guitars:

Gibson, 36, 37, 72; Guild Stratford X–350, 72, 199, 237, 238; Harmony flat top acoustic, 28, 29, 236; lessons, 29–31, 34, 36, 129; technique, style, 36, 38, 39, 43, 58, 83, 84, 86, 87, 92, 99, 100,111, 127, 179, 193, 224, 230, 236–238

high school, 40–42, 44, 45, 48, 49, 56, 58, 130; *Jamboree* (movie), 2, 92, 118, 123, 124, 202, 233, 271n; junior high school, 31; marriage, 131–134, 136, 138, 151, 152, 186; musical influences, 26, 27, 44;

performances & gigs, live:

55–58, 63, 65, 66, 85, 88, 89. 91, 98, 102, 118, 124, 126, 130, 133, 138, 141, 150, 154, 159, 160, 163, 164, 167, 172, 175, 176, 178–184, 191–193, 199, 201–210, 223, 228, 231, 232, 236–243, 245–247, 249, 250, 269n; Alan Freed's "Easter Jubilee of Stars." *See* Freed, "Easter Jubilee of Stars"; "American Heroes," 203–205; British Theatres, 109, 138–140, 161, 162; Cadillac Show Bar, 73; "Carroll's Café," 63–66; early performances, 40, 41, 45, 56, 58, 130; Club Avalon. *See* Wildwood, NJ; Flannery's Constellation Lounge, 181, 182; Gay Haven (Detroit), 59, 60, 269n; "Johnny Night," Connie Mack Stadium, 89–91; lack of, 167, 168, 172, 187, 189; London Hippodrome, 3, 97, 102–105, 107; London Palladium, 3, 108, 160;

New Jersey shore, 192:

173–177184, 185, 200, 202–204, 206, 208, 209, 220, 222, 239–243, 249–252, 173n;

recordings:

"All Over Town," 47; "Angel of Love," 146; "Angela," 174; "(Be My) Baby Doll," 250–254; "Because I Love You So," 158; "Boogie Woogie Blues," 43, 44, 54, 268n, 269n; "Box on," 200; "Butterfly." 1, 68, 70, 71, 73, 74, 76–79, 81–83, 85, 86, 88, 89, 91, 93, 115, 117, 119, 122–124, 132, 145, 202, 204, 214, 220, 232, 235, 243, 245, 269n, 270n; sheet music for, 162. *See also* Gracie, Charlie, record companies, Cameo; Gracie, Charlie, royalties, record sales; Lowe, Bernie; "Cool Baby," 92, 118–120, 123, 124, 126, 127; "Crazy Girl," 127, 132; "Doodlebug," 145, 146; "Dream," 112, 185; "Dressin' Up," 127, 132; "Fabulous," 1, 77, 83–85, 88, 89, 91, 93, 96, 115, 202, 214, 220, 221, 228, 230, 231, 235, 243; "Frankie and Johnny," 62; "Go Man Go," 220, 221; "Guitar Boogie," 39, 111, 112, 229; "Head Home Honey," 61; "He'll Never Love you Like I Do," 175; "Hold On," 200; "Honey, Honey," 62; "Hurry Up Buttercup," 145; "I Love You So Much It Hurts," 92, 114, 115, 127; "I'm a Fool That's Why," 146; "I'm Gonna Sit Right Down and Write Myself a Letter," 43; "I'm So Glad It's You," 273n; "Just Like Us (Come Noi)," 173, 174; "Just Lookin'," 83–85; "Ling Ting Tong," 112, 185; "Love Bird," 127, 128, 141; "Makin' Whoopee," 169, 170; "My Baby Loves Me," 61; "Night and Day, USA," 173, 174; "Ninety-Nine Ways," 70, 71, 73, 78, 270n; "Oh Well-A," 158; "Plaything," 83, 271n; "Race, The," 166, 167; "Rockin' 'n' Rollin,'" 47, 48; "Rockin' the Boogie," 208; "Snuggle Up Baby," 273n; "T'Ain't No Sin in Rhythm," 48; "Tenderness," 184, 185; "That'll Be the Day," 175; "Tootsie," 273n; "Trying," 92, 141; "Walk With Me Girl," 184, 185; "Wanderin' Eyes," 91, 115, 141; "W-Wow," 169, 170; "Yea Yea (I'm in Love With You)," 273n; "You Got a Heart Like a Rock," 119; "You Mostest Girl, 208

residences:

Drexel Hills, 185–187; 515 Carpenter Street. *See* South Philadelphia; Havertown, 2, 124–126, 153, 155–157, 160, 161, 163, 167; Llanerch Hills, 159, 160, 163, 172, 181, 182, 185, 186, 213; 731 & 735 Pierce Street. *See* South Philadelphia;

royalties, record sales, 62, 70, 71, 73, 74, 79, 81, 82, 89, 91, 92, 118–122, 124, 132, 133, 142–144, 162, 165, 167, 174, 176, 177, 184, 208, 209, 235, 243–245, 248. *See also* Lowe, Bernie; ABKCO; songwriting, 43, 47, 48, 61, 62, 71, 84, 158, 165, 167, 173, 174, 230,

H

N

O

P

R

S